THE DEMONS OF 9/11

ALAN SCARFE

SMART HOUSE BOOKS

Heidi von Palleske/Smart House Books
100 Bain Ave, 35 The Oaks, Toronto, M4K 1E8
www.smarthousebooks.com

Publisher's Note: This is a work of fiction. Although many of the people and events described were real, the entirety is a work of the author's imagination.

Book Layout © 2018 Smart House Books
Cover design - Aaron Rachel Brown
Cover concept - Barbara March

The Demons of 9/11/ Alan Scarfe -- 1st ed.
ISBN – 978-1-988980-07-2

This is a revised edition of the novel previously published as The Vampires of 9/11 by Clanash Farjeon (Trafford Books, 2010) and *I vampiri dell'11 settembre* (Gargoyle Books, Rome, 2011).
It is now the only author-approved version.

Also by the same author:
The Revelation of Jack the Ripper
The Vampires of Juarez
The Mask of the Holy Spirit

Praise for The Demons of 9/11

"With all due respect to Steve Alten's *The Shell Game*, Alan Scarfe's *The Demons of 9/11* is the real McCoy . . Scarfe's central sympathetic characters all know what went down on 9/11 - no ifs, ands or buts . . What went down was an inside job with twisted grin Dick Cheney at the black and bloodthirsty centre of a nasty cabal including a foul-mouthed Condoleezza Rice and the darkest prince of all, Henry Kissinger. No aliases, no excuses, no mercy - except some sympathy for a haunted George Bush and his loyal Laura, possessed of some decency as befits a former school librarian . . What we know at the end is that a subject taboo within the cocoon of mainstream media can be accessed outside that cocoon through the art of the novel. As Picasso said, 'Art is a lie that makes us realize truth' . . Stieg Larsson would approve."

> **- Barrie Zwicker**,
> author of *Towers of Deception: the Media Cover-Up of 9/11*

"Scarfe's narrative rhythm is exemplary with stunning scenes that are effective and credible. His strong ethical thrust is sharpened by the horror and creates a perfect balance of denunciation and entertainment."

> **- Sergio Riotino**, *L'informazione*

"Scarfe convinces and thrills with his rapid-fire invention. He never lets you forget the leitmotiv ever-present in all his books which pushes one to ask - is everything truly as it seems?"

> **- Susanna Raule**, *Cut-up*

"A book to read, reflect on and understand the perversity of power. But also to enjoy the lively and amusing style of an author unafraid to call George Bush a degenerate war criminal."

> **- Simone Scataglini**, *Horror.it*

"The spiral of the story captivates the reader in a disturbing alternate reality."

> **- Igor de Amicis**, *Thriller magazine*

"Anyone who loves mysteries and brilliant writing will not fail to find food for their desires."
> - **Andrea Turetta**, *Free Art News*

"Scarfe's novel opens the door to a world of darkness even more terrifying than the daily news."
> - **Stefania Auci**, *Diario di Pensiero Persi*

"Macabre and enjoyable as *Doctor Strangelove* . . political horror fiction at its best."
> - **Maurizio Crispi**, *Italia Informazioni*

"It is certainly conventional wisdom now that September 11, 2001, is the ultimate American 'day of infamy' but getting to the truth of it has been consistently and successfully avoided.

Did the fools who perpetrated the horror of that day care nothing for the victims? Did they have no concern for the disasters that would follow for everyone they loudly and publicly proclaim they are elected to protect?

Scarfe's savage satire exposes the infamy of nation states that shout their innocence no matter what they do to bodies and to minds. His whole trilogy is a rolling, roiling tribute to the powerful fact of absurdity in all contemporary life."
> - **Eric Ross Green**,
> *Awash with Blood, an Awake and Arise Call to All Goths*

Dedicated to
the millions whose
lives have been destroyed
by the deception of
9/11

and
the lifelong friendship
and
humanity
of
Eric Ross Green

"It will have blood.
They say blood will have blood.
Stones have been known to move and trees to speak:
augurs and understood relations have by maggot-pies
and choughs and rooks brought forth
the secret'st man of blood."

Macbeth
Act 3, Scene 4, 121-125

Vamp in basso ostinato

This is a work of shadows, by shadows, for shadows. It had no beginning and will have no end. We are now and always shrouded in its penumbra. To fashion a starting point we need only drive a stake at random into the ground of time.

Imagine a massive government building the day after the turn of the current century. Black glass windows reflect the early morning sun. Snow-dusted cars fill a vast parking lot. In the distance, barren trees and a glimpse of frozen river.

The furniture of a spacious office on the top floor has been moved aside and a strange ceremony is in progress. Thirteen people lie flat on their backs in a wide circle with their feet pointing to the center. Two are women, the others men of a similar middle age. Their arms stretch outward as they stare intently at the ceiling. They are all naked. Their clothes hang from chairs a few feet beyond their heads like the hours on a clock. Three hold military drab, eight a dark civilian blue, only the women's clothes have any conspicuous color.

As one celebrant intones a phrase the group repeats and each follows each.

They appear equals with no obvious leader.

"We are the egg . . "

" . . and the ego."

"We are the germ."

"We are life."

"We are the only gods."

"Proud . . "

" . . and predatory . . "

" . . who define all truth . . "

" . . and disseminate . . "

" . . all fantasy."

"We know no heaven . . "

" . . nor hell . . "

" . . but praise immortal death . . "

" . . our master."

The words become an improvised fugue which continues until,

without any audible cue, their voices join in calm finality.

"We who will make all else bow down before us."

After a long moment of quiet contemplation they get to their feet and dress in modest silence.

Passacaglia Buffa - Stanza One

§

"What the hell is a 'transhumanist', Michael?"
His sister always called him by name when going for the jugular.
"Well, what?" she insisted.
"Someone who believes in the transhuman."
"And what is that?"
"Um . . "
"You mean like transcendentalism?"
"No. Well, yes, something like that."
"Like the sixties? Someone who does yoga, or drugs?"
"No, more like someone who believes in that which may be beyond human."
"Like E.T.?"
"Maybe."
"Don't be idiotic. All the wine-soaked waffle about humanism is bad enough without . . "
"Well, there are people who'd like to believe there's something more . . we can achieve . . or partake of . . day to day than . . "
"Our muddled little lives?"
"Yes. Well put."
"Is that why you're going to New York?"
"You can come if you want."
"No, thanks. Been there, done that. Besides it'll still be a mess."
"I understand."
"What makes you think they'll let you in?"
"It wasn't a problem. The magazine got me a ticket. The airports were open within a few days. Things seem to be getting back to normal."

"So you're going to see a transhumanist?"

"No, no. Something strange happened. I don't mean the attack. There was a curious report amongst all the other strangeness. John tossed it across his desk at our meeting last week. He wants me to find out more about it."

"What?"

"You'd just laugh."

Michael had for many years written the occasional article for a magazine called 'Enigma' which was dedicated to a rational and dispassionate examination of any and all occult and so-called supernatural phenomena.

"Just tell me it's not political."

"It could be *quasi*-political. But it's most likely nothing."

"God, if I have to listen to any more of that sophomoric crap!"

"Some of it might not be crap."

"Oh, come on, Michael."

Michael Davenport and his sister and only sibling Helen, who had once made the mistake of hitching her youthful fortunes to an aspiring American art dealer and suffered through some bleak years in Brooklyn Heights, were sitting at breakfast in their small shared flat in Chalk Farm, London, some five and a half weeks after the tragedy of 9/11 shattered the naive assumptions of the western world and the 'crap' was the growing multitude of conspiracy theories that now dominated everyone's dinner conversation. Everyone in London with any kind of left-wing persuasion, that is.

Helen was ten years and three months younger than Michael, she was not quite yet forty-two, and since her disappointments in the New World had become a self-proclaimed and loudly outspoken realist and perhaps rather too automatically pooh-poohed what she termed 'flabby thinking'.

He, on the other hand, had been transfixed that fateful afternoon as the last driblets in his soup bowl lay desiccating on his desk. It was just after lunchtime in London when the first plane hit and Marta called to alert him. He stood stock-still for hours in front of the one remaining functional television set in his cramped but to him wonderfully comfortable and comforting study, watching the spectacle the whole world was watching and muttered almost without hesitation, "This gives the bastards everything they need."

Marta was Hungarian and Michael's wife but, though they were very fond of each other, for a variety of reasons always lived separately.

However, for Michael, it wasn't whether the horrifying carnage was self-inflicted to further some witless and nefarious purpose, that was a given to a man of his experience and instinct and awareness of the all too frequent instances of such blatant skullduggery in America's past. He knew very well that, no matter how constant the pressure of earnest souls to unearth the truth about them, they would forever remain mired in obfuscation. It was painfully obvious to any outsider that such things had deformed the country's inner life and made honest dealing in its politics impossible. No, what Michael had become interested in were those three paragraphs on the thirteenth page of Al Jazeera claiming that two salvage workers had seen something decidedly unusual emerging from the rubble of Ground Zero twenty-six days after the towers fell.

A mirage most probably. A figment of over-tired imaginations. A wisp of smoke or some kind of silly American gag. Very unlikely to be of consequence but there was just the slimmest possibility it might be 'transhuman'.

§

On the plane to New York Michael couldn't help reliving the bizarre events of his last trip to America four and a half years previously. Events that, due in part to a nasty English winter cold but mostly to some inherent pig-headedness in his proud Saxon ancestry, had very nearly cost him his life.

He had a great fondness for cats and desert landscapes and one morning, while traveling by bus from Miami to Los Angeles to visit an expatriate couple of screen-writer friends, he waded, in reckless hungover excitation, across the shallow trickle of the Rio Grande from El Paso to Ciudad Juarez while filming a huge white Siberian tiger.

Half an hour later he was observed capturing a shadowy image of the tiger's owner as it obediently curled itself into a long white imousine.

This man, Amado Portillo Perez, turned out to be the billionaire *patron* of the Juarez drug cartel. He had just faked his own death by the complex ruse of having his brother killed during cosmetic surgery in a Mexico City clinic and dispatched his thugs to recover the tape. They found Michael as he was approaching the border crossing and threw him to the ground, took the cassette from his camera and stole his passport.

Michael couldn't bear the thought of losing his precious footage of the tiger and was obsessive enough to try and retrieve it which resulted in his being taken to Portillo's magnificent villa above Juarez, dressed up as someone called 'Bartolomeo Vespucci', a mysterious panjandrum whose reality or unreality Michael had never been able to verify, and forced to portray him at a meeting with two high-ranking members of the Russian Mafia in the penthouse suite of Portillo's hotel in El Paso.

The Mafia dons wanted to stash a large quantity of contraband plutonium in the Samalayuca desert south of Juarez and needed Portillo's help. At the end they had performed a revolting, and to Michael quite absurd, sexual ritual with Portillo's sister and a black American woman resembling Condoleezza Rice who was there to act as interpreter. Afterwards, as all four stood unabashedly naked before him, still flushed and dripping seminal fluid, the Russians made a toast which Michael had struggled to remember and which Marta easily translated for him on his return to London.

'Besssmertnaja smert' nash vladelec!'

'Immortal death, our master!'

That same evening, during the televised gala finale of the Miss Texas Pageant which the drug lord was hosting at the hotel in the guise of his false *persona* Amado Barragan, Michael had assisted a two-day's-old acquaintance, a former agent of the American Drug Enforcement Administration, in 'outing' Portillo while hanging him helplessly off his seventeenth floor balcony.

Portillo was number one on the DEA's most wanted list but when Michael and the courageous agent exposed his true identity for all to see and made him so vulnerably available for arrest there were no takers. It was plain some hidden power had other fish to fry and, to Michael's lasting sadness, the agent got himself killed.

The American media had for years painted Amado Portillo as a 'vampire' in the metaphorical sense but Michael had been shown proof there was a terrifying lick of reality to it. Both Portillo and his sister told him without hesitation they truly were vampires and the horrors they forced him to witness were stark testimony their weird belief couldn't easily be dismissed. Even the ritual with the Russians had involved an exchange of blood.

Michael attempted afterwards, in a series of articles for the magazine, to give a full account of the experience but when your readership worldwide is something like five or six hundred certifiable oddballs you can't really consider your work has vaulted the palisade of the Collective Consciousness.

§

After three days of being given the runaround, Michael was able to locate the two salvage workers, Luciano Perretti and Jim Gonzalez. They had been taken off the job because it was found they were suffering from 'stress'.

Gonzalez lived in the Bronx and Perretti in Hoboken but they agreed to meet him in a coffee shop near his hotel. Affordable and New York are oxymorons but, at Michael's suggestion, the magazine booked him two weeks at the Belleclaire on West 77th Street. It was scruffy, as he knew, but the most tolerable of a bad lot and the location provided many memories of another old and very dear friend who once lived on West End Avenue. It was also a kind of homage because the friend suffered a massive heart attack and dropped dead at the corner of 9th Avenue and 42nd Street while riding his bicycle to the first reading of a play he had written.

Well, alas, not quite dead. At his wife's pleading in the emergency room the attending doctor made a fifth reluctant attempt with the paddles and, after more than half an hour in the afterlife, his heart magically resumed its beat. But, as the doctor warned his wife, he would never come back to himself. He lived on for two more years and, though he confounded the experts and eventually walked again and would do so for hours in an eerie robotic fury along the paths of Riverside Park with Michael holding him by the arm, steering him by main force in a futile attempt to avoid the sea of dog droppings, this most articulate of men, who to any passer-by must have seemed the very reincarnation of peripatetic Socrates, never uttered another word. He could sit calmly in his recliner and stare at Michael for an entire afternoon with unblinking eagle eyes and not give the slightest indication whether he knew who he was.

This reminiscence filled Michael's mind as he walked over to the Manhattan Diner on Broadway which he recalled serving a dark, almost European blend unlike the insipid bogwater usually dished up in Middle America.

A headline caught his eye at a newspaper kiosk, 'Toxic Nightmare at Disaster Site', and though he wouldn't normally have delved into a rag like the Daily News he bought a copy. It was an article lambasting the city government for not coming clean about the witch's brew of sulfur dioxide, benzene, chlorinated dioxins, glass and asbestos fibers, polychlorinated biphenyls, chromium, copper, lead and zinc lurking unseen in the gray dust that still blew in choking clouds from every ledge and rooftop in Lower Manhattan and which ever since the tragedy had been posing a serious health hazard to both residents and rescue workers alike.

Michael was reading this and muttering with disgust as the two men came in. He had his back to the door but though the diner was very crowded they had no trouble picking him out. It puzzled him why no one seemed to have that difficulty. Surely his manner of dress was nondescript enough. He finally decided, like Jack up the beanstalk, he must simply have the 'smell' of a bloody Englishman.

His mild disgruntlement was assuaged somewhat to observe that Perretti fitted the cliché image of an Italian to a fare-thee-well. Short and stocky with thick dark hair and a five o'clock shadow at ten in the morning. Gonzalez, on the other hand, was a bit of a surprise, a tall second-generation Filipino.

Perretti took in the headline as the two men settled into the booth.

"It's not funny, I'm telling you. Everyone is sick from it. Burning lungs, skin, eyes, throat. We haven't been down there in two weeks and we're still bad."

"I'm sorry to hear it. Our government displays the same callous indifference when it comes to the safety of its citizens."

A perky young waitress arrived and Michael told the men if they were hungry to please order whatever they liked. They both wanted coffee and Perretti asked for a cinnamon roll which the girl avowed were the best in the city and departed.

"I'm sure we could commiserate all day about the ills of the world," Michael went on, "But that's not why I'm here. I told you I write for a magazine in London. I'd like you to describe exactly what you saw."

It was evidently a tale that was hard to begin and the men looked at each other with discomfort for a moment.

"It didn't start with that."

"No?"

"No, we think it started 'cause we didn't like what was going on."

"We told the foreman."

The cadence of their speech was typical New Yorker.

"What?"

"Well, for starters nobody gives a shit about safety or protection."

"Hundreds of guys have got hurt."

"Working without hard-hats or masks even."

"But worse than that, they're making us go too fast. There's still thousands of bodies under that rubble."

"It takes time. You have to move careful. Piece by piece."

"It's a matter of respect."

"We only found maybe five hundred so far."

"But they keep pushing us to cut the stuff up and haul it away. It's a shame and a sacrilege."

"We think they're scared about it really being investigated."

"Examined by experts, you know."

"They're down there but they don't let 'em in."

"Too dangerous, they say."

"The fires are still burning unbelievably hot."

"Like the inside of a volcano. Nothing puts it out. I'm telling you, there's still molten metal everywhere."

"But it's bull. I mean, we were there, weren't we?"

"And you complained about all this to the foreman?"

"Darn right. We told him we were gonna talk to the reporters."

"A couple of weeks ago they started letting small groups of them inside the frozen zone."

"What's that?"

"The area that's off limits to the public. It's been slowly getting smaller since it happened."

"To start with they were allowed to take photos but a few days later Giuliani put a ban on it."

"Why?"

"Who knows? All the same reason, I guess."

"And did you talk to them?"

"Well, we were going to . . "

"But the foreman got mad and told us to do our job."

"So you never talked to them."

"Not about that."

"This other thing took over. They let us talk about that."

"What other thing?"

"You know already."

"I know what I read but I want you to tell me."

The girl brought their coffees and the cinnamon bun and the men paused.

"I gotta say, it was weird," Perretti continued.

"We thought at first it must be some freak looking for the gold."

"What gold? The article didn't mention gold."

"No. We didn't tell him. We couldn't prove it."

"That maybe a billion dollars worth of gold and other precious metals was in vaults under the ruins."

"But the bigger deal was the rumor that some of it had been stolen."

"You mean, since the towers fell?"

"Yeah. Crazy, ain't it?"

"Some of it was being moved through a tunnel under Building 5 on the day."

"Anyway, we never saw it but one night, it must've been three or four in the morning, we were working together clearing debris under Building 4. We guessed that was where one of the vaults was supposed to be . . "

"Because they were really putting the pressure on to get through it . . "

"And we both saw . . "

"What?"

"We know it's totally nuts."

"But we both saw it. The same thing."

"What exactly?"

"There was a sound, I don't know how to describe it, a kind of electronic clicking and buzzing . . "

"I heard it like loud finger-snapping . . "

"And what happened?"

"Something came out of the rubble on the far side."

"Came out . . how? From some sort of hole?"

"No, there was no hole. The stuff is so compacted from the collapse you wouldn't believe it. It just kind of formed up in front of it."

"Like a ghost?"

"Exactly like that. Like in the movies."

"It's crazy but we both saw it."

"And it seemed like a person?"

"Yeah, definitely."

"Was it solid?"

"Sort of solid and not solid."

"It came toward us for a second and then stopped like it had seen us."

"It pointed at us and opened its mouth like it was laughing but there wasn't any noise. Other than the snapping and buzzing."

"How long was this?"

"Long enough so we knew what we were looking at."

"Then it moved really fast out of sight."

"We shouted at it to stop and went after it."

"But it just flat out disappeared."

"How did it move?"

"Fast. It was running. But it didn't make a sound."

"So it had legs?"

"Oh yeah, legs, shoes, everything."

"There were some other guys working close to where it must have gone by but they said they didn't see anything."

"There was no place to hide. There was either rubble or where we'd cleared it away."

"And then it was quiet again?"

"Yeah, well, the noise it was making stopped. There was a lot of other noise to do with the cleanup all the time."

"What did it look like?"

"You read the paper."

"The guy wanted to know everything."

"You spoke to him only?"

"No, no, there was a whole bunch of them. From everywhere."

"But I couldn't find any reference other than the one in Al Jazeera."

"Maybe because it was so completely nuts."

"No one else reported it."

"They yanked us off the job the next morning."

Michael took a sip of coffee and tried his best to seem serious.

"You said it looked like a vampire."

"It did."

"I'm telling you no lie. We both saw it. It looked just like that old vampire movie. The one with Bela Lugosi."

"Dracula?"

"That's it."

"Black cape and all?"

"The whole thing, white face, black cape, white gloves, long teeth."

"And you said this thing looked like the vice-president."

"Exactly. We both saw it."

"It looked right at us. You couldn't mistake who it was."

"Was it wearing some kind of mask?"

"No."

"No, we don't think it was a mask. No, definitely not."

"And it just disappeared."

"It's impossible to get on the site without a security check so there's no way it was some kind of prankster."

"And nearly a month before Halloween," Michael observed wryly, "I'm not surprised they took you off the job."

They shared a small laugh.

"No, sure, we can see how it looks."

"But why would we make it up?"

"You think we want everyone making fun and saying we're loony."

"People do strange things."

"What, like for money?"

"Or their fifteen minutes of fame."

"That wasn't what we were doing."

"We told some of the other guys what we saw and we said the same to the foreman and he told us why didn't we go tell that to the reporters. We thought, hey, this might be our chance to talk about all the other stuff."

"But when we started in one of them said the foreman told them we were a pair of nut-jobs who thought they just saw Count Dracula so most of them moved away after a few kind of derisive questions, you know. Just this Arab-looking guy, well, he was well-dressed and all that, anyway, he got interested and we stood around talking to him for over an hour."

"So why do you think this thing appeared to you? Why the vice-president?"

"How the hell do we know?"

"They say we're delusional but it's not true."

"So you think Dick Cheney came all the way down into that basement to point at you and smile?"

"No, of course not. Not the guy himself."

"What then, his spirit? His doppelganger?"

The two men didn't seem to quite understand and shrugged.

"No, I'm not sure what it means either," Michael said with a smile. "And this all happened early in the morning of October 7th according to your story."

"That's right."

Michael found it mildly interesting that only a few hours later the attack on Afghanistan had begun but he didn't bother to mention it.

"So why do you think you two particularly would see this?"

"We don't know."

"You're not Dracula fans."

"No."

"Have you got something against Mr. Cheney?"

"No."

"You haven't got some sort of political axe to grind?"

"No. Nothing to do with him, anyway."

"Have any of your co-workers seen anything like this since?"

"No. Not that we know."

"And you swear to me this is not just a put-on."

"We swear."

"We've decided maybe we *are* crazy."

Michael looked at them carefully. There was nothing at all suspicious about the way the two men were behaving.

"Tell me again about the cleanup."

"They're forcing us to go too fast. There are three hundred firefighters down there looking for bodies but one of them told us once we get the gold out they're gonna be cut back to just twenty-five."

"They don't care about the people who died anymore."

"Like we say, they just want us to scoop and dump. They won't let anyone in to check it out. We're cutting all the steel up, loading everything onto trucks and it all gets taken away. They're melting it down and selling it to China someone said."

"One of the truckers stopped for a sandwich before he got to the dumpsite and they fired him on the spot."

"Maybe it's being examined somewhere else," Michael suggested.

"How would that work? Wouldn't you need to see it in place first?"

"They've definitely got something to hide."

"Who?"

"How the hell would we know? It's hard to believe. But it's like the biggest thing that's ever happened. The biggest attack ever on American soil. You'd think they'd want to go over every little thing with a fine-tooth comb."

"With tweezers even."

"It's a crime scene. A murder scene. A slaughter scene. We don't get it."

Michael did only too well but he didn't elaborate since that wasn't the subject of his investigation. He thanked the two men for coming and told them he would write up their story for the magazine and would be in touch.

As Michael walked back to the Belleclaire he chided himself for not telling them there was really nothing to write about. At least the ghostly manifestation part and the political conclusions to be drawn from the hasty and secretive cleanup, though monstrous, weren't really the kind of thing that interested the readership of Enigma. The appearance of 'Dick Cheney' in a vampire suit was either a ridiculous prank or pure nonsense and though the men were clearly honest and not trying to gain anything from it as an isolated circumstance their obvious hallucination could only be of marginal interest. A curiosity the perspicacious would relish but hardly serious aficionados of the supernatural.

Stanza Two

it takes billions or fame to admit ya
or power unless it has quit ya
the point of it all
is to keep this round ball
in our thrall no we wouldn't shit ya

§

At approximately the same time that Michael bade farewell to Jim Gonzalez and Luciano Perretti, George Walker Bush, quondam founder of Arbusto Energy, soon after known as 'El-Busto', and then owner and managing partner of the Texas Rangers baseball franchise, then the first governor in Texas history to be elected to two consecutive four-year terms and now the 43rd president of the United States, was strolling from the Palm Room onto the West Colonnade and pausing outside the Press Corps offices to breathe the scented air wafting from the Rose Garden with his vice-president, the aforementioned Richard Bruce Cheney, avid fisherman, multiple heart attack victim, former Chief-of-Staff to the 38th president, five-time Congressman from Wyoming, Secretary of Defense during the reign of the current First Father and erstwhile CEO of Halliburton, the world's largest oilfield services corporation, and, a pace or two behind, the slim, immaculately dressed figure of the current Presidential National Security Advisor, the unassailably loyal, famously gap-toothed, multi-talented Condoleezza Rice, promising ballerina and figure-skater in youth, accomplished concert pianist in adulthood, fluent speaker of the Russian language, ex-Provost of Stanford University, Special Assistant for National Security Affairs in the first Bush White House, former board member of Chevron and future Secretary of State, whose given name memorialized a loving mother's playful inspiration with the musical term *con dolcezza* and now proudly graced the prow of a supertanker.

'Shrub', as George was affectionately known, had just been seated on a stage in the East Room of the White House Residence, surrounded by an impressive assembly of law enforcement officials, politicians and national and international media, putting his scrawl, a signature analyst's dream, the 'George', short, cramped and indistinct, the 'Bush' a long squiggle racing to the finish line, to H. R. 3162, the Counterterrorism Bill, thereafter commonly dubbed The Patriot Act.

This bill, which the president assured the American public in his follow-up remarks was an essential step in defeating terrorism while protecting constitutional rights, had passed two days previously in the House of Representatives by a vote of 357 to 66 and in the Senate the day afterwards by a vote of 98 to 1 despite the fact that virtually none of those dignitaries had actually read it. Hardly surprising since even the short version of the document, which must have been many weeks or more likely months in the drafting, ran to well over a hundred pages. Nonetheless, the president thanked them all for their hard work and bipartisanship and went on to give plaudits to almost everyone in attendance, the vice-president, the Secretary of State, Colin Powell, the Secretary of the Treasury, Paul O'Neill, the starch-collared, hymn-crooning Attorney-General, John Ashcroft, who wasn't one to take chances and had prudently avoided commercial airline flights since mid-summer, and the Directors of the CIA and FBI, for waging their "incredibly important two-front war, one overseas, one here at home."

Terrorists cannot be reasoned with, the president expounded, because they recognize no barrier of morality and have no conscience and then, to prove his point, cited the ongoing anthrax scare and the recent deaths of two Washington area postal workers.

Envelopes contaminated by a suspicious white powder containing spores of the lethal bacillum had been headline news since the commencement of the attack on Afghanistan at the beginning of the month but their dissemination must have started weeks earlier. The outbreak affected postal facilities up and down the east coast, most particularly in Florida, New Jersey, New York and Washington, one of which sorted mail for the White House though the president confidently asserted he 'didn't have anthrax', and spread to the offices of NBC news, the New York Post, Microsoft, Capitol Hill and the State Department and that very day had infiltrated the mail room of the CIA. To date there were three confirmed deaths and thirty-two serious exposures but over ten thousand people had been tested and the British pharmaceutical giant GlaxoSmithKline and German Bayer had pledged to assist the Department of Health and Human Services in amassing a stockpile of enough Cipro antibiotic to treat twelve million Americans.

This, he opined, added extra urgency to the current legislation which would give the police, the FBI and ATF agents and federal marshals, the customs officers, Secret Service and other intelligence professionals the tools they needed to identify, dismantle, disrupt and punish terrorists before they could strike, put an end to their counterfeiting, smuggling and money-laundering and allow unimpeded surveillance of their communications, including email, the Internet and cellular telephones. The vice-president had pronounced that this imperative to secure the homeland was no temporary thing and would become 'permanent in American life' and the president seconded the motion to thunderous applause.

"We will enforce this law with all the urgency of a nation at war," he told the gathered multitude. It was 'essential' for 'preventing more atrocities at the hands of the evil ones.'

After their brief pause to smell the roses during which they couldn't help but share a sly moment of triumph, the three became all business again and walked into the West Wing, took an immediate double left turn and entered the Cabinet Room where a crew was ready and waiting to tape the president's weekly radio address. It would not be broadcast until the following day and was little more than a rehash of his recent words but it would underline their message to a frazzled American public and an apprehensive world.

§

Back at the Belleclaire, Michael had an impulse to look up his sister's long lost art dealer husband. Helen would be furious with him but she needn't know. It was nearly twenty years since they last met and, though Michael had nothing against the man personally, the meeting had been far from cordial.

'Was he still in New York, or even alive?' Michael wondered. He would be in his late forties by now. Michael punched the name 'David Giudice' into his laptop search engine and it took only a fraction of a second to find something promising. There was a David Giudice connected to an art gallery called 'White Noise' which claimed to specialize in Canadian art. The address was on Spring Street in the Soho section of Greenwich Village which Michael found amusing because he lunched the day before at a natural food restaurant only a few doors away.

'Who else could it be?' he thought.

Since he always avoided telephone conversations if at all possible he decided just to turn up at the gallery and see what happened.

It was a glorious autumn afternoon, unseasonably mild with a clear blue sky, a fresh breeze blowing off the Hudson and russet leaves scudding everywhere, but as Michael rounded the corner onto Spring Street from Lafayette an upsetting sight greeted his arrival.

David Giudice was standing in the doorway of the gallery shouting at the top of his lungs at another man. A small cluster of onlookers had gathered beyond the parked cars on the opposite curb.

"Because the world is fucking crazy!" he yelled, "And there's no fucking way to penetrate the white fucking noise, that's why!"

The other man stood his ground and apparently wasn't much affected by the ongoing tirade. Michael judged him to be at least ten years older and, despite the evident expense of his tailoring, rather rotund and squat in comparison with David, whose aristocratic leanness had grown more chiseled with the years.

David turned on the group peering from across the street and took a few paces toward them.

"What are you all staring at?! We live in a mad house! Our government blew up our fucking city and killed our families and we run around waving fucking flags! We're dupes, patsies, babes in toyland!"

A young woman, who had not stopped to listen but was merely making her way past the others, responded in a normal voice saying, "What are you shouting for? You think we don't know?" David observed her retreating form for a moment and quieted and the onlookers slowly began to disperse.

Michael was impressed no one called out 'Commie!' or 'Traitor!' or any of the usual mindless kneejerkery but then this was the Village.

David turned to the other man and spoke in a softer tone.

"You're not a creep. I take it back. You loved my sister. You loved Ruth. And I love you for that. God damn it though, the pain is unbearable. We're in the black bloody night now and we're on our knees. On our sad complicitous fucking knees!"

With that David left him and went back into the gallery and the round-faced little man turned away along the sidewalk passing Michael and nodding politely and for the briefest fraction of a second as he did so

Michael saw his features transform into the spitting image of Richard Cheney!

In truth, beyond the dark overcoat, black hat, cropped white hair and pale complexion, there was little similarity. Michael instantly put the apparition down to the combined effect of his conversation with the two salvage workers that morning and jetlag. It didn't yet constitute any kind of confirmation but nonetheless it had been extremely vivid, if short-lived.

It was still flashing in a strange retinal aftershock as he considered that this might not be the moment to turn up on David unannounced. On the other hand, his emotional vulnerability could prove fortuitous. Michael decided to wait a few minutes before following him into 'White Noise'.

David was nowhere to be seen as Michael entered so he took a slow turn around the empty gallery. He had never been much interested in Eskimo soapstone or walrus tusk carvings nor all those earnest and repetitive thunderbirds and totem poles from the rain forest but there were a few quite good contemporary pieces. An egg tempera of a ballet dancer and a seascape and a nude leaning over a bathtub by someone called Darcus whom Michael assumed to be French-Canadian which, to him, explained the quality. Though English, he had an anti-English bias. Despite the quantity available he didn't sense the place was prospering.

He heard footsteps coming rapidly down a flight of wooden stairs and David burst through a door at the rear of the small but well-ordered space. He was nearly out the front before he noticed Michael.

"I'm sorry, sir, I have to close for a while. If you want something you'll have to come back."

Michael could see pain and fatigue in his eyes.

"David? It's Michael. Davenport. Helen's brother. Do you remember? I know it's been ages."

David suddenly laughed.

"Good Christ. Yes, I remember. Too well. I saw you outside and thought you looked familiar but I couldn't place you. Sorry. What are you doing here?"

"I work for a magazine. In London. I'm here on assignment."

"Oh yes? What kind of magazine? Look, I've really got to go. My lover is sick and throwing up like you wouldn't believe. I have to get him some medicine. Walk with me. The drugstore's just around the corner."

They left the gallery and David locked the door behind them.

"What kind of magazine?"

"It examines, it tries to rationally examine, out of the ordinary phenomena."

David laughed again.

"Like what just happened here?"

"Not really. Maybe partly."

"How's the little monster Helen?"

It was Michael's turn to laugh.

"Still monstrous. She never remarried, you know. We share a flat."

"She's not with you, is she?"

Michael smiled at his sudden concern.

"No, not lurking round the corner waiting to pounce."

"That's a relief. And you never married, is that right?"

"No. Several close calls but no. Well, I am married to a Hungarian. We did it years ago to get her out. We're good friends but we've never lived together."

"Helen was right to leave me. It was stupid. I didn't realize. I spent the whole time trying to pretend I wasn't gay. It was hard for her."

They walked into the drugstore and Michael waited. He could see David in conversation with the pharmacist, an elderly Chinese, and it was obvious the man knew the situation very well. It took only two or three minutes for him to make up what was needed. As they left to go back Michael said, "I heard you in the street before I came in."

"I don't see how you couldn't have."

"I assume you were referring to the horrors of a month and a half ago. Were you in New York?"

"Right here. We could see the towers from the roof."

"It must have been utterly extraordinary."

"Worse than that."

"Yes, yes, of course."

They walked on in silence until they reached the gallery.

"This is probably not a good moment to catch up if . . "

"No, no, don't worry about it. This happens all the time. Fernando's dying. He won't care."

They went inside and David locked the door and turned the sign to 'closed'.

"I don't see much of a queue," he said ruefully, "Come on up."

It was two flights of stairs and at the top a revealed brick archway led into a large and remarkably tasteful room filled with an eclectic assortment of comfortable furniture, plants, hundreds of books, paintings and memorabilia.

"Nando?" David called.

A tiny groan came from the bathroom and David went in and shut the door. Michael examined the book selection and mused with approval that, after all, they might get on. Why had they not all those years ago? No idea. People change.

The bathroom opened again.

"Make yourself presentable. We've got company," David commanded over his shoulder as he came out.

"Who?"

Michael detected a Spanish accent beneath the croaked monosyllable.

"Relax. You've never met him," David replied and said to Michael, "He'll be out when he's ready."

"Are you certain it wouldn't be better . . "

"I said don't worry. He likes company. So, is it too early for a drink?"

Music to Michael's ears.

"Not for me."

"Good. These days I'm ready before breakfast. What would you like?"

"What are you . . ?"

"Red wine."

"That'll be perfect," Michael said, too polite not to lie.

David shouted into the bathroom.

"A glass of *vino rosso*, sweetheart?"

"Don't be a little prick, you little prick," came the hoarse reply.

"That's why he's been puking. Even the mountain of medication he has to take doesn't stop him. He's got galloping HIV and three weeks ago had a massive heart attack. Circulation problems are a well-documented side effect of the AIDS meds. His doctors have told him he's on death row."

Michael couldn't think of a response but one came from the bathroom.

"Why are you such a little prick anyway?"

"Could it be because . . ?"

"You have such a little prick?"

The wine was open and David put a glass of it in Michael's hand.

"Thank you." He took a big swallow. "Mm, ambrosia."

"Almost as good as blood. It's Italian."

Michael's eyes suddenly focused on a small, framed photographic portrait of the vice-president on the top of a bookshelf against the opposite wall and it made him nearly jump out of his skin. Cheney was staring straight at the camera and snarling like a vampire. There were specks of blood at the corners of his mouth. It was exactly the expression on Amado Portillo's face as he howled in agony after his sister gut-shot him. One more coincidence like this and it would definitely have the makings of a story. It took Michael a few seconds to regain his composure.

"I was a little surprised at first the people in the street seemed to agree with what you were saying. There are a lot of people in London who do too. It's very hard not to think it was some kind of inside job. Though it seems to me, if it were, they could hardly expect to hide it for very long. There would have to have been literally thousands of people who knew. At least part of it."

Fernando wheeled out of the bathroom in a chair wearing flaming pink silk pajamas and a heavy yellow bathrobe. The olive skin of his face was mottled purple and his cheeks and temples were skeletal hollows.

"Of course there would have! David thinks everything is a conspiracy. Hi, I'm Fernando."

They shook hands.

"My mother was Irish but it's hard to tell. I was born in Havana and I'm going to die in New York but please, please, please, don't let that bother you."

"I'll try. I'm Michael."

Strange, he thought, that the first and only other Fernando he could recall having met in his life was connected to a gallery. In Juarez he had been stunned into silence by his photographs of murdered women, *'las desaparecidas'*. They still corresponded from time to time.

"I figured it out in there while I was gagging on magnesia," this so similar and yet so sadly different Fernando went on, "You're the brother of that poor girl whose life he did his best to ruin."

"He didn't manage it entirely."

"He's a vampire himself so he thinks everyone else is. That's why we've got that awful new addition."

Fernando pointed to the Cheney photograph. Curiously, Michael had talked about vampires with Fernando Rios as well.

"Please help me get him to throw it out. He may not be a vampire or guilty of anything but stupidity and greed but he is deeply ugly. It's not healthy having a little altar of hate smack in the middle of the living room not that David hasn't got a right to be upset. Did you tell him?"

David poured Michael some more wine.

"No."

"Tell me what?" Michael asked.

"His sister was in the second tower."

He never made her acquaintance but Michael remembered David had a twin sister named Ruth when he heard him speak about her to the man in the street.

"They were on the phone. She would have been killed instantly. At least we hope so. She was on the 81st floor."

"How dreadful. I'm sorry."

David nodded and took a sip of wine.

"We went up on the roof after we heard the first plane hit. We didn't have any idea what it was until we turned on the news. I had to try five or six times but I did talk to her. We were still talking when the second plane . . "

He had to pause to control his emotion.

"I heard the most unearthly howling on the other end of the line and . . I felt her die."

Once again, silence was the only possible response.

"God bless the magnesia," Fernando said finally, "Pour me a big glass of that life-giving young Italian blood, you little prick, I'm cured."

David did and refilled Michael's glass and the bottle was gone.

"Don't worry. We never run out," he said and opened another and they sat together while he opened five more and explained all the reasons he could think of that made it irrefutable the 'attack' was an inside job.

The ridiculously slow reaction of the Air Force when on sixty or more other occasions during 2001 aberrant flights had all been intercepted within ten minutes; the speed and precision with which the twin towers collapsed; the unexplained and inexplicable collapse of Building 7; the fact that structures of that kind had never before been brought down by fire; the haste and clandestine nature of the cleanup; the still raging fires and molten steel; the lack of any serious investigation; the uncollected put-options on the two airlines; the secretive evacuation of the Bin Laden family members; the impossible trajectory of whatever it was that hit the Pentagon; the total absence there of any believable plane debris and at the crash site of flight 93 in Shanksville, Pennsylvania; the hole in the Pentagon wall being far too small to accommodate the wingspan of an airliner; Bush's guilty face as Andrew Card whispered the news of the second plane into his ear in the pet goat classroom; the Secret Service's serious breach of protocol letting the children go on reading to him with America under attack; the immediate accusation of Osama Bin Laden and Bin Laden's denial in both Al Jazeera and Ummat when he would obviously want to take credit for a such a spectacular success; the race to blame Iraq and the extraordinary readiness of the Afghanistan bombardment, which were both according to David the direct result of the imperialistic ambitions of a neo-conservative and preponderantly Jewish cabal within the American government whose desire for a world controlled by the United States coupled with their Zionist sympathies had made a catalyzing catastrophe of such magnitude a cynical necessity and justified in their sick minds the appalling brutality they had inflicted on their fellow citizens; and on and on and on. And Fernando rebutted every one.

Finally at two in the morning Michael pronounced, "If you want to redress the death of Ruth and everyone else who died that day and who are dying since and will die in the future because of these undeniably corrupt heartless swine . . sorry, Fernando, you make an eloquent case for the defence but I think they did it, any 'jihadists' that may have been involved were just patsies . . you have somehow to prove exactly how they plotted and oversaw the whole unbelievable thing . . and that, I'm afraid, is a virtual impossibility without an army of lawyers and whistle-blowers and I don't see anyone hurrying to take the stand. Everyone knows in their heart, even the few incorrigible optimists like Fernando, the official version of the Kennedy assassination and all the other ones is artfully concocted rubbish but the only effective refutation can come either from Congress or the mainstream media initiating an unbiased investigation and both are chock-a-block with cowardly careerists who've sold their consciences. Lobbyists always have more stamina than the man in the street and I predict with complete certainty this will turn out just the same. People believe one thing in private and another in public and more than anything else are too lazy and too scared maybe to keep on looking the awful facts in the face for any length of time. The great snowball of crap always buries their resolve eventually."

At that, Fernando started to choke with laughter as he had often done during the evening, they were all puffing away on cigarettes too as the wine went down and the hours went by, but this time he couldn't stop and

David thought he better put him to bed and Michael couldn't help but agree so he gave them both a hug and just as he was leaving he thought to ask where the photograph of Cheney came from.

"He printed it from some paranoid webzine," Fernando said, still wheezing, "But don't believe what he's about to tell you."

Michael looked at David questioningly.

"It's true," David demurred with an impatient tone, "Two weeks ago it was just a cleverly exaggerated photograph. I can't remember what site I found it on. But the blood appeared later."

Now here, at last, was something worth writing about.

"What do you mean appeared?" Michael asked with a chill tickling his spine.

"Just that. I haven't touched it. I kept it because I hate the man and I think he was behind the whole thing. The blood began appearing a few days ago and little by little has become what you see. I swear on Ruth's soul I haven't moved it from behind the glass since I framed it."

Michael turned to Fernando but he threw his hands up in a mock gesture of innocence.

"Don't look at me. If I cut myself I'll bleed to death. Despair has made him a tad psychotic, that's all," he joked but he wasn't really smiling. "It's our own little shrine. Like Lourdes. At least he hasn't suggested we pray to it."

Stanza Three

§

At eleven the following morning Michael returned to the gallery and found David re-arranging a sculpture exhibit. They both commented on how the other looked surprisingly 'chipper' and 'bright and bushy-tailed', as the respective English and American colloquials have it. Michael, in particular, was one of those fortunate, or unfortunate, individuals who seem able to consume almost limitless quantities of alcohol without obvious damage.

"I forgot to tell you last night," he said, "But when the chap you were talking to in the street walked past me after you went back inside for a split second I saw him as the vice-president. I don't mean I thought he resembled him. I put it down to jetlag or indigestion but his features actually morphed into the exact image of this man Cheney. It was brief but crystal clear."

"That's weird."

"Particularly since you told me about the photograph. And I didn't tell you last night either that the reason I'm in New York in the first place is because two salvage workers at Ground Zero told a reporter from Al Jazeera they had seen an apparition while they were clearing debris in what used to be a part of the basement under Building 4. They were there to unearth a vault containing gold bullion and this thing they saw looked like a cross between Bela Lugosi as Count Dracula and, you guessed it, Dick Cheney."

David looked at him and chuckled.

"Weirder and weirder."

"Who was the man yesterday?"

"I'd only met him a few hours before. We were both walking toward

Ground Zero. I do it a lot. In the first couple of days family members could get close but they put a stop to it. Now there's chain link and green mesh so no one can see. The frozen zone they call it but it changes daily. They're going to open it tomorrow for a memorial service. Anyway, we stopped at a corner on the west side of Broadway at Cortlandt. I was looking through a slit in the mesh. The site was visible a block down the street. We'd been more or less walking side by side since we crossed Vesey and he started to talk to me. We had breakfast and after we chatted for a while it came out that he and Ruth were lovers. I knew nothing about it. I still can't believe the coincidence. He's going to the Breeders' Cup at Belmont racetrack this afternoon and invited me to come along."

"What's his name?"

"Louis. Lamy, I think. Something like that."

"Lamy, as in French for friend? Or Lamia . . the mythological demon who devoured children. Half serpent, as I recall. Keats wrote a poem about her."

"Let's assume possible friend."

"Did you find out much about him?"

"No. He's the CEO of a construction and engineering company. Semi-retired. Rich as hell. And he had an affair with my sister."

"How did he come to know her?"

"She worked for a company he did business with."

Michael nodded.

"And how is Fernando today?"

"Still sleeping."

"I'd like to have another look at the photo but it can wait. Do you think the blood specks might be some sort of stain? Does the photo have a backing?"

"Just plain cardboard."

"Do you think some dust from the collapse might have got in and reacted with the paper? Or didn't it get up this far?"

"Oh, it did. It wasn't that much, not like south of Canal, but I had the whole building professionally cleaned. There really is no rational explanation."

"So what do you think is causing the red spots?"

"I have no idea. The subcutaneous pressure of overwhelming guilt. Erupting like pus from a pimple."

Michael laughed.

"In a photograph?"

"Why not? You saw Lamy morph into Cheney. The workers saw Cheney like Dracula. What did they say it did? Did it speak to them?"

"No, it just pointed at them and opened its mouth like it was laughing but it didn't make any sound. They said they heard some kind of clicking noise but after a few seconds it went round the corner and vanished. Some other workers were there but didn't see anything."

"When was this?"

"October 7th. Three o'clock in the morning."

"The day that lamebrain Ridge was put in charge of 'homeland security'. The same day the bombing started. We had fifteen thousand people in a protest march from Union Square up to the theater district. The Times barely reported it. Did they see this thing again?"

"No, they've been laid off. The foreman said they were suffering from stress but they'd also complained about the lack of safety precautions and how everything was being carted away without any proper examination."

"That would do it."

"They tried to talk to the press but only the correspondent from Al Jazeera would listen."

"And you read that story in London?"

"My editor did."

David thought for a moment.

"Come to Belmont with us if you have time. Who knows, the horses could morph into the whole Cabinet."

§

At that moment in the President's Dining Room in the White House, which is just a few steps past the President's Lavatory down a carpeted corridor from the Oval Office, he was settling in for an early lunch and a butler was popping the cork on a bottle of the First Lady's favorite Becker Vineyards red, the Texas Iconoclast Cabernet Sauvignon, which she felt would be the perfect companion for their rib-eye steaks as long as he confined himself to no more than a few sips.

Seated with the First Couple around the beautiful inlaid walnut table, which had the leaves out to be made circular and more intimate for the occasion, were the vice-president, who since the implant of a defibrillator under the pectoral muscles of his chest four months previously had been more than willing to once again savor fresh meat, and the primly-clad Ms. Rice.

The room, like the entire magnificent edifice, was oriented in line with the cardinal points of the compass and the president as always sat with his back facing the high antique mirror that adorned the wall between the door and window at the south end of the table. The door led to the Oval Office Patio which afforded a fine view of the Putting Green and the South Lawn but it was seldom used because the president preferred to keep it more or less permanently locked.

A second door beside the fireplace once opened into a hall from which one might enter the Roosevelt Room but it had been closed off at the president's wish and there was only one entrance remaining which caused no slight difficulty for the kitchen staff because they had to bring everything required through the Oval Office itself.

The First Lady sat opposite her husband with her back facing the fireplace and the vice-president slouched in his characteristic fashion on the west side of the table with the National Security Advisor neatly perched to the east.

One might assume such an elite gathering would be deep in the discussion of earth-shaking topics like the president and Condi's recent trip to the APEC Summit in Shanghai and his colloquies with Jiang Zemin and Vladimir Putin or his phone conversations that morning with Jacques Chirac, Egypt's Mubarak or Chancellor Schroeder or how their assignee Giffen had just sweet-talked Nursultan Abishuly Nazarbayev into letting Chevron and ExxonMobil slurp up the vast pool of black gold under Kazakhstan's Tengiz or how best to keep the wool over the eyes of the Secretary of State or whether it was now time to lay off blaming Al Qaeda for the anthrax scare or the fate of Abdul Haq or the president's meeting with the National Security Council and his briefings with the CIA and the FBI's Mueller and Ashcroft and Ridge or what to do about that loose cannon Rumsfeld or the Taliban or all those pesky conspiracy theories that threatened to boil over or even the weather in Oklahoma or the imminent World Series, but no, they were reminiscing about youthful indiscretions. A painful subject which never failed to flush the Mona Lisa smile from the First Lady's face, not only because of driving through a stop sign and causing the death of a high school classmate but also because Barbara and Jenna, her twin daughters, had recently been having some very public problems with the demon drink. Particularly Jenna who had just completed her freshman year at the University of Texas and been sentenced to thirty-six hours of community service for the trivial offence of trying to purchase alcohol at a popular Mexican restaurant with false identification using the maiden name of her basilisk paternal grandmother, 'Barbara Pierce'.

The president and vice-president were fond of congratulating themselves for their avoidance of any serious military service and also their arrest, Bush at thirty, Cheney in his early twenties, for 'operating a motor vehicle while intoxicated' but on both counts Cheney had the edge. Not only had he ducked the army altogether by an artfully-timed sequence of student, then married-student, then fatherhood draft deferments while the president was forced to an undistinguished stint in the Texas Air National Guard but he had the added prestige of having been nailed not once but twice for drunk-driving and the glorious happenstance the two of them were now giggling like sophomores about as the butler filled their glasses was the fact that he had actually been punished to a lesser extent on the second occasion. He had been handed a thirty-day suspension of his driver's license and ordered to forfeit one hundred and fifty dollars bail by the first judge in Cheyenne but eight months later in Rock Springs had escaped with only a one hundred dollar fine.

In those far off days the police in one county did not have the means to check with another whether someone in their custody was a repeat offender.

"They could've arrested Jack the Ripper back then and had no idea who he was or what he'd done!" the vice-president concluded with delight.

The president chuckled and raised the Cabernet to his mouth and had taken a tiny blissful sip when he happened to glance up at Healy's classical 1860's portrait of John Quincy Adams on the west wall. It was a personal favorite because Adams was the first and only other presidential son of a president and thus he felt they had a bond. Adams was seated under a Grecian portico on a gilt and leather armchair with his right hand outstretched among some papers on a table and his left hand holding a small book on his lap with his index finger marking a page. The arms of the chair were supported by sphinxes with bare breasts.

The painting hung directly behind the vice-president and as Shrub swallowed the wine and stared in astonishment Adams' outstretched palm and the pages of the book began to bleed and the stern features of his face and shining hairless pate that sat with jowls squeezed upward like a milk-fed crystal ball upon the high platform of his collar changed slowly but unmistakably into the perfect likeness of the man before him with the driblet of rib-eye juice on his chin.

§

It was five minutes to noon and David was upstairs checking on Fernando as Michael observed a dark blue Mercedes station wagon coming to a stop outside the gallery with Louis Lamy at the wheel. There was no available parking spot on the street and Lamy looked toward the windows and gave a couple of brief beeps on the horn so Michael decided not to wait and went out to introduce himself.

"Hello," he began, "My name is Michael Davenport. David is . . "

"Weren't you here yesterday?"

"I was."

Michael was half expecting the alarming transfiguration of the day before to reoccur and struggled to maintain a level gaze but the man had quite a pleasant face, nothing of the vice-president's nasty lop-sided sneer, and appeared more like an aging cherub now that he saw him clearly.

"Are you a friend?" Lamy asked.

"An old acquaintance. David was once married to my sister. I haven't seen him for donkey's years."

Lamy made no discernible reaction.

"Is he coming?"

"Yes, yes, he's just seeing to his . . room-mate. He wondered if you wouldn't find it too much of an imposition if I joined you."

Lamy's eyes narrowed ever so slightly but he seemed otherwise untroubled by the suggestion.

"Sure. No problem. Hop in."

"Marvelous. Thanks."

Michael skirted around the car and dithered for a moment whether to get in the front or the back and then thought what the hell did it matter and got in beside Lamy.

"You a fan of the nags?"

"Ah, no, not really," Michael answered, "Formula One is more my ticket."

"Is that so."

"I had a distant relative who developed a racing car called the Elva back in the fifties. I've become more and more fascinated by the sport as the years have gone by."

"Same with me and the nags."

The gallery was on the north side of Spring Street which was one way going east. There were vehicles parked along both curbs and a stream of cars, mostly taxis, were slowly squeezing by Lamy's Mercedes on the right. One of the drivers hammered on Michael's window and looked past him to swear at Lamy but Lamy made no response and the immediate cacophony of honking horns that swelled up from behind as the man stopped to bellow forced him to move on.

"You live in New York or just visiting?" Lamy asked.

"Just visiting. From London."

"How did I guess."

Lamy tapped his horn again.

"I figured David could use a little diversion. You saw how upset he was."

"With good reason, I think."

Lamy didn't answer.

"What is the Breeders' Cup?"

"The World Thoroughbred Championships. Richest day in all of sports."

"Really. Forgive my ignorance but what is a thoroughbred exactly?"

"A race horse."

"Ah," Michael said and smiled apologetically.

"Goes back a couple of centuries to your neck of the woods. Three Arabian stallions were introduced to some English mares and sired the whole breed."

"Ah," Michael repeated, "Sorry, but my knowledge is pretty much limited to Secretariat and the Triple Crown . . "

"The Belmont Stakes is the third leg. After the Derby and the Preakness. In June. I was at the park in '73 when that fantastic chestnut set the course record. Two minutes twenty-four. Led the pack by thirty-one lengths. Fastest time over twelve furlongs of dirt in history."

Michael was about to ask 'How long is a furlong?' but at that moment David came out of the gallery and locked the door. He walked quickly to the car and bent to see where Michael was sitting and got in the back seat and slid to the center.

"No apologies. From either of us, right?" he said to Lamy.

"No apologies," Lamy agreed and put the Mercedes in motion.

"Elva. That stand for anything?" he asked.

"It's French. *Elle va.* She goes."

Lamy chuckled.

"Makes sense. What was your relative's name?"

"Frank Anderson."

"Can't say as I've heard it."

"It was a long time ago. He sold the company in the early sixties."

"My name is French. Lamy. The friend. The family originates from Brittany. Some from Normandy also. Beaumont. In the *Pays d'Auge.* Famous for apples and Calvados. *Auge* means trough. The old circular stone troughs where they pressed the fruit. Incredibly lush and beautiful countryside. Beaumont and Belmont are the same name."

He chuckled again.

"Meaningless connections amuse me."

"We have that in common. Someone called this the Age of Trivia."

"It is," Lamy seconded with a broad smile, "Just like every other 'age'."

"Yes, I suppose so."

"The trick is making enough connections for meaning to appear. Otherwise," he began declaiming in a cod French accent, "One will never be able to perceive the full glory and terror of the wood for the isolated sameness of the trees, as the saying she goes."

He guffawed at his silliness and Michael knew he was going to like him.

"Too true and the wood has infinite depths," he said.

"And pitfalls."

Michael glanced back at David before going on.

"I have friends who bought an eight bedroom manor in Brittany some years ago. They sold an antique business in Whitstable and moved there lock, stock and barrel. It was obscenely cheap. They have an orchard and make their own cider. He raises sheep and she paints. Utterly idyllic. I'd hate it."

They all chuckled at that.

The Mercedes was ascending the ramp onto the Brooklyn Bridge.

"New York," Lamy grunted, underplaying the words, "Some people it drives insane. Some people it drives sane. Things have changed since those Hollanders and Walloons turned up with their Reformed Protestant vision and started the whole crazy ball rolling. Twenty or thirty people died building this bridge. Including the designer. Suffered a crushed foot before construction even began and died of lockjaw. His son took over and after a dive to inspect the pilings got crippled with the bends. Took thirteen years to complete. The longest suspension bridge in the world. A national monument. A work of art. 'It will forever testify to the energy, enterprise and wealth of that community which shall secure its erection.'"

Lamy quoted in a suitably grandiose tone and they grinned at the schoolboy humor.

"We're the beneficiaries," he added with a sly wink.

They were nearing the middle of the span and Michael, always an avid sight-seer, turned his head to look back at Manhattan. Clouds of gray-white smoke were billowing upward from Ground Zero.

"Hell of a view," Lamy said and Michael nodded in agreement.

"There's still a surprising amount of smoke."

"A lot of it's steam today. They're really hosing it down because there's a memorial service at the site tomorrow afternoon. Makes it look worse than it has been."

"Amazing that it keeps burning."

"Office products. We're a culture addicted to paper."

Michael could sense David's discomfort and Lamy must have been able to observe his eyes in the rearview mirror but ploughed on nonetheless.

"The Dutch were astute business people but what a mistake they made when they sold that island. The hub of the world's creative energy. The gap in the skyline behind us will be filled in before you know it. I dearly wish one person who was in those towers had not been. Selfish of me. Selfish of us, I'm sure. I wish with all my heart it never happened but it did. Whatever the explanation. Think of all the wars of human history now lost to memory. Strange how irrelevant in any lasting sense most of them were."

They fell silent for a while as Lamy took the Cadman Plaza exit at the end of the bridge and made a few turns through what Michael thought a rather derelict section of Brooklyn before climbing another ramp onto the I-278 E.

"You know," Michael took up the thread, "Beneath all that enterprise and energy and the belief in boundless wealth, whenever I visit I find everything in this country has the aura of an endgame. Particularly in Los Angeles. It feels to me like some weird party is taking place. A party for the end of the world."

Lamy laughed.

"That's because you're a stuffy inbred English cynic," he said pleasantly.

"I'll have you know I'm Saxon," Michael riposted with a smidgen of genuine pique, "And Saxons are far from stuffy. The royal house of Windsor may be a lot of inbred twerps but they've nothing whatever to do with the real England. They're expatriate German mutants. Betty Battenberg we call her. Less than affectionately, I might add. They're a freak show and a total joke. Do you think David is cynical to believe the house of Bush is responsible for Ruth's death?"

Michael instantly regretted the question and Lamy didn't reply but David did.

"Some writer compared Bush One with Caligula," he said calmly, but there was a threatening edge to his voice, "A horse-lover too, by the way. He tried to destroy all trace of earlier accomplishments, even Homer's Iliad and Odyssey, so no one in the future could compete with his self-declared godhead. Laughable, sure, but I wish I could say the wars of either Bush are an irrelevance, Louis. I agree with Michael. We're headed for catastrophe on an unimaginable scale and the rich bastards . . I'll make you the exception, if you like . . us the exception . . just want to go down partying."

"Rich bastards are only poor bastards with money," Lamy replied.

"Now who's being cynical," Michael said.

"I think we'll see martial law soon," David went on, "It wouldn't surprise me if we've had our last election. They've wanted to set up a military dictatorship since the 1930's. Maybe the extreme fringe is right and Papa Bush was an adopted fascist plant. Maybe Pauline Pierce was 'sex-magicked' in Paris by the 'Great Beast 666' and Dubya is the grandson of Aleister Crowley and George H. Scherff. Who the hell cares? All I know is they and their corporate cronies are going to make a hell of a lot of money out of it. And there's your motive. The biggest motive there is."

"You got that right," Lamy agreed.

"Well, since you're part of that world, Louis, can you tell me how it came to pass?"

"What?"

"The absolute chasm that separates the game being played and compassion for the victims. Do money and power always extinguish the soul?"

"Not always."

They were no longer traveling north toward the Triboro Bridge but Lamy had taken the I-495 E which Michael assumed from the signs was also the Long Island Expressway and he didn't notice at first that David was suddenly brandishing a small hand-gun.

"I'm glad to hear you say that, Louis, because I'm going to put it to the test."

Lamy caught sight of the pistol out of the corner of his eye and was shocked for a moment and the car swerved slightly and then Michael turned and saw it and realized it was nothing but a plastic toy.

"Oh, for god's sake, David . . "

David giggled and stuck the barrel up his right nostril.

"Don't worry, I'm not going to kidnap you. I thought of it though because I'm too far gone for persuasion."

Lamy was smiling but it was hardly mirthful.

"Why are we going to bet on horses, Louis? You told me you loved my sister. Why aren't we driving to Washington to stand outside the White House and scream bloody murder? Ruth has to have some kind of justice, don't you think? We can't let her just become forgotten collateral damage."

Lamy remained silent.

"I need you to help me, god damn it!"

David was shouting now.

"Or were you a part of it, Louis? Did you know it was going to happen? Did you make a big fat pile on it like the others?"

Lamy reacted by putting the Mercedes into a sudden savage slalom and they careened back and forth across the freeway barely missing several other cars and causing a stream of justified profanity from their drivers. David and Michael were thrown violently from side to side, particularly David who banged his forehead on the car door and started to bleed.

"Jesus, Louis, what the fuck are you doing . . !"

"Here, I say, steady on old chap . . !"

"I don't like being insulted," Lamy said as he steered normally again, "And I don't like threats. I was kidnapped in Colombia years ago and held for ransom. Two million. They didn't get it. You know fuck all about me."

They drove on for several minutes without speaking until Lamy turned onto the Cross Island Parkway and broke the ice once more.

"Collateral damage and friendly fire. Terrible phrases. Mindless euphemisms. The creations of a culture of avoidance. How friendly can death be? Assassination? An old story in America. Lincoln, McKinley, the

Kennedys, King. The dervish dance of brief authority. Nothing changes. It's just so fucking boring to bitch at the level of television's idiocy, don't you think?"

"Bitching?!" David erupted again, "I lost my sister, you waffling prick, and it is not possible for me to sit back and philosophize about it!"

This time Lamy laughed out loud.

"I'm one of those people you love to hate," he said with satisfaction.

David was dabbing his forehead with a handkerchief.

"I don't hate you, Louis. I'm just tired of the talk. I thought you might like to help me break through the white noise of lies that has swallowed our country, that's all. Naïve of me. Michael's sister used to call me an innocent."

"She still calls me that," Michael added lightly, hoping to ease the tension.

"How do you think I would be able to help?" Lamy asked.

"You must have plenty of politician friends. I could be wrong but I'm guessing you vote Republican. I'll bet you have clout with the press. What about some kind of public forum? Something that would last more than two seconds and wouldn't end with us getting killed. Ruth was murdered by our own government, Louis. Her blood inside me won't be still."

"That's what scares me about you. I don't trust idealists who wax rhetorical about blood. You think you can force some earth-shattering consequence? A mass awakening, to what, the truth? People have been shouting some version or other of it throughout history. No one stops long enough to hear. What can a couple more fools like us do? The great broom sweeps everyone along. We're just aggregations of soil and slag on the floor."

It was David's turn to laugh.

"Jesus Christ, Louis, you are one evasive and depressing son of a bitch."

"We said it all last night, David," Michael chimed in, "It's not really that we couldn't do anything. We could go to Washington and pour gasoline on ourselves and be flambéed. That would certainly make a statement but, speaking for myself, I don't have the guts. We could shoot someone we assume to be guilty or strap on a bomb and risk blowing up the innocent but we'd have joined the ranks of those we despise. The point is no matter what we did it would be insignificant. Louis is right, we're powerless because our corporate-owned media won't listen and politicians won't act because being re-elected takes precedence over everything else."

His trite attempt at mollification at least had the salutary effect of numbing the combatants into another silence as they traveled along the Hempstead Turnpike and then Lamy exited and made another bewildering sequence of turns and Michael noticed a Sussex Avenue and a couple of other theatrically-named streets in passing and suddenly they were on a landscaped driveway with a paddock to their left and the backside of the racetrack before them.

"That's a statue of Secretariat over there," Lamy told him.

"Ah, yes."

Michael could just make out a gray plinth in the distance lost among a swarm of people and on top a gray horse at full gallop without saddle or rider. He found it surprising that it seemed almost a miniature.

Lamy drew up to a sign that proclaimed Executive Parking and a uniformed valet hustled to the car.

"OK, no more hacking away at each other," Lamy offered as they walked by the trophy display in the Clubhouse lobby, "We should celebrate. This is the first big international event in the city since the shit hit the fan. I invited you to have a good time. You need a little R and R."

"Nothing a jug of martini won't cure," David responded amicably but the ominous undertone was unmistakable.

Michael could hear distant bugles as they got on an elevator.

"The call to the post. Timing is everything," Lamy told them and pressed the button for the Garden Terrace.

§

Seeing the blood and the hallucinatory visage of his campaign partner, which once he looked away and blinked and looked again completely disappeared, made the president unusually taciturn. Laura had to pick up the slack in the conversation and by the time they boarded Marine One on the South Lawn for their accustomed weekend retreat to Camp David in the Catoctin Hills she too was feeling more than a little sulky.

Stanza Four

§

Lamy led Michael and David down the myriad tiers of white-clothed circular tables in the Garden Terrace and through to an enclosed private lounge called the 'Belmont Preferred Access Area' which afforded a spectacular view over the entire racetrack. Michael judged it could accommodate no more than a hundred and he could see a mouth-watering buffet spread out along the whole length of one wall. Lamy told them the area was reserved for owners and their guests as he was greeted with a familiar gusto by the *maître d'* who ushered them to a table by the window.

"Very impressive," Michael said, but Lamy shrugged it off, "I take it I can safely assume you're an owner?"

"For many years," Lamy answered.

"And also that one of your 'nags' will be running?"

"Two. The fifth and then the last race. I'll let you know."

There were programs on top of the menus at each place-setting and Michael picked one up to read it. A waiter arrived and Lamy introduced him as 'Danny' and they ordered drinks. David, as threatened, a double Belvedere Martini, Lamy a Manhattan with no cherries and Michael was pleasantly surprised to find they had draught Guinness on tap.

"So what were you doing in Colombia to get kidnapped, Louis?" David asked when the waiter had gone, "I can't believe it was just bad luck."

"No, but it was arbitrary. I wasn't anyone's dupe or patsy. There was nothing suspicious or mysterious about it. I was part of an international consortium there to develop a nickel mine that everyone including the rebels seemed to want. A sudden deluge wiped out the road and my partners and I diverted over a mountain pass. A bad mistake. When our captors found out we weren't drug dealers they decided to hold us for ransom. As simple as that."

"How did you escape?" Michael asked, "You mentioned they didn't get the ransom."

"After a few days we were able to surprise our young guards and killed them. Three of them. Not much more than boys. It was ugly and I felt bad about it. Woke up for years screaming."

Michael was tempted to share his own experience of being kidnapped but he had never yet been able to tell the story of his abduction by the vampire drug lord of Juarez without becoming, in Helen's words, 'ridiculously overcomplicated.'

"Were you helping the rich or the poor, Louis?" David asked with an edge of malice, "Or just your shareholders back home? The world is being destroyed by our meddling. Do you think we're bombing Afghanistan because we're the good guys? The Taliban cut poppy production by ninety percent but it'll soon be back to normal. The CIA and Wall Street need the profits. Were you part of it in Colombia, that's all I'm asking? Were you meddling where you shouldn't have been?"

Lamy gave him a tired look but didn't bother to reply and Danny arrived and served their drinks. Lamy asked him why the first race was so late in starting and he told them a filly named Exogenous got spooked by something and injured her head and neck on the way to the track and had to be sedated but it wasn't fatal. Michael enjoyed the man's strong Brooklyn accent though he caught no more than half of what he was saying.

"Too bad," Lamy said, "A thing like that can end a promising career," and added as Danny handed out betting forms, "Anyone feeling lucky?"

David ignored the question but Michael was interested.

"I've never known what the difference is between an Exacta and a Trifecta," he said, perusing the form, "Infacta, I don't know what either of them are."

"How about win, place and show?" Lamy asked with a smile.

"That would be gold, silver and bronze."

"Exactly. So the Exacta is betting on gold and silver at the same time and the Trifecta is all three at once. There's also a Superfecta, that's the top four. And other things like Quinellas but don't worry about them yet. Why not start by taking a stab at the winner?"

"Good idea. So what's your advice?"

"Well, Spain is the defending champion. Pick whatever you think."

The horses were finally in position at the starting gate and Michael decided to bet two dollars on Spain and see what happened. Lamy filled in a Trifecta and put a hundred dollars on it but David, having nearly finished his first Martini at a gulp, was paying no attention and ordered another.

Suddenly the horses were off and accelerating away from them down the dirt track.

"Which one is Spain?" Michael asked.

"Number twelve. It's in the program."

"Ah, yes," Michael said, but he could only see their backs and they were too bunched for him to discern any numbers until the middle of the far stretch.

"She's taken an easy lead," Lamy observed, gesturing Michael to the small pair of powerful binoculars Danny set for them on the table.

"Well, well," Michael answered and was already excited enough to rise to his feet but in the last eighth of a mile number six seemed to appear from nowhere and nipped Spain on the outside by a nose at the finish line. Too close for Michael to tell which horse actually won and he was about to ask when the results were called out over the loudspeakers. But, whether it was the twang in the announcer's voice or the mental static that always seemed to befuddle his otherwise acute faculties at such moments, he couldn't fathom at all what had been said.

"What was that?" he enquired when the voice stopped.

"Number six took it," Lamy told him.

"Ah," Michael said and sat down.

"Better luck next time."

"Did you get yours right?"

"No. Not even close," Lamy answered casually.

"It went by so fast. I barely had time to get the horses in focus."

"Less than two minutes. One minute forty-nine seconds."

"They didn't even run a whole lap."

"No. The finishing post is the same for every race but the lengths are different. The track is a mile and a half. This one was only a mile and an eighth."

"Ah," Michael said and then ventured, "And how many furlongs is that?"

"Nine."

"And why is an eighth of a mile called a furlong?"

The waiter returned with David's second double Martini. He was sitting with his eyes closed but somehow they popped open as the waiter put the drink down.

"That's your neck of the woods again," Lamy answered, "Somewhere back in the dark ages it meant 'long furrow'. Like our friend here's brow."

David came back to life and downed half his new cocktail with one swallow.

"You didn't answer my question, Louis."

Lamy stood up.

"I'm going to get food. I suggest you do too," he said calmly and walked off toward the buffet. Michael started to follow but thought he'd better have a crack at easing the tension and leaned over the table close to David.

"Look here, old chap," he said quietly, "Do stop needling him. He invited you to enjoy yourself. What's the point?"

"To each their own enjoyment," David replied dismissively, swigged the rest of his drink and looked around to try and catch the waiter's eye.

"Well, I think you're being damned silly," Michael said and went to join Lamy.

On the way he noticed two middle-aged men sitting with a group of younger women at a table not far from theirs by the window and one of the men was staring at him. Michael hadn't any idea who the man was but he found the face strangely familiar and when he came up to Lamy he asked if he knew.

Lamy was busy loading up a plate but glanced over and said, "Sure. General McWhirter. Why?"

"I got the feeling he recognized me."

"Shall we go ask him? He's not such a bad guy. Retired from the army quite a while ago. Under a bit of cloud. Runs a consulting firm now. It's what people like us do when we get old. Except he's on TV a lot."

"Doing what?"

"You know, giving his opinion about this and that."

"A pundit."

"That's right."

"Yes, now I remember. That's where I must have seen him. I can't think why he was looking at me that way."

"Why not say hello and ask him."

"No, no," Michael said, "Heavens, no."

"Suit yourself."

Lamy moved off toward their table and as Michael found a plate and began sizing up the astonishing array of sumptuous choices he saw Lamy and the general exchange a friendly wave.

By the time he returned to his seat David was already half way through his third Martini and in the middle of a growing harangue.

" .. Some answers *are* black and white, Louis. True or false. Yes or no. Like did members of our own government know it was going to happen? Yes. Did some actively plan it? Yes. Did others simply look the other way? Yes. Are they frantically trying to cover it up? Yes. Was it the greatest crime in American history? No. Hiroshima and Nagasaki and Viet Nam were far worse. But should those who were responsible be tried and sent to jail? Yes. Will they be? No .. "

Up to this point David had kept his voice down but nonetheless the intensity of his gestures and facial expression were drawing some attention, particularly from the general's table which Michael could see over Lamy's shoulder.

" .. Should we be doing something about it .. ?"

Lamy finally got fed up and cut David off.

"Look, you adolescent little prick," he whispered, "I'm tired of your bullshit. If you can't do anything but repeat yourself, fuck off."

David threw back his head and roared with laughter and then gulped the rest of his drink.

The horses were lined up for the second race and Michael could see that the starting gates had been positioned even further around the track than last time. He missed betting at the buffet but what did that matter. He was desperately trying to think of some way to stop things from becoming a total embarrassment.

"You think I don't care," Lamy went on, "But I don't just feel horror for what happened that day. I feel absolutely sorry for what it says about all mankind."

"So what, Louis, so what? All I'm looking for is a tiny gesture. I can't live in my skin any longer if I do nothing. I'm sure my ideas are stupid and doomed to failure but I can't just sit back and enjoy the show!"

David got slowly and a bit unsteadily to his feet. His voice had risen above the ambient hubbub of laughter and chitchat and people were definitely turning to look at them now.

"Maybe I should kidnap this whole room full of rich bastards!" he shouted and faced them, "That could start a chain reaction, eh, Louis, why not?! Look at you all stuffing yourselves! What's the matter, need to bury your guilt?! Too bloated to deal with the truth?! You know damn well it wasn't a bunch of Arabs who attacked us! They couldn't have flown those planes! It was Cheney and Wolfowitz and Perle . . !"

The room had been relatively silent but the second race started and at the mention of Arabs someone yelled, "Sit down and shut up!" and a swelling chorus of boos and jeering quickly drowned David out.

" . . Open your eyes and look at the evidence . . !"

"Where's your patriotism?! Get a life!"

"What are you, nuts?! Dick can't fly!"

"This is a race meeting not a debating society!"

"Go home! Nobody cares what you think!"

The *maître d'* was on the phone to security and told a couple of the waiters to try and get David out but before they were able to reach him he stopped shouting and abruptly strode from the room. Michael had an impulse to go after him but thought better of it. He would call when he got back to the hotel.

The horses crossed the finish line and a sequence of bewildering numbers began flashing up on the long black board across the track behind it and as Michael was about to ask Lamy if they were amounts of money being won, as the numbers scrolled larger and larger, the entire structure of the message changed and instead of counting dollars the digits began to jump about and started forming the letters of the alphabet, huge capital letters that finally spelled the words 'RICHARD BRUCE CHENEY'.

Michael saw the letters of the name dash in a rolling sequence from first to last at least a dozen times across the whole length of the board in quick succession and he turned to his host but Lamy was cutting a slice of glazed ham on his plate and seemed entirely oblivious. He looked over at the general and his guests who appeared so too and then around the room to see if anyone at all had noticed this incredible occurrence but they were talking and eating and drinking and laughing as if absolutely nothing out of the ordinary had happened.

He turned back to look at the board and it was just numbers again. Numbers he assumed bore good news for the lucky and bad for the unlucky. An afternoon at the races. Everyone enjoying a roll of the dice. Everything normal, commonplace. Perhaps, like David, he was going out of his mind.

Michael took a deep breath and a last swallow of Guinness.

'Thank god for it,' he thought, 'I might just have another.'

He was about to sample a first bite of his meal when he sensed the general staring at him again. A hard level searching stare and as Michael caught his eye the man held the look for a moment before grinning and turning away and Michael had the peculiar feeling as he did so that perhaps he was not the only one who had been aware of those capital letters.

"So, what brings you to New York?" Lamy asked.

Michael was still reeling inside and fearful the vice-president would suddenly be sitting in front of him but mercifully it was just Lamy.

"Ah, well," he stammered, "That's rather a long . . look, um, before I answer, didn't you notice anything strange happen just now?"

"Other than being insulted, you mean?"

"Yes, sorry about that." Michael had no idea why he was apologizing. "I told you I haven't seen him for years. He's obviously in grief. I'll call him later and see if he's all right. No, I meant on the sign out there with all the numbers."

"Like what?"

"Well, I saw the numbers change and form up into a name. It scrolled across the whole board a dozen times."

"What name?" Lamy asked with sudden interest.

It crossed Michael's mind that he might regret mentioning this mysteriously reoccurring motif but strange phenomena were his stock in trade and he was here to investigate precisely this one, wasn't he?

"The name of your vice-president," he said carefully.

An uncharacteristically revealing expression flickered across Lamy's face. The tiniest of elfin smiles that betrayed some hidden and dangerous knowledge. During the entire afternoon's exchange, except for the two instances of justifiable anger at David, his demeanor had been one of perfectly disinterested affability.

"Do you normally suffer from hallucinations?" he asked.

"It's not just me," Michael ventured, "Something quite similar happened to two workers at Ground Zero a few weeks ago. I suspect there may be many people here who have been seeing such things."

"You mean here in this room?"

"Possibly. But no, I meant more generally in your country."

"Is that right. So what's your interest in it?"

"I write for a little magazine that examines matters of this kind. Since you ask, it's what brings me to New York."

"Fascinating," Lamy said and a momentary silence fell between them. "The third race will get going soon. Want to try again?"

Michael assumed Lamy had just neatly pigeonholed him with David in the madman compartment so he nodded and picked up his program. He had always been very fond of gambling and was a keen student of the workings of chance.

"Some of these horses have magnificently eccentric names," he chuckled, "Just in the last race we've had Shesastonecoldfox. That's quite marvelous. Imperial Gesture. Take Charge Lady. What more could one want? And Bella Bellucci, for heaven's sake. An eponym for that dishy Italian actress, I wonder?"

Lamy shrugged, "I don't know but she came in third."

"Did you win anything, by the way?"

Danny came to collect their forms for the third race and Michael quickly glanced down the list and saw the name Forbidden Apple which was altogether too good to resist, though Speedster City Zip certainly came a close second, and he placed another two dollar bet.

"Yes," Lamy answered, "Win and place were both Godolphin."

"What?"

"Both out of Godolphin Stables."

"Ah. Why does that sound familiar?"

"I have no idea but they're owned by a friend of mine. The beard in the corner under the *keffiyeh*. Sheikh Mohammed bin Rashid Al Maktoum. Maybe you heard of his stud farms. He's got two in England. Crown prince of Dubai. Worth billions. I put a hundred into a Trifecta and came out with a hundred and ninety thousand."

"Dollars?"

"Not a bad return. The prince's purse will be around six hundred thousand."

Michael was speechless.

The third race began and he watched through the binoculars. For whatever reason it was taking place on a grass track inside the dirt one but, as in the first, another horse nipped Michael's choice at the finish line.

"Too bad. Maybe you should try a place bet next time," Lamy said and then, without being prodded, translated the gist of the announcer's words for him. Val Royal had won the race in record time. The track was exceptionally fast because of the recent dry weather. Michael's Forbidden

Apple placed second and Bach was the show. Speedster City Zip had shot his bolt right out of the starting gate.

Michael couldn't keep his eyes off the rolling numbers on the board but to his relief no further names appeared.

"So was that another zillion?" Michael asked.

"No," Lamy answered with a smile, "I sat that one out."

Suddenly the general was standing over them. Michael hadn't been aware he had moved. He was taller than Michael would have guessed with cropped gray hair and pale watery eyes and his lips were unusually thick and slackish. Like Lamy he was dressed in a navy blazer over a sport shirt open at the neck.

"Hey there, Lou," he said, "Who's your friend?"

Michael observed with amusement the habitual false infusion of warmth into an otherwise reptilian demeanor.

"Oh, hello Larry, yeah, this is Michael. Michael Davenport, he tells me. From jolly old London. Michael meet General Larry McWhirter."

Michael got part way out of his chair and extended his hand and the general shook it and repeated his name as though in an effort to commit it to memory.

"Michael Davenport. Davenport. Pleased to meet you, Michael. What are you doing here with this son of a bitch?"

'Good lord,' Michael thought, 'The man either has a speech impediment or his back teeth are awash in saliva.'

"Um, a longish story. Suffice it to say he was kind enough to invite me."

"Good, good. Winning anything?"

"Not yet, I'm afraid."

"Well, keep at it. Get the son of a bitch to put you on the inside track."

"Go to hell," Lamy said pleasantly and the general laughed.

"Well, nice talking to you, Michael. You staying in town long?"

"No, just a fortnight."

McWhirter chuckled through his slopping dentures and repeated the quaint phrase.

"Just a 'fortnight', huh? But what the hell, you live in London," he said and brushed Michael's shoulder with his knuckles as though sharing the remembrance of some delicious whorehouse escapade, then turned to Lamy and asked, "Did you know that other guy?" making it sound like in idle afterthought.

"Only met him yesterday."

"What was his problem?"

"Lost a sister in the second tower."

"Shit. No wonder," McWhirter said and whistled at the obvious magnitude of the tragedy, "That'd be enough to fuck with your mind."

He appeared overcome with the thought of it and walked slowly back to his table nodding agreement to the empty air.

"I didn't get the impression he knew you," Lamy said when he had gone.

"No. Well, he may have been hiding it."

"Why?"

Michael didn't have an answer and raised his hands in a gesture saying so.

"You know, if David had been in any kind of mood to listen," Lamy went on after chewing and swallowing another mouthful, "I would've told him the whole event today is dedicated to the victims of 9/11. It was one of the reasons I invited him. A bunch of us set up a Heroes Fund. Everything I win is going straight into it. The Sheikh and the general and plenty of others too. I'd guess twenty million by the end of the day. The Sheikh already gave five million of his own."

"Heroes Fund?"

"To help the rescue workers and the families."

It wasn't easy to make Michael feel genuinely sheepish but he did. Perhaps all his dire suspicions were unfounded and Americans were as innocent and generous-spirited as the man before him seemed to be at that moment. Perhaps.

"Wow," he said, "I'm sure he had no clue. I'll tell him. No wonder everyone booed. The Sheikh can't have been too pleased, I would imagine."

"Why? He said it wasn't Arabs. Finish your food. After the next race, I'll take you down to meet my people."

"That would be splendid," Michael said and looked at the program, "What are the chances for Squirtle Squirt?"

"Good, I'd say. Jerry Bailey's a great jockey. One of the greatest."

Danny came again and Michael asked if he could provide another Guinness as fast as possible and as he was handing him two dollars for Squirtle Squirt Lamy said, "Why not try for more?"

Michael looked at him and wondered if this strange man truly knew the inside track as the general had joked and then fished out a ten-dollar note from his billfold. Lamy nodded with approval and must have read the question in his mind because he told him he was a bit unsure about the condition of the horses this time and played it safe with a Quinella on Squirtle Squirt and Xtra Heat.

"How does that one work?" Michael asked.

"It's a way to hedge your bets if you can't decide. You choose both horses so you win either way."

"Good lord."

Danny hustled back with his Guinness and the race started. It was called the Sprint and only covered six furlongs and was over before it had barely begun but in the last thrilling seconds Squirtle Squirt came positively hurtling down the stretch and overtook Xtra Heat on the outside.

There was a burst of applause from the room and hoots of joy and whistling at one of the tables.

"Bobby Frankel finally beat the jinx," Lamy explained, "He's never had a winner here until now. Congratulations. You just won a hundred bucks."

"And what about you?"

"Not much. Ninety grand maybe. Come on, I'll show you the inside track."

Lamy got up and Michael downed half the Guinness. Lamy could see he was hesitating and said, "Don't worry about the money, we'll get it later. I'll give you a good tip for the last race."

"Clearly I could do with one. Thank you. I'll think about a donation."

As they walked toward the door he was sure the general's eyes were drilling into his back but he didn't turn to see him pick up his cell phone.

"The fifth is turf again," Lamy went on, "Eleven furlongs. Fillys and mares. Three years and up. My baby is Scamthemall."

§

It was a beautiful afternoon in the wooded hills of Maryland too and twenty feet above the treetops one of four identically glistening VH-60N Whitehawks broke formation with its hovering entourage and dropped out of sight to touch down on the helipad at Camp David and the First Couple jumped into a golf cart and sped to Aspen Lodge.

They treasured their moments in this glorious spot because they could enjoy the freedom of the open air without the suffocating presence of security and they immediately changed into something comfortable. The president donned a ratty old sweatshirt and shorts and the First Lady a soft pink tracksuit and he went for a jog and she for a walk along the same winding leaf-strewn trail.

Even the fresh air and exercise didn't lighten his mood however, nor did the thought of watching the first game of the World Series between the Yankees and the Arizona Diamondbacks that evening, and before she returned and he got in the shower he guiltily knocked back a large Jack Daniel's.

§

The general excused himself from the women and made his way outside onto a broad terrace beyond the Preferred Area to make his call and dialed a cell number in Belfast. He was pleased when a deep authoritative voice answered.

"Connie," he said, "How's the beer treating your digestion?"

"Not good."

The general chuckled.

"Look, I'm at the track. You'll never guess who turned up with Lou Lamy."

"Who? You'll have to be quick. I'm at supper. Patten's chewing my ear off."

"What about?"

"The frogs and krauts won't play ball on Iraq."

"Never thought they would. Bunch of pansy chickenshits."

"So who turned up?"

"Michael Davenport."

"The limey who was with Portillo?"

"That's him."

"So what? We tracked him. His identity checked. Except the bull about being a movie director. Other than that there was nothing."

"Then what's he doing here with Lamy?"

"Why don't you try and find out?"

"Don't bark at me, Con. I'm doing it. You think that boyscout Hutchinson knows anything?"

"Hell no. It was taken out of our hands. I don't even know what happened."

"Good. Better for us they didn't use it."

"There's always next time."

"Bye now, Connie. I can hear the rain's got you down."

The general snapped off his phone and stood for a moment thinking.

Loomis Consterdine, the unhappy voice on the end of the line, was for many years the Superintendent of the New York State Police and had been appointed by Bill Clinton, at about the same time the general was made his Director of Drug Control Policy, as head of the Drug Enforcement Administration. He retired from the position before George Bush was elected and was now helping to reorganize the Royal Ulster Constabulary into the new Police Service of Northern Ireland.

He and the general had been ghostly shepherds behind the meeting between the Russian Mafia and Amado Portillo which Michael was forced to attend in the disguise of 'Bartolomeo Vespucci' and the 'it' the general spoke of was the stash of fissionable plutonium that, as far as they knew, still lay buried beneath some ancient petroglyphs in the Samalayuca desert.

Several times during the months that followed his escape Michael had the creepy sensation he was being shadowed through the streets of London.

§

Down in the 'backside' of Belmont Park, the paddocks and stables where the horses and jockeys and trainers and handlers and the two thousand or so groundskeepers and cleaners and various support staff that sustain them hang out, Michael was briefly introduced to a few of Lamy's 'people'. His trainer, whose name was Max, and the jockey for Scamthemall, a truly tiny gentleman not over four foot nine whose name was something like Croucher or Crotchet or Croquet, and two others in suits whose names Michael instantly forgot. He had then been left to his own devices and Lamy disappeared for a private conference with them. Lamy had shown him where to stand so he wouldn't get hurt or be in the way and he was enjoying the bustle and the wonderful smells and unaccustomed sounds, the uniquely American argot of the denizens and, most of all, the overwhelming beauty of the animals when suddenly Lamy was by his side again. It couldn't have been more than three minutes.

Lamy had filled in some history as they descended. Scamthemall was a four-year-old mare bred from his stable which was way out on Long Island near a town called Mattituck on the shores of Peconic Bay. He named the stable in honor of his brother who was the current Trade Commissioner for the European Union. It was called 'Le Seigneurie Pascal'. Unlike him, Pascal was an extremely disciplined man and a patrician son of a bitch. They were both born in suburban Paris but Lamy had come to America in his late teens and 'lost his Frenchness'.

"So, is the 'inside track' sorted?" Michael asked in jest as they began making their way back across the paddock.

"There is no fix, Michael. At least, none with my horses."

"Why Scamthemall then?"

"I like irony, haven't you noticed?"

"Will she win?"

"I hope so."

"Should I bet on her?"

"If you want."

Michael laughed and Lamy smiled.

"Would you advise the general to bet on her?"

"He has his own horse running, Spook Express."

"Ah. How long has he been retired from the army? You said it was under a bit of a cloud."

"There were allegations he overstepped his authority and pushed his men to commit atrocities during the First Gulf War. I don't think they were true. Later on Clinton appointed him as his Drug Czar."

Michael felt pinpricks of excitement all over his skin. Things were starting to fall into place.

"What did that entail exactly?"

"The Director of Drug Control Policy. Something like that."

"You don't mean the DEA?"

"No, that was different. It was run by a guy named Consterdine at the time. I guess they worked together."

"And when was that, do you remember?"

"Round about the late nineties, I'd say."

Michael was pretty sure now why McWhirter had come to their table and repeated his name. He didn't tell Lamy but it must have been connected to the Miss Texas Pageant at Amado Portillo's hotel in El Paso. The judges had originally been Portillo and the beloved Country and Western singer, Tanya Tucker, and Laura Bush, who was then First Lady of Texas, but Miss Tucker's flight from Nashville was delayed by a massive hailstorm and, at the last minute, Michael, who, due to the drug lord's lies, was assumed by his beauty queen girl-friend to be a famous British movie director, was chosen as the songstress's emergency replacement.

The whole absurd event had been broadcast on live television. Michael was seated at the head table with the other judges and, to his horror, Portillo quickly invented a list of ridiculous movie titles that were read out by the pageant's hosts as his directorial resumé. It was impossible to protest any of it without risking his life so he comforted himself with the thought that an American audience, particularly at a beauty pageant, wouldn't know the difference.

However, before the pageant was half over Michael's new acquaintance, the ex-DEA agent Chuck Bowman, had taken Portillo hostage and they hung him off the seventeenth floor balcony and shortly thereafter Chuck was killed by a sniper and both Portillo and his sister were dead. It happened during the weekend of the vernal equinox in 1997 and was big news. The general and the DEA head must have been watching! That was why he sauntered over so innocently to their table and now Michael was walking straight towards the man again past the buffet. This would call for another Guinness at the very least, if not something stronger.

By the time Michael and Lamy took their seats by the window the horses for the fifth race were off and Lamy said, "Don't worry. I took the liberty of placing a bet for you downstairs."

Michael couldn't summon an appreciative response because he wasn't sure he liked the idea and, rather churlishly, picked up the binoculars and followed the race without comment. Saxons are rugged individualists and believe they must be forgiven the small luxury of pride. As it turned out Scamthemall began well but was nowhere to be seen at the finish and came dead last.

Michael put the spyglasses down and squinted in puzzlement at Lamy as the loudspeakers announced the result. Congratulatory hugs were in progress at the general's table and Lamy was smiling too.

"She blew them away last year but she's getting old," he said.

"How much do I owe you for the bet?"

Michael reached for his billfold but Lamy gestured him to put it away.

"Oh, to be sure, I didn't wager on my old gray mare," Lamy intoned with a lilting Galway accent, "I put your two bucks into a Trifecta and, glory be, it worked. Worth a pretty penny, if you want it."

'Why is it Americans seem to love putting foreigners on the spot?' Michael thought rather ungratefully.

"How much would you say?"

"Five," Lamy teased.

"Hundred?"

"Thousand."

Michael stared at him in disbelief.

"Good lord. I don't quite know what to say. Thank you. Very much. How on earth did you guess it right?"

"Just lucky."

"Really?"

"I told you I don't do fixes."

"Did you bet your hundred on the same thing?"

"No. I put a hundred thousand on Spook Express to place and that's just what she did. It'll pay back five fifty."

Michael was more and more off balance. He had never been with anyone in his entire life who could risk such sums as if they were small change, to say nothing of his suspicion Lamy and the general had engaged in some subtle and secretive communication about him. But what? And how could that be since Lamy had no prior knowledge he would invite himself?

"You just won five hundred and fifty thousand dollars?"

"Well, minus the original hundred, four hundred and fifty-eight to be exact."

Lamy got up and walked over to McWhirter and clapped him on the back and they laughed and leaned in to exchange a few whispered words in each other's ears and Lamy hugged one of the young women that were with him and kissed her on the cheek then shook the other man's hand, patted the general on the shoulder again and returned. Was their colloquy solely to do with Spook Express?

The waiter was at their side and Michael asked Lamy politely if he was going to have another drink and he said, "Sure, why not?"

"Same again, gentlemen?" Danny asked.

"Same for me," Lamy nodded.

"I'll make a change and have what he's having."

"Make them doubles."

"But I'll have the cherries with mine," Michael added.

"Did our noisy friend leave the building?"

"Sure did, Mister Lou. Slick as you know what."

The mention of David's rude exit increased Michael's paranoia. Why was a man like Lamy spending time with a perfect stranger? Surely he had many friends and business associates here whose company he would have preferred.

"I must say this is all very good of you."

"Why's that?"

"Well, I was a rather a gatecrasher. Perhaps none of it would have happened if I hadn't invited myself to come along."

Lamy waved off the notion as unlikely.

"He needed to get it off his chest," he said.

Michael would like to have asked about the relationship with David's sister but an inbred sense of propriety forestalled the question.

To Michael's surprise, however, Lamy reintroduced the subject of the two workers at Ground Zero and asked what they had seen and then listened carefully as Michael told him in detail not only about that but the bloodstained photograph as well and how he turned into the vice-president before his eyes on the pavement outside the gallery and once more described what just happened with the sign. The new information propelled Lamy into a lengthy, and to Michael quite extraordinary, monologue about the government's notorious Carnivore spyware and how, if one were truly interested in flushing out the guilty, the technology could be utilized in reverse to orchestrate occurrences like the toteboard flashing the vice-president's name and if this were done over and over again on the Internet and key public occasions and major sports events with greater and greater frequency and from a sufficiently secure location it might have the effect David was craving.

Michael was stunned by such a complete shift of gears and mesmerized by the quiet intensity of his host's voice and they drank their Manhattans and ordered another round and let the sixth and seventh races pass without betting.

"So you agree with David?" Michael said at last.

Lamy smiled his elfin smile.

"I couldn't say who ordered who to do what when, but the basic picture is pretty damn clear."

"You weren't part of it?"

Lamy shook his head.

"I'm not on the 'inside' inside track."

"What about . . ?"

Michael made a tiny nod in the general's direction.

"Not as far as I know. He's some way out of the loop now, I'd say."

It was utterly weird but at precisely that moment McWhirter looked over at Michael and winked. They had been talking very quietly and the noise level in the room was so high he couldn't possibly have overheard.

"OK, we have to make our bets on the Classic. It's the big one."

"Which horse is yours?"

"Number eleven."

Michael looked down the list and found the name, Ruth's Pity. He had never met her but it brought tears to his eyes.

"What do you suggest?" he asked.

"He's a great horse."

"He?"

"The Classic is for boys only."

"Ah, yes, I see. So I should bet on him?"

"I am. Go for the Exacta, 11-6."

The waiter was there and Michael didn't have the hundred dollars that he was now willing to splurge but Lamy said he'd cover it and the race began. It was a mile and a quarter over the main dirt track and four magnificent horses vied neck and neck for the finish line. First Tiznow was leading, then Sakhee, then Albert the Great but in the last fifty yards Ruth's Pity came from behind and took it by half a length.

Michael was so stirred with excitement he was trembling. It didn't matter to him that he might have made a few dollars. It was the sheer beauty of it.

"Fantastic. Utterly fantastic. He won. What a horse. Congratulations."

Suddenly the general was beside them again.

"I hope the cunning bastard told you to bet on him," he said.

Michael nodded that indeed he had.

"Good, good. Son of a bitch is kind of tight-lipped sometimes."

Lamy just smiled benignly.

"Whupped my horse's butt but I figured he would," the general went on and then turned to Lamy and asked, "Did you get all three?"

"All four."

McWhirter chuckled in envy.

"Son of a bitch."

"Sorry about that."

It had been Ruth's Pity, Albert the Great, Sakhee then Tiznow at the post and Michael assumed the interchange meant Lamy had won the Superfecta. God knows what that would be worth. Michael knew from the program that Albert the Great was the general's horse and the others were owned by the prince and couldn't stop himself from asking, "Did you name him after the great Dominican scholar?"

"How's that?"

He could tell from the general's blank expression it was idiotic but it was too late to change course.

"Your horse. Albert the Great. Was his naming to do with Albertus Magnus, the famous Medieval theologian and scientist?"

"Shit no. Albert was my grandfather. Died in the second battle of the Marne."

"Ah. Sorry. Silly of me."

The general turned back to Lamy.

"What's up for you tonight, Lou? Want to join the party? Girl's idea."

"No can do," Lamy replied and waved in apology to an attractive blond sitting with the other women at the general's table.

"That's a shame. Well, see you in the spring. You'll enjoy the rest of your trip better, Mr. Davenport, if you find some way to lose this jerk."

They all laughed and McWhirter walked away.

Lamy won over a million dollars on the Classic and, on his advice, Michael won close to fifteen thousand but not even as he paced in mortal dread at Amado Portillo's villa had he ever felt so completely like a lost duck bobbing helpless and alone on an unfathomable sea.

Stanza Five

§

By late afternoon the president was stinking and his normally patient spouse slammed the sliding patio door on him twice, the second time nearly severing the fingertips of his left hand, and told him in no uncertain terms if he kept it up she would have no alternative when they returned to Washington the following day but to decamp either to Prairie Chapel Ranch or the fucking Mayflower Suite at the fucking Marriott Renaissance because the fucking Hay-Adams, which she preferred because the Federal Suite afforded a fine view of the White House, was closed for fucking renovations.

§

Lamy got to his feet and told Michael he had to go down to celebrate with his people and that Danny would bring him a check for his winnings which would be an incredible twenty thousand dollars or thereabouts and if he felt like donating any of it to the Heroes Fund Danny would be happy to oblige. He offered to come back within the hour and drive Michael to his hotel but Michael said he had done quite enough for him for one day and would be fine on his own.

"I'd like to meet again though if you have time," Michael said as they were shaking hands in farewell.

"Sure," Lamy replied, "My wife died last July and my kids are both on the west coast. I'm going to the memorial at Ground Zero tomorrow. I'll pick you up on the way if you want. Maybe we'll swing by David's gallery. See how he's doing."

"That would be splendid. I'm at the Belleclaire on West 77th Street."

"I know it. I'll see you outside at noon. *A bientôt.*"

Lamy turned and made his way to the door stopping for a few moments to say hello to the prince and his entourage before walking out.

Michael's head was spinning, not so much from the delicious mix of sweet vermouth and bourbon or the exhilaration of the racing as the happenstance of meeting the general and the inexplicable weirdness of the sign flashing Cheney's name, and he sat down again to gather his thoughts. He wondered where David was now and if he shouldn't leave it as long as tomorrow to find out whether he was all right. He tried to remember everything Lamy had said, particularly about the spyware. What an amazingly appropriate and terrifying name. Carnivore! He was very anxious to find out more about his mysterious host and what he knew.

Danny came to the table and asked if he would like anything else and he said he'd have another of those delectable double Manhattans, if that was all right. He asked what brand of whiskey they used and Danny said Maker's Mark which didn't mean much to him and, in a gesture of largesse with which he quite surprised himself, he told the hardworking little man that he would be pleased to donate five thousand of his winnings to the Heroes Fund. He couldn't believe there would be fifteen thousand left over. It would allow him to remain in New York beyond the two weeks allotted by the magazine if his investigation began to bear fruit.

When Danny returned, holding a tray with an envelope and a single elegant cocktail glass brimming with glorious nut-brown liquid, Michael asked for the bill for the afternoon's refreshments and was told not to worry about it, Mister Lou never let his guests pay.

"May I offer you a gratuity then?" he asked.

"How's that?"

"Some form of tip. As a thank you."

"Don't even think about it. Mister Lou takes good care of everyone. Oh yeah, I almost forgot. I filed the donation. In your name. Hope that's OK."

"Yes, of course, that's fine."

"Receipt's in with your check."

"Ah. Splendid. Well, thank you again. You've been very kind."

The envelope wasn't sealed and though Michael wanted to resist having a peek at the contents and put it straight in his jacket pocket without a glance it was quite impossible. He slid it nonchalantly off the table into his lap when he was sure no one was looking and slipped the check half way out. Wonder of wonders, his name was spelled correctly and the amount was fifteen thousand, one hundred and thirty-two dollars! What about taxes? No one had asked. He replaced the check in the envelope, folded it and tucked it carefully into a zippered compartment inside his shoulder-bag.

As he sat sipping his drink, watching the room slowly empty of its patrons and the daylight fade, he became aware the attractive blond woman who Lamy had kissed on the cheek was looking at him quite brazenly. Michael was no shrinking violet when it came to opportunities of the kind and returned her look with equal openness of intent and she gestured him to join their table. What the hell, he was a stranger in a very strange land.

The other two women were still with her but the general and his male cohort had left the room shortly after Lamy. However, Michael assumed from his previous invitation that he would be coming back and he picked up his drink and walked over and shook the ladies hands politely, introduced himself and sat down in their midst. The blond woman, who was not just attractive but stunningly beautiful now he saw her at close quarters, something that was normally the reverse in Michael's experience, introduced herself as 'Brandy' and her two companions as 'Cindy' and 'Melissa'. It had been abundantly clear to him already and the unlikely nominations confirmed what they were but as their subtle perfume wafted about him Michael was surprised to find them all pleasantly soft-spoken and intelligent.

"Do you work with Mr. Lamy?" Cindy asked.

"No. I just met him. This morning, as a matter of fact."

"But you're in the same business?"

"No, no, not at all."

They didn't pry further. Obviously discretion was an essential asset.

"Tell me something about the general."

"It depends what you want to know," Melissa responded.

Michael joined in their smiling and said, "Aren't you all going to some kind of post-race do?"

"No, well, not Dwayne. He's pretty busy these days."

"We were surprised to see him."

Michael could only assume Dwayne was the other man.

"Is he a retired general too?"

He certainly seemed far more the ramrod archetype than McWhirter.

"He's got so many medals he has a hard time standing up."

"The president just appointed him to take over from someone. Who was it, Brandy?"

"Richard Clarke."

Michael knew very well who that was. He was a counterterrorism expert. He had been brought in as an advisor by Bill Clinton but was apparently unhappy with his diminished role in the Bush White House and had resigned a day or two after Operation Enduring Freedom, the attack on Afghanistan, began. Michael had seen him interviewed by the BBC and was particularly interested by the tidbit that he had arranged the date of this retirement in early June. So Dwayne, whoever he was, was his replacement. Michael remembered Clarke had merely been moved sideways and become an advisor on cyberspace security or something like that. Congress had recently been told of the havoc a determined terrorist hacker could wreak on the telecommunications and financial systems, on power and water supplies by such means, and an already shell-shocked American public warned that the potential was 'beyond frightening'.

"Yes, I can see why he might be rather occupied," Michael said.

"This anthrax thing is really scary."

"Does he know who's behind it?"

"Saddam Hussein."

"He said there's no doubt about it."

"Ah," Michael said, nodding his head gravely, "That is scary," but as far as he could tell they were oblivious to his double meaning.

At that moment the general came back into the room but Dwayne wasn't with him. Michael could see he noticed immediately where he was sitting but it was hard to gauge his reaction. In any case, Michael had finished his drink and had no intention of intruding.

"Girls looking after you, Mr. Davenport?" he inquired pleasantly as he got to the table but didn't sit down or wait for a response. "Good, good. My buddy had to get back to D. C. Should have gone with him but I promised these lovely ladies a party. If Lou's buggered off on you why not join us, whaddya say?"

It took a fraction of a second for him to change his mind. An indefatigable curiosity was Michael's *bête noire* but he didn't sense he was in any danger. Surely if the general had needed him to disappear it would have happened years ago.

"Am I dressed well enough for the occasion?" he asked. He was wearing his usual tweedy sport jacket and slacks and they were none too stylish.

"You'll be fine," McWhirter replied with a dismissive gesture.

"Then I'd love to."

"OK, let's do it, ladies," the general said, snapping his fingers at them in jest, and the women gathered their things and stood.

"You don't mind me calling you Michael?"

"Please."

McWhirter put a friendly hand on his shoulder as they walked to the door.

"Girls've been tee-heeing all afternoon how cute they think you are."

§

Even if Michael had known David was arriving back at the gallery at just that moment and running up the wooden stairs to the apartment to find Fernando lying semiconscious on the kitchen floor in a pool of vomit and blood he would most likely not have refused the general's invitation. He was a fatalist at heart and shared with the great Elizabethan poets the precept of letting cards and sparrows fall as they may.

§

On the way down to the Clubhouse lobby McWhirter made a call on his cell to his driver and asked Michael about his line of work. Michael told him he was a writer but didn't divulge anything about the reason he was in New York. He said he had been visiting David who was his sister's ex-husband and was planning to attend tomorrow's memorial service with him at Ground Zero.

"What kind of writer?"

"Anything and everything. I'm a journalist."

"Ever written or directed any movies?"

"No."

Michael was enjoying watching the general's mental gears grind.

"Ever been in any? Girls figured you for an actor."

"I'm sorry to disappoint them. Good lord, no."

McWhirter shrugged and let it drop.

"So how does Lou fit in? I know he loves writers."

"Really?"

"Oh yeah, yeah. He's a literature nut, didn't you know? He's passionate about it. Gives away thousands to struggling authors. I can't believe you didn't know."

"I only met him this morning."

"You gotta be kidding me. Is that right?"

"David knew him," Michael answered but didn't tell him why.

"Yeah, but just for a coupla days he said. What does he do?"

"He has a gallery of Canadian art in Soho."

"So what's his connection to Lou?"

"It's a bit delicate. I'd rather not say."

"Something to do with the sister who died?"

"I'm afraid you'll have to ask him."

A long black Cadillac DeVille limousine was waiting outside the lobby and the driver was standing ready to open the doors and they all got in and as they set off slowly through the mass of departing traffic McWhirter told Cindy and Melissa to fix drinks. The men were in the rear with Brandy between, the other two in seats facing them. Bourbon on the rocks was the choice except for Brandy who wanted a simple Coke.

"How long have you owned horses?" Michael asked.

He wanted to pinch himself to make sure this was really happening. The luxurious interior of the limousine was an entirely alien world. The only other time he had ever been in one was with Amado Portillo and on that occasion he had been certain the trip would be his last.

"Hell, I'm strictly a dabbler, not like Lou."

"He told me you'd retired from the army."

"Yup, long time ago."

"What do you do now, if you don't mind my asking?"

"Golf and fuck," the general replied and roared with laughter and each in their fashion followed suit.

"Were you part of the Heroes Fund?"

"Sure, sure. Hope you threw some in."

"I did."

The car was accelerating up onto a very busy but still moving freeway.

"And, of course, you know the prince," Michael said ruminatively.

"If you know thoroughbreds you know the prince."

"It was all new to me. I thought it was quite fantastic."

Night had fallen and the motion of the headlights all around them traced lurid patterns on the women's faces as they picked up speed. The silky smoothness of the car's suspension combined with the bourbon made Michael imagine himself injected with Demarol, being whisked on a hover-gurney by three scrub nurses in cocktail gowns to some subterranean operating theater.

"I assume from what you said you live in Washington."

"Arlington. Across the Potomac in Virginia. The girls all live in Maryland."

"Did you drive here?"

"God no, came into JFK. Gonna have to make the last flight now."

"Maybe we should have gone back with Dwayne," Cindy said.

"Did he have his own plane then?"

"Yup, government jet. Only way to fly."

Michael could see from the skyline they were heading back into Manhattan.

"Do you come to the States often?" Brandy asked, "Lou told Larry you're from London."

It was an innocent enough question but Michael wondered if some unseen ball had been passed and it was her turn to do the digging. Obviously McWhirter wasn't yet convinced he really was who he said he was. No doubt, Michael mused, he has been living with lies for so long that truth can only mean deception.

"I come as often as I can but the last time was four and a half years ago. I went to Texas. I love the desert in the southwest."

"Whereabouts in Texas?"

"El Paso."

"Where you there on business?"

"No. Just on my way through to Los Angeles to visit friends."

"Did you get to Mexico?"

He pronounced the 'x' as an 'h'.

"Only Juarez."

"Juarez is horrible!" Melissa grimaced, "My uncle retired to San Miguel de Allende. It's beautiful."

"Where is that?"

"In the mountains of Guanajuato. It's kind of like Santa Fe."

"I'd love to go there then. I agree Juarez is horrible."

"What do people in London think about George Bush?" Cindy asked out of the blue, leaning across to top up Michael's glass.

"Well, London is very different from England," he explained carefully, "In England they don't really mind him so much. In London most people think he's a dangerous idiot."

"Most people in New York too," she confirmed, but Michael couldn't tell if she was in agreement.

There was a momentary silence.

"Were any of you near the Pentagon?"

"No, where we live is nearer Baltimore," Cindy answered.

Unfortunately Michael's rather hazy sense of geography made her reply quite meaningless to him.

"Ah. Yes."

"I was about to give a lecture," Brandy mentioned casually.

"Oh?"

"She's a sociology professor," Cindy said proudly, "Brandy the Brain."

"Good lord."

The general was so silent Michael thought he might have fallen asleep but he suddenly came back to life.

"He's a dangerous idiot all right but not the way most people think. He says he's gonna track down the evil-doers in their caves, that he's gonna shock and awe. Cheney, Rumsfeld, Myers, that little weasel Rove, your faggotty mama's boy Blair, the whole useless pack of them, they all beat their meat to the same damn drum. But none of them have the guts to use the full force that's required. They're going to fuck it up, I promise you."

"What exactly?"

"The Taliban. Hussein. You name it."

"You mean Iraq is next?"

"Course it is. Been the plan since day one. Georgie boy thinks God is telling him to do it. Rumsfeld sprinkles his memos with biblical quotes."

"I'm sorry to say Blair is of the same persuasion."

"Yeah, I know. Is he a little prick, or what?"

"Both," Michael answered and the general laughed.

"What about bin Laden?" Michael ventured.

At that the general got sly and leaned across Brandy's lap.

"I'll tell you a little secret about bin Laden," he said, putting a bony hand on Michael's knee, "He's an asset. They're never gonna find him 'cause they don't *want* to find him. Anyway, he had pretty much zero to do with it."

"I thought he had everything to do with it," Michael said

disingenuously.

"Well, he fucking didn't and that's all I'm gonna say."

The driver must have taken a different bridge than Lamy because Michael could see a heavily built-up island in the river below them which he hadn't noticed on the way and they descended into the city in silence.

After a few twists and turns they arrived at Central Park and the driver took a left on Park Avenue and then another on 63rd Street and stopped in front of a dimly-lit restaurant called *'Fin de Partie'*. The coincidental appropriateness of the name made Michael smile. It was down a dozen stone steps from the pavement and from the outside looked quite empty and forlorn but inside it was another story altogether. It had been booked for the occasion by a very similar-looking bunch to those in the Preferred Access Area at the track and was already extremely crowded as they entered. Michael hoped he might meet the prince but soon realized the thought was naïve. The people he struggled to converse with over the loud music of the band and the bray of vacant laughter for the next two and a half hours were not in that league. A snippet from Samuel Beckett ran repetitive laps through his brain, ' . . that's what hell will be like, small chat to the babbling of Lethe about the good old days when we wished we were dead.' They were rich, some no doubt extremely so, and the only subject of any interest to them was money and they couldn't get away from Michael fast enough after an initial polite interchange. All, that is, except Brandy.

She seemed to know nearly everyone and certainly did her duty and made the rounds but she kept coming back to Michael and making sure his glass was filled and he found out quite a lot about her and she about him. She was from a working-class family in Portland, Oregon, and wanted to be a veterinarian but got pregnant in her teens and raised two children. Her childhood sweetheart whom she married turned out to be a typically abusive jealous bastard and she left him with toddlers in tow and had somehow managed to attend four years of college in San Francisco and gone on to earn a double PhD in sociology and biology from the University of Southern California. She was now, as Cindy informed them on the way, an assistant professor at the University of Maryland. But she also had a wild side and satisfied it by bestowing her favors on a growing number of Washington heavy-hitters among whom, she was not shy to admit, was the vice-president.

By the end of their lengthy and frustratingly intermittent intercourse

Michael was quite, quite drunk and she had the general's permission to escort him to his hotel in the limousine and they took their leave of the party.

All Michael could remember the next morning of their East Side to West Side passage was his boyish fantasy, as the car glided like a greased serpent through the darkened byways of the park and he lay gazing up at the rosy pastel flicker on her bare shoulders and the now nearly leafless trees, that the woman stripping her clothes off above him was the reincarnation of Marilyn Monroe and his fervent prayer, as this goddess rode him to a blinding blissful orgasm, that she was not suddenly going to blossom into Richard Cheney.

§

He wasn't the only one floating in Bacchic limbo, however, because at about the same time George Walker Bush might have been found snoring and half-buried in a pile of damp maple leaves if the beam from the flashlight in the faithful hand of his National Security Advisor had chanced to land upon him.

Ms. Rice, the president's Chief-of-Staff and his wife Kathleene Card, who was the Associate Pastor of Trinity United Methodist Church in McLean, Virginia, accompanied the First Couple to Camp David most weekends and had proved an indispensable comfort to their gently snuffling boss since the crisis began.

Having staggered away from the patio doors sucking his fingertips he hit the circular wrought iron railing hard and flipped straight over it into the sloping rock garden below but, as happens sometimes with the massively inebriated, he had remained miraculously upright and stumbled headlong through a patch of autumnal shrubs to the lawn and, having reached it, plunged forward in a zigzag wobbly dash all the way to the putting green where he finally lost his balance and slumped down disconsolately on his bottom.

He was still clutching his half empty bottle of Jack Daniel's and demolished several more ounces of it before making a decision and lurching to his feet.

He made his way unsteadily past the pool through the gathering gloom to a small rustic lodge named Witch Hazel and, chuckling to himself, pried up a window with an axe like a cat burglar. The opening was small and he nearly got permanently wedged with one leg in and one out but at last folded himself through it head first. He drew the curtains and switched on a low-wattage lamp beside the couch in the living room and found some firewood stacked by the back door. It took a while to construct a workable assembly in the grate and even more to light it but eventually he had a satisfying blaze and turned on the old black and white television and after some irritable twiggling of the dials found the Fox channel.

A young blond Alaskan pop star named Jewel was in the middle of singing the national anthem and the president sat heavily on the low-slung couch with his forearms dangling from his knees and chugged the last of the bottle and watched blearily as the record-breaking home run king Barry Bonds threw the ceremonial first pitch and Derek Jeter got clocked by Mike Mussina and scored on Williams' double and almost made it through the top of the first inning before his eyes rolled upward in his head and his body toppled sideways and he sank into a deep slumber.

Now the president was not the simple man that some supposed although it might be true to say he would have been happier had the hand of fate led him to a simpler kind of life. He was the eldest son of ambitious parents and it seemed to him he was always being either pushed or mocked and this fostered an insecurity which revealed itself in an habitual and edgy resentment at any kind of questioning. Pushed first and foremost by the 'special relationship' with his 'Gray Fox' gorgon of a mother and mocked by the reptilian elder of Kennebunkport, his famous father, Texas Congressman, CIA Director, Chairman of the Grand Old Party, two-term vice-president and 41st president, current special advisor to the Carlyle Group of private equity managers, who coincidentally were meeting with bin Laden's brother Shafig in their sanctum on Pennsylvania Avenue that bright September morning. Then pushed and mocked and hounded by a procession of phonily rectitudinous ancestors beginning with his tall Nazi-sympathizing grandfather Prescott and dating all the way back to the marriage of Elizabeth Plantagenet with the Chief Constable of England, Humphrey de Bohun, on November 14th, 1302! And, as well, by his business partners and political contemporaries over so many, many years.

There was also the subtle but insistent pressure from his soft-spoken wife and the empty sermonizing of that pompous fake Billy Graham and a gladhanding battalion of brokers, backers, bankers and bullyboys who provided loot by the barrelful, who stifled their snickers and sucked up to his face because they needed a stooge for their schemes of power.

All of this had given him bad dreams which even bourbon could not temper. One recurring nightmare took place before the huge statue of an owl in a great forest echoing with hoots of mirth. He was lying helpless and disheveled with his belly on a campground picnic table as a naked and bespectacled Henry Kissinger huffed and snorted and fumbled to penetrate his anus from behind with a flaccid greasy member and the grotesque distorted faces of everyone who had ever eased his passage to high office frolicked about them pointing soiled fingers, cackling like witches on the Sabbath and jabbing in triumph at the stars with white hot branding irons tipped with the letter W.

But that was not the torment of tonight. It was, if anything, even worse and he forced himself to rouse from the horror of it to torpid semiconsciousness from time to time and on each occasion the Arizona Diamondbacks were scoring.

It started with the painting and the blood but then he was suddenly in a watery dripping disused tunnel that led from Camp David beneath the sleepy town of Sabillaville six miles to Raven Rock, Site R, the 'back-up Pentagon', the National Military Command Center, hewn deep into the substrata of porphyritic granite in order to sustain the continuity of government during all possible levels of nuclear incident, and the undisclosed location of the vice-president on 9/11.

And as he stumbled through the shimmer of this sewer the ground began to shake beneath his feet and the whole tube lurched and swayed and split asunder and he was falling like Indiana Jones into an underground lake filled with fiery dragons and thick with gore. And all the dragons had faces like the members of his Cabinet but dressed as Arabs with long beards. And there was Rumsfeld chasing his identical twin with a Bedouin's dagger. And pale Wolfowitz in a *keffiyeh* strangling sweat from Richard Perle with a Yale necktie. And they reversed and each became each and there was Condoleezza mincing about his feet like a two-headed bitch in heat. And the news came that the oil was gone! And now they were all dressed in top hats like Victorian gentlemen at the club and the dark stone pool below was writhing with gigantic octopi tearing the white innocent flesh of naked babes. And he was one of them crying out in agony to the pallid, implacable ghouls above!

And there was Gonzalez homering and four more runs in the bottom of the fourth and he was watching a film of the vice-president and a dozen hooded figures toasting with blood in pewter goblets to an audience of smiling rattlesnakes. And a jet was coming in to land at an Air Force base and the disoriented passengers were met by Waffen-CIA and hustled to murky gas chambers.

And the towers were melting like crimson popsicles and everyone was falling and chasing their terrified doubles down a molten concrete waterfall.

And the seventh inning stretch and Irving Berlin and stand beside her and guide her and again the two Condoleezzas were lapping at his feet and trying to bite off the buttons of his jeans and he was back in the tunnel and all the two-headed dragons, one head smiling a brain-dead smile, the other with bloody fangs snarling and vicious and unstoppable, came rushing pell-mell toward him and trampled him over and over and over until the pain was gone and he was nothing but a thick black ooze under their shit-encrusted hooves.

He woke himself in a panicked wide-eyed sweat and the game was over but the dream was not because as Joe Buck and Tim McCarver chattered on about the highlights and the winning pitcher Curt Schilling's great seven innings and his boast about the dancing nightclub twins, the lost Mystique and Aura of the Yankees, they were joined in the broadcast booth, despite some offscreen protest, by a starkly pale Dick Cheney who sat down between them, throwing away his suit jacket to the floor manager as he did so, removed his tie, unbuttoned his collar and shirt to the navel and, staring them into silence with a malevolent smirk, thrust it provocatively off one shoulder to reveal his breast and the still livid scar from his defibrillator implant. And as the vice-president was instructing them with a growl to kiss it the camera cut away to their faces and both their faces were his own! And the horrid growl grew louder and more insistent and the two of him stared in disbelief but then stooped to do as they were bid. And as his two pairs of lips made unwilling contact with the rancid skin the clammy wound began to gurgle and pulse and swell and the pudgy white torso stretched slowly to breaking and burst, exploding like a supernova right through the television screen, shattering it into a thousand pieces and filling the living room with a steaming sludge of body parts and blood and he lost all control of his bladder and bowels and had bolted with a shriek out into the misty night.

Stanza Six

the cream of this world's dignitaries
we esteem the great owl not canaries
through our shiny red robes
poke tiny hot probes
we're infantasized ritual fairies

§

As Michael slowly surfaced in his bed at the Belleclaire the next morning he was troubled, not so much by the momentary unfamiliarity of his surroundings nor the puzzle of how he came to be there but the nagging feeling that he had divulged some secret he should not have. He sat up and couldn't shake it and went into the bathroom to relieve himself. As he appraised his nakedness in the cabinet mirror, scratching his stubbled chin, the fog slowly cleared. Her scent was still thick upon him and their glorious Valkyrie ride came flooding back.

At the height of their passion she had questioned his identity, gasping that she couldn't believe he was really who he said he was and now he remembered that he had mischievously whispered of a doppelganger, an identical twin whose name, or code name, was Bartolomeo Vespucci. The bourbon had brought forth a jesting James Bond prankster to further plumb the general's mind. Michael knew perfectly well Brandy had not straddled him because she thought he was cute, though he flattered himself she had not remained totally unaffected by his charms. He was still in fighting Saxon trim! Not bad, he thought, for a fifty-two-year-old semi-reclusive intellectual.

However, despite his amusement at the drollery of it all, though he couldn't yet be certain McWhirter was connected to Chuck's murder nor the other horrors in Amado Portillo's penthouse, nor whether the general even knew the name of the bizarre figment Portillo forced him to portray, there was no doubt Brandy would have reported her findings on the flight back to Washington and Michael was well aware his incorrigibly flapping tongue might have put him in jeopardy once again.

After looking in the pocket of his shoulder-bag to check if the envelope with his winnings was still there and finding that it was and briefly wondering if he might be able to cash it somewhere if necessary, he showered and went out for breakfast at Arty's delicatessen at 84th and Broadway.

He was feeling remarkably well considering the circumstances and ordered a refreshing bowl of chicken soup, followed by chopped liver on rye, smothered in mustard with pickled cucumbers and carrots and French fries and then asked for a slice of cinnamon apple pie with vanilla ice cream and a cup of dark blend coffee and sat back to read the papers. He noticed during the feast his watch was an hour fast and it wasn't until the middle-aged waitress reminded him Daylight Saving had ended at two o'clock that morning that the mystery was resolved. The headline in the Daily News proclaimed the Arizona Diamondbacks' trouncing of the defending champions nine to one and Michael was tickled by the story of Aura and Mystique. He felt he had been blessed by both at once.

There was a front page article notifying the American public that top FBI and CIA officials now believed the anthrax attacks were not connected to Osama bin Laden or Al Qaeda but were more likely the work of a single male domestic terrorist with a scientific background and experience handling hazardous materials. There was confirmation of the execution of the mujahideen commander Abdul Haq at the hands of the Taliban and of the continued pounding they were taking from American warplanes. And a report that a multi-billion dollar aid package had been put together for Pakistan as a reward for its support. And a small item on a later page admitting that ten civilians had mistakenly been killed by an errant bomb in a village north of Kabul. And something unreadable about Barry Bond's divorce leading to prenuptial agreement reforms in California. And that a magician named Lance Burton would be performing an upside-down straightjacket escape in the Monte Carlo Casino in Las Vegas tomorrow to publicize the unveiling of a Harry Houdini stamp by the Post Office but Michael could find no further news of the Patriot Act signing nor its frightening ramifications and nothing at all about the memorial service at Ground Zero that afternoon.

Michael delved into the weekend Guardian, which he had been pleased and somewhat surprised to find at the kiosk, and discovered Prince Charles had met with Muslim leaders in an effort to improve British-Islamic relations, whoop-de-do, he thought, good for the chinless wonder, and that Abdul Haq had very likely been betrayed to the Taliban by double agents of the CIA and Pakistan's equivalent ISI and that the CIA had refused to send a helicopter to rescue him even though it would have been quite routine. And a feed from the Boston Globe revealing that the National Security Agency had been busy destroying data pertinent to the 9/11 investigation. And that ten thousand jihadist warriors were heading from Pakistan to the Afghanistan border in a convoy of trucks and buses. And that Israeli troops had delayed their promised withdrawal from Palestinian areas citing ongoing gun battles as the reason. All things that had not been reported in the Daily News but really of precious little interest and he put the papers on the next seat and paid the bill and walked out.

What was of interest to Michael, as he strolled back down Broadway to the hotel and his meeting with Lamy, was that sign at Belmont flashing Cheney's name and all the other inexplicable yet possibly transhuman manifestations. What on earth was causing them to happen? He wondered how many citizens of this great city and across the whole country might also have seen such things and assumed they must be delusional because they involved the vice-president or someone else in a position of authority and power.

§

The president had at last been found and taken on a stretcher to Aspen Lodge and put to bed and in the morning before chapel he lay with his sorry head in Laura's lap and asked her for the thousandth time for understanding and forgiveness which for the thousandth time she freely gave and they donned their church clothes and went up the hill hand in hand and listened with humble hearts to Reverend Kathleene's prayer.

The 'Evergreen', as it was called, was a non-denominational facility which had been dedicated by the First Father ten years previously and the regular navy chaplain was always happy to involve visiting pastors in the service. It was a friendly space built from wooden beams and local stone, conducive to the intimacy of worship, and a small cleancut assemblage of camp officers and staff, wives and children, privates and politicians, exalted, lowly, or somewhere in between, knelt in expectant silence.

"Dear God," she began quietly, "You are the Sovereign Lord of our nation and we thank You for Your eternal blessings. We are confident that nothing can separate us from You. That even in the face of recent challenges You are always with us.

"We come to You in humble surrender from many faith traditions, yet united as one truly ecumenical body, aware that we are vulnerable alone.

"We need You, God, as we need each other. We seek Your guidance for our beloved president and those who work with him as they strive to protect the people of the United States of America. We know that You care personally for each one of them and we ask You to open our hearts and minds so that we can discern Your will for our nation in this time of tremendous grief and loss. Please deepen our ability to love and understand each other. Let us see this remarkable world of Yours without fear.

"We come also seeking your sacred intercession for the men and women who have been placed in harm's way while serving to defend our nation.

"For those who are kneeling before You here in this chapel, help them by Your grace to be wise leaders, Lord. Let them be led by You and may all honor and glory be Yours, our God. Amen."

The president and his doe-eyed sweetheart and everyone present repeated the word in all humility and then proceeded to the canteen together for a brunch of chicken-fried steak.

§

When Michael walked up to the waiting Mercedes and peered in through the open window of the passenger door Lamy asked, "So, did she show you a good time?"

"What? Who?" Michael stammered in astonishment.

"Don't just stand there. Get in."

Michael did so and gazed at Lamy, attempting an innocent smile.

"Perhaps you'd like to tell me what you're talking about."

Lamy chuckled.

"You've got that well-screwed look."

Michael was silent and Lamy started up and eased the station wagon from its parking spot outside the hotel down the block toward West End Avenue.

"I'd like to know what you know," Michael said, "I'm not a fool."

"Nothing at all. Just guessing."

"Too good a guess to be coincidental, I'm afraid. Did you and the general plot the whole thing together?"

"I didn't mention the general, did I?"

"Oh, come off it. Yes, the women invited me to join their table when you and the general had gone and I did but I had no intention of anything beyond that. When the general came back he said there was a party and that I'd be welcome to come in your place."

"And you did."

"Ha, ha, yes. In a manner of speaking."

"She's a gorgeous woman."

"Without a doubt."

"So did you tell her what the general wants to know?"

Michael didn't answer.

"Who was the other man? General Dwayne."

"Dwayne Cronin. A real hard-assed son of a bitch. President just made him another of his attack dogs on Iraq."

"Yes, replacing Richard Clarke."

"Don't let Clarke fool you. He's a son of a bitch too."

"Look here, Louis," Michael said impatiently, "I'm going to call you Louis from now on. Look here, Louis, old chap, I don't give a fiddling monkey's fart who is a son of a bitch according to you and who is not, as far as I can see you all fit the mould, but I would appreciate knowing if you are somehow collectively plotting my demise. I'm not interested in who the guilty are, everyone's guilty, I'd just like to understand what is going on. Particularly with the Cheney manifestations. Whether they're spontaneous or being orchestrated by some reverse Carnivore wizard as you intimated."

"I think maybe you better tell me why the general is so interested in you. You could be getting yourself in a whole lot of trouble."

"Do you expect me to believe you don't know?"

"You can believe what you want but I don't."

"Really?"

"Really. Other than horses the general and I move in different worlds. We're not what he would call buddies."

Michael took a deep breath.

"All right," he said, "Have you ever heard the name Bartolomeo Vespucci?"

Lamy looked at him blankly.

"Nope. Was he Amerigo's brother or something?"

His ignorance appeared to be genuine but it was hard for Michael to be sure.

"You know there's a big question whether America was actually named after him," Lamy went on, "Some people think the origin is *'Ommerike'*, an old Norse word for 'farthest outland', others that John Cabot had a benefactor in Bristol named Richard Ameryk which is kind of funny because as far as I know Cabot just thought he had discovered an island off the Chinese coast. And there are the Amerrique mountains on the Caribbean side of Nicaragua, some say the origin was Mayan or Carib or even African. And, come to think of it, I did read a book years ago by a historian named Bartolomeo de Las Casas who sure didn't like Vespucci and claimed he'd changed his name from Alberigo after the fact. But it was really Vespucci who established what they had all discovered was a new world so in the end Las Casas didn't have much of a case the continent should have been called Columba instead. Maybe you got the names mixed up."

Lamy was negotiating the Mercedes around a car full of gawping tourists in Columbus Circle at that moment but neither of them commented on it.

"Good lord have mercy," Michael groaned, "You're worse than I am. I've never known such an unnecessarily loquacious mine of useless information."

"I'll take that as a compliment."

"What world do you move in then if not the general's?"

"My own."

"And what is that?"

"Hard to define, old chap."

"Give it a try."

"OK, but don't blame me for loquacity. I'm sixty-four next Sunday and since I emigrated from France my whole adult life has been centered on the world of AEC. Architecture, engineering, construction. Got an undergraduate degree in commerce and economics from Columbia in '59 and a PhD in chemical engineering from MIT in '62 and went south. Created my own company after a few years and cut my teeth on a bunch of crazy high-risk projects all over Latin America. Spent twenty-seven years down there all told. Made a fortune and got married to a fantastic woman from Lima who turned out to be a terrible nag in her old age. I told you she died last July. Of cancer. But mercifully quick. Both my daughters are married to guys I don't care for particularly. One's a rich movie lawyer in Beverley Hills, the other's with the border patrol in San Diego. They have children and the girls stay home. Are they happy? I doubt it but what can I do. I met David's sister Ruth a few months before I retired in '96 and it turned out to be the most fulfilling relationship I ever had. She was a lot like him in some ways but much more reasonable, though that's unfair because I only met him two days ago. I've never moved in political circles other than being sucked into it by my wealth and I try to avoid functions of that kind. I prefer giving my time and money to young writers who need them. It's probably what I wanted to be."

At the corner of 42nd Street the traffic stopped dead. A cadaverous figure dressed in ragged black with a top hat and long cape, straggly hair and a stark white face was striding on enormous stilts among the cars wearing a sandwich board with the words '9/11 VAMPYRE' written on the front in large dripping red letters. Michael was so anxious to discover what might be on the back he jumped out of the car and just as he did the figure raised its gloved palms to heaven with a gesture imploring justice, rolled its staring eyes in an expression of infinite sadness, bared a full set of wickedly sharpened teeth and then turned slowly around with a sly feral grin as if it knew exactly what he wanted and Michael began cheering and clapping in excitement and delight as gory hand-painted capitals were revealed proclaiming the name 'LON CHENEY'.

A stroke of genius. The elder Chaney in his makeup as the sinister tenant in 'London after Midnight' with the quite obviously intentional alteration of the vowel pointing a gnarled finger at the vice-president.

"Fantastic!" Michael exclaimed as he hopped back in.

The lights changed and the stilt-man strode away and the traffic moved on.

"Another manifestation?" Lamy asked ironically.

"No, no, of course not, not at all in the same way, but you have to admit it was fantastically clever. It's like everyone knows but . . "

"But what?"

"They just won't tell each other or something."

"Maybe it wasn't really there."

"Oh, bollocks, we both saw it. There was a whole crowd watching."

"Did they join in your applause?"

"One or two."

"OK, tell me. Who is Bartolomeo Vespucci?"

As they continued on past Madison Square Park and the Flatiron Building at 23rd Street Michael did his best to describe in as uncomplicated a fashion as he knew how the sequence of events in Juarez four and a half years ago and he had just started on the meeting in Portillo's penthouse with the Russians when Lamy tried to turn left onto Spring Street and their progress was halted by a roadblock.

They could see the flashing lights of emergency vehicles in the distance and a gurney being wheeled out from the door of David's gallery by paramedics.

"Good lord," Michael said, "Something's happened."

An NYPD officer was there and waved them to move on.

"Go and see. I'll wait for you down the far end."

Michael nodded and got out.

"I think I know the people involved," Michael offered but the officer clearly didn't care and didn't try to stop him and he was able to walk to within a few yards of the gallery entrance and join a small group of people that had gathered to watch on the opposite side of the street. There was a young woman amongst them and her eyes were moist with tears and Michael made his way close to her.

"Do you know the owner of the gallery?" he asked quietly.

The woman looked at him but didn't answer.

"I do. David Giudice. I've known him for many years. He was once married to my sister. And I know Fernando. Can you tell me what's going on?"

At that moment a second gurney was brought out onto the sidewalk. The face of the body was covered.

"Good lord," Michael said, "I thought perhaps Fernando . . "

"They're both dead."

Michael paused in shock and the young woman began to weep openly.

"How? Do you know? I just saw them yesterday."

"A friend found them this morning and called the police," a middle-aged man told him, still in pajamas and a bathrobe and holding sections of a newspaper to his chest, "They think it was a double suicide."

"David and Fernando?"

The man nodded gravely.

"Did you know them?" Michael asked.

"Very well."

"Are they sure it was suicide?"

"They were on the bed together. Nothing had been disturbed. There was no break-in. The gallery was locked. A friend in the neighborhood had invited them for brunch and got worried when they didn't show up or answer the phone. Everyone knew Fernando didn't have long."

"Yes. How terrible. Where will they take them?"

"The medical examiner, I guess."

Michael suddenly couldn't think of the word he was looking for.

"For an . . autopsy?" he managed finally.

"I'd guess that's the procedure."

They stood in silence as the ambulances drove away.

"What will happen with the gallery? Do they have the key?"

"Warren over there'll look after it. He's the one that called the police."

A man who Michael judged to be in his seventies at the least was on the other side of the street talking to an officer and Michael waited until they finished and the officer walked away before crossing over and introducing himself but he didn't find out anything much beyond what the other man had told him except that there had been no blood and no weapon had apparently been used. He found them lying in each other's arms and that was all. Michael asked about the funeral and the man scribbled his telephone number on the back of one of Michael's Enigma cards and said to call him tomorrow when he would know more about the police report and Michael thanked him and walked slowly down to the corner to find Lamy.

The roadblocks were being cleared away and traffic was moving along Spring Street again and at first Michael couldn't see the Mercedes station wagon anywhere but then an insistent horn sounded and Lamy pulled up behind him.

"Nowhere to park. Had to keep circling," Lamy said as he got in.

They started off again toward Ground Zero and the memorial service and Michael told the awful news as briefly as he could and when he finished they had just passed Foley Square and the Court House and Lamy turned off onto a side street and was lucky enough to find a car just leaving its parking space and he drew into it and switched off the engine and thought for a little while.

"Maybe it was suicide and maybe not."

"What, you think . . ?"

"I wouldn't put it past them."

"Why, what reason could they . . ?"

"Maybe he shot his mouth off in the wrong place."

"You mean the general . . ?"

"No, it wouldn't have been him."

"Who then?"

"Could have been a lot of people. If it wasn't suicide I'd say you stand a good chance of being next. Go on with your story."

Michael described in detail the sexual ritual of blood the two Mafia dons had performed with Portillo's sister and the black woman who was there to interpret and reminded him of Condoleezza Rice and the excruciating tape of the Russian henchmen being dissolved in acid and the agreement about the plutonium and then the Miss Texas Pageant and how he had been pressed into service as the third judge and Chuck Bowman and the balcony and the deaths of Bowman and the sister and Portillo in the jaws of his tiger and his arrest and night in the El Paso jail and the following morning's suspiciously quick release and how the whole terrifying affair was inseparably intertwined with the Portillo's belief they were vampires, something that to this day Michael had not been able to either conclusively prove or disprove.

"Interesting," Lamy mused quietly when the tale was done, "Why in hell did Portillo need you to be there?"

"I've never been able to answer that. I was instructed on pain of death not to say a word but to nod my head in approval whenever he looked at me. I can only assume the presence of Bartolomeo Vespucci, whoever he really is, was somehow necessary to smooth the way, to give a kind of blessing to the transaction. Portillo told me to act like the Pope and the Russians certainly deferred to me in that way."

"They obviously didn't know what he looked like."

"Obviously."

Lamy paused to consider.

"You know what," he said, "I think there's a damn good chance McWhirter and Consterdine were behind the deal to stash the plutonium and Portillo and the Russians didn't even know it. Pulling strings to make sure it happened."

"Good lord, that never occurred to me."

"I doubt they really gave much of a shit about Portillo being outed. Enough to off your friend Bowman maybe but these guys kill if you sneeze the wrong way."

"The morning I was released the newspapers were all praising Chuck as a hero for what he did. That he'd performed a great public service for exposing this wicked drug lord. The lawyer for my friends from Juarez who were arrested with me pointed out an article buried on an inside page reporting that a rival gang had taken over Portillo's villa that same night and murdered his mother so he wasn't going to be of any more use to them. We knew someone high up must have given the order to let us out. From the way the El Paso police behaved the night before I thought I might be incarcerated for life."

Lamy made a decision and started the car.

"I think we should forget about the service. What will it be but tear-jerking bullshit and platitudes? Andrea Bocelli and your creepy little composer who keeps inundating Broadway with pap, what's he called now, Baron Webber. Giuliani and Pataki and Hillary Clinton. Fuck it. I loved Ruth but fuck it. Until we have proof how David and his partner died and we probably never will know for sure, I say we get you out of town."

"Where? This is all too fascinating to go back to London now."

"My place on Long Island. I've got something I want to show you."

"What about the hotel room and my bags?"

"We'll get them later if we have to. It's better that you don't check out."

"Why would they bother about me after all these years? I often felt like I was being followed in London. For quite a number of months when I got back. They must have found out everything about me and when they were satisfied I hadn't made the connection you just did they let it drop."

"Yeah, but 9/11 may have changed that."

"How so?"

"What if the plutonium was once part of the plan?"

Michael was dumbstruck and felt an uncomfortable twinge of fear.

"The general could have forgotten all about you but then he saw you with me. Maybe the black woman didn't just look like Condoleezza Rice. Maybe she actually was the bitch. If so, it's even more of a miracle you're still alive."

"I suppose even they realize they can't kill everyone."

"If it was her then they definitely know about your pal Bartolomeo."

Michael cursed himself for his stupidity. Why, oh why, had he succumbed to that infantile impulse and whispered the name in her ear? Because he imagined it might 'fuck with the general's mind' to use his own phrase? And now Lamy had made it abundantly clear this man who he thought he could play cops and robbers with was very likely the ruthless accomplice of mass murderers.

"Last night," he began his shamefaced admission, "The young lady asked me who I really was and for some utterly idiotic reason I did mention that I had a kind of alter ego. I don't know what the devil I thought I was up to but I did say the words Bartolomeo Vespucci to her."

Lamy laughed out loud.

"What webs we weave," he said with a knowing smile, "You are deep in the brown stuff now."

"Surely they found out I wasn't this man long ago."

"No doubt, no doubt, but then, like I say, the general saw you with me."

"What difference would that make? I told him we'd only set eyes on each other a few hours before."

"What if he didn't believe you? They don't like me because they know I'm not one of them but they have to make nice because I'm number nine on the Forbes list of American billionaires. I've got more money than Silvio Berlusconi but I make them feel nervous. They don't trust me and never will."

Michael knew this mind-boggling leprechaun was rich but a billionaire! And how odd for him to mention the ill-gotten gains of the recently re-elected and notoriously corrupt Italian prime minister when so many homegrown comparisons might have served. Such quibbles, however, were hardly the matter of the moment.

"So you're saying that because I was with you they'll think I actually am this man and everything else is some kind of elaborate cover?"

"Could be. As a species they don't have much imagination."

"Or too much."

They were speeding down the Long Island Expressway. Michael recognized more or less where he was but had been too engrossed to notice how Lamy got there so quickly. Why was it whenever he came to this blasted country everything always got complicated, not to mention lethal? Life was so simple back home.

"Where are we going? The racetrack again?"

"No, that was the last meet this fall. Starts up again at the end of April. I told you my stable is near Mattituck. I live there too. Relax and enjoy the ride, it'll take another hour and a half."

Michael thought of yesterday and David and the toy gun, he had brandished it at about this point, and was overcome with sadness. Surely, despite what Lamy conjectured, it was much more likely David orchestrated a painless suicide because of Fernando's illness and his own despair. He didn't relish the idea of phoning Helen but, in all decency, he didn't have much choice. What if she decided to come over for the funeral? Well, he didn't know yet if there would be one. He would try and put her off in any case. He didn't want to involve his beloved baby sister in what was rapidly becoming a very dangerous muddle.

"I owe you a hundred and two dollars, by the way," he said idly, suddenly remembering the bets Lamy had placed for him.

"Don't worry, I haven't forgotten. How do you think I got so damn rich?"

Stanza Seven

it's a boy's club for schmoozing and glee
no bitch gets in here sits to pee
but one day a year
to prove we're not queer
we invite our prime cuts in to tea

§

Unlike Michael the general had enjoyed his extra hour of sleep. When the last flight landed at Dulles it was four minutes to midnight and his head didn't hit the pillow in Arlington until two o'clock. His estranged wife Alice, who still owned a nineteenth-century Colonial Classic in Georgetown but was completely helpless and bedridden with rheumatoid arthritis and required twenty-four seven nursing care, had forced him to let her move back in with him and he could hear her racking snores as he tiptoed past her bedroom door.

Dulles International Airport, which was named for the Secretary of State of the Eisenhower era, John Foster Dulles, a man who fervently desired to liberate the world from Communism and was largely responsible for the fatal idiocy of Viet Nam and the brutal despotism of Iran's Shah Reza Pahlevi, is located in Chantilly, Virginia, where the next annual Bilderberg conference was scheduled to take place at the luxurious Westfields Marriott the following June. The Bilderbergs, named for the hotel in Oosterbeek, the Netherlands, the site of their first meeting in 1954, are a secretive group of the rich and powerful who do their best to shape the broad outline of the human experiment and, among many another nefarious scheme, to ensure the quadrennial enthronement of their chosen candidate in the Oval Office. Permanent members of this insidious clique include David Rockefeller and Henry Kissinger and their last meeting in Gothenburg had been attended by Pascal Lamy.

The general left a note on the kitchen counter for Cecilia, his live-in Costa Rican maid, to wake him at nine which she dutifully did and as soon as he had wiped the crusts from his pale gray eyes and gargled with a mouthful of cherry-flavored Listerine, inserted his teeth and taken a swig of the coffee on his breakfast tray he dialed the cell phone of Condoleezza Rice. There was no answer and he had pressed redial several times to the same lack of effect before remembering it was Sunday morning and therefore where she must be.

At six minutes past eleven he tried again and got through.

"I'll call you back," she said.

He had to wait another fifteen irritating minutes before his phone rang.

"About time you got up off your knees," he teased.

"Fuck you, Larry, what do you want?"

"Where are you now?"

"The office in Laurel. Everyone's gone to brunch."

"How's the boy?"

"Behaving badly. I had to dig him out of a ditch last night."

The general chuckled.

"Any idea why?"

"He mumbled some bullshit about seeing Dick in a painting and being half naked on the post-game show. What do you want?"

"Seen your buddy Yaponchik lately?"

There was an icy silence. Vyacheslav 'Yaponchik' Ivankov was the second of the two Russian Mafia dons at the meeting with Portillo in Juarez and the one with whom she had exchanged various vital bodily fluids at the ritual and she didn't appreciate the reminder of humbler days.

"Or Bartolomeo Vespucci?"

His teeth weren't in quite snug and the surname came out slushy.

"I've never met him."

"Ever get the Roman contingent to confirm or deny?"

"Nothing. They're even better liars than the Jews. Like stabbing a mirage. I've decided he doesn't exist."

"What about Michael Davenport?"

"Would you please just fucking well explain yourself."

"I bumped into him yesterday. With Louis Lamy."

"Who?"

"Davenport."

"What in hell were you doing with Lamy?"

"Not me, chipmunk. Davenport was with *him*."

"What?" she said incredulously, "I hate that smug little fucker. Where?"

"Belmont. They were with some guy whose sister died in the towers. He got smashed and sounded off about it."

"Lamy? Davenport? The guy? Who?"

"The guy."

"So?"

"Well, so you tell me why Michael Davenport, the piss-ass nothing, is with Lamy if he isn't Bartolomeo Vespucci?"

"For Christ's sake, Larry, get your damn teeth fixed. What are you doing, your Sylvester the puddy-tat imitation? Lamy's a jerk. He gets off befriending people like that. Davenport's a penniless writer, remember?"

"OK, so we're gonna leave him alone, is that the decision?"

"Why is he in New York?"

"Visiting the drunk, he said. The guy looked queer to me but Davenport told me he was married to his sister."

"Davenport was married to the woman in the tower?"

"No, genius, the other way round. The faggot was married to Davenport's sister."

"Well, get your fucking story straight. Why are you bothering me with this crap?"

"Thought you might like to tie up an old loose end."

"What did the drunk say exactly?"

"The usual. Started on about no Arabs being in the planes and all that but he didn't get far before everyone yelled at him to shut up."

"What was his connection to Lamy?"

"Davenport wouldn't say. The sister's my guess."

"Which fucking sister?"

"The drunk's, who else?"

"This is really starting to bore me, Larry. I'm only talking to you because I don't like chicken-fried steak. Where is Davenport staying?"

"Some cheesy fleapit on the West Side."

"Does it have a name?"

"The Bellucci. No, hold it, I'll find out. What time is good if I call you at work tomorrow?"

"Eleven fifteen. We've got Security Council after the briefing and, God spare me, Shimon Peres all afternoon. The old shyster will pretend to be concerned about peace and George will get his earnest glazed look and try not to nod off. What in hell is the point when no one in the room intends to make good on anything they say?"

"You wanted the job."

"And what'll I spend my lunch hour doing?"

"What?"

"Catching pitches in the bowling alley."

The general laughed so hard his upper plate nearly dislodged completely.

"Why do you put yourself through it?"

"He's nervous about the fans on Tuesday."

"Couldn't be stopped though, huh?"

"Fat fucking chance."

The general was still chuckling.

"You know, chickadee, maybe it's time to get religion after all."

§

Michael could see planes coming in to land to their north and a broad expanse of green and some kind of sports venue in the distance beyond and a lake of sorts to the south.

"Where are we now? We came this way to the track, didn't we?"

"Flushing Meadows. If you like tennis, it's where they play the US Open. And you can see the top of Shea Stadium."

"I thought that was for baseball not tennis."

"It is. Home of the Mets. Arthur Ashe is where they have the Open."

Michael didn't know why he had asked the question in the first place and went back to what was really on his mind.

"But how can it possibly have been Condoleezza Rice? Why would a woman in her position have involved herself in such a thing? I couldn't swear it was her. The Russians mounted them like animals."

Lamy smiled.

"She's a Soviet expert. Traveled there a lot for Poppy Bush. He called her his 'warrior princess'. Knows Gorbachev and Yeltsin. All the new oil jillionaires. Plenty of opportunity to meet some useful people on the seamier side. I don't have enough fingers for the private sector boards she sat on before being elevated to the White House. Transamerica, Chevron, Carnegie, Charles Schwab, Rand, Hewlett Packard, you name it. Not bad for a segregation era preacher's kid from Alabammy. Did you know her father's name is John Wesley Rice? You'd be surprised what lurks behind that prim Presbyterian veneer. Not 'Christian perfection', I promise you that."

"But surely she could have sent someone else."

"Not if the Russians insisted."

Michael thought for a moment.

"So I was Portillo's counterbalance?"

"Maybe. If I knew who your alter ego was I could tell you."

"I don't remember her showing any reaction to me. We never spoke or shook hands. I don't even think we met eyes. She was deadpan throughout, even when the Russian was fucking her. She must have known I was a fraud the whole time."

"Maybe. Maybe not."

"It's very strange though. The two Russians were utterly obsequious towards me. They were as skittish as if I'd been Dracula himself."

"In rituals like that, Masons, Templars, the College of Cardinals electing a new Pope, the Inquisition, the KKK, all boy's clubs basically, I think women have always recognized keeping a low profile is the safest policy."

"Of course, but afterwards she and the general must have spoken and even if she didn't know who I was she certainly would have found out soon enough. Why didn't she have me killed?"

"You said it already. Like everyone, they have to choose their battles. I guess you ultimately didn't matter that much."

It's a strange thing, the human ego, though not mattering had without doubt saved his life Michael suffered the fleeting rankle of belittlement.

"And what?" he began again, "Do you really think the plutonium might once have been part of an alternate plan for 9/11? To make a 'suitcase nuke', is that it?"

"They may have been weighing the options but I suspect, in the end, even they couldn't bring themselves to that level of devastation and their Arab surrogates probably weren't up to it anyway. You remember the name Ramzi Yousef?"

"I think so. Something to do with the earlier bombing, wasn't he?"

"That's right. February 26th, 1993. I've got a feeling that first time they were acting on their own which is why it didn't work all that well and why it was so easy to use some of the same dummies this time without their knowing it. Yousef hoped the explosives in the van would be powerful enough to undermine the structure and make the towers fall into each other. After that he was involved in a foiled assassination attempt on Benazir Bhutto and then Bojinka, which was a plot to kill John Paul II on a visit to the Philippines, blowing up two American flights from Bangkok to Tokyo at the same time to divert attention. He did a successful test run and started to think he could blow up even more planes and the Pakistanis caught him. They flew him back to the States and the FBI have been dining out on this quote recently. They say as his plane came in over the towers he looked down and said, 'It is not yet finished.' Bullshit baffles brains. He's gonna rot in solitary out in Florence, Colorado."

"Why are you telling me this?"

"No reason. Just that your little Miss Warrior Princess has been denying and denying that anyone ever imagined terrorists might use planes."

"Transparent nonsense."

"But people buy it. Prescott Bush's favorite mantra was, 'Claim everything, explain nothing, deny everything.' His seed has learned it well."

"So give me your take on what happened."

"Am I allowed a modicum of loquacity?"

"If you must."

"OK, I'll be brief. They caught wind these Jihad Joes were plotting it, they may even have put the idea in their heads, helped them along with visas and money and flight schools and at the same time made their own plan as a surround to make sure it wouldn't screw up this time. The planes were guided for the last minutes from a remote command center in Building 7. Everyone in them was dead before they hit. The towers were brought down by a controlled demolition operated from the same location. Building 7 was pulled to destroy the evidence. The fires are still burning because the thermite incendiaries that were used to cut the steel melted it in huge quantity. They're carting it away fast so this won't get out or, at least, can never be proved. An air-to-ground missile blew the hole in the Pentagon and the same for the charred field in Shanksville. The passengers on those two flights were all murdered. I can't say exactly who gave the order but what I have to show you will give you a pretty good idea."

"Bravo for brevity. And who is they?"

"There are thousands. Most who had a part in it have to deny it even to themselves. Some might have the guts to admit it but would claim they only knew the whole picture later and never suspected it would turn out to be something so fucking barbarous. The courageous few who were so upset they'd risk blowing the whistle are getting silenced one by one. Who knew all of it? A small inner circle. Maybe a hundred at most. You know the names and none of them did any of the dirty work."

"Never. Not even in the good old days."

The highway had dwindled from six lanes to four and was bypassing built-up areas and bordered with trees and farms and Michael would have been amused, had he noticed them, by the green signs pointing the way to towns like Amityville and Babylon, Jericho, Brightwaters, King's Park, San Remo, Stonybrook, Half Hollows and Ronkonkoma, but he was suddenly feeling tired.

"Will it be all right if I make a call to England when we get there?" he asked, "I must let my sister know about David. We'll have to find out if there's a funeral. God, I hope she won't want to come."

He was overcome by a yawn and the attempt to stifle it made his eyes water.

"Do you suppose there were any Cheney apparitions at the memorial?" Lamy chuckled.

"The only one that puzzles me is the two workers. You and David are born fantasists but Bela Halloween Cheney beneath the buildings, that I can't figure."

"David had a perfect explanation, what was it, 'the subliminal', no, a word for 'under the skin'."

"Subcutaneous?"

"Yes, that's it, 'the subcutaneous pressure of overwhelming guilt squeezed out like pus from a pimple'."

Lamy smiled and nodded his head in appreciation.

"Couldn't have put it better myself."

§

Before the president's digestive juices had begun their work on the chicken-fried steak the four Whitehawks took off again for Washington. Laura had arranged a prayer meeting in the Yellow Oval Room in the White House residence for three-thirty that afternoon because, even though her wayward boy was very private about such matters and had made his desire to keep the Reverend Graham at more than arm's length known, she hoped that under the rapidly deteriorating circumstances some further spiritual counsel might prove beneficial. Given her threat to decamp forthwith he had little choice but to obey.

The Yellow Room was her favorite for entertaining and she had instructed the staff to clear a space under the chandelier. Normally two plush yellow couches and a pair of Louis XVI armchairs were set before the fireplace but today called for a more open configuration. She was already planning special new ornaments for the great Christmas tree that would be framed in the curving windows of the Truman Balcony. Decorations that would epitomize the hopeful future she earnestly wished for all Americans.

She had asked that two large television sets be brought in for the occasion and positioned underneath and a few feet in front of the portraits of John A. P. Millet as a little boy and the artist Jane Emmet de Glehn and a female companion languorously reading in a sunlit garden on the Greek island of Corfu, by the great American, John Singer Sargent, which were on loan from a private collection and hung to either side of the mantelpiece.

The Reverend Kirbyjon Caldwell was going to join them via satellite from the 'Power Center', his mega-church in Houston, Texas, which had been fashioned inside the shell of a K-Mart to accommodate weekend crowds of fifteen thousand, and, as well, the leonine evangelist and his wife Ruth had graciously agreed to have their rustic mountaintop retreat in the Black Mountains of North Carolina invaded by a television crew for the same purpose. Both the Grahams were in their eighties and ailing. He had been fit enough to join the president and lead the prayer at the National Cathedral Remembrance Service on September 14th but broke his foot in a fall at the Bulldog Stadium in Fresno during a more recent Crusade to California's Central Valley and his doctors insisted further engagements involving travel were out of the question.

In the room with the reluctantly pacing president and his wife, sipping tea and nibbling on a variety of sandwiches and cakes, were Kathleene Card and Jim Towey, the newly-appointed director of the Office of Faith-Based Initiatives, a recipient of the Papal Cross and a member of the Knights of Columbus and thus, needless to say, Catholic, as well as representatives from the Wesley Theological Seminary, the Church of God in Christ, the National Capital Baptist Convention and the Episcopal Diocese.

As soon as Reverend Kirbyjon and the Grahams were with them and hellos had been said all round, the eight who were bodily present knelt down in a circle and held hands and Caldwell led an opening prayer in praise of 'the name above all other names, Jesus the Christ.'

Then the Reverend Graham, with flowing white hair and famous voice still rich and strong, looking like Moses but trembling slightly from Parkinson's disease, intoned a few carefully chosen words about sin being the only thing that's wrong with the world and faith in, and obedience to, the will of that same Galilean being the only way to fix it. He was seated on a rough-hewn rocking chair beside the bedside of his crippled wife and he turned to her and said, "But Ruth has always been able to convey my thoughts more succinctly than I," and she opened a slender volume and read one of her poems in a soft lilting croak.

"Lord, when my soul is weary
and my heart is tired and sore,
and I have that failing feeling
that I can't take any more;
then let me know the freshening
found in simple childlike prayer,
when the kneeling soul knows surely
that a listening Lord is there."

It was a tough act to follow but Laura had placed a Bible on the carpet by her knees and she let the president's hand go and picked it up and gave it to him.

"Read it to us, George," she said with a loving voice, "The page is marked. It will make you feel strong again."

It was his favorite, the twenty-seventh psalm of David, and, once the sweating red-faced Commander-in-Chief had opened the book, he stared into the gently urgent eyes of his beloved and smiled his crooked smile in gratitude.

He cleared his throat and began.

"The Lord is my light and my salvation, whom shall I fear?"

She had been right, he was feeling better already.

"The Lord is the strength of my life, of whom shall I be afraid. When evil-doers came upon me to eat up my flesh . . "

But it wasn't to last because the image suddenly struck him as though he had never heard it before and it made him shiver and at the same moment he heard a crackling sound emanating from the fireplace where no fire had been kindled and he paused, too fearful to look up.

" . . even mine adversaries and my foes . . "

The crackling was joined by an insistent drumming.

" . . they stumbled and fell."

He dared a peek to either side and all heads were bowed and still.

"Though an host should encamp against me, my heart shall not fear . . "

The drumming got louder and the crackling was joined by a sizzling noise and the pungent smell of seared meat.

" . . though war should rise against me, even then will I be confident. One thing I have asked . . "

He stopped. He could feel an inexorable presence moving toward him and instinct forced him to look. Forming from nowhere like a malevolent blur between the serenely beatific televised faces of the Reverend Kirbyjon Caldwell and the aged couple, who both appeared to be enjoying forty winks, dressed in the full regalia of a Shawnee chieftain with a red bandanna and eagle feathers entwined in his long black hair, a bear-claw necklace, knee-length buckskin boots and ceremonial robes of rawhide, lined with elk's fur and attached at the shoulder with a taloned clasp, yet sporting a familiar twisted leer that was unmistakable, came the impossible figure of Wyoming's current favorite son, Richard Bruce Cheney, and the vision floated into the center of the prayer circle drawing a sharp knife from a beaded sheath.

Laura reached out and tugged at his sleeve to continue but he could not for as he stared up at the patently ridiculous delusion towering over him, and tried with all his might to will it into oblivion, the knife in the vice-president's tawny callused hand began to drip thick gouts of blood upon the verses of the psalm.

The others in the room were looking at him from under their eyelids and Laura shuffled on her knees to his side and, pretending he had been overcome with emotion and moved to speechlessness, began reading from where he left off. The dumbstruck president heard her words through the drumming as though they were static coming from the dark side of the moon.

"Hide not thy face from me. Cast me not off, O God of my salvation . . "

His lips were moving indistinctly to the sound but in his mind the book was nothing but a spongy mottled clump of gore.

§

The vice-president was about to have a spot of trouble of his own. He had just kicked back in his custom-built Chippendale recliner to watch a fly-fishing special filmed along the banks of the South Fork of Idaho's

Snake River when the telephone rang by his side. It was his Chief-of-Staff, Lewis 'Scooter' Libby, calling from the Eisenhower Executive Building and he knew from the treble pitch of his voice it was something serious.

"What are you doing there?" he asked.

Daily business was normally conducted in the West Wing and the EEOB, as it was called, was for overflow and the occasional ceremony or press interview. Beside that, it was Sunday afternoon.

"I don't know why," Libby told him, "I was feeling nervous about the tape and had to come and check. There were three copies in the safe, right?"

"Right."

"Well, now there's only two."

The chunky son of Wyoming, who attended Yale but flunked out after only three semesters and relayed the precaution from Raven Rock to the White House staff as well as those in employ at his residence at Number One Observatory Circle to start taking Cipro antibiotic on the evening of September 11th, was silent.

"I thought maybe you . . " Scooter chirped hopefully.

"No. I didn't," came the measured reply.

The tape in question reflected a desire on the vice-president's part to share some amusement, and more importantly gain some respect and kudos, at both the forthcoming Bilderberg get-together and the annual funfest at Bohemian Grove in July. He figured it would make a perfect accompaniment for the Cremation of Care ceremony and the Great Owl would surely hoot in approbation.

"Who else knows the combination except you and me?"

"No one," the boy from Casper answered darkly, reaching into his cardigan pocket for some nitroglycerine.

Stanza Eight

the cremation of care starts our frolic
light years from the church apostolic
round the statue of moloch
with greased buttock and bollock
stumble ghastly white ghouls alcoholic

§

The threatening Shawnee chieftain and his crimson knife began to lose their form and slowly atomized into a harmless kaleidoscope of psychedelic globules as the First Lady's soft voice neared the psalm's end.

" . . Deliver me not over to the will of mine adversaries, for false witnesses are risen up against me and such as breathe out cruelty. I had fainted unless . . "

The president turned in relief to his helpmeet and swallowed hard to moisten his larynx and after a brief pause they were able to speak in unison.

" . . I had believed to see the goodness of the Lord in the land of the living."

And everyone in the room and on the television feeds from Houston and Montreat joined in muted but inwardly fervent conclusion.

"Wait on the Lord: be strong, and let thine heart take courage; yea wait thou on the Lord."

Though his awful vision had evaporated, or perhaps metabolized, and the Good Book was restored to its former bleached purity in his hands and for a quasi-miraculous moment his heart actually did feel less burdened, it wasn't easy for him to get through the remainder of the afternoon's pleasantry and when at last he had managed grateful goodbyes to the distinguished guests, whose web of encouraging platitudes and unsolicited advice as they departed was so obviously pitying it would have choked the gaiety from a walrus, he told Laura with a wan smile he was going to the Oval Office to think. He wasn't particularly hungry he said and, if anything, the valet could bring him a light supper at game time and she gave him a bolstering clasp on the shoulders and let him shuffle off toward the West Wing.

"I'll be watching it in bed," she said to his departing form, "If you .. "

But she didn't finish the sentence and walked briskly through the doors to the Truman Balcony lighting up a Newport 100 as she went.

George slouched forlornly down the stairs and along the carpeted hallways amid the Sunday silence of his house wanting nothing more than to run out to some local bar and drown his sorrows with some carefree good old boys but he could not. Why, oh why, had that motherfucker appeared to him as a Shawnee chief and what had kissing his wound been all about? He had no idea. He did know that ever since he was a boy he had always found it difficult to keep a perfect poker face when telling lies and these recent mental aberrations, if that was indeed what was happening, sure as hell weren't going to make it any easier.

He passed through the Oval Office to the Dining Room and sat quite still in front of the portrait of John Quincy Adams daring it to do what it had done but it did not and when his supper came the room was dark. The valet, however, was a sensitive man and given to a certain strange shyness himself and quietly switched on two shaded side-lamps, laid out the contents of his tray neatly on the mahogany table beside the slumped president's reclining arm, turned on the television set and found the Fox channel and went out again without uttering a syllable.

The one-time pitcher for the Yale Bulldogs hadn't moved nor was he moved by Ray Charles' soulful rendition of 'America the Beautiful' and when the game was over he didn't even care the Diamondbacks had won.

§

At very nearly the same second that the Shawnee sagamore made his spectral and unwelcome appearance in the Yellow Oval Room and a fattish man in a cream-colored cardigan, dreaming of younger days and paddling the unpredictable waters of the Snake River from Deadman's Bar to Moose, had his snatched moment of relaxation interrupted, Michael was standing on a sandy bluff above Long Island Sound, looking at the waves gently lapping a pristine stretch of private beachfront with a mild Atlantic zephyr caressing his salt-and-pepper hair, dialing Lamy's spare cell phone.

They spent the rest of the drive to Mattituck in idle chatter that deepened their knowledge of each other and the subjects of their mutual concern but it was mostly rehash and no really new idea had been introduced. Michael was well aware he could be falling into an elaborate trap just as he had done in Juarez. There was no real reason to trust the genial gnome at the wheel but then again there was no evidence to suspect him of any malicious intent either.

He had been utterly bowled over by their arrival at Lamy's estate. Seventy secluded west-facing acres that overlooked nothing but rolling meadows and the sea. Fully half were devoted to matters equestrian but the main house, which Lamy told him was built in the style of Stanford White and enclosed eight bedrooms, nine bathrooms and a ballroom within twelve thousand square feet of living space, was separate and surrounded by an extensive agricultural preserve of its own.

During a jaw-dropping tour of the house and grounds, Lamy couldn't resist digressing about White's murder at the hands of a jealous husband named Harry Kendall Thaw, spoiled heir to a Pittsburgh mine and railroad fortune with a long history of mental instability, who was rumored to have thrashed his wayward bride on their honeymoon with a dog whip.

There was no income tax and little to put a brake on the rampant greed of the Morgans, Rockefellers and Carnegies in the Gilded Age, very like the Wild West of unregulated hedge fund management today he went on to observe wryly. White had designed the second Madison Square Garden, the New York Herald Building, the Washington Square Arch and First Bowery Savings Bank as well as luxurious summer homes for the Astors and Vanderbilts and the astonishing 'Rosecliff' in Newport, Rhode Island, for a silver heiress from Nevada, modeled after the Grand Trianon of Versailles, and dwelt in maharajan splendor on the Garden's top floor where the infamous red velvet swing dangled seductively from a golden ceiling. It was at an after-theater supper club on the roof that the enraged Thaw drilled three bullets into the magnificently mustachioed architect and he died at the age of fifty-two on June 25th, 1906.

Lamy's encyclopedic exposition of the event took the entire three quarters of an hour of their walk and Michael burst into quite genuine applause at such bravura when he was done.

Michael asked if he might stroll down to the shore and Lamy pointed out the best path and gave him the cell phone for the necessary call to his sister. It was half past nine in the evening in Chalk Farm and it took five rings for Helen to answer.

"Were you in the tub?" he asked with a slightly impatient tone.

"No, I just got in the door. Where are you?"

"Still in New York, well, out on Long Island actually but I won't bore you with a complicated story. Look, for a lot of different reasons, and it doesn't matter now, a day or two ago I took the opportunity to give David a ring and . . "

"Why in hell would you do that?"

The irritation in her voice was expected.

"At a loose end I suppose. I don't know, I was interested after all these years and it seemed a reasonable enough thing to do. Look, it doesn't matter. What matters is, well, you see, he's dead."

There was a brief silence.

"How long for?"

"No, no, you don't understand. I saw him. We talked. I saw quite a lot of him as it turned out. But now he's dead. Just last night. As far as I know he and his lover committed suicide."

A longer silence.

"Oh."

"Yes. I'm fairly sure that's what it was. I'll know more when the police have completed the autopsy tomorrow."

"The police are involved then."

"Well, naturally. A friend found them lying on the bed together and called. I arrived just as the ambulances were taking them away."

An even longer silence.

"Heavens. It's a bit of a shock."

"I know. I'm sorry."

Michael could see two freighters passing each other on the distant horizon.

"What was his lover like?"

"A delightful fellow. From Cuba. He was very ill."

"With what?"

"AIDS."

"Ah."

"Poor chap was on his last legs, I'm afraid. And, oh, yes, I almost forgot. I don't know if you ever met her but David's sister Ruth was in the second tower when the plane hit. She was killed instantly, he said."

"Jesus. Shit. Of course I knew her. God almighty. Is there anything else?"

"Not about that. When I saw David yesterday he was still very upset about it. Understandably. I think that's why they did it. The suicide.

Because of Fernando's illness and then, you know, the death. That's what I'm assuming."

"Is there some other possibility?"

She had him cornered and he took a deep breath and proceeded to explain as much of what had taken place over the last week as he felt was necessary.

"Good god, Michael," she said with a mirthless chuckle as he finished, "You always manage it, don't you?"

"What?"

"Getting yourself in a hopeless jam jar."

"Ah well now, if you could see where I'm standing, you'd sing a different tune. Look, sweet thing, I'll call you tomorrow evening. I'll know better how the land lies. What the police know and the funeral, if there's going to be one, and all that."

"Ah yes, the funeral. Why, do you think I ought to come or something?"

"No, no. It's getting on for twenty years, for heaven's sake."

"Well, I'll think about it. Call me tomorrow same time. And please be careful whatever you're doing! Jesus, aren't you a trifle old."

"Not at all, not at all, you rude little sod. How's Tigger-cat, moping?"

"Pure fantasy, sweetheart. She loves it when you're gone."

"Bah, you deserve each other. Pair of nasty bitches."

She chuckled again and Michael crooned, "Bye," in a singsong voice and shut the phone. He was amazed at the rapidity with which the two freighters had moved beyond each other. He was also surprised, now he came to think of it, that he could discern no opposite shoreline. He had only the vaguest sense of his bearings at the best of times but the drooping sun told him he was facing west or thereabouts and ought therefore to be looking at the American mainland, the state of Connecticut or something like it, and yet nothing could be seen but open sea. Clearly, he mused, Long Island was aptly named.

He loved the ocean, having grown up beside it on the south coast of England, and decided his host wouldn't mind him being absent a bit longer. He clambered down the sandy cliff to the water's edge and rolled up his trousers, took off his shoes and socks, left them on the shingle above where the waves could reach and, just as though he had been a child again on the beach at Worthing, went for a glorious refreshing paddle.

He made his way back to the mansion beside a field of dry corn stubble and another of winter wheat, beneath the neatly trimmed branches of an apple orchard and through a gate in a towering lilac hedge which led into a manicured rose garden and then out onto the azure Italian tiles by the swimming pool. What magnificence! Years ago, almost too long to remember, he and Helen and Marta had dreamed of scraping together all possible resources for the down payment on a property that was faintly similar and far, far less opulent in the rolling coastal hills of his native Sussex but, alas, fate had not pedaled in tandem with their fantasy.

He walked across the flagstone patio and through the sliding French doors by which he had left, traversed the vast living room with its balustered balconies leading from the floors above, passed under an arch and had to open two more sets of double doors at either end of a long hallway before turning right into a private study and finding his host where he said he would be watching the news.

As soon as he entered Lamy switched off the television with the remote and motioned him to sit wherever he liked. There was a lovely blaze in the fireplace and Michael rubbed his hands in the warmth of it, then chose an armchair nearby that faced his mysterious host.

"Enjoy yourself?" Lamy asked pleasantly.

"Very much."

"Was she in?"

"Yes."

"Good. Care for a drink? Anything goes."

"What about one of those . . ?"

"Manhattans?"

"Yes. I thought they were delicious. Danny told me they use Maker's Mark."

Michael congratulated himself on having recalled the name correctly. All was not lost with the old brainpan.

"It's not bad as bourbons go. I prefer a Kentucky Straight Rye."

"I'm sure I wouldn't know the difference. The only one I'd ever heard of until yesterday was Jack Daniel's."

"Tennessee whiskey. Filtered through sugar-maple charcoal. God-awful stuff. Do you know what a Sazerac is?"

"No."

"The first cocktail ever made. And the name of the company in New Orleans. I stock an eighteen-year-old Sazerac rye. Makes a fine Manhattan. But maybe you'd like to try something different."

Michael was more than ready for alcohol of any description.

"Perhaps. What's in it?"

"The original was cognac and bitters. Before the Civil War. The cognac came from an outfit in Limoges where Sazerac is a fairly common name. The bitters was the secret recipe of a Creole apothecary from Haiti called Antoine Amédée Peychaud who settled in the delta around 1795 .. "

"I'm sure I'd love one," Michael interrupted.

He had to overcome his innate politeness but another lengthy historical rumination was clearly in commencement.

Lamy looked over at him with a Cheshire cat smile.

"Forgive my loquacity," he said and pushed one of the buttons of a console on the table by his elbow, "Only just got started. It's an interesting story."

"I'd like to hear it. Sorry. The walk made me thirsty."

An aged but very light-skinned African-American man with straightened hair as orange as a tabby cat's suddenly materialized from nowhere in the open door and rapped quietly on the frame. His function was obvious though he was dressed in a soft open floral shirt and pale slacks.

"Two Sazeracs, Charlie. Large."

The old man gave a tiny expressionless nod and vanished again.

"Don't know much about Limoges," Lamy said, picking up where he left off, "A Roman settlement in Gaulish times, they make oak casks today and fine porcelain. In the 1870's wine production through all of France was cut by two-thirds due to the insatiable appetite of a tiny root-chawing aphid and cognac became too expensive so they changed to the local whiskey and added a splash of absinthe but since you can't get the real thing now they use Pernod or Herbsaint or whatever. Charlie makes a fantastic homemade anis of his own. A dash of old Amédée's gentian bitters mixed with a sugar cube and a double shot of Kentucky over crushed ice poured into a fresh glass rinsed with a whisper of Charlie's liqueur, toss in lemon peel and you've got the quintessential flavor of Cajun decadence. You'll understand in a minute. Ain't for nothing they call it the Big Easy."

Charlie reappeared and came into the room carefully holding a tray with two large simple upright tumblers perspiring from the chill of the deep amber concoction within and two small crystal bowls brimful with what Michael soon discovered were shelled pistachio nuts dusted in jalapeño pepper.

He set one of each down on the dark polished wood of the tables beside them and slid coasters expertly underneath. He stayed standing with his back to the fire to watch Michael's reaction at the first sip.

"Mmmm," Michael murmured gratefully as an aroma of spice islands and citrus groves coupled with the bittersweet bite of the liquor assailed his palate. The aftertaste was smooth despite the strength and the hint of licorice not in the least unpleasant.

He looked up at Charlie and added, "Wow. Unique. Splendid. I like it."

The old man didn't smile but Michael caught a tiny gleam of satisfaction.

"Enjoy," he said in a gentle fluting voice and made for the door.

"We'll eat before the game, Charlie," Lamy said to his departing back.

"I told her. Camilla got everything set to go."

"Bring us another in ten minutes."

"Okey-dokey."

Michael had never heard an accent quite like it. Cajun, or Creole perhaps. His hair color was truly extraordinary and without a fleck of gray. It was surely a safe assumption that he dyed it. Michael tried to guess his age as he disappeared without a backward glance into the hallway.

"He's eighty-seven," Lamy said.

Michael was startled. Once again he had read his mind.

"Everyone always asks. Would you have preferred a Manhattan?"

"Yes, probably, but this is very good."

"It'll grow on you."

"Yes, I'm sure it will. Charlie has negroid features but his skin . . "

"Charlie and Camilla are Peruvian mestizos. They've been with my late wife's family since she was a child. Carlos Felipe Arturo Jorge Monte y Liston de Madera. One of his great-grandfathers was a *condottiere* from Seville, another came on a slave ship from Guinea. Our Dominican friar who didn't like Vespucci, Bartolomeo de Las Casas, was an early champion of slavery in Spanish America and then one of the first to denounce it as he saw the horrors mount. He was also born in Seville."

"You can't stop, can you," Michael cut in with an appreciatively teasing tone, "Any more connections and I might join the priesthood myself."

Lamy smiled and took a sip of his cocktail and then stood up.

"OK," he said, "Show time. If you'll go on humoring me I'll give you the intro."

He began pacing slowly back and forth as he spoke.

"I have something I want to share with you. I'm not sure why. Maybe because there are so few others who would believe it's not a fake. It's hard for me. A tape has come into my possession from a secret source. A person I trust completely which is why I know it's real. It confirms what I said earlier about the Pentagon and the crash site in Shanksville. Part of it's horrifying, part comic. It was foolish that it was made at all but I understand why and why the makers thought it was safe. The camouflage of monsters has always been their own monstrosity. A place where ordinary mortals dare not go. That criminals are drawn back to the scene of their crimes is true. Like all clichés. Sadism delights in revisiting its own ghastliness. That's what this tape is and, of course, a quick way to gain respect from other infantile bastards of the same kind.

"It won't matter a damn if my friend puts it on the Internet. The evidence for a conspiracy is already boiling over from countless websites but the average American can't bring themselves to look. And won't. The whole personality of the country has been corrupted by the distorting mirror of its own success. The result is phony sentiment concealing unjustifiable arrogance and unacknowledgable guilt. The most relentlessly self-congratulatory nation on the planet and therefore the most blind."

"I said much the same thing to David and Fernando two nights ago."

Lamy retrieved his Sazerac and took a thoughtful swallow.

"Sorry to labor the point. The curse of all loquacious assholes. How much do you know about those two flights?"

"Not a lot."

"No, they're kind of vague for most people because the footage of the towers was so dramatic. Anyway, stop me if I'm boring you. American Airlines 77 went off the radar over the southern tip of Ohio and the FAA just drew a dotted line on the map leading it to the Pentagon. United flight 93 got about as far as Cleveland before turning round and crashing in Pennsylvania. I know you're not much on geography but bear with me. Wright-Patterson is the name of a huge Air Force base in Fairborn, a suburb of Dayton, Ohio, about the same distance from where flight 77 was lost to radar and where they claim 93 turned. It honors the Wright brothers who had their workshop in Dayton and the Patterson brothers who bought the patent for the first mechanical cash register. Invented by another saloon owner of French extraction called James Ritty to keep, as the saying goes, his employee's fingers out of the till. His machine had no cash drawer and he called it, 'Ritty's Incorruptible Cashier'."

Michael chuckled.

"I knew you'd like it. Anyway, around 1884 the Pattersons bought him out and founded the National Cash Register Company. Helped to crack the Enigma code during the war. That connection ought to amuse you. Made polonium triggers for the A-bombs we dropped on Japan. Gone worldwide now with retail data systems and bar-code scanners and ATMs. Gobbled up by AT&T in '91 and spun off again six years later. Good friend of mine's the CEO, a Swede, Lars Nyberg. Yeah, yeah, I know, I'm unstoppable. Point is Wright-Patterson is very high tech. Home to a major systems center and research lab and a big USAF hospital. Seven thousand residents and a work force twice that. OK, the first thing . . "

"Hang on," Michael said, "I've got a piece of trivia about Dayton for you."

"Not the Dayton Accords, they were held at Wright-Patterson."

"No. The Speedwell Motor Car Company. In 1911 they . . "

"Invented the first sedan, yeah, their factory was next door to the Wrights."

This time Michael laughed out loud.

"You are quite, quite obnoxious but wonderfully entertaining."

"Well, wait 'til you get a load of this," Lamy went on with a cod Marx Brothers wiggle of his eyebrows, "OK, the first thing on the tape is both planes coming in to land at the base. One right after the other which is very strange considering the time they both took off. The FAA ordered every flight in the country to land at the nearest available location starting at 9:26 and you'll see the clock on the tape shows 9:47 thru 9:49 as the planes touch down. The official version tells you flight 77 crashed into the Pentagon at 9:37 and 93 into the farmer's field near Shanksville at 10:03."

Charlie appeared with two fresh cocktails as instructed and set them on the tables as before. He held out the tray for Lamy's empty glass and took the other from Michael's hand.

"Shut the door, Charlie, will you," Lamy said as he was leaving.

Before he went on Lamy walked to the fire, shifted the placement to allow better combustion and laid on another log.

"I like birch wood," he said, "Burns clean and quiet."

"Yes, it's very pleasant indeed."

"Last thing. I'm sure you know every plane has its own tail number."

"Yes, I think so, like a license plate."

"Well, you'll notice these two don't. How they made them disappear I don't know. The base is open to a residential area on the south side. The back end where the planes wind up is hidden by trees along the Mud River but some local yokel with a camera could have been looking as they came in so they needed to cover their ass."

Lamy sat down again and pressed a button on his console.

"Come over here. You'll see better."

The L-shaped couch was facing the television and Michael went to sit on the opposite end to his host. He had been nibbling on the pistachios and found them delicate and delicious and took his bowl with him. The drink was also beginning to have a most interesting effect. Very mellow but slightly hallucinatory.

Lamy pressed another button to dim the room lights, not quite to darkness but to allow better viewing, and the tape began.

"It may amuse you to know while you watch that the USAF has for many, many years carried the cryptic phrase, 'Global Power for America,' embossed on its official stationery. Bold statement of fact or blatant agenda or both, it lacks a certain subtlety, I'm sure you agree. That fatal absence of humility we spoke of earlier."

As Lamy had foretold the first two minutes showed the planes landing with trees behind them in the distance. They were quite small in the frame to begin with but the camera followed their progress until they came close and turned away and then picked them up from another angle as they taxied past a line of a dozen parked Stratofortress bombers.

"One of those could have dropped the first hydrogen bomb on Bikini Atoll," Lamy said, "B-52s, 'the long rifles of the Air Age.' Crews call them BUFFs. Big Ugly Fat Fuckers."

The planes turned again and inched their way down a narrow dead end with their wing-tips nearly grazing the hangars on either side and came to a stop. They were both 757s, one United and one American. Michael didn't find it all that strange, or even notice at first, but it gathered an eerie power because the entire sequence was without sound and had the style of an old home movie.

Thirty or so uniformed personnel were waiting on the sand-colored tarmac by each plane, not in any kind of formation, looking quite relaxed in their short-sleeved shirts, and exit stairways were rolled out and as the doors opened and the passengers disembarked they met them and escorted them into the hangar. Though they were evidently being asked not to use their cell phones, and their unheard conversations were animated with excitement and concern, the atmosphere was more one of relief than danger. There were several men who appeared to be of Arabic descent but they seemed calm and were treated exactly like the others. There were clearly no hijackers among them. The pilots, co-pilots and cabin crews were the last to deplane and were met and escorted in the same way.

Inside the hangar a couple of hundred folding chairs had been set up and once all the passengers were seated they were addressed by an officer. What they were being told was hard to tell exactly but it appeared to be something about a medical security check.

"My guess is possible anthrax spores on the plane," Lamy said.

After the brief address all the passengers began talking at once and one by one they were taken away through a door. No one argued or made any kind of protest.

The tape then suddenly cut to a darkened room and showed four horrifying examples of what happened to them. The first was a frail elderly white woman in a light blue summer suit, the second a chubby black boy who Michael estimated to be ten or close to that, then a fat man who had sweat through the armpits of his open white shirt and was carrying his sport jacket and the last happened to be a pretty young stewardess in her United Airlines uniform.

The room was rather like one where you might have your eyes tested with similar-looking equipment and a figure who appeared to be an examining doctor spoke a few words to each of them as they came in and then arranged them on a cushioned seat with their foreheads touching what looked like a lens of some sort. There were two assistants standing by. The doctor told the examinees to be still and they obeyed and he touched a button and all instantly slumped dead. The assistants caught them by the arms and dragged them out some double swinging doors and two others came in and threw their hand luggage after them and then took up the same positions. At no time did the camera reveal the faces of the murderers.

However the lens, or whatever it was, snuffed out their lives it left no mark on their foreheads that Michael could see but a thick ooze reddened the sockets of their ears and colored the vitreous humor of their eyes.

"Molecular dissociation beam. Instant brain jelly," Lamy conjectured.

The deaths were cut together in quick succession and gutwrenching in the extreme but the next sequence of images was from some abattoir in hell.

In contrast to the dark clinical precision of the execution room the chamber to which the attendants dragged the hapless victims was brightly lit and had white walls. The cold brutality was beyond sickening and reminded Michael of the tapes Amado Portillo's vampire sister Cecilia had shown him in Juarez and of his friend Fernando's photographs. In some ways it was even worse.

The four bodies were laid one after another on a long stainless steel table and stripped of every vestige of their clothing, then bound by the feet and lifted onto a hooked conveyor line that transported them limp and swaying upside down like so many animal carcasses through to another room where their dangling heads were sliced off by the whirring blade of a machine that quickly adjusted itself to the varying heights of their necks and, in the same instant, the twitching decapitated corpses were grasped tightly between the curving fingers of a press and one long squeeze was all it took to rid them of the major quantity of their blood.

"Automation," Lamy observed quietly, "Henry Ford's wet dream."

The blood gushed from their necks in a pulsing unbroken stream and passed through a mesh that sieved any solid particles of vein or muscle or bone that might have been forced loose before being channeled away in a trough that led one knew not where.

Finally the exsiccate shells of what three short minutes before had been living beings were unhooked by gloved hands and tossed onto a conveyor belt that trundled them upwards and dumped them into the compacting jaws of a waiting garbage truck along with their heads, crumpled clothes and belongings.

"Thus endeth part one," Lamy said and stopped the tape, "Need a breather?"

It took Michael a moment to control his emotion and respond.

"Um, ah, no, not really. I'm supposing part two will answer my big question. Why they were killed in that particular way."

"It'll give you a small part of the answer. I'll let it run and explain what I can over dinner."

Lamy pressed the button beside him and the tape started again.

The next sequence ran at high speed, even faster and jerkier than a Keystone Kops silent movie. It began at dusk on what looked to Michael like a putting green on a golf course. Two plain white vans were being unloaded by four young men in overalls. Again no faces could be seen.

From the first van came something midway between a huge bath and a hot tub spa. Flat bottomed and circular and obviously made of heavy metal because it took all four to heft it onto a waiting dolly and wheel it up a slight hill to reach the middle of the green. They left it there and raced back to fetch a stand and a pair of gleaming steel cylinders that eventually provided two adjustable rows of flame. The men set the stand in place with the cylinders underneath the center. The legs of the stand were of sufficient height and breadth for them to place what looked like logs around the cylinders so they disappeared.

"You're not making it go this fast, are you?" Michael asked.

"No, it's the intent."

When everything was to their satisfaction the four men hoisted the tub onto the stand, Michael was thinking of it as a massive cauldron, and took some time to ensure it was perfectly balanced. Then from the other van they brought two curved metal step units in sections that they assembled around opposite sides of the tub. When they were done there were seven steps up with the top step broader and level to the lip to allow bathers, if such there were going to be, ease of access.

Then two of the men hopped in the cargo compartment of the second van and a third backed it up the hill against the tub with the loading doors open to a position between the step units and the men inside began carefully maneuvering six forty-gallon blue plastic drums from the front of the van's cargo space to the rear.

As soon as Michael saw the first barrel he knew what was about to happen and said, "In goes the blood."

The driver and the fourth man came around to help them and stood in the narrow space between the van and the tub and they emptied the drums into it.

"How long after was this?" Michael asked, "It poured like water. Did they use some form of, um, you know, something to stop it clotting?"

"Anti-coagulant. Yeah, sodium citrate, I imagine."

One of the men lit the gas lines under the tub and the vans drove away and the sequence ended. It had taken no more than ninety seconds.

There followed a rapid jumble of indecipherable symbols and curlicues, like the ones Michael remembered flashing across the screen in his local cinema years ago when the film broke or the projectionist changed reels too slowly, that had obviously been added to complete the desired effect and then virtual darkness.

The last section began with headlights approaching down what was evidently a bumpy path in the distance and the images running at normal speed. It was murky but before long Michael counted four black limousines coming slowly toward the camera's vantage point which was just above and beyond the tub. As the cars came to a stop beside a fifth that was already there the headlights reflection cast a somber glow on the velvety liquid filling the bottom of the frame. Heat from the canisters was gently circulating the blood and a soft mist was rising from it.

This time there was sound and as the headlights were switched off car doors could be heard slamming and drunken laughter and muffled conversation.

"Who the fuck has the brands?"

"They do. Up there."

"Does that make sense? I can't fucking well see anything."

"Get your asses down here! We're gonna kill ourselves it's so fucking dark!"

The camera started down the hill and fifteen or more people were revealed in the light of burning torches stumbling about by the limos in medieval ankle-length monkish robes with hoods. It was impossible to glimpse a face long enough to make any kind of sure identification as most were given a brand by someone off to the left of the camera which was then lit from another by someone standing on the right.

One of the hooded figures suddenly noticed the camera.

"Shit, what the fuck, Dick, is Scooter filming this?"

"Of course."

Was it the vice-president's voice? Michael couldn't be sure.

"Are you out of your mind?"

"What's the problem? There's no problem."

"Are you crazy . . ?"

A deep guttural German accent cut the protestation off.

"Shut up, Rummy. You always piss your pants for nothing. Let's go."

The gaggle of ungainly figures made their way awkwardly up the slope, some stumbling and tripping on the hem of their robes, and a few grumbling words and jocular responses were muttered but they were now being filmed from behind and Michael couldn't decipher what was said.

As they reached the area where the cauldron stood simmering with the flame from the hidden gas canisters making the phony logs around them appear to burn, four went to the bottom of the steps, two on each side, while the rest formed a wide circle around them and held their flaming torches high.

There was a moment of silence and stillness but, just as one of the figures put a foot on the first step and began to ascend, it was broken by a stifled giggle.

"Wolfie, get a grip," the deep German voice admonished.

"*Heil* Hitler," the giggler said in mock acquiescence.

There were more giggles from several others and the figure on the first step waited until silence was restored then continued to the top of the stairs.

"*Mein Führer*," a second ironic jester whispered fervently.

"Ach, put a fucking sock in it, Richard," the figure growled.

The interchange caused an extended sequence of giggles and guffaws until what was certainly the vice-president's voice cut in with mock parental gruffness, "It'll be dawn if you all don't can it. Get it over with, Henry, for Jesus' sake."

The figure at the top of the steps raised both its arms to the brilliant starlit sky, causing a momentary loss of balance, and nearly toppled backwards but after a hushed second or two of flailing it miraculously recovered its equilibrium.

"All hail the sperm of fantasy!" a female voice exclaimed.

"All hail the sperm of fantasy!" the group followed in unison and the figure's arms dropped to its side and let loose the robe which slithered down behind it to the bottom of the steps and there in all his hairy sagging bloat stood a stark naked Henry Kissinger.

"Immortal Death, Our Master!" came the resounding chorus.

"No fucking kidding," Kissinger said.

The hooded figure at the bottom of the steps came part way up to lend him a hand and the 56th Secretary of State and winner of the Nobel Peace Prize, arch-meddler in other nation's affairs and wanted accomplice to Operation Condor, took off his glasses, entrusting them to the assistant's care, then, after briefly testing the liquid's temperature with ill-shapen toes, made a slow, almost regal descent into the warm blood.

Once he was settled in to the neck a figure from the bottom of the steps on the other side ascended and stood at the top and in the same way struggled to maintain its footing and a similar sequence unfolded.

"All hail the egg of falsehood!" shouted an as yet unheard male voice.

"All hail the egg of falsehood!" the celebrants repeated.

This time when the homespun robe was doffed the pudgy smooth whiteness of the vice-president shimmered like a ghostly mirage in the torchlight.

"Eternal Strife, Our Destiny!" came the paean of praise.

"Blow me," Cheney said quietly and the worshipers whistled and hooted and clapped in a mockery of polite applause and with an offhand wave of dismissal, and the aid of his hooded compatriot who took his spectacles also, he stepped gingerly down to join his hirsute companion in the gently bubbling gore.

At this, the circle of votaries turned their backs and fumbled the burning faggots into cradles on stakes that had been set in the ground behind to hold them, then turned again and pulled enormous plastic Super-Soaker squirt guns from deep pockets in their robes, letting them fall to the ground at the same time, and charged naked toward the bathers, whooping like Hollywood Indians around a wagon train. They had obviously gone barefoot since alighting from the limos.

Michael could glimpse other faces now if only fleetingly. He didn't recognize most but in the remaining minutes of their infantile game he was certain he saw the current Secretary and Deputy Secretary of Defense as well as the Chairman of the Defense Policy Committee, the Deputy Secretary of State and the National Security Advisor though he knew them more by their faces than their names.

"Do you know who they all are?" he asked.

"Unfortunately," Lamy replied, "The nexus of Bush's foreign policy. They call themselves the Vulcans. Plus a few idiots from the PNAC."

As they approached the tub and attempted to fill their guns the two bathers rose to their feet with an even bigger pair and mercilessly soaked them from head to toe with blood. But eventually the attackers succeeded and there followed an all-out battle with everyone up and down the stairs and in and out of the tub and squirting and splashing and slithering over the skin of everyone else and at last too many were in at once and the tub began to slip slowly sideways off the stand and seven occupants went with it and it tipped and spilled the entire contents over the green grass accompanied by hysterical shrieks of mirth and terror. By some lucky chance the tub rolled free without crushing anyone and accelerated down the hill into the darkness barely missing the limos and as the fallen lay sprawling on the ground the others came and emptied the last of the gore from their guns on them and in the midst of their doing so the tape abruptly ended.

Charlie knocked on the door and opened it a crack.

"Camilla say come on to supper now if you ready."

"Right away, Charlie."

Lamy got up and went to the television and removed the tape.

He looked at Michael as if to gauge his reaction, then put the tape in a desk drawer and locked it.

They didn't speak as Lamy led the way to the dining room.

Stanza Nine

§

Contrary to Michael's expectations Camilla was large and effusive and quick, quite the opposite of her shuffling husband's loose-limbed boniness. Her frizzed hair was iron gray and stuck out in all directions from a bandanna of brilliant red with a vibrant blue zigzag running through it. There was nothing African about her face and the skin was as smooth as a baby's despite her age. The high aristocratic cheekbones and the intensity of her manner were decidedly Spanish.

The dining room was clearly her domain. It was large like everything else in the mansion but not coldly elegant as many such are. The grand table wasn't highly polished and the upholstery of the chairs didn't match. The shelves and sideboards were cluttered and needed dusting but everything seemed delightfully comfortable and wonderful smells from the kitchen made it even more inviting.

Introductions were made and Charlie served wine as Camilla bustled out and came in again immediately with an appetizer which Michael was happy to see was primarily potatoes. The Sazeracs had put his sometimes tricky stomach on edge, or perhaps it was the horror of the tapes and the unaccustomed stress of the last forty-eight hours. Lamy called the dish *'Papa a la Huancaína'*. A favorite with Camilla, he said, because she was born in Huancayo which meant nothing to Michael but Lamy didn't explain further.

"Camilla is a princess," Lamy teased as she put the plates down in front of them, "On both ends as she likes to say. Entirely apocryphal but a charming story. A love match between a conquistador from the minor nobility in Córdoba and the granddaughter of Atahualpa, the Inca emperor who Francisco Pizarro put to death by garrote in the summer of

113

1533."

"Yeah, yeah, Wicho," she said, "You know too much for your good."

"And speak too much," Lamy agreed.

"Siempre, siempre, cierto. Es muy triste."

She winked at Michael from behind him and put her big arms around Lamy's neck and kissed the top of his head as though he were her son.

"You are welcome in this house, Miguel. Ignore him if you can. He is bad for the digestion."

Charlie had set the bottle of wine on the table in front of Lamy and gone off to the kitchen and she followed him and left them alone.

"She's eighty-one," Lamy said, "A great survivor."

"Amazing. You're a fortunate man."

"I'm lucky to have them as my friends. Let's eat a little before we talk."

§

As Michael was enjoying the sliced potatoes and the gentle tang of the cheese sauce, two of New York's finest were knocking on the door of Room 137 in the Hotel Belleclaire.

Michael had a bizarre liking for the number 137. It began with the number of the double-decker bus he took home to the flat in Battersea he shared with a wild young Canadian when they were students at the Rose Bruford Academy of Dramatic Art and ever since he always booked rooms with that number if it was at all possible. It had become an obsession and invaded his life in many odd ways. They were the last three digits of his telephone in Chalk Farm and had appeared without request on several credit cards and in a host of other places and some years ago he had discovered satisfying confirmation of its importance during a lecture by a renowned physics professor at Sussex University who had examined the number's profound correlation with Einstein's cosmological constant.

The detectives were following up a lead from a business card they found in David and Fernando's apartment. 'Enigma' was embossed on it in red Gothic script with the name Michael Davenport beneath and the address and telephone of the magazine's office in Tottenham Court Road and on the back Michael had scribbled 'Belleclaire West 77th'.

Michael gave it to David in the wee hours of the morning after the three of them had enjoyed the half dozen bottles of Italian red wine and he had completely forgotten about it.

The two officers had been instructed to question him because the results of the autopsy on the gay couple brought in from Spring Street that afternoon had not confirmed the double suicide theory but were now pointing toward the possibility of double murder.

§

The second dish Camilla served was a spicy ceviche made from white sea bass and at the first taste Michael was quite unsure he could do it justice. The chilis and lime were an overpowering combination and there was a strange tasting green vegetable with it that Lamy told him was a local seaweed which didn't do much for its appeal but, after he discovered the sauce it swam in was called *'leche de tigre'* and was considered both a hangover cure and a potent aphrodisiac, with a few draughts of Charlie's excellent wine he finally managed to wash it down.

"So let's start with where they were and then tell me who they were."

"My guess is the Great Serpent Mound in southern Ohio. Maybe an hour or hour and a half drive from Dayton and Wright-Patt. Anthropologists would call it an effigy mound. An earthwork in the form of a snake that may have been started by the local Indian tribe as long as three thousand years ago. I think our goons were standing in the middle of the head. Like Stonehenge it has countless interpretations. Was the snake their sacred totem, was it for burials, was it calendrical, does it reflect the star pattern in the constellation Draco or the trail of a comet or the alignment of the moon. Many geologists believe it's the site of a Permian asteroid impact, others an ancient volcano. Why those fools chose it I have no idea except this is the Year of the Snake in the Chinese calendar."

"And they went all the way there just for that?"

"It seems so."

"Why?"

"A victory party? These guys love triumphalism."

"And Rice was the only woman."

"Looked like it to me. Not sure she had the biggest mams though. Fucks like a mongoose, so they say. Been carrying a torch for Dubya for years. Not alone there. Karl Rove, the advisor Bush likes calling 'turdblossom', same deal. Bush has a lot of charm if you fall for it. The common touch. Never learned much at Yale but knew everyone by name in the frat house and Skull and Bones. That's why the neo-cons groomed him so carefully to follow his god-awful father."

"When did the bloodbath . . sorry . . when did the ceremony happen?"

"9/12, 9/13, not later."

"Do you think one of them gave explicit instructions about the horrific way the passengers were killed?"

"I doubt it. Sadists are everywhere. Some little fucker probably jumped at the chance. Bet they enjoyed it when they saw it though. Gave him instant promotion."

Michael smiled at Lamy's cynicism and thought, 'How else can one deal with such ghastliness?'

"I was gobsmacked when they all shouted at Kissinger, 'Immortal Death, Our Master.' *Bessmertnaja smert' nash vladelec!* The Russian toast in El Paso."

"Weird but not surprising. For vampires who don't know they're vampires."

"What do you mean 'don't know'?"

"I'm saying none of them think they're in any way malicious. Not even as they play games in other people's blood or give their blessing to mass murder. They look at it as natural and necessary curative procedure."

"Like the drafters of the Wannsee Protocol. Incredible."

"I wish it were."

"You don't mean that one half absolutely doesn't know what the other half is doing. Totally schizophrenic like O. J. Simpson."

"You think he was a split personality? I think he knew exactly what he did and it terrified him. Like George Bush. People like them still have a vestige of conscience. With Kissinger and Cheney and their kind the halves coexist quite comfortably. They have no guilt at all. David put it very well. The absolute chasm between the game being played and compassion for the victims."

The sad events of earlier in the day came flooding back. After what they had just witnessed a double suicide seemed vanishingly unlikely.

"So these were the actual originators of the plot, the tight-knit little cabal who knew everything."

"Maybe not originators. It could go way, way back. But yeah, some. Kristol and Kissinger and Cheney, for sure."

"What did you call them? It sounded like something from Star Trek."

"The Vulcans were a foreign policy advisory group surrounding

Condoleezza Rice during the last election. Bush rewarded them with key appointments after the Supreme Court stole it for him. Nothing to do with spaceships or futurism. There's a huge ugly statue of Vulcan in Birmingham, Alabama, where she was born. It's a steel town like Pittsburgh so some dumb committee figured the Roman god of fire and metalworking would make a suitable emblem."

"And what is the PNAC exactly?"

"The Project for a New American Century. Bully pulpit of the neo-cons. The brainchild of two Zionists. You saw one of them. Regular columnists in rags like the Times and the Post. One little prick is an associate of the Carnegie Endowment for International Peace which might once have been a vaguely laudable concern but that changed in the '50s with the Dulles brothers and George Frost Kennan. That son of a bitch is still alive by the way. His so-called 'doctrine of containment' has justified the brutality of the last fifty years. These pooh-bahs were always fishing around for a catastrophe big enough to cow the public so they could put their imbecile agenda in place. 'American leadership is good for the world,' blah, blah, blah. Full-spectrum dominance. Globalization and militarization. Way too stupid and venal to discuss. Continuous wars clearing a path for the biggest corporate feeding frenzy the world has ever seen. You know all about it."

"And they made the tape to show it, you said. For a laugh. To who?"

"It goes on and on. You wouldn't believe the number of little boy's clubs on the planet. Thousands in the US alone. But this gem is reserved for the elite. The Bilderbergs, Bohemian Grove, groups like that. And even there it'll only get shown to a select few. My brother goes to these pathetic shindigs sometimes, he's been a sucker for politics since we were kids, but they'd never let someone like him see it."

Camilla arrived with the main course. Glory be, it looked like stew. Charlie brought in a bottle of red wine to accompany it but he didn't bother to change their glasses.

"We call it *sancochado*," Lamy said, "Beef with cassava and sweet potato."

There was a side plate of Lima butter beans in a kind of salsa which Michael also thought looked perfect. English broad beans were his very favorite. As a boy he loved to peel and devour them straight out of his mother's garden, along with raw broccoli and cauliflower. She admonished him that too much would ruin his stomach but he never listened.

"There have always been people who want to play god," Lamy went on when the old couple had gone again, "History is littered with them. This new bunch is no different. And the public swallow their arrogant bullshit just the same."

"I was fascinated they went through with the mumbo-jumbo even though it was quite clear none of them take it seriously."

"No, they don't. In my book it makes them even worse. It's one thing to be an ignorant Macedonian out to conquer the world because what else is there for a young guy to do but these bastards cause agony and anguish and giggle about it. It's what I meant before. They use vampire ritual lingo although none of them really think of themselves as vampires but the truth is that's what they are."

"You mean more than metaphorically?"

"Shit yes."

Michael had to think about that and took a mouthful of stew but let it drop for the moment.

"Fascinating," he said, "And utterly macabre. I thank you for sharing it but, as you pointed out, it's nothing new. I want to know about the sign at the racetrack and the appearance of Cheney's doppelganger under the ruins. It's the inexplicable that interests me, not sophomoric pranks however appalling."

§

There was something else the officers had found in David and Fernando's apartment and news of it was quickly percolating upwards in the direction of the Department of Homeland Security and the FBI and would find its way into one of a hundred memos on the desk of the assistant to the Deputy National Security Advisor in the White House the following morning and one would assume it was certainly not worth bringing to the attention of the esteemed Dr. Rice unless one knew of the rapidly proliferating number of related objects already overflowing the shelves of a locked storeroom in the Eisenhower Building.

§

The general was resting bare feet on a silken pouffe in his paneled study in Arlington and puffing contentedly on a Cuban cigar preparing to watch the game. He had spent much of the day on the phone and by six o'clock successfully called in a favor for an unofficial stakeout at the Belleclaire to begin that evening at nine.

He had to use all his considerable powers to persuade the party involved that his person of interest would be easy to spot and a physical description enough until he could provide an up-to-date photographic image. He promised to get something lifted from the Miss Texas Pageant tape or better still from the miles of surveillance footage from four years ago in London but, no matter what, he wanted immediate feedback on the subject's smallest movement.

He had dallied with yet another Internet search for 'Michael Davenport' and found the same boring articles in Enigma and the ancient reference to a play he had done in Arbroath on the east coast of Scotland in the winter of 1974 called 'The Rattle of a Simple Man' and several slightly more recent about the few episodes of 'Coronation Street' he had appeared in during the autumn of 1977 that did contain one small picture of Michael with long sideburns but he was only twenty-eight and virtually unrecognizable and the mention of his comments at a town hall meeting in Hastings about the construction of a sea water spa hotel, all of which the general had seen many times before and it had quickly strained his limited patience. Yet it was far less frustrating than searching for 'Bartolomeo Vespucci' about whom there was precisely nothing except that he was a nephew of Amerigo and a professor of astronomy at Padua and had written a letter concerning the influence of the fixed stars on free will to Niccolò Machiavelli in June, 1504.

§

"Sorry but I don't have an explanation for the inexplicable," Lamy said, "I only suggested technologies were available that might produce such results. I didn't say I thought they were the cause."

"Tell me about Skull and Bones."

"Not much worth saying. Too much has been made of it. Sure the members help each other out and think of themselves as important. If they want to fantasize that they run the world, so what. Prescott, the Bush patriarch, the senator who had a thing for Hitler along with many of the American moneyed class in the '20s and '30s, was one of the bunch that went west to dig up and steal what they claimed was Geronimo's skull.

Seventy years later some tribal chairman from Arizona tried to get it back which was also pretty silly because it was bullshit in the first place. A typical frat house lark, nothing more. The only thing I've ever found amusing is the name they gave George W. Boy's clubs love having secret names for each other, Baal, Beelzebub, Gog, Magog, and that dire punishments will follow if any member reveals them. Anyway their name for Dubya was 'Temporary'."

Lamy burst out laughing.

"Why?"

"Because when they asked him what he wanted to be called he couldn't think of anything and the name stuck!"

Lamy laughed so hard tears came to his eyes.

"I don't know why I find that so damn funny," he said, wiping them with his napkin, "But something about the name is perfect, don't you think?"

Camilla came to fetch their plates and Michael complimented her for the fourth time on her cuisine which she shrugged off for the fourth time but each time he could see she was pleased and Charlie set a small stemmed crystal glass in front of him and poured a shot of brown liquor into it and stood back to watch as he had done before in the study.

"Charlie also makes his own *pisco*," Lamy told him, "He wants you to try it."

"What is it, a dessert wine?"

"No, neither my wife nor I ever liked dessert so we never have it. Camilla will find you something if you want."

"No, no, thank you, that was wonderful."

"*Pisco* is kind of like brandy. It's grape. In Peru the aficionados say it has to be made from a single variety but Charlie's is a blend. *Acholado*. Half-breed. Try it. It's sweeter than most brandies but deceptive."

Michael took a swallow and looked at the old man and nodded.

"It's very mild tasting. But very good. Thank you, Charlie."

"I know English people like drink," he said with a tiny smile, "Enjoy."

He set the bottle down in front of Michael with a gesture that was too small to be called a flourish and ambled away after his wife.

"They like you," Lamy said.

"I like them. Aren't you having some?"

"No, I don't care for it. It's all yours. Bring it with you. It's game time."

They got up and returned to the study and Lamy switched on the television again from the console and turned to the Fox channel.

"I hate Rupert Murdoch but I love baseball," he said.

The second game of the World Series also took place at Bank One Ballpark in Phoenix before a standing room only crowd and the great Ricky Henderson threw out the ceremonial first pitch. He had returned to the San Diego Padres for the 2001 season and broke three major league records. He surpassed Babe Ruth in walks, Zack Wheat in games played in left field and Ty Cobb in runs scored and on the last game of the season he made his 3000th career hit. Even more remarkable for an aging veteran of forty-two he had stolen twenty-five bases and he received a well-deserved ovation at his appearance.

Lamy told Michael all of this as they watched and continued throughout the game with an onslaught of anecdotal trivia that was breathtaking.

The game, however, was less than thrilling except for the performance of the Diamondbacks' Randy Johnson, who pitched a complete game shutout fanning eleven Yankees and allowing just three hits. The only offensive excitement came in the bottom of the seventh inning when third-baseman Matt Williams hit a three-run homer off the Yankee starter Andy Pettitte and sent him to the showers but by then Michael had consumed a large quantity of Charlie's *pisco* and barely noticed. The final score was Diamondbacks 4, Yankees 0, and at the end of the game Lamy turned to the news.

After lead items that concerned another New Jersey postal worker diagnosed with inhalation anthrax and gunmen killing sixteen people in a Christian church in Behawalpur, Pakistan, and footage of Israeli tanks withdrawing from Bethlehem, there was a brief report about the memorial service at Ground Zero and, though no comment was made by the newscaster, Lamy and Michael saw three completely inexplicable things taking place.

A crowd estimated at eight or nine thousand were gathered to mourn and there was seating for perhaps half of those facing the skeletal remains of the towers and platforms for the speakers and performers. Above and behind them was an enormous television which initially showed a full screen of the Stars and Stripes with 'God Bless America' written across the bottom.

The first bizarre occurrence, made much more so by the fact that no one in the audience appeared to see it, happened toward the end of the national anthem.

The final words are 'Oh, say does that star-spangled banner still wave o'er the land of the free and the home of the brave' and beginning exactly on the word 'free', and continuing for perhaps five seconds during the customary *ritardando* on the last phrase, the image of the flag morphed into a tight close-up of the vice-president's face and hands behind thick jail bars. There was no sound but he was sweating and screaming for help and violently shaking his cage in a futile attempt at escape.

Michael was jolted from his drowsiness and instantly looked at Lamy.

"Yes, I saw it," he said with a smile.

"Christ, it's about time!" Michael exclaimed, "Why in hell doesn't anyone else?"

There was a cut of Andrea Bocelli singing Schubert's 'Ave Maria' and before Michael could say anything more there were a few seconds of Metropolitan Opera soprano Renée Fleming singing 'God Bless America' clearly unaware that Kissinger, Cheney, Rumsfeld and Rice were prancing about behind her in outlandish vampire costumes, swinging and swaying like backup singers at a Tina Turner concert.

"What the fuck is going on?" Michael shouted.

Hard on the heels of that impossibility came a clip from the invocation given by the Archbishop of New York, Edward Egan.

"They were innocent and they were brutally, viciously, unjustly taken from us," he was saying solemnly, "Their lives and futures were snuffed out by villains filled with violence and hate," and Michael's near-hysteria could only mount as he watched the same ghoulish foursome walking up and down behind him like some picket line in Hades holding placards aloft on poles that read, 'Ha! Ha! Ha!', 'Get a Life!', 'The Joke's on You!' and 'Catch Us if You Can!'

The whole segment took less than a minute and at the end of it the newscast went on with a much longer report on the World Series game but Lamy turned the sound to mute on his console.

Michael was out of his chair and gesticulating like a maniac.

"How, how, how is it possible they don't see it?! Are you telling me we're the only ones? Everyone watching on television must have seen that!"

"I'm telling you they do and they don't."

"What the devil does that mean?"

"I've told you. They do but they won't go there. Like O.J. and George

Bush."

"But you said you didn't see the name flashing on the sign at the track."

"I didn't. I was eating."

"Have you ever seen anything else like this?"

"No."

"Well, perhaps now you'll believe me."

"I always believed you."

"You didn't. You suggested I was having hallucinations."

"Maybe we're both having them now. Maybe you've infected me."

"Oh, come on!"

Lamy was flipping through the channels looking for other news reports of the memorial and didn't immediately find any but they waited for the New York stations to begin their local broadcast and twice they caught similar clips, one of the cardinal and one of the anthem, and they both saw the same impossible things happening in the background.

Finally Lamy switched the television off and said it was time for him to retire and though Michael was still bursting with excitement from this virtual proof of the transhuman he had to agree. For the third night running he was far from sober.

Stanza Ten

it's the greatest boy's party on earth
you're not here might as well died at birth
we fritter the days
mounting babies and plays
and compute our collective net worth

§

Michael rose bright and early the next morning and came down after a quick shower to find his host already at breakfast in the dining room reading the morning papers. Daylight allowed him to admire the vista from the huge bay window which looked out beyond the swimming pool to the orchards and rolling fields and a tiny glimpse of Long Island Sound in the far distance.

"I have to go to the city. You can stay here if you want," Lamy said.

"Well, what do you think? I'll have to ring their friend to see if he knows yet about the autopsy or the funeral. I promised my sister I'd phone this evening. I'm sure I'll be fine if I go back to the hotel."

"I don't know about that. The best idea would be to drop you at Kennedy and you don't even go there."

A teapot had been set on the table in front of him and Michael could smell its fresh-brewed warmth and gave it a swirl and said, "Good lord," and poured himself a cup. He was astonished to find a bowl of sugar and a jug of milk also and looked at Lamy with an appreciative smile but his head was behind the newspaper. Michael could see the headline, 'Diamondbacks Take Game Two, 4–0', as he added a teaspoon of sugar and a splash of milk and stirred.

"What, you think I should go straight back to London?" he asked after he had taken a sip, "Without even fetching my things?"

"Might be wise."

"I can't do that. Good lord, no, this has all become too interesting for me to do that. No, no, I'll take my chances at the hotel. I'd have to go anyway to collect my passport."

Lamy looked at him and shrugged.

124

"I figured you might have it. OK. I'll give you my cell number in case."

"If they want to get me being in London won't help."

"No, I guess not. Might make them think twice about it though."

Camilla bustled in with a plateful of eggs and sausages and baked beans and fried tomatoes and another piled with three slices of toast and big mounds of butter and marmalade on the side.

"*Buenos días*, Miguel," she said cheerfully, "Did you dream good dreams?"

"Not particularly, I'm sorry to say," Michael replied, glancing at his host, "You're wonderful to have made this beautiful English breakfast though. It's truly amazing and you're amazing and I can't thank you enough."

"*De nada,*" she said with a twinkle and then asked, "You stay with us longer?"

"I'm afraid not. But I would be more than delighted to come again."

"That will be soon, *espero*," she said, walking briskly back to the kitchen door and gesturing toward the bay window, "Carlos stays out there with his fruit. Don't worry, I say your goodbye," and she was gone.

Lamy took the last sip of whatever he was having and got up.

"Sorry to run out on you but I have some things to do and we have to leave in fifteen minutes. Think you can make it?"

"Of course."

It was a pity to hurry such a glorious repast but Michael did and met Lamy by the garage. It reminded him of a mews with its six large rolling doors in a row. There was also a putting green out the front he hadn't noticed before and he could see some of the stable's white-painted barns and paddocks with jumps and a field with a dozen horses in the distance and a trainer riding one at a gallop.

"My wife took up golf when we came back to the States. Played four or five times a week. I never got much good at it."

"I went once with an old friend in Scotland and lost thirteen balls."

"That's about my speed," Lamy said as they got in the Mercedes.

The return trip to New York was eerily quiet. Michael could see Lamy had something on his mind and was uncharacteristically monosyllabic but in some ways it was a relief not to have to be on one's intellectual toes and in any case he had a lot to think about himself.

Outside the hotel Lamy said, "I'm busy later and tomorrow daytime but I'll be here after that. I'll pick you up at six. Call if it's inconvenient."

He handed Michael a business card and, barely giving him time to close the car door, zoomed off down 77th Street.

§

Sixty seconds after Michael's arrival at the Belleclaire the telephone rang at the Arlington offices of L. R. McWhirter and Associates. It had taken Lamy just over two and a half hours for the drive into Manhattan from Mattituck but all in all the traffic hadn't been too bad for a Monday and it was now seventeen minutes to eleven.

"Your boy's back," said the general's laconic informant.

"Whaddya mean back? Back from where?"

"Back. Never saw him go out."

"And you've been there all night?"

"Yup."

"You're sure you didn't miss him?"

"Look, buddy, we do our job."

"OK, OK. Let me know right away if he goes out again and tail him."

"Yeah, yeah, yeah."

The phone clicked off and the general immediately looked up a number in his Rolodex and dialed and after two rings she answered.

"I thought I said eleven fifteen."

§

Michael went to the desk to ask for the key to Room 137 and was informed in hushed tones by the clerk, a prematurely balding young man with a pronounced lisp and suffering a serious outbreak of rosacea but who clearly didn't like authority figures, that two NYPD detectives came looking for him yesterday evening and had returned with a search warrant not more than twenty minutes ago and were in all probability still there.

"Good lord," Michael said, "I'd better see what they want."

The young man eyed him with surprise but said nothing further and Michael bounded up the stairs to the first floor.

"Can I help you?" he said irritably upon entering and seeing the mess that had been made of his belongings. The clothes from the closet were now in disarray on the bed and his suitcases lay open on the floor and, worst of all, the careful piles of books and newspaper clippings and notes and tickets and identification that he had organized on the writing desk had all been rummaged through and among the muddle he couldn't find his passport.

One of the officers was on his cell phone and gestured Michael to wait.

"No, there's nothing . . no, well, if you wanna send forensics . . no, what's the point . . look, the guy just came in . . give us a minute and we'll call you back."

The officer hung up. Both men were in suits with their ties loosened.

"You Michael Davenport?" the one with the phone asked.

"Yes, I am. Would you mind telling me . . ?"

"Here from London, England?"

"Yes, just last Wednesday. You know that already from the . ."

"Ever been in an apartment at 69 Spring Street?"

"Yes, I think so, if it's . . "

"Belongs to one David Giudice."

He pronounced every possible syllable of the surname.

"Yes, I know him, he used to be . . "

"When was the last time you were there?"

"Um, well, yesterday afternoon but only outside because I . ."

"Were you there the night before that?"

"Um, no, no, I wasn't."

"Where were you?"

"Um, I was at the races, at Belmont. David was there but he left . ."

"To go where?"

"Home, the apartment, at least that's what I . ."

"What time was that?"

"Oh, um, I think it was probably about half past three . ."

"And you didn't go with him?"

"No."

"What time did you leave?"

"I'd say, um, something like half past six."

"Was anyone with you?"

"Yes."

"Who?"

"I was in the company of General Larry McWhirter."

At the mention of the name the rapid-fire interrogation stopped and the two detectives looked at each other.

"Now see here, I'd like to know what . ."

"You a friend of his?"

"No, I'd only made his acquaintance that very afternoon."

The response engendered another silence.

"Would you please explain what gives you the right to . . "

"This does," the second detective said and waved the search warrant.

"Then explain to me why . . "

"This yours?" the second man asked.

"What?"

He held out Michael's business card. Michael looked at the card and turned it over and suddenly remembered and cursed himself.

"Um, oh, ah, yes. Yes, I see now. Yes, it is."

"You say you were outside Giudice's apartment yesterday afternoon?"

"Yes, I saw the ambulances and the bodies . . "

"Were they friends of yours?"

Michael could see the sexual smirk in the man's eyes.

"Yes. David was once married to my sister."

"You don't say."

"Yes. But he realized during that time that he was gay."

The officer threw up his hands in a yielding gesture.

"Hey, bud, whatever turns you on, you got no problem from me."

"So," the first officer began again, "Where did you go after the races?"

"I went with the general and his party to a restaurant."

"Which restaurant?"

"It's somewhere over there on the other side of the park. It was called *'Fin de Partie'* if I remember correctly. French. It means 'endgame'. A chess term and a play by Samuel . . "

"And how long were you there?"

"Not very. Two or three hours."

"Until when?"

"Well, I'm not sure what time I actually returned to the hotel. I'd had a little more to drink than usual. Probably tennish."

"Did you take a cab?"

"No. I was driven here in the general's limousine."

"And you didn't go anywhere else after that?"

"No, I went straight to sleep. Out like the proverbial . . "

"When do you plan on getting back to London?"

"You've had a good look at my ticket, I'm sure. November 7th."

"No ideas about leaving early?"

"None."

The men were silent again and the first nodded to the second and he handed Michael his passport.

"OK, my friend," he said and they made for the door.

"So you think they were murdered, is that it?" Michael asked.

The second officer turned back and gave Michael a card.

"Call that number, they'll fill you in."

§

The general and the National Security Advisor also decided no drastic action was required for the moment. They would continue Michael's tight surveillance and see how things played out.

"I bet he spent the night with that shit Lamy."

"Who can say, chickpea. How's Mister Fastball this morning?"

"A zombie. Sat there popping a ball into his mitt during the briefing. It's why I'm already back in the office. We had calls to Mkapa in Tanzania and that new Zia woman in Bangladesh. He was supposed to talk about cooperation but basically just handed me the phone after he said hello. Mueller and the singing senator wanted to get approval for their new terror alert at the end but he just wandered off."

"Was the Vaderman with you?"

"There's something going on with him too. Said he wants a private word after lunch."

§

What neither of them could have guessed, nor the NYPD detectives, nor the general's seedy sleuth staked out in his tired old Mustang outside the Belleclaire, nor Michael or Lamy, was that the vice-president, an expert double-hauler of Montana's Big Horn River whose favorite fly was the 'Chernobyl Ant', was at that moment in the storage room at the Eisenhower Building staring over the top of wire-rimmed spectacles at a very nervous Scooter. His eyes glistened malevolently and the utterly mirthless smile was even more crooked than usual. He was holding a small, framed image of himself that was dribbling blood from beneath the glass and spotting the linoleum at their feet with a spatter of tiny droplets.

People born in the Year of the Snake are not natural collectors but it was not yet possible to lay blame for the extraordinary clutter of objects lining the shelves and filling every corner of the room except upon Cheney himself. It was he who ordered the FBI to bring them here but could never have imagined the trickle of six weeks ago would turn into this daily flood.

"Why was he killed?" he demanded, "Did you order it?"

"No," Libby replied, "I'm pretty sure it was Mueller."

"What the fuck is his problem? We can't kill everyone."

"I think this guy was particularly vocal."

A spot of crimson suddenly soiled the vice-president's pinky and he jammed the frame in amongst an array of similar knickknacks on a nearby shelf and wiped his finger on his trembling aide's sleeve with revulsion.

There was every conceivable kind of object, action figures, ceramics, stuffed animals, a moosehead and a glazed fish wall-hanging, movie posters, magazines, book covers, a hunting knife, a desk set, mugs, cups, saucers, souvenirs, T-shirts, sweatshirts, a G-string, liquor bottles, a hubcap, seven cell phones, four suitcases and a gym bag, a football, two tennis rackets, a throw rug, a car blanket, eighteen license plates, a soccer shoe, five baseball caps and a bat, twelve gloves, a piece of velvet art, a toolkit and a tacklebox lining the walls of the long narrow room from floor to ceiling. Every one sporting an image of the vice-president dressed either in his customary suit and tie or baggy military fatigues or some absurd costume like a bikini or a wizard's hat, an executioner's mask or even diving gear with goggles, flippers, spear, wetsuit and breathing tank. Sometimes he brandished a weapon, a pistol, machine gun, dagger, yoyo, axe, cutlass, light sword or bazooka but in every case without exception blood was either dripping for real or spurting in a sculpted cascade from his mouth. There were rags under every shelf to sop it up that needed changing several times a day.

"They delivered over a hundred pieces of shit like this in a goddam wardrobe box this morning. We've got overflow now in a locker downstairs. A lot of the stuff is so big it has to be destroyed on site."

"Some jerk emailed a home movie with Condi, Rummy, the Doctor and me carved on the face of Mount Rushmore and it wasn't a fake."

Scooter thought that might actually have pleased his boss and tried sharing a conspiratorial wink but it wasn't reciprocated.

"Wouldn't it be better to get rid of all this?"

Cheney grinned slyly.

"I'm going to wait until the building's crammed full then pull the fucker and blame it on you-know-who."

Libby chuckled sycophantically but then became serious.

"What are we going to do about the tape?"

The descendant of Radulfus of Quesnay, the ancestor from the oak groves of Normandy who trampled through Saxon Sussex with the army of William the Conqueror in 1066 and stayed to be immortalized in the Domesday census, gazed at his flunkey with scorn.

"Nothing," he snarled, "None of it matters."

§

Michael immediately rehung his clothes, put his suitcases away in the closet and reorganized his paraphernalia on the desk and he was now looking at the cards. Lamy's couldn't have been simpler. The word 'Lamy' embossed in deep aquamarine dead center with a phone number beneath. The other read, 'OCME Main Office, 520 First Avenue, New York, NY 10016, (212) 447-2030.' Whatever 'OCME' stood for Michael knew he would never make the call. He was allergic to officialdom in any media.

He looked in his billfold and found the number that 'Warren' had written on the back of another Enigma card along with his name. Michael kicked himself for not having demanded the officer return the one he had foolishly given David. He thought of all personal possessions as the Orunda do nail-clippings, not like the Turk or the Inca who hide them in wall nooks believing they will come in handy at their resurrection but much more realistically that some conniving bastard might use them in this world to monkey with his juju. He would love to have been able to redress his feeling of violation but what could he do?

After a few deep breathing exercises and a long sojourn in the bathroom and a shave and a change of clothes he was calm enough to venture once more onto the street and this time he took his ticket and passport with him.

§

As Michael ambled up Broadway to 79th Street and turned right to enter the Dublin House which he had been very pleased to see was still there, Condoleezza was squatting by the pins at the far end of the White House bowling alley, wearing a catcher's mask and wielding a padded mitt, waiting for a woozy-looking president to throw his first pitch. The single lane was the lovechild of Richard Nixon but it had to be squeezed in under the driveway to the North Portico and it was stuffy and claustrophobic. She tried to get him out onto the South Lawn but he would have none of it.

He had changed into a tracksuit and his old Bulldogs cap and spent several minutes bouncing up and down and swinging his shoulders around to warm up.

"Come on," she barked finally, "My knees are killing me."

"Gotta get loose," he said, "Can't risk pulling a muscle."

"Fuck-a-doodle, just throw the damn thing."

"You don't understand. The whole country'll be watching."

"Well, they ain't watching now, which is surely the point, so throw it!"

"OK. Ready?"

"Bring it on."

The president went into his windup and faltered and then did it again and let it go but it was so tentative it clunked onto the lane two-thirds of the way down.

"Way to go, bubba, that'll show 'em," she said as the ball rolled to a stop at her feet and she rolled it back, "One more time."

"I'm a tad out of practice," he muttered sheepishly.

"Give her the old college try."

He shook his shoulders and blew through his rubbery lips and threw the ball again and it was much more powerful but far too high and caromed off the ceiling about ten feet in front of her, knicking out an upside-down divot of plaster and paint. It was heading straight for the blown-up photographic fresco of the stately presidential mansion on the wall above her head but she could tell from the spin its trajectory would be much lower and as she ducked on all fours it slammed into the top of the headpin behind her and with a weird drunken reeling motion every one of the ten slowly and miraculously keeled over.

"Ha!" she yelled encouragingly, "Steeeee-rike!"

§

The Dublin House was darkly comforting and old-fashioned and reminded Michael of home and he ordered a pint of draught Guinness which he remembered being excellent here. His system was still parched from the *pisco* and the humiliating encounter with the detectives had unsettled him. Mercifully the bartender was an Irishman who didn't try to be jolly.

He had purchased both the Daily News and the Guardian on the way and since the patronage was sparse even though it was lunchtime he was able to find a table near the window where there was sufficient light to read them.

He noticed a small man of Mediterranean complexion enter as he sat but didn't think much of it.

§

After a couple of dozen throws the president found a smidgen of his old form and finished off with three genuine strikes in a row.

"When are we doing Peres?" he asked as she peeked round the door into the basement hall to make sure no tour was in progress.

"Two-thirty."

"I'm gonna take a nap."

She accompanied her worrisome charge past the Secret Service office to the family elevator and even leaned in to press the button to the second floor for him.

"Sweet dreams," she said.

As soon as the doors were closed she raised her eyes to heaven and hissed menacingly, "Any suggestions?" and she took it as God's revenge that immediately afterwards she bumped into the vice-president in the Rose Garden arcade.

"OK, good a place as any," she said, "What's up? I need a sandwich."

Cheney fixed her with a steely stare and pondered.

"Come on, Dick, I haven't got all day."

"Someone's been messing in my safe across the road."

"So?"

"We seem to have misplaced a copy of the tape."

"Which fucking tape?"

"The tape of us all with the Doctor in Ohio."

"So?"

"You wouldn't know where it was, would you?"

"How the fuck would I? I never ever go there."

His cold grey eyes examined her closely.

"Did you know we were on TV yesterday?"

"I was told about it. A lot of shit like that has been happening. Look, say what you want to say."

"Have you been talking to the general?"

"Which fucking general?"

"McWhirter."

"Yes, a couple of hours ago. We talk all the time."

"What about?"

"Whatever we need to talk about. What the fuck do you want?"

"You were talking about Vespucci."

"How do you know that?"

"A little birdie told me. She said he was here."

"We don't even know he exists."

"Oh, I think we do. He was with Louis Lamy at Belmont and a faggot friend who has since turned up dead."

She pretended it was news to her.

"What was his name?"

"David Giudice."

"And you say he's dead?"

"Him and his lover."

"When?"

"Found them yesterday morning."

"How?"

"Scooter said Mueller. I thought maybe you."

"Why would I care about this guy?"

"He was upset about his sister and making a lot of noise."

"They're a dime a dozen."

"I know but someone must have screwed up because the NYPD are looking into it as a homicide."

"Mueller will already have told them to drop it."

"I'm surprised he didn't tell you."

"Everyone around here keeps too damn many secrets."

The vice-president fell silent.

"So what's the problem?" she went on irritably, "We've got Vespucci under surveillance. He was gone all night but was back this morning. Anyway, he's not Vespucci, he's some twit from England called Michael Davenport who writes crap for a crummy magazine."

"Oh, I beg to differ. But, whoever he is, we can't take chances. He's with Lamy. Lamy's brother is the EU Trade Commissioner and maybe next boss at the WTO. Giudice could have been much more than he seemed. We have to be sure of the connections. There are a lot of people out there just waiting for us to fuck up."

"I know all this. So?"

The one-time House Minority Whip dabbed the corners of his mouth with the knuckle of his forefinger.

"We have to be sure," he repeated ominously.

§

In a conference room in the massive Department of Justice Building, which after twenty-three years was about to honor the slain Robert Kennedy, the current Attorney-General, a fervent member of the 'Singing Senators' and often referred to by his colleagues as 'that nitwit', was bursting to regale the assembled press with his song, 'Let the Eagle Soar'. Sharing the platform was the Director of the FBI who had pleaded with him to refrain but the lyrics were swirling uncontrollably above the starched strangulation of his collar in his blood-starved brain.

"We've fought for freedom on the distant shore.

Paid a price, a sacrifice you can't ignore.

Let the mighty Eagle soar like she's never soared before,

From rocky coast to golden shore,

With healing in her wings as the land beneath her sings,

'Only God, no other kings', let the mighty Eagle soar!"

He was muttering the words under his breath like a prayer but finally a stern throat-clearing from the FBI Director caused him to stop and begin.

"Good afternoon. The administration has concluded, based on information developed, that there may be additional terrorist attacks within the United States and against United States interests over the next week. We view this information as credible but unfortunately it is not specific as to the type of attack or target.

"Consequently, a terrorist threat advisory update has been issued to 18,000 law enforcement agencies across the country to continue on highest alert. We ask for the patience and cooperation of the general public if they encounter additional measures by those who are charged with securing their safety and we urge them to report unusual circumstances and inappropriate behavior to the proper authorities."

He went on to list the government agencies involved which included the Immigration and Naturalization Service, the Nuclear Regulatory Commission, the FBI, the Environmental Protection Agency, the Federal Aviation Administration, the Departments of Transportation and Energy and the governors of all fifty states.

Director Mueller repeated the request in different words and concluded that, despite the total lack of specifics, "It will give us a force multiplier that could well prevent another terrorist attack."

A woman asked whether the threat advisory on October 11th had helped to avert such an attack and Mueller admitted it was very difficult to tell.

"What should Americans do with this information then?" she queried, "You never rescinded the last one and my assumption is most Americans already are on a heightened state of alert."

"I think that is . . that is true," Mueller agreed, "However, we have received this additional information, specific as to time but not as specific . . not specific as to other details and we think it is important to put it out there."

"May I just make a comment here?" Ashcroft broke in, "We have decided to share with the American people that we have alerted law enforcement. And that's important. Because we are alerting law enforcement and conferring with them we think this gives people a basis for continuing to live their lives the way they would otherwise live them with this elevated sense of alertness or vigilance.

"I trust the American people to be able to understand in this context of conflict where there is a front overseas and another front here in the United States that they can make good judgments and can understand this kind of information. And we are sharing it exactly in the context that the director has indicated. It is not specific but it is information that we think the American people have a good mature judgment and capacity to accommodate and to understand."

Someone else stood up and wondered if they had briefed the president about this and whether he agreed to the release of the warning and Ashcroft and Mueller looked at each other for a moment and then Ashcroft said yes, they had made him aware of the situation earlier in the day.

The woman had remained standing and asked, "Do you have any concerns that if you issue these alerts and nothing happens then people will start not to take them seriously and next time . . ?"

"No," Ashcroft cut her off, "If people take these warnings seriously, they go about their lives, but they participate with patience in the additional steps that are taken by law enforcement authorities, they are very likely participating in the prevention of terrorism and the disruption of terrorism. There is no reason for a success on the part of the people in forestalling or otherwise delaying or interrupting terrorism, for that to lull them into a false sense of indifference. It's important to understand that these are to be taken seriously but by taking them seriously on a continuing basis we can have the good outcome of avoiding very serious additional terrorist problems."

The woman was momentarily dumbfounded. Such incoherent nonsense, she mused, positively defined the term 'Kafkaesque'.

Then another reporter stood and asked Mueller if this current warning was related to the ongoing anthrax situation.

"I would be speculating if that were . . on that issue," he mumbled, "I have no reason to believe at this point in time that it is related."

"*Do* you have reason to believe," the woman chimed in again, "That this is a more credible threat than the last threat that you . . ?"

Again Ashcroft cut her off, "I think we clearly stated we believe this threat to be credible and for that reason it should be taken seriously," and without further explanation he and Mueller walked out of the room.

As they did so, the Attorney-General resumed his mumbling.

"Oh, we're far too young to die, we can make it if we try,
We've not yet begun to fly, it's time to let the mighty eagle soar
Once more."

"Tweedledum and Tweedledee," the woman snorted in derision but very few of the hastily departing assemblage seemed to get the reference.

§

After his third pint Michael got up to look at the chalkboard menu behind the bar and chose steak and kidney pie. He washed it down with a fourth Guinness and decided to take the subway to Soho again and call Warren from a paybooth. It was clearly unwise to use the phone in his room at the Belleclaire. Perhaps the opportunity would present itself for a face-to-face chat, one never knew, and then he would ring Helen, have another glass or two and return to the hotel for a much-needed early night.

He didn't notice his swarthy shadow get up and follow as he left the Dublin House and strolled down 79th Street blinking in the pale autumn sunshine.

Stanza Eleven

§

After a brief exchange Warren didn't hesitate and asked Michael to come to his apartment. It was not more than a hundred yards from the White Noise gallery near the corner of Wooster at 137 Spring. After so many coincidences of this kind Michael was not really all that surprised at the number but it did add zest to his step as he mounted the stairs to the first floor.

"Come in, come in," the old man said jovially as he opened the door.

The sitting room was tiny but every square inch of space had been utilized. It was obvious its inhabitant had lived there a long time and was a person of artistic sensitivity and great intelligence and something indefinable in the atmosphere made Michael instantly feel at home.

"Thank you for being so kind."

"Of course, of course, please have a seat."

An aging wicker basket chair, exactly like one his Canadian flatmate bought at a Saturday morning flea market in the Portobello Road and lugged all the way to their digs in Battersea those many years ago, was the only apparent choice.

"Can I get you a cup of coffee? Or tea? Or a glass of wine?"

"Do you know, I'd love a cup of coffee, thank you."

"Come with me while I make it."

The kitchen was not classifiable as a room. Perhaps a deep closet or corridor with the sink and appliances and cupboards all on one side and a window at the far end that peered into a gloomy air shaft in the building's interior.

"So Helen is your baby sister."

"Yes."

138

"Isn't that interesting."

"Did you know her well?"

"Quite well, yes. David was a student of mine before he went off to London. I was surprised when he came back married. I don't think he made her very happy."

"No. She was shocked and moved when I told her though."

"She's not with you, is she?"

"No, no. She doesn't like New York."

"Yes, I remember. She went back to England right away after they split up. We had lunch the day she left."

"She was devastated by it."

Warren was fidgeting with an ancient espresso machine and didn't respond.

"Would they tell you any details about how they did it?"

"No, they've been swamped since 9/11 trying to identify thousands of bits and pieces. They confirmed it was suicide by an overdose of barbiturates. Fernando was addicted to Seconal. With the cocktail he was taking it's amazing it didn't kill him sooner. They're going to state suicide on the death certificate and they'll release the bodies to the funeral home tomorrow. Their wills make it clear they want to be cremated and their ashes mixed and scattered in the sea."

The espresso was suddenly bubbling forth into two simple white demitasses below the forked spout.

"Sugar?"

"Yes, please."

"Like the Italians."

"I'm afraid so. Thank you. Will there be a service?"

"Hell no. They were both atheists. I've arranged a direct cremation at a place five minutes from here on Bleecker. The only ceremony will be at the beach."

"Where do you plan to go?"

"They'd probably like it if we just tossed them off the Brooklyn Bridge or the Staten Island ferry but I think somewhere more private."

"How many people are you expecting?"

Warren chuckled amiably.

"Me. And you if you want. David's sister's dead. His parents died decades ago. Fernando was the only one of his family to ever leave Cuba. I called his father in Havana. David and Fernando went there a lot. They took what they called their farewell tour in August so Rafael knew the situation. He said he'd been expecting to hear from David every day and was speechless with tears when I told him what had happened. Fernando's mother is still alive but even if they had the money, which they don't, it's impossible for them to make it."

"Didn't they want the ashes?"

"No, they understood."

They both nodded their heads and took a sip of the espresso.

"Oh shit!" Warren exclaimed, almost choking on the hot liquid, "How can I be so senile to have forgotten. David left Helen everything in his will. The gallery, the apartment, everything. They're mortgaged to the max and there may be nothing left if she sells but it's all hers, lock, stock and barrel."

§

Michael's shadow, who was standing across the street watching the doorway of 137, had called in a replacement. He was pissed off he would have to take the subway back to the Upper West Side to retrieve his car. Nonetheless, he used the time while he was waiting to call Arlington and report and the general immediately called the White House. It was half past four in the afternoon but the meeting with the Israeli Foreign Minister was over and, to his surprise, the receiver was snatched up almost before he heard it ring.

"So?" she snapped.

"He's gone back down to Soho."

"Soho what?"

"Two NYPD detectives interviewed him at the hotel."

"Jesus Christ."

"They found out the faggot and his tootsie were murdered."

"I know. Dick told me. He's mad as hell."

"Can't blame him. Who *is* responsible?"

"Mueller," she answered, lying.

"Not again. Are you sure?"

"I asked him point blank twenty minutes ago."

"That son of a bitch is dumb as dogshit. Isn't there anyone over at Hoover anymore who has a goddam clue? How the fuck did they let the NYPD into it? Never mind why did they do it in the first place. The guy was the definition of harmless."

"Reflex. They don't think about it. Just kill, kill, kill. It's easier."

"Did you tell Mueller to fix it?"

"He has."

"But now Bartolomeo Davenport knows it wasn't suicide."

"He would have known anyway. The point is he'll get the message."

"And we can always sick Mueller on him if he doesn't."

There was nothing reflective about their pause. A solution is a solution.

"How was the old pitching arm?"

"Pathetic. I'm worried. He got through OK in Shanghai because the Chinese speak his kind of speak. You should have seen his little face beam when Zemin said, 'There is no isolation from evil,' but I have no idea how he's going to hold up in front of the UN. That's less than two weeks. The zombie act worked like a charm on Peres though. Got him really spooked. He's used to being the dude with the long silences. Loves the technique. Today they were like two old geezers in the park playing chess. I started to fantasize they'd turned to stone but finally I gave them the prod and they kind of woke up and agreed to differ as they both knew they would and after a quick cup of tea and the photo op and the blither about progress for the media the old bastard was happy as hell to bugger off."

McWhirter chuckled.

"So peace on earth is just around the corner. Glory hallelujah."

§

When the president spoke about the Foreign Terrorist Tracking Task Force he told the reporters, "We will make sure that the Land of the Free is as safe as possible from people who come to our country to hurt people. We welcome legal immigrants. We welcome people coming to America. We welcome the process that encourages people to come. What we don't welcome are people who come to hurt the American people. So we're going to be diligent with our visas and observant of the behavior of people who come," but now he was running as fast as he could on a treadmill in the workout room on the third floor of the Residence because in his fevered mind he was being pursued by a band of whooping turbaned ayatollahs all brandishing scimitars and wearing wire-rimmed spectacles and all of them clones of Richard B. Cheney.

As his panic grew he saw his running shoes catch fire and suddenly he wasn't a man but a frightened dog and the howling pack behind him were enormous undulating snakes that thundered across the ground like stampeding water buffalo and as the flames engulfed him, burning off his fur and causing his skin to erupt in bubbling welts, the snakes began to clank and he could see they were made of huge jointed steel flanges and their fangs were molten tamping irons that were about to devour him.

He tried to duck the hideous fantasy and lost his footing and the relentlessly whirring machine threw him backwards and he hit the floor and the wall behind it with a bone-shattering thump but his bruised hands and knees managed to scuttle like a frightened crab to the bathroom and he hung his sweat-soaked face over the toilet just in time to vomit.

His words bounced madly in the bowl, "Americans who unwittingly helped people that hurt Americans regret it now. Americans who were willing participants to hurt America will be brought to justice. Anyone who helps a terrorist is equally culpable as a terrorist. We've got a new law now that will help us to pursue those who would harm Americans and those who would help them harm Americans. People need to be held accountable in America and we're going to do just that."

§

"Good lord," Michael said, utterly flabbergasted, "Will she have to come?"

"I don't suppose so. Not if you want to handle it."

"Good lord, this is quite astonishing. What time is it?"

Warren consulted the oven clock.

"Four thirty-three."

"Good lord, I promised I'd ring her just about now. I have no idea what she'll want to do."

"Be my guest," Warren said, gesturing to the phone in the sitting room.

"Are you sure? I'll reverse the charges."

"Don't even think about it."

"That's very kind."

"I'll leave you some privacy," Warren said, putting on a windbreaker and a scarf and a tam over his wispy white hair, "I need some things at the store anyway."

"Please don't on my account."

"It's fine. Really."

"When do you think we'll be scattering the ashes?"

"Whenever you want. I'm picking them up the day after tomorrow."

"And you've obviously spoken to their lawyer."

"He asked if I knew how to contact her so I was glad you called."

The old man stepped out the door and Michael sat at his desk.

"Good lord," he muttered and took a deep breath and dialed.

There was no ring whatever but suddenly Helen answered.

"I've got one hell of a lot of news," he said.

"Where are you now? I've been worried sick."

"Why? I'm fine."

"Because you said they were murdered."

"I didn't say I knew that. Unfortunately I do now."

"What?!" she shouted, "So they were?! Jesus, Michael!"

"Yes, I believe so. The official verdict is suicide but that's another story. Look, this is what you'll never credit, David has left everything to you in his will."

There was total silence.

"You're fucking joking," she said almost inaudibly.

"No, it's absolutely true. I'm down in Soho near the gallery with an old friend of theirs. You know him, for god's sake. Warren. I'm in his apartment. You must've been here. You've probably sat right where I'm sitting."

"Warren? I love him. How is he?"

"He looks in splendid shape."

"He must be well over eighty."

"Could be. What's his name, by the way? I only know him as Warren."

"Warren Allen Jones. He's famous."

"What as?"

"Lots of things. He's a great artist. And writer. He knows everybody."

"Well, I'm happy to get to know him. Look, what do you want to do? Warren has arranged a cremation and they wanted their ashes mixed and scattered in the sea and we'll probably do that the day after tomorrow. I'm going to suggest we go out to Long Island where I was yesterday."

"Well, what do I have to do? What has he left me exactly?"

"I don't think he had any money. Oh yes, I forgot to tell you, I won twenty thousand dollars at the races so we've got some."

"You're pulling my leg."

"No, it's true. The cheque is burning a hole in my billfold. I haven't talked to the lawyer, just Warren. As far as I know it's only the apartment and the gallery. I'll try and discover more in the morning. It's silly but Warren went out to the shops to give us some privacy. I don't know why he didn't stay and talk to you himself."

"Why were they murdered? Was it a robbery? Who did it?"

"That's a ridiculously long story."

"Are you in danger? What are you doing there, for heaven's sake?"

Michael could hear the sound of footsteps coming up the stairs.

"Hang on, he's back. I'll let you talk to him," he said, then added an urgent afterthought, "But don't mention the murder thing. I'm not sure he knows."

Warren came in with two paper shopping bags and Michael gestured him to the phone.

"Hello, my sweet one, how are you?"

"I'm awful," she said, "How are you?"

"The reason is terrible but it's wonderful to hear your voice."

"Yes, I know. This is mad. Why on earth did he do it?"

"Oh, my dear, Fernando had no more than a few weeks left and David was seriously depressed. Did Michael tell you about Ruth?"

"Yes, he did. But I don't mean that. I can understand that. I mean why did he leave everything to me?"

"It shouldn't be hard to guess but maybe I'm being sentimental. Maybe there was no one else."

Helen was silent for a moment.

"Do you think I should come?"

"It won't matter to David but I would love to see you."

Michael was now resigned to it and perhaps it was for the best. There would be much to do and why shouldn't a woman say goodbye to her only husband.

Warren could tell he wanted to say something and held out the receiver.

"Look, we can use the money from the races for your ticket. Why don't you see if you can get a flight tomorrow or Wednesday and ring us back."

"It's too late to call Barbara. I doubt she'll let me off."

"Bugger Barbara and bugger the college. Just tell them it's happening. You've had a bereavement, for fuck's sake."

§

The Chinese believe that 'Metal Snakes' like the vice-president are proud, vain, vicious and cunning and will always be antagonistic to 'Fire Dogs' like the president who are sexy, charismatic, popular and open-hearted.

A Fire Dog is also supersensitive to unfair treatment and neither will ever forgive a stab in the back.

But the vengeance of a Metal Snake is sharp and silent and his mortal enemy is the 'Earth Pig'.

§

"I think someone is following you," Warren said.

Michael had just rung off with the agreement that Helen would call as soon as she had flight information and an arrival time.

"How do you know?"

"When I went out there was a short olive-skinned man smoking a cigarette across the street and when I came back from the store he was saying a few words to another man who you can see standing there now. I could tell they were talking about this building."

Michael went to the window and peeked out from behind the curtain. There was a tall fair-haired man, who he thought looked Ukrainian or certainly Eastern European of some sort, in the doorway opposite and though he wasn't looking up Michael felt he had sensed his presence in the window because after a moment the man began pacing up and down.

"Hmm," Michael said.

"Tell me about why you're here."

Michael began the story and it wasn't more than a minute or two before he mentioned Lamy and Warren smiled.

"You've met him then?" Michael asked.

"Oh yes, I know him well. We are what you call chalk and cheese. I decided to respect him because of my love for Ruth."

"He has the most amazing encyclopedic mind."

"Yes, indeed, he is very intelligent."

"But . . ?"

"There is something a little sinister."

"I thought so at first but having spent the best part of two days with him . . "

"Did he take you to Mattituck?"

"Yes. I was there last evening and stayed the night. He drove me back to my hotel this morning. He said he would pick me up again tomorrow at six but didn't give a reason."

"Ruth was very much in love with him."

"He told me their relationship was the happiest of his life."

"Perhaps it was. I wouldn't know."

Michael went on with the story and once or twice checked to see if the tall man was still outside and he was. Inevitably his narrative led him to describe some of the events in Juarez and to the name Bartolomeo Vespucci but it meant as little to Warren as it did to everyone else.

"You seem to have become a character in someone else's novel," Warren observed with a wry smile when Michael finished, "The whole thing is positively Sicilian."

"And completely daft," Michael added.

The telephone rang and it was Helen. She had booked a departure from Heathrow on Wednesday morning at 10:25 and would be arriving at JFK at 1:15 that afternoon. She felt she ought to return no later than Saturday and Warren said it shouldn't be a problem to meet with David's lawyer on Thursday. She worried it was going to cost over three hundred pounds but Michael assured her that his race winnings were real and that he would happily pay for it. She could either stay with him at the Belleclaire or Warren would somehow make room if she preferred. They would both come to meet her at the airport and as they said goodbye they were all suddenly very excited about the prospect.

Michael decided he had to let Warren know about his visit from the NYPD and was quite surprised by his response.

"I knew it as soon as I saw them on the bed together. Fernando was a great lover of our miraculous existence. He would never have agreed to shorten his life by a single second. The pain and misery of his disease were just part of it."

Michael nodded.

"How do you think it was done then? The people I talked to in the street said there was no sign of a struggle."

"No, there wasn't. Another thing that told me they hadn't done it themselves was that they were both naked. Fernando was once very beautiful and he despised what had happened to his body. He would never have allowed himself to depart for the great beyond without covering up. And also the two pill bottles beside them on the night table were totally empty which I thought was a bit odd and then I found a half-dissolved Seconal tablet floating in the toilet. You say David was drunk when he left the racetrack?"

"Not drunk. He'd inhaled several martinis but I suspect he was drinking a lot after Ruth died. It was just enough to make him reckless."

"Someone probably followed him home and put a gun in his back at the door. They've got all kinds of nasty ways to kill you. Maybe there were two of them and David was dead before he got upstairs. Fernando was helpless and it wouldn't have taken much to dispatch him. Then whoever it was arranged them on the bed like Romeo and Julio, the typical ignorant assumption of a gay suicide."

Michael thought for a moment.

"It's interesting," he said, "What time did you talk to the examiner's office?"

"I had to try half a dozen times but probably noonish."

"The detectives were in my room when Lamy dropped me and that was about twenty to eleven so in between someone must have told them to change their story."

"They wouldn't have said they were suspecting murder anyway."

"No, I suppose not. One of the officers was talking on the phone when I got to the room and I remember him using the word 'forensics' but then he said, 'What's the point?' and that they were going to talk to me and call whoever it was back but they didn't grill me very thoroughly considering the situation. What I absolutely don't get though is why it was necessary to kill them. What on earth had they done that was so dangerous or so different from anyone else?"

"David was very active in a group that's pressing hard for a full congressional investigation."

"Yes, but so are hundreds of others. I'm sure half the population of New York knows the official version of what happened is a pack of lies."

"Did Lamy say what he thought about it?"

"Neither of us were certain it was murder yesterday. He said if it was then maybe David just said the wrong thing in the wrong place."

"I don't think they pick their victims arbitrarily. They know who they want to intimidate. Did the possibility occur to you their warning was for Lamy?"

Michael was startled.

"No, good lord, I never thought of that. He never said he thought that."

"And maybe not only Lamy."

Michael's surprise turned to horror.

"What, you mean they were . . ?"

"Sending *you* a message, yes. You and whoever they imagine are behind you. It makes a nasty kind of sense, does it not, Signor Vespucci?"

§

It was hard for Michael to absorb the awful implications and by the time he left the apartment the sky was dark and the street lighting in the area so muted they couldn't tell from the window if the man was still watching across the street. Not that it mattered, Michael was far too upset to care.

Life is miraculous, yes, but its labyrinthine curlicues profoundly meaningless. If Cheney's apparition had not appeared to Perretti and Gonzalez and the reporter from Al Jazeera had not spoken to them then he would never have come to New York and decided to look David up and they wouldn't have gone to the races and David and Fernando would still be alive! To go even further back it would never have happened if he hadn't been stupid enough to cross the Rio Grande while filming that blasted tiger because he would never have been linked to this vampire-blessing, politician-obsessing, doppelgangrenous figment!

Michael was not one of those puling numbskulls who believe shit happens for a reason nor was he so infantile as to pin such things on the malign playfulness of the gods. Chance is blind. Perfectly, miraculously blind.

As he came out the door of 137 into the street there was no sign of the man. It was almost a pity because he was just in the mood for a confrontation. What a lot he had learned and so much of it was delight. Warren was, if anything, even more remarkable than Lamy and somewhat more genuinely humane. He was first and foremost a teacher but he had also owned a recording studio and nurtured the careers of many talented musicians. He was president of the New York Goethe Society and the Thomas Paine Club. He was a painter and author and the publisher of the American Humanist and had recently completed editing the Encyclopedia of Freethinkers, a four-volume opus celebrating the lives of those valiant few who maintain their sanity despite the imbecility of their fellow man.

Beyond that, he was fluent in Italian, French and Cantonese and had been a captain in the American 5th Army that landed at Anzio and was surrounded by the Germans for a week in the caves of Pozzoli and went on to the liberation of Rome. He was also proudly gay and a lifelong activist and had taken part in the Stonewall protest of June 1969 in Greenwich Village which began the gay rights movement. But even more important than any of those things he had been kind to Helen when she needed it.

And now Helen was going to be involved in this madness. Perhaps he could get her away from New York again by Saturday and nothing awful would happen. What on earth were they going to do with David's belongings and the apartment and everything in the gallery? Sell them, he supposed. Let the lawyer sort it out.

But the overshadowing question was whether or not their death was to do with him or rather his 'shirt of Nessus', the Italian mirage. Had the black woman in El Paso actually been Condoleezza Rice? If so, were she and General McWhirter still in collusion? And if they were, why on earth would they be sending a warning about 9/11 to Bartolomeo Vespucci? Well, of course, it wasn't him, but only their mistaken version of him doing the things Michael Davenport was doing. If he was at Belmont with a man pressing for a congressional investigation and shooting his mouth off. If he was in the company of a loose cannon billionaire whose brother they assumed was one of them. Yes, that was it, they had no idea how to interpret his actions and like all people guilty of grievous crimes they were convinced unseen enemies were subtly plotting against them.

The thought of their nervous confusion, whoever they were, made him laugh out loud and the bystanders on the subway platform where he was waiting moved a few paces away. He was caught up in an absurd game of cat and mouse in which he was neither. What a joke. What a nasty tragic joke.

The C train rattled in and stopped with a deafening squeal. It was about half past eight on a Monday evening and thus not overly crowded and Michael was able to find a seat for the trip uptown between a large black woman with copious bags of shopping and a teenage boy with long curly hair and headphones blaring music in his ears so loud that Michael could hear the tinny outline of its monotony even above the clack of the wheels.

Nonetheless, he enjoyed riding the rails and observing his fellow passengers and it didn't take more than a moment or two for him to notice that the tall man who had been outside Warren's apartment was standing by the central door of the car. He tried to catch his eye but the man didn't fall for it and since he was very comfortable he decided to watch closely and confront him later.

The man followed him off the train at 72nd Street and Central Park West as he knew he would and Michael could hear his footsteps all the way to Broadway and 76th. There were several subway routes that would have brought them closer to the Belleclaire from Spring Street but they involved changing trains and he found that a bore. He liked to walk in the cool night air and the soft architecture of the brownstone houses was always pleasing.

In the brighter lights of the main thoroughfare Michael stopped abruptly and turned to look at the man. He was not more than twenty paces behind and stopped also. There was no one in between them.

"I'd like a word with you, young man, if you don't mind."

The shadow tried to look as if he were examining the contents of a shop window and Michael walked back in his direction.

"Would you care to tell me why you're following me?"

The man eyed him blankly and turned away.

"You were watching me outside 137 Spring Street, were you not?"

There was no reaction.

"Do you work for the government?"

Still nothing.

"Or the FBI?"

The man turned to look at him again and grinned a nicotine-stained grin.

"What about the CIA? When did you last speak to General McWhirter?"

The man's eyes betrayed a tiny blip of recognition. Michael prided himself in his ability to read faces and stared at him levelly.

"Well, when you do, give him this message. We are not amused. Have you got that? We are definitely not amused."

The man decided to speak at last and Michael had been right, the accent was strongly Eastern European, not precisely Russian though and hard to place.

"I don't know what you talk about, you crazy prick," he said, without a trace of animosity.

"Oh, I think you do. Where are you from?"

The man smiled again. A two pack a day habit at the least, Michael surmised, and the untrained teeth of a Hollywood dental surgeon's best nightmare.

"I am American. Where you from, you crazy prick?"

"England. Most people tell me that's obvious."

"Yes, is obvious."

"So, where are you from? Your accent is interesting."

"I am from New Jersey, crazyman."

"New Jersey, let me think now, is that on the Black Sea or the Baltic?"

"New Jersey on Hudson, prickyprick."

Michael was finding the idiocy of their interchange highly entertaining and gave a little snort of laughter.

"How long have you been in the States, two months or three?"

"I was born here, prickyman."

"I'll tell you what, I'm going to call you Nikolai. I'd be willing to bet you're not even registered with the Immigration and Naturalization Service, Nicky, and haven't been more than two weeks off the boat from Romania. I think I'll have to have your residency status looked into if you keep calling me names."

The man turned away again and was silent.

"Yes, I think we'll have you deported to Pennsylvania."

Michael could see the man wanted to laugh.

"Or perhaps you'd prefer Florida."

He was definitely on the verge.

"What about Italy?" Michael asked.

The man suddenly turned back and nodded, joining in the improvisation.

"Sure, why not, I love Italy."

"Everyone loves Italy. OK, if you tell me your name, I'll make sure you go to Italy."

"OK, you are right, I am Nikolai," he said and they both chuckled.

It was getting sillier and sillier. Michael was starting to like him. It was time to go.

"OK, Nick, just remember what I said. I don't really mind you following me. Hell, I'd invite you for a drink if I weren't so tired. I'm going straight to bed and then I'll be at Arty's Deli for breakfast about nine. I'd take the night off if I were you."

Michael walked away, crossed to the median and waited for the oncoming line of taxicabs to pass. He didn't look back at the man as he entered the hotel and asked the clerk for his key. He wasn't the one from the morning with the rosacea but even though he didn't say anything Michael could tell from his face they must have talked.

As he trudged up the stairs he was amused to think of the general's reaction if indeed such a reaction there was to be and the thought suddenly struck him that, if he was clever enough, he might become the one playing the cat.

Stanza Twelve

there's no way to stop us don't try
we've sucked mammon's tits cracked and dry
the good and the poor
the saint and the whore
we crush milk rape or crucify

§

"He knows we're on his tail," McWhirter slurred into the mouthpiece.

"Way to go. You and your stupid underworld connections. I told you to leave it to me."

"Don't get uppity, chitlins, our connections are the same."

It was ten past six on Tuesday morning and they were both still in pajamas. His had pale white and blue stripes and were flannel and crumpled and she wore a frilly little girl's nightshirt made of light green silk so short that it exposed both the lower curve of her buttocks and a cheeky hint of curly black pubic hair as she paced up and down in bare feet.

"Are you brushing your fucking dentures, or what?" she groaned.

The general swallowed obligingly before going on.

"He said he was none too happy about it. He said 'we' to be exact. 'We are not amused.' He spent four hours yesterday afternoon with Warren Allen Jones."

"Who?"

"The faggot devil-worshiper. The old guy who's always stirring the shit."

"For Christ's sake, spit in the sink, you're making my ear wet."

McWhirter swallowed again.

"Was Lamy with them?"

"No. I called you last night. Where were you?"

"None of your damn business."

"I thought you only had eyes for Mr. Baseball."

She was silent.

"What's up for you today?"

"Don't ask. I'm holding his hand while he talks to Azerbaijan first off and then Kocharian in Armenia about Nagorno-Karabakh. He can't even say it, for Jesus' sake. Then the usual and then the NSC. He's going out to some high school in Maryland at lunchtime with Bob Dole and Principi and Paige and I've told him he's on his own for that but it's his little Lessons in Liberty initiative and he'll be fine. Bullshitting kids is what he's best at. When he comes back we've got a bunch of House members with aviation concerns and the Commission to Strengthen Social Security which is nothing to do with me, thank god. After that, we're off to the game."

"Got time to join me for lunch at the El Paso?"

"OK. Twelve fifteen sharp. I'll only have half an hour."

§

The vice-president was on the way from Observatory Circle to Langley in his chauffeured limousine by seven thirty and was just crossing the Potomac south of the Little Falls Dam and the Snake Island fishway. It had been completed in 1959 but never adequately fulfilled its purpose due to incompetent construction and the huge amount of debris regularly washing down the river and though he was vaguely aware of the new design put in place during the last year, thanks to the efforts of Maryland Senator Paul Sarbanes and the Fish and Wildlife Service, the fate of spawning Atlantic shad was not what occupied his mind.

He was making yet another visit to the office of George Tenet, the Director of the CIA, a man of Greek heritage like Sarbanes and a hangover from the Clinton Administration, who would have been replaced after the 'intelligence disaster' of 9/11 had it been up to him and who hung onto his job only because his boss was impervious to argument and stubborn as a mule and continued to favor the man for some unknown reason. Yet his position was vulnerable and the equally willful oilman from Casper intended to keep making him aware of it and thus force him to manufacture evidence of weapons of mass destruction in Iraq which the plotters had required from the very beginning.

The Foreign Terrorist Tracking Task Force was entirely the vice-president's brainchild. As far as most were aware, it was set up to allow Tenet and his band of superannuated schoolboys to focus on Al Qaeda but was really another mechanism for unhindered domestic surveillance.

With it he hoped to flush out the traitorous cruds responsible for his hangarful of blood-boltered simulacra.

§

Michael spent a very restless night and, as so often happens when there is too much to occupy the mind, fell into a deep sleep only when morning began its ineluctable creep round the curtains so he was more than a little irritated when the maid knocked on the door at a few minutes past eight.

"Can't you read?" he mumbled groggily, "What does 'Do Not Disturb' mean to you?"

"Sign say 'Please Make Up Room.' You want me make up?" replied the polite but merciless trill.

Was it conceivable he hadn't placed the sign on the handle properly?

"No! Later! Tomorrow! Go away!"

"Not need towels?"

"No! Nothing. Tomorrow will do. Please."

"Hygiene tissue?"

"No!"

"OK. I turn sign for you."

The chirpy singsong seemed Oriental but he couldn't be sure.

"Thank you," he added in sour imitation.

He lay back heavily but the pillow was damp with sweat and just as he was struggling to flip it to the dry side the telephone rang.

"Hell and damnation," he muttered, fumbling for it by the bedside, "Yes?"

It was Lamy.

"Just checking. Sorry to wake you," he chuckled.

"You didn't. 'Housekeeping' already managed that. Checking what?"

"That you're still with us."

"Ah. Yes. Well, I am. But it's been interesting."

"How so?"

Michael's mind was gradually regaining focus.

"The police were here when you dropped me. I'd forgotten I gave David my card with the name of the hotel written on the back."

Lamy laughed.

"What's so funny?"

"Did they book you for murder?"

"No, they just asked a few pointless questions and went away."

"And they haven't bothered you again?"

"No."

"I was in Bernie Kerik's office, he's the New York Police Commissioner, maybe forty minutes after I left you when he got a call from the mayor."

"Yes, what's his name, Rudy Giancana."

Lamy laughed even louder.

"Giuliani, but you were close. They're both sinister sons of bitches. Anyway, to start with Kerik was willing to talk about the possibility of murder but after the call, which he lied about and told me was from the medical examiner, he said it was firmly established as a double suicide."

"All to be expected, I suppose. The way of the world. I went to see the man who's looking after the funeral."

"Yes, Warren."

Michael was barely awake enough to be astonished but he was.

"How do you know?" he spluttered.

"He called me. He told me about the will and your sister. I'm going to take you both to JFK tomorrow."

Michael was having a hard time keeping up.

"Did he tell you I'm being followed?"

"Yeah, that too. Look, I'm having lunch with my brother but I'll see you at six, is that still OK?"

"Yes, why not, did Warren mention . . ?"

"Try and stay out of trouble," Lamy said cheerily and was gone.

Michael managed to get the phone back on the hook and flopped exhausted on the adjusted pillow. He wondered what else they had talked about. He wanted to ask Lamy about the warning and who he thought it was for, and who the hell was having him followed and why, but that would have to wait now until the evening. It was childish he knew but he couldn't help feeling suspicious of their conversation and somehow slightly betrayed. His two new acquaintances were obviously not so chalk and cheesy as Warren had led him to believe.

§

Laura hadn't slept well either. After finding George babbling incoherently in the workout room, and patching up the carpet burn on his hands and knees, she had put him to bed with Barney and Spotty and a heavy dose of Sonata sedative and placed an emergency distress call to the Reverend Kirbyjon in Houston.

Barney, who had not long ago celebrated his first birthday, was a grateful gift from the former governor of New Jersey, Christine Todd Whitman, the president's recent appointee as Administrator of the Environmental Protection Agency and she had hastened to do her benefactor's will by downplaying the stream of dire toxicology reports from her staff and ensuring the people of Lower Manhattan that their air was safe to breathe and their water to drink.

Both Barney and Spotty were of the species *canis lupus familiaris*. He was a feisty Scottish terrier and she an aging English Springer spaniel who had been born in the White House some dozen years previously and been a friend and companion to the First Mother but it was he who became known as the First Dog, which was only right and proper according to the First Family because he had the good sense to take an instant dislike to the vice-president.

Since it was a Monday evening the reverend was putting his slippered feet up in the palatial splendor of his Houston mansion. His ministry proclaimed the 'virtue of prosperity' and the Almighty's admiration for those blessed to link their 'spiritual wholeness' with their 'financial wholeness'. The good pastor was firm in his belief in what he called 'entrepreneurial faith' and he didn't really want to be disturbed but it was the president's wife calling and he instantly agreed to be in Washington first thing in the morning. He rearranged his schedule and ordered his private jet to be ready for a 4AM departure and he was now kneeling on the carpet in the Yellow Oval Room with her. The subject of her distress was too sore to kneel and was slumped down rather awkwardly on his left buttock beside them.

"Being therefore justified by faith," the reverend began with a favorite quote, "Let us have peace with God through our Lord Jesus Christ."

Then they spoke the words of a well-remembered prayer together and, ever so slowly, the mood of the stricken president seemed to rally.

"Blessed Father in heaven, we thank you for sending your Son, Jesus, to die on the cross for us, and for His blood that was shed to redeem us and to cleanse our sins.

"Lord, we are sorry and we repent and we pray humbly for Your forgiveness. We understand that we must change the course of our lives.

We are determined in our hearts to follow only You.

"We invite You to become the Lord of our lives forever. We openly proclaim and confess that from henceforth You are so.

"We believe that You have been raised from the dead and that therefore we are saved and are new creatures. The old things have passed and all things have become new. We are the children of God.

"In the name of Jesus, Amen."

They remained silent for a moment and the president wiped his tired eyes.

"OK, George, what in hell is going on with you?" the reverend asked.

There was no reply.

"Come on, hon, Kirby came a long way," Laura urged, "If you won't speak to him how can he help."

The president raised his head and stared mutely into the face of his beloved, his lips and chin trembling to control the incipient tears.

"I . . am persecuted . . and . . and pursued," he managed at last.

"Pursued by what?" the investment banker demanded with fraying patience.

"By . . by . . blood."

"Whose damn blood?"

The president's brow furrowed as his mind strained for clarification.

"Just . . plain old blood," he said with a shrug and offered a silly sideways self-deprecating smile, "Gobs of blood . . and . . and . . that bastard Cheney!"

§

Michael was unable to go back to sleep, not least because of the constant chatter and commotion in the hallway outside his door, and eventually realized he was ravenously hungry. He had nothing to eat since yesterday's lunchtime pie, so he showered and dressed and went downstairs to the lobby. The morning clerk with the rosacea was there again and greeted him with undisguised curiosity.

"Everything OK today, sir?" he lisped.

"Yes, thank you very much, no problem."

"What did the effing dicks want?"

Michael was momentarily stunned by the boldness of the question.

"Ah, the effing dicks, yes. They were wondering if they should arrest me for a double murder but thought better of it."

The young man gave him a ladylike gaze of interrogation while scratching his flaking scalp, then let out a strange braying wheezing sort of laugh at the assumed joke and didn't enquire further. Michael could hear sporadic snorts of amusement all the way to the street.

He looked for any sign of 'Nikolai' and there was none but after careful scrutiny he noticed someone sitting in the driver's seat of a car halfway down the block and set off nonchalantly toward breakfast. It was only a dozen steps from the Belleclaire entrance to Broadway and he turned as he got to the corner and cast a subtle glance back and as he suspected a man was getting out.

Now he came to think of it he wasn't sure Arty's Deli would do eggs and bacon quite the way he fancied, and he wanted to see whether his new shadow was expecting him to go there, so he ducked quickly into the Manhattan Diner where he met with Perretti and Gonzalez. It was almost directly opposite the hotel and he walked straight to a vacant rear booth without waiting to be seated. There was no way the man could have seen him enter and the booth allowed a reasonably clear view of the front window and the door. He saw the man hurry past and was just about to congratulate himself for losing him when he reappeared and came in. Well, of course, it was obvious, he told himself. He was no longer to be seen on the street and where else could he have gone. So much for the cloak and dagger stuff.

An older gruffer waitress, clearly not the kind to enthuse about cinnamon rolls, arrived with a menu and a glass of iced water and eyed him critically.

"Sign says 'Please wait to be seated', sir."

"Yes, yes, sorry, I was being followed."

It clearly failed to impress her or even penetrate her consciousness.

"You want coffee?"

"Yes, please. Thank you."

The man was waiting at the front counter but Michael couldn't tell where he was looking because of his dark glasses so decided to eat first and test him later. He seemed strangely familiar but it wasn't until Michael had half finished his bacon and eggs that he remembered he had been in the Dublin House.

§

"You chose the man, George," the reverend said, "It seems to me that means you have no earthly choice but to live with him. What in heck has he done that's so wrong?"

Alas, George knew that to provide the barest beginning of an answer to the question would have been to end both a presidency and a marriage at a stroke.

"I just want . . I just need the visions to stop," he replied.

At that moment the National Security Advisor popped her head in and said she had Aliyev, the Azerbaijani president, waiting on the line in the Oval Office for the last five minutes.

"If we want him in the coalition you better come now."

The president nodded and obeyed. He was more than relieved to escape.

"I've never ever seen him like this," Laura confided when they had gone, "It almost makes me want to laugh it's so bad."

"It does have its funny side," the ever-attentive boardmember of Continental Airlines agreed, "How long has it been going on?"

"I thought he acted a bit strange the day and night of the tragedy and, of course, the last few weeks have been terrible so I put everything down to that but since lunch on Saturday it's got way, way worse and so fast it's making my head spin."

"Has he described the visions he talked about?"

"No. Just blood. And Dick. Blood and Dick. I think he sometimes feels that Dick overshadows him. He's not a very confident man, you know, and Dick can be kind of overwhelming."

"He's been through a difficult time. We've all been through a difficult time. I think he just cares too much about everyone."

"I know. Isn't he a wonderful guy?"

Kirbyjon put his big black hands on her shoulders and lovingly kissed away a tear from her cheek.

§

Since he had nothing particular to occupy his time until six o'clock and as the weather was clear and bracing Michael decided to take a stroll down the length of Broadway to Times Square to see if the stilt man might be there. He would find a booth to phone Warren and ask how things were going with the transport of the corpses. His shadow was perched on a revolving stool at the front counter and was nursing an espresso. Michael poked him on the shoulder and nodded with his head to follow as he left.

As he walked he wondered whether he should contact Perretti and Gonzalez to see if any more visions had appeared to them but he thought it wasn't very likely. Surely the materialization of Richard Bruce Lugosi in a vampire suit beneath the towers had been something to do with the location. The overwhelming pressure of subcutaneous or subterranean or even subatomic guilt. It seemed sensible that such phenomena would only become manifest to people who believed in the culpability of those whom the visions implicated. Perretti and Gonzalez had claimed neutrality about the vice-president but they certainly had growing suspicion about the sinister motives lurking behind the whole business and, as far as he knew, David and Lamy and himself were the only other people who had provably been aware of any of the other peculiarities and they had never been in doubt about the real perpetrators.

No, wait, there was Fernando. He poohed-poohed all conspiracy and yet he could see the blood in the Cheney photograph. And what about the general? Was he right in feeling McWhirter too had seen the sign with the name flashing across it at the racetrack? He should have asked Brandy if she had seen it instead of being coy about his blasted double identity.

What about the utterly extraordinary appearances of Cheney behind bars and then with Rumsfeld, Kissinger and Rice at the memorial service? Was it possible he and Lamy were the only people who saw them? And how was it that they had seen exactly the same thing? It was inconceivable unless the four were actually present at Ground Zero in some inexplicably transhuman fashion. Surely, if it was the morbid joke of some Carnivore hacker then thousands of viewers must have seen them.

When he reached Lincoln Center he decided to give his mind a break from these imponderables and made a diversion across the plaza to see what was playing at the Met. He was very fond of opera. It was one of the greatest disappointments of his life that his voice, however pleasant the timbre of his everyday speech, had never been able to produce more than an unmelodious croak when he attempted to carry a tune.

The performance that evening was Verdi's 'Luisa Miller', a work about which he knew very little other than that it was based on a play by Schiller and concerned a count who had risen to power by murdering his cousin. But the night before it had been the glorious 'La Boheme' directed by

Franco Zeffirelli and starring the ravishing Romanian soprano Angela Gheorghiu as Mimi and her husband Roberto Alagna as Rodolfo. He had seen them in the same roles at Covent Garden some ten years previously and how he would love to have attended this production.

"Che gelida manina! Se la lasci riscaldar.. "

He launched into Rodolfo's aria at the top of his lungs and two elderly ladies seated on a bench waiting for the box office to open turned to look at him without expression and put their fingers in their ears.

"Ah, Mimi . . *mia bella* Mimi!"

Though he could talk forever without tiring, even so brief an attempt as this strained his vocal chords to raggedness. He remembered the pained expression on the singing coach's face at Rose Bruford and swallowed sadly. Someone behind him was applauding and he swung round at the noise to see his shadow leaning on a wall twenty paces away with a cigarette dangling from his mouth.

"Bravissima," the man mouthed sarcastically at the last slow clap.

"You may have to pay for that," Michael threatened with a dry rasp, "You might be amused but I am not, I promise you. I told your other half that yesterday. If you keep it up I'm going to introduce you to Count Dracula."

The man stubbed out the butt beneath his foot with an unmistakable gesture of Latin indifference and Michael returned his insolent stare for a long moment before nodding a polite farewell to his aged critics.

"Ladies," he said, but they were rummaging in their bags for breadcrumbs to feed a gathering flock of obliviously strutting pigeons and barely noticed.

He continued on to Columbus Circle and tried to shake his somber mood by risking life and limb in a mad dash through the whirligig of taxis and buses to get onto the hub below the statue. His shadow didn't bother to give chase and watched from the safety of the Time Warner building.

Michael shaded his eyes to squint at Columbus on his pedestal and thought he looked more than a bit swish standing there hand on hip in his Genoese gown. He had to read the plaque beneath several times before he could make head or tail of its meaning.

"To Christopher Columbus. The Italians resident in America . . "

Yes, all right, he assumed they had passed the hat round to pay for it.

"Scoffed at before, during the voyage menaced, after it, chained, as generous as oppressed, to the world he gave a world."

Ah, he said to himself at last, it all refers to Columbus and not the Italians. But 'as generous as oppressed' was pure revisionism. Michael knew that after his third voyage both he and his brothers were arrested on Hispaniola for committing atrocities and returned to Spain for the barbaric and indiscriminate use of torture. But Ferdinand and Isabella pardoned him after only a few weeks in jail and he died a wealthy man.

There was another monument on the other side of the circle at the corner of Central Park and Michael decided to give it a look as well. It was enjoyable keeping his tail on his toes.

He was amused to discover it was yet another piece of historical mendacity. A memorial to those who perished on the USS Maine, an American battleship that sank in Havana harbor on February 15th, 1898. President McKinley was quick to blame it on a Spanish mine and dubbed it an 'unprovoked attack', thereby arousing the ire of the always gullible American public and allowing him to declare war on Spain even though the captain of the ship swore the cause was simply an explosion in the coal bin.

There was a plaque cast in metal from the ship bearing the improbable image of an ancient Greek warrior complete with shield and an inscription to the valiant seamen, 'by fate unwarned, in death unafraid,' who died that others might be free. 'Lordy, lordy,' he mused, 'The usual guff.'

He could cite dozens of examples. The motive is always transparent and yet ignorance remains wilfully spellbound. Hitler used the same ploy in a Gliwice radio station on August 31st, 1939, and three days later his Panzers stormed into Poland. Lyndon Johnson used a phony torpedo incident in the Gulf of Tonkin to gain congressional approval for his escalation of the war in Viet Nam and now the neo-cons had come up with a vicious charade of their own to trump them all.

As he continued down Broadway into the theater district it was possible to read a double meaning into every marquee. 'Mamma Mia!' No kidding, he thought. 'The Rocky Horror Show.' 'Les Miserables.' 'The Phantom of the Opera.' 'The Producers.' Springtime for Hitler, indeed. 'Thou Shalt Not.' 'The Dance of Death.'

Where had he read that the two British stars of Strindberg's masterpiece had been bumped from an appearance on 'Charlie Rose' so Charlie could interview Henry Kissinger?

Beyond Times Square at 43rd Street he laughed out loud at 'Urinetown' and couldn't resist going for a closer look. It was playing at the Henry

Miller. He didn't know but assumed the theater must be named in honor of the author of 'Tropic of Cancer'. Miller was a New Yorker, wasn't he? How would he have characterized the perennial blindspot of humankind? 'Tropic of the Myopic'?

'Urinetown' was a musical. Of course, he opined, doesn't everything in this country become one sooner or later? He found out from a bystander it was about a water shortage so severe that a law gets passed barring the use of toilets in private homes. The populace must use public conveniences only or face prosecution and these were now the monopoly of the ruthless Caldwell B. Cladwell. Which merely proved the truism, the bystander added without a trace of irony, that there's always some nattily-dressed son of a bitch who can shake a profit from other people's distress. There was a song in it, the poster said, titled 'It's a Privilege to Pee' which made Michael laugh again and realize he was suddenly feeling the need.

He hurried on to look for an available coffee shop, crooking his finger at his shadow in a 'follow me' gesture.

"Let's go," he said, "The next one is 'Dracula, the Musical'."

This inevitable concoction had recently been staged in California but was not as yet destined for the Great White Way.

There was a Starbucks on the corner and, though their ubiquity was nearly as offensive as those abominable hamburger chains, he thought he might manage to avail himself of the restroom without being accosted by some officious waitress. It was crowded but amazingly enough the facility was free. As his bladder emptied he wondered whether the name was a reference to Melville's mate of the Pequod or Nash's rainmaker or was it that the bucks being made outnumbered the stars in the sky.

His shadow was waiting at the door and followed to the corner of 42nd Street and Seventh Avenue but the stilt man was nowhere to be seen.

Down 42nd a huge billboard of Disney's 'The Lion King' adorned the New Amsterdam theater and a neon sign proclaimed New York's 'Madame Tussaud's'. It beckoned above the competitive garish clutter and he went along in that direction thinking he might as well catch the subway back uptown from the Port Authority Bus Station at Eighth and to his delight and surprise, as he wandered through the cavernous mall within it, he bumped straight into 'Lon Cheney' courageously plying his eloquent message amid the passing bustle near a shop with red banners outside on which Noah's dove was depicted holding its olive branch.

He stopped to stare in renewed admiration and the man recognized him and stopped still too. Michael turned to his shadow and pointed meaningfully up at the 'vampire' and the white-faced figure gasped and threw its palms wide in terror.

"I come in peace," Michael assured him, "Can I buy you lunch?"

§

The general's office in Arlington was conveniently located not more than a five iron shot from the Army Navy Country Club of which he was an honorary life member. It was just another mile down the Henry G. Shirley Memorial Highway to the Pentagon and two miles up Glebe Road to the El Paso Café on North Pershing Drive. The heart of Arlington is the National Cemetery, as everyone knows, and he had a choice plot picked out for himself amongst the fallen comrades of Operation Desert Storm.

The El Paso had become famous almost overnight because the president and his wife ate supper there two weeks after the horrors. The president had enjoyed a cheese enchilada and the First Lady chicken fajitas. They told the waitress they'd surely come back soon and left her a fifty-dollar tip.

The general was sitting at the table graced by the presidential party though not on the same chair as the president. That had been whisked away by the owners, painted red, white and blue and was now hanging from the ceiling above a mural of a saguaro tree and two sombreros. He was sipping a double Hornitos margarita and mulling over the call he received two minutes ago from Michael's shadow. Why in hell would Bartolomeo Vespucci be at the Chock Full O'Nuts in the food court of the Times Square Hilton with a known dissident and perennial troublemaker eating a date-nut bread and cream cheese sandwich and drinking a peach iced tea?

He had positioned himself with a view of the entrance and since the dial on his Panerai Luminor submersible wristwatch told him it was thirteen minutes past noon he was expecting her at any moment but the perplexity caused by the phone call was suddenly compounded on seeing Louis Lamy walk through it with his tall gaunt aristocratic-looking twin.

Lamy caught his eye and they came over to the table.

"Larry, meet my brother Pascal."

"A pleasure," the general said, half standing to shake his hand, "What brings you to Washington?"

"Lunch," Pascal replied with chilly *hauteur*, "Or, rather, for me it is dinner. I have arrived from Luxembourg less than one hour ago."

"Can I buy you both a drink?" McWhirter asked pleasantly.

"Another time," Lamy said, "We haven't had much chance to catch up lately and I've got a date with our buddy Davenport at six in Manhattan."

The general's eyes narrowed.

"He's quite a character."

"That he is," Lamy concurred, "Did you know the other guy's dead?"

"What other guy?"

"Shot his mouth off. Sister died in the tower. That one."

"Dead? How?"

"Bernie Kerik told me suicide but my guess is murder. Him and his lover together. Surprised you didn't know."

"Why in hell would I?" the general responded levelly.

Condoleezza entered on the word 'lover' but he was too occupied to notice her change direction and make a beeline for the powder room.

"I got the feeling Davenport interested you. I can't believe he fit in too well at the party. I know you put a tail on him. What I don't know is who for. People like us don't really retire, do they?"

They both smiled and the general looked at Pascal.

"Was he always such a conceited son of a bitch?" he asked jokingly, nodding his head at Lamy, and then turned back, "I'd love to humor you, Lou, but you're dead wrong. I didn't know a thing about it."

Lamy laughed.

"Too many secrets are bad for the bowels."

"Thanks for the tip. I'll give you a call sometime. Enjoy your stay in our little town, Pascal," McWhirter said with a wink in farewell.

"I will. There is always something to amuse the mind if not the soul."

They walked away and the general's gray eyes followed them with concern. Lamy was about to get his answer because there was Condi on her way toward him but then he thought, fuck it, so what.

"Did you see who that was?" he asked as she sat down.

"No, who?"

"Lamy."

"No shit."

"With his snot-nose of a brother. Fresh in from Luxembourg."

"That was quick. He was at the EU council early this morning. Chris

Patten's on the Commission with him. Hates his guts."

"I never could stomach that lofty French horseshit either. Lamy asked about Davenport. He knows we're shadowing him. Now he's seen you he'll know why."

"What will he know? Our interest in it? How?"

"What if they've talked? What if Lamy knows about four years ago? What if all of fucking Europe knows?"

"What if they do? They're not going to come right out and say it."

"Some of them might."

"So? They'll get trashed as fanatics like everyone else."

A waitress arrived for her drink order.

"It's about time," she said, "I want a Vampire's Kiss and make it snappy."

Stanza Thirteen

the future is ours just forget it
we've pampered and powdered and pet it
we've feathered our bed
with soft skins of the dead
necrophilistine perverts don't sweat it

§

"I know who Bartolomeo Vespucci is."

"Who?" Michael asked.

It had taken an amazingly short time for 'Lon Cheney' and he to get to know each other. His real name was Maxwell Forman and he was an actor and mime who sometimes worked for the various avant-garde theater companies that always spring up like mushrooms in places like New York but who mostly did his own thing on the street. He had been performing a solo work at the Pompidou Center in Paris on 9/11 but hurried home because, like Michael, he knew instantly who the culprits were and how difficult it would be to get anyone to believe it.

Michael told him about Enigma and the apparitions and sketched in the events that led to him being followed. His shadow was sipping yet another espresso at a table not fifteen feet away.

"Him," Maxwell said, pointing at the man.

Michael smiled at the outlandish idea and turned to face him.

"Yes, well, I grant you he certainly does look Italian. What's your name, by the way? We've decided you're Italian."

"Nikolai."

"Oh no, Nikolai was last night."

"We are all Nikolai."

"Very funny. My friend here thinks you're Bartolomeo Vespucci."

The man's face beneath his sunglasses seemed suddenly pale.

"Maybe him too," he responded, but with a peculiar lack of conviction.

"Gosh, you're funny as a barrel of monkeys. The existential Mafioso. That's what you are, isn't it?"

"I am what you wish."

Michael turned to his new companion.

"What can you do with such irrefutable logic?"

Maxwell was smiling.

"He's right. That's exactly what I meant."

Michael was momentarily befuddled.

"What?"

"That he's necessary but you don't know why. We'll never know why."

"What, like God? Even if he doesn't exist it was necessary to invent him?"

"In a way, but not really God or Jesus. More like their antimatter correlate."

Michael was silent. He'd heard a lot of drivel in his life but this was starting to take the whole loaf of nut bread.

"The glue that binds," Maxwell said by way of clarification.

Michael was finding it worrying that he never seemed to blink.

"Why would a gang of international drug-dealers need the 'glue that binds'? You sound like a blasted advertisement."

"The grease that makes the wheels spin smoothly."

"Christ almighty, glue, grease, next you'll be saying the gum that never stops giving. What the fuck are you talking about?"

"Just trying to help. Every chemical reaction needs a catalyst."

"What, you mean they couldn't have done it without me? You might as well say everyone is necessary. That we're all Bartolomeo Vespucci. That all's for the best in this best of all possible worlds. To say it is to say nothing."

Maxwell smiled and shrugged.

"We should change the subject. Your shadow here is tailing you to report back to someone what you're doing. He made a call as we were ordering."

Maxwell had eaten a veggie wrap with a cup of New York Decaf.

"I know. I'm not entirely daft."

"Maybe he isn't your guy Vespucci," Maxwell went on, "Maybe that's who was at the other end of the line."

"No, I've got a pretty good idea who that was."

"If it was anyone at all."

"Don't be stupid."

"It's a prerequisite for working at the Ontological-Hysteric theater."

"Cute name, whatever it's supposed to mean. But look, enough buggering about, I want to know how people in the street react to you. I'm stunned that there haven't been demonstrations. A mass uprising. Lynch mobs descending on Capitol Hill."

"You should check out Union Square. That's where the action is."

"I will, thanks. Tell me this. We haven't talked about this one. Did you go to the memorial service at Ground Zero after I saw you on Sunday?"

"No."

"Did you see the reports of it on television?"

"Don't have one. But I know what you're going to tell me. I have friends who saw it too."

Michael was thrilled.

"What did they see?"

"That Cheney was on the screen screaming from behind bars. That Kissinger and Rice, Rumsfeld and Cheney were dancing about behind the speakers holding 'fuck you' signs."

"That's it exactly! How many people you know saw them?"

"Maybe two. Two different groups."

"So were they there or not?"

"What, you mean at the service?"

"That too, but were the four of them actually there or were they an illusion? And if they were an illusion, why did we all see the same thing?"

"No one I know who was at the service saw anything. My friends who told me about it saw it on television."

"So it could have been rigged. Or selective somehow. But how?"

"I don't think it's either. It's beyond that."

"Explain."

"They're transhuman phenomena."

"Like ESP, ghosts, action at a distance, the general heading 'paranormal'?"

"Obviously. Transhuman but with a human cause."

"The subcutaneous pressure of overwhelming guilt pushing up like pus from a pimple."

Maxwell chuckled.

"Cool. I love it. How else can you explain it? I've got friends who've had stuff happen like the thing with Cheney's picture. I've got a feeling there's a whole lot of that going on. Someone told me there's a photograph circulating on the Internet of Mount Rushmore with the four of them and they say it's not a fake."

"Of course I've heard of Mount Rushmore but what is it precisely?"

"Some guy named Borglum and his son carved four president's faces into a mountain in South Dakota. Washington, Jefferson, Lincoln and Teddy Roosevelt, I think. Between the wars. It pissed off the local Sioux enough to put up something like it with Crazy Horse instead."

"And the faces have turned into Cheney, Rumsfeld, Kissinger and Rice?"

"Not permanently. Probably only for a second or two. But someone caught it happening on camera."

"How big is this thing?"

"Enormous. I don't know, a hundred feet high. At least. And solid granite."

Michael started to laugh at the wondrousness of it.

"How absolutely, utterly fantastic. So, how do people react to you? I have to say I admire your courage."

Maxwell was still in his costume and makeup though without the cape and hat and wig and sharply filed false teeth he didn't look all that alarming. His sign was folded against the wall behind their table.

"Most do their best to ignore me. Religious people get upset and say it's a sacrilege and disrespectful to the dead and the real airheads call me a pinko commie faggot traitor and yell I should be strung up or stoned to death or have my balls cut off. Very few get it or agree. At least not vocally."

"Why? When it's so obvious. Like watching the Magruder tape or the towers fall. I find the lack of reaction even more astonishing than all the weird stuff."

"I believe it's called the engineering of consent. Goes back to Bernays and way beyond. Bread and circuses. You name it."

"*Béarnaise?* Who was he? I thought he invented steak sauce."

"Ha ha, no, different guy. Edward Bernays was Freud's nephew. Brought his ideas about manipulating public opinion to the States. Became the guru of Madison Avenue. Inspired Goebbels and every hooey salesman since."

Michael had always been a slow ruminative eater and washed down his last bite of sandwich.

"Fascinating. It's like a Dali painting or Krazy Kat comic where a cannonball goes right through someone's stomach and you can see the world on the other side through the hole but the victim doesn't even notice. So you haven't personally seen any of these transhuman manifestations?"

"Nope. Reality is weird enough for me."

"Good lord, yes, I know what you mean."

Michael took out his billfold and extracted an Enigma card.

"I'll be here for another week or so at the Hotel Belleclaire."

He started fumbling in his shoulder-bag for a pen to write the name on the back but Maxwell said he knew it.

"I'd love to talk to you some more but I have to phone and find out about a funeral and maybe go down to the Village and then I'm meeting someone at six. Do you know Warren Allen Jones, by the way?"

"Of course. He's famous. Ask him about Bernays. He did an interview in the Voice with him before he died. Bernays was a hundred or something like that. I took an art class with Warren in the '70s."

"What about Louis Lamy?"

"Yeah, I've heard of him. Rich bastard. But he helped a friend of mine become a successful novelist. Hal Jason France."

"Don't know the name."

"Spooky thrillers. I've never liked them."

"So what will you do with the rest of your day?"

"Keep on walking. I've got a gig next week in Minneapolis."

"What doing?"

"A mime show. I call it 'Humpty Dumpty'."

"Is that what you were performing in Paris?"

"Yeah, I've taken it a lot of places. West Africa even."

"What's it about?"

"Whatever I want. I've never done it the same twice. In Minneapolis I think Humpty'll be George Bush."

"A fabulous idea. What about him? How much was he part of it?"

"Who the heck knows. My take on him is that, like Humpty, he shouldn't be misunderestimated."

Michael laughed in agreement.

"Do you have a phone so I can keep in touch?"

"Nope. No TV, no phone, no computer. But, hey, I do go to the movies."

§

Michael watched his strange new acquaintance with admiration as he expertly remounted his stilts leaning on the facade of a Money Exchange outside the Hilton entrance, reassumed his identity as 'Lon Cheney' and strode off without a backward glance toward his more customary station at the corner of Broadway. He couldn't help but wonder if Lamy had known who he was when they passed him on their way to Ground Zero. He was irritated with himself that the presence of 'Nikolai' had stopped him from mentioning David and Fernando's murder because Maxwell might well have known them and been able to shed his own peculiar light on it. Everyone seemed to know something about everyone else in this dreamscape. And what could one make of the Mount Rushmore phenomenon? It epitomized the whole bizarre business. Two separate realities. Two different universes maybe, how could one know?

His shadow was smoking by the curb twenty feet away and Michael suddenly noticed the giant clock above his head was tilted thirty degrees counterclockwise out of vertical and laughed at its eloquent confirmation of this topsy-turvy world.

§

It was nearly half past two as he leaned sideways to read the time and on the stage of Thomas S. Wootten High School auditorium in Rockville, Maryland, a surprisingly calm and unruffled president was in the middle of his address to the student body. He had managed to banish the horrors from his mind temporarily and dropped off for a twenty-minute snooze in the presidential limo on the way.

The relatively affluent suburbs in the rolling hills of Montgomery County, where native agriculturalists had cultivated sunflowers and marsh elder for millenia before invading Senecas and Susquehannocks gradually depleted their numbers and they disappeared altogether in the 1700's beneath wave after wave of European settlement, had voted two out of three for Al Gore in the disputed 2000 election but that was of secondary importance to the president's handlers. The subject of his talk was patriotism and it was being broadcast live on CNN.

"We're a nation of patriots," he began, acknowledging the applause from the assembly, smiling down at the enthusiastic faces of the marching band below him in their stovepipe toy tin-soldier hats and turning to nod his head at the dignitaries seated behind him on the flag-draped platform.

Members of the American Legion and the Veterans of Foreign Wars and the Military Order of the World Wars in their cheesecutters as well as the liberal Republican congresswoman for Maryland's 8th District, Connie Morella, who voted consistently against her party on abortion, gun control, gay rights, immigration and the environment and had been one of only five Republicans to oppose all four articles of impeachment against Bill 'Slick Willy' Clinton during the Monica Lewinsky scandal. Beside her sat Robert Dole who had given the introduction. The senator, a former presidential candidate and decorated war hero, had his right arm paralyzed by German machine gun fire in northern Italy in April, 1945. Beside him the Secretary for Veterans Affairs Anthony Principi, who once served on the destroyer USS Joseph P. Kennedy and commanded a river patrol in the Mekong Delta in Viet Nam, and the Secretary of Education Roderick Raynor 'Rod' Paige, who was in the classroom at Emma E. Booker Elementary in Sarasota, Florida, as Chief-of-Staff Card whispered in the president's ear that the second plane had smashed into the South Tower.

"The attacks of September the 11th," he went on, assuming an appropriately somber expression, "And the attacks that have followed were designed to break our spirit. But instead they have created a renewed spirit of patriotism in America. We see it in the countless flags that are flying everywhere. We hear it in familiar phrases that move us more deeply than ever before.

"We know that this is one nation under God and we pray that God will bless America, the land that we love, regardless of our race or religion or where we live.

"We have a renewed appreciation of the character of America. Our country has been an incredibly generous country, the most generous country in the world. We're generous with our universities, we're generous with our job opportunities, we're generous with the . . "

His face went momentarily blank and something internal made him shudder but then he recovered the thread of his speech.

"What a beautiful system it is, that if you come here and you work hard, you can achieve a dream. Never did we realize that people would take advantage of our generosity in the way they have. That our enemies have no values that regard life as precious. They hate what America stands for. They hate our success. They hate our liberty.

"We are a generous people, a thoughtful people, who hurt and share the sadness when people lose their life or when people are hurt. As we pursue the enemy in Afghanistan, we feed the innocent. As we try to bring justice to those who have harmed us, we find those who need help. We have helped each other in every way we know, in donations, in acts of kindness, in public memorials, in private prayer. We have shown in difficult times that we're not just a world power but a good and kind and courageous people.

"On the Korean War Memorial in Washington are these words, 'Freedom is not free.' Our commitment to freedom has always made us a target of tyranny and intolerance. Anyone who wants to destroy freedom must eventually attack America because we're freedom's home and we must always be freedom's defender .. "

He stopped for the applause and took a sip of water.

"We gave those who harbor the Al Qaeda organization ample opportunity to respond to reasonable demands. Our nation's demands were just and they were fair. We said very simply, 'Turn over Al Qaeda, send the terrorists out of your land, let the innocent Americans and other hostages you hold in Afghanistan go free and destroy all Al Qaeda training camps.' And they chose the wrong course and they will now pay the price .. "

More applause.

"This country has always been able to count on men and women of great courage. From the day America was founded 48 million have worn the uniform of the United States. More than 25 million are living today, some of whom are with us at Wootten High and you may know some of them in your families.

"I know one such veteran. He fought in World War II like Senator Dole. My dad."

He acknowledged the ovation and a genuine tear misted his eyes but beneath it all, despite the massively positive feedback, he could feel himself running out of steam and the nervousness and uncertainty crept in again and he began to sweat into the armpits of his dark gray suit.

'Oh God,' he prayed, 'No more visions!'

"We must remember that many who served in our military never lived to be called veterans. We must remember that many had their lives changed forever by the experiences or the injuries of combat. All veterans are examples of service and citizenship for every American to remember and follow.

"In twelve days, on Veteran's Day, we will honor them. We will remember the Bob Doles of the world. We will remember a generation that liberated Europe and Asia and put an end to concentration camps. We will . ."

He could hear his voice continuing to speak about service and sacrifice and courage and the hard lessons every new generation must learn about liberty and the challenge of the mission but his heart and mind were far away.

'Oh please, dear God, no more visions! I beg You let me get to the end of this bull without them! Who cares about global supremacy anyway?! Only my father and his bigshot corporate cronies who sneer behind my back! And that pasty-faced sidewinder sack of shit Cheney!'

§

The ophidian quirks of the 46th vice-president were also very much on the mind of the hairy fat man born in the Year of the Pig, a disciple of Metternich and the Viscount Castlereagh, who was at that precise moment sitting beneath a portrait of the Emperor Franz Joseph and his wife Sisi at a secluded corner table in the Restaurant Imperial in Vienna. Tiny bubbles of slaver on his lower lip glistened in the muted glow as he watched renowned executive chef Hans Jürgen Schauer serve his famous fillet of turbot with goose liver with *Maître D'* Reinhard Christ standing stiffly to one side.

He left his sanctuary in Kent, Connecticut, early Sunday morning and had flown by private jet to the Austrian capital at the invitation of President Klestil and Chancellor Schüessel in order to chair and moderate a variety of panel discussions on global media issues at an elite worldwide forum of communications executives such as Greg Dyke of the BBC, Fedele Confalonieri of Mediaset, Edgar Bronfman Jr. of Vivendi Universal, Robert Hormats of Goldman Sachs, Joel Klein of Bertelsmann and Vice-Minister of the Chinese State Council Information Office, Gouqing Wang, and, though he would much rather have hurried home on this final day and gone straight to Yankee Stadium to catch the last few innings of the game, he had reluctantly accepted an invitation from Conrad Black. Black was newly titled the Baron of Crossharbour since renouncing his Canadian citizenship and neither he nor his journalist wife Barbara Amiel were much to be recommended as dinner companions but as it happened he was secretly plotting to dump both of them in a legal morass which would provide an entertaining *schadenfreude* to their chitchat and they had promised the still handsome Dina Merrill, now vice-chairman of RKO pictures, would complete the quartet.

The Year of the Snake, 2001, had been an unpredictable *annus periculosus* for the Nobel Peace Prize winner from Fürth, Bavaria, and was only now beginning to show signs of improvement thanks to the distraction of 9/11.

His difficulties began in February with the serialization in Harper's magazine of an article by Christopher Hitchens entitled 'The Case Against Henry Kissinger' which was subsequently expanded and published in book form in May as 'The Trial of Henry Kissinger'. Hitchens accused the former National Security Advisor of war crimes, crimes against humanity and genocide, and rumor had it negotiations were already underway for the film rights, so it was not without reason he identified with Viscount Castlereagh and had even gone so far as to imagine a facial resemblance with the revered Irish Presbyterian and co-subject of his Harvard doctoral thesis. Castlereagh was also reputed to be a hugely successful diplomat and had been, with Metternich, the guiding force behind the Congress of Vienna which in 1814 had redrawn the map of Europe in a form which essentially lasted for the next hundred years but he was loathed in England on the domestic front and vilified by the poet Shelley thus: -

"I met Murder on the way.

He had a face like Castlereagh.

Very smooth he looked, yet grim.

Seven bloodhounds followed him.

All were fat and well they might

Be in admirable plight

For one by one and two by two

He tossed them human hearts to chew

Which from his wide cloak he drew."

And Byron thus in a mocking epitaph: -

"Posterity will ne'er survey

A nobler grave than this.

Here lie the bones of Castlereagh.

Stop, traveler, and piss."

Doggerel and unconscionably unfair rubbish groused the one-time sergeant of the 970th Counter Intelligence Corps and then congratulated himself that such was frequently the fate of those who are ahead of their time. He also knew he was made of sterner stuff than the delicate lord.

Castlereagh had been driven to slit his throat with a letter opener on August 12th, 1822.

What Hitchens claimed was that he had subtly undermined the peace talks in Viet Nam in 1968 in order to increase the chances of Richard Nixon becoming the 37th president thereby causing more than half the American casualties in the war by prolonging it, not to mention millions more throughout Indochina since he was the undoubted *eminence grise* behind Nixon's merciless bombing of Laos and Cambodia. Also, in 1971, against the advice of the National Security Council, he had supported General Yahya Khan in Bangladesh which resulted in the murder of five hundred thousand civilians when Khan overthrew the democratically elected government. Third, that he was deeply involved in the destruction of Salvador Allende's socialist experiment in Chile in the early 1970's and, among many others, the murder of General René Schneider during a botched kidnapping in the streets of Santiago in 1970 and the assassination of Marcos Orlando Letelier del Solar, who had served successively as Allende's Minister of Foreign Affairs, Interior and Defense, in a car-bombing in Washington in 1976. And last, by refusing to recognize the legitimate nationalistic aspirations of the people of East Timor after their independence from Portugal, and giving tacit approval to the corrupt Suharto regime, he had indirectly caused the slaughter of yet another quarter million innocently yearning souls.

The musical satirist Tom Lehrer quipped that political lampoon had become obsolete when he won the Nobel Peace Prize with Le Duc Tho for negotiating the ceasefire in Viet Nam in 1973, an award Politburo member Tho rejected but the great-great-grandson of Meyer Löb accepted 'with humility'. He was thick-skinned about jibes and accustomed to controversy, he had to decline an endowed chair at Columbia University in New York in 1977 because of unrelenting student protests, but never before had he experienced anything quite like this.

On May 31st while he was staying at the Ritz Hotel in Paris, on the heels of the publication of Hitchens' book, a French judge named Roger Le Loire requested a summons served in order to question him about American involvement in the brutal campaign of murder, kidnapping and sabotage during the 1970's, not only in Chile but also Paraguay, Uruguay, Brazil, Bolivia and Argentina, that was known as Operation Condor and he was forced to flee the country.

Then in August an Argentine judge named Rodolfo Canicoba sent a letter to the State Department requesting a deposition from him about the same events.

And on September 10th a civil suit was filed in Washington against him and then CIA-Director Richard Helms by the two sons of General Schneider asserting that he and Helms had given the order for their father's murder and demanding a settlement of three million dollars.

And on September 11th, twenty-eight years to the day after the *coup d'état*, a group of Chilean human rights lawyers filed a criminal case against him, along with General Augusto Pinochet, former Bolivian general and president Hugo Banzer, former Argentine dictator Jorge Rafael Videla and former president of Paraguay Alfredo Stroessner, on behalf of fifteen victims of the same clandestine operation.

Further, he had just received advance warning from Paul Bremer, his former managing director at Kissinger Associates, that the Brazilian government was about to renege on a lucrative forthcoming speaking engagement in São Paolo because they could not guarantee him immunity from judicial action.

Heinz Alfred took only small comfort from his recent creation with fellow Defense Policy Board members Richard Perle and Gerald Hillman of a Delaware-registered company called Trireme Partners that was about to make a killing in the current successfully orchestrated escalation of the 'war on terrorism' and the long-planned conquest of Iraq, despite the fact that Bremer was chairman of a National Commission on the subject, because the vice-president was being incomprehensibly cavalier in handling the public scrutiny about his conflict of interest as ex-CEO of Halliburton. The corporation was paying him a million dollars a year collectable at the end of his term in office and the indirect result was that it now risked exposure for padding its budget and fleecing the Pentagon of many millions more.

Worse than that, a coded fax had been delivered to his suite before breakfast that morning. Its origin was Little Odessa in Brighton Beach, though it had taken a necessarily circuitous route, and it contained potentially disastrous news.

It was now almost certain, the message said, that Bartolomeo Vespucci was in New York and some rash fools around the vice-president were toying with the idea of eliminating him.

Stanza Fourteen

§

Michael dialed Warren's number from a booth at the Port Authority station but reached only his answering machine. He didn't mention Lamy's plan to drive them both to Kennedy the next day because he wasn't sure which of the two old mystery men might have suggested the arrangement. In any case, he was meeting Lamy again at six and presumably Lamy would tell him then so he made his way down to the subway thinking it might be a good idea to return to the Belleclaire for a nap. Who knew what the evening would entail?

His shadow sat directly opposite on the swaying car as it sped northwards, staring brazenly at him from behind his sunglasses. Michael could see the glint of his eyes and fancied the look seemed suddenly tired and even a trifle shy and got up and took the empty seat beside him.

"So, Nikolai," he said in the man's ear, just loud enough to be heard above the clatter, "Whereabouts in Italy are you from? Napoli? Brindisi? Palermo?"

Like last night's 'Nikolai', the man initially ignored him.

"Ever heard of Semion Mogilevich?"

He was the obese *capo di tutti capi* who mounted Amado Portillo's beautiful drunken sister Cecilia in El Paso.

"No? What about Vyacheslav Ivankov?"

It was hard to pronounce the name with any accuracy, especially for Michael, but he was the Russian *vor v zakone* of Brighton Beach who spent himself in the doppelganger of Dr. Rice.

"No, nothing? What about Alberto Anastasia?" Michael went on, arbitrarily pulling names from memory, "Sammy 'The Bulbul' Gravano? Rodolfo Giuliani?"

The man turned and looked at him with undisguised disdain.

"He's the mayor," he said.

Well, at least it had broken the ice.

"Ah, yes, silly me."

"And I'm not Italian."

He had a surprisingly cultivated accent now Michael came to notice it.

"You have to admit you look Italian."

"You look English."

"But I am English."

"If you say so."

"Saxon English."

The man paused as if he didn't understand and then said, "I think you're the Italian," and turned away.

"Who told you that?" Michael asked, trying to conceal his interest.

The man gave a small dismissive shrug but otherwise made no response.

"OK," Michael said, "Since you're not the Italian, does the quaint expression *'Bessmertnaya smert' nash vladelec'* ring any bells?"

"I don't understand Russian. I am Albanian."

Michael laughed out loud.

"Where have all the goodfellas gone?" he exclaimed, waving his hands at the graffiti-smothered ceiling in a gesture of mock despair, "Why are there no Italians in the mob any more? Why are you all Russians or Albanians or Jews?"

"Times have changed."

"So your name really is Nikolai."

"Of course. Why should I lie?"

"Why should any Nikolai lie?"

The man only grunted at Michael's awful attempt at alliterative humor.

"And it was Nikolai last night too?"

"You called him Nikolai. His real name is Vladimir."

Michael laughed again but his delight in the absurdity was starting to pall.

"All right then, why did you look strange in the coffee shop when I told you my companion thought you were Bartolomeo Vespucci?"

"He talked a lot of shit. You know you are this man."

The train was stopping at 72nd Street and Michael smiled wanly and decided it was useless to say more.

§

The harried president had returned to Washington from Rockville and after a meeting with three members of the House of Representatives, who wanted to discuss their new aviation security bill, he took a quick shower and now had his hand dutifully placed at his mother's elbow as they made their way slowly down the steps of the North Portico to the first of a line of waiting limousines with Laura and the Reverend Kirbyjon close behind. This second presidential entourage of the day was leaving for Andrews Air Force Base and the flight to New York and then the helicopter ride from Kennedy to Yankee Stadium.

Though he was not without curiosity he would probably have found it of only tangential interest that several previous aircraft once serving as Air Force One, FDR's 'Sacred Cow', Harry Truman's 'Independence', 'Columbine III' that Mamie Eisenhower named after the state flower of Colorado and 'SAM 26000' which had carried JFK to his death in Dealey Plaza, were all proudly on display in the National Museum of the United States Air Force at Wright-Patterson.

One of a phalanx of reporters gathered beyond the great marble pillars asked the casually-dressed Commander-in-Chief whether he preferred the Yankees or the Diamondbacks and he replied rather feebly that he just hoped the Series would go the full seven games but when another enquired after the health of his pitching arm he managed to conjure the semblance of his famous winning smile and leaned over as if to read an imaginary catcher's signals and mimed throwing the man a ball.

Condoleezza came hurrying down the stairs with the Cards a few moments later glancing at a text message she had just received from the general asking her to call and saying it was urgent. Once she was alone in her limo and the cavalcade of armorclad vehicles was well away from the White House grounds she speed-dialed his number.

"I just got a rocket from Doctor K saying he believes Davenport is Vespucci and that no one but no one is to touch him. He thinks Dick wants him out of the picture."

She was silent for a moment.

"I don't know where he got that idea. Dick agrees with him. OK, fine. If they both like it with their heads up their butts, fuck it, why should we care?"

"He's also demanding a list of everyone outside the circle who knows."

"Knows what?"

"Who Davenport is."

The overworked and undersatisfied Warrior Princess sighed heavily.

"That's fucking impossible."

"Sure is, chess pie, sure is."

"For the love of god, Larry, swallow before you go on."

The general swished his gums and took a big gulp.

"And stop with the soul food shit."

"OK, sugar plum."

"Fuck off."

"I told him about Lamy and the races and the dead homo and the fact that he's meeting Davenport again tonight."

"So?"

"I guess Lamy'd be number one on the list."

"A hit list? Don't be stupid."

"He should be. But people like Lamy don't worry him."

"No, duh. Come on, Larry, where are you going with this?"

"He's worried about my girls."

The graduate of St. Mary's Catholic Academy in Cherry Hills, Colorado, who was described by old flame Jasper Carrott as a 'ferocious kisser', let out a malicious squeal of laughter.

"That is your fucking problem, hornytoad!"

§

Michael was roused from the thick caress of afternoon slumber by insistent knocking and was puzzled, after staggering to the hotel room door and fumbling to open the security latch, to see not Lamy but a chuckling Warren.

"It's five past six," he said jovially, "We thought maybe you'd forgotten."

"Good god, sorry, I fell asleep. You'll have to give me a minute. What are you doing here? I tried to call you. Where are we going?"

"Put on something warm and come down when you're ready. Lou wants it to be a surprise."

Warren disappeared down the hall before Michael could ask more.

His brain was throbbing.

'Lou'? Is it 'Lou' now? Lou the blasted Lamia wants what to be a surprise?

§

The vice-president's Chief-of-Staff, 'Dick Cheney's Dick Cheney', who's investment banker father Irving Liebowitz nicknamed 'Scooter' after the Yankee's great shortstop, Phil Rizzuto, and who had also recently been dubbed 'Germ Boy' because of his obsession with universal smallpox vaccination, a subject on which he had expounded in a novel about a smallpox epidemic in Japan in 1903 which had received favorable comparison with the work of Hal Jason France in the New York Times book review not least because its author had been savvy enough to include saleable dollops of bestiality, pedophilia and rape, was positively hurtling down the steps of the Eisenhower Building. He sprinted across West Executive Avenue and dashed through the door into the West Wing where he made an immediate left turn and found his boss alone in his office in short shirtsleeves with tie loosened peering through an enlarging viewfinder at a film clip. It was no more than ten seconds in length but it had captured his image and blood cascading from between stony lips down the granite face of Mount Rushmore.

"The third tape's there again!" Libby whispered in breathless confusion.

A feverish clamminess on the vice-president's brow was evident to the jittery erstwhile legal counsel for defense contractor Northrop Grumman as he pulled his face back slowly from the eyepiece and looked up with a most peculiar expression flickering across his pallid features.

"I don't know how or who but it's been returned!"

"Well, that's good, isn't it?" the Metal Snake purred.

§

As Michael came out of the Belleclaire he was indeed surprised to see not the expected Mercedes wagon but a silver-haired and uniformed chauffeur holding open the rear door of a glistening white stretch limousine and gesturing him toward it. He came forward slowly and peered in. His new acquaintances were beside each other on the back seat with drinks in hand wearing the annoyingly bland expression of co-

conspirators.

"What are you looking at? We're late," Lamy barked.

"Mind your head, sir," the chauffeur said politely as Michael clambered in.

"Sorry, yes, I'm afraid I dropped off for a minute," Michael apologized and tried to make himself comfortable in the equally luxurious leather seat facing them.

Lamy handed a document from his breast pocket to the chauffeur.

"Yankee Stadium, Mike," he said, "Here's the security clearance."

The chauffeur nodded and closed the door.

"Third game of the Series," Lamy explained to Michael with a grin, "Our boy Dubya's tossing out the first pitch. Gotta see that."

Michael had to admit all possible aspects were exciting.

"Warren's on Perrier but I'm having a Manhattan. Want one?"

"Perhaps I'd better begin with water," Michael replied.

"Suit yourself."

Lamy opened a fresh bottle and handed it to him with a tumbler full of ice.

"Game won't start until around eight-thirty but it's going to be a zoo. Got over a thousand police officers assigned. Never been a Series that went so late in the year. Regular season got delayed in September."

Michael looked between their heads at the dimly lamplit street behind as the chauffeur drove away expecting some version or other of 'Nikolai' to pull out and follow but there was no one.

"Guess they called off your tail," Lamy observed.

"Since you seem to know everything," Michael said, looking at Lamy wryly, "Perhaps you'd like to tell me exactly who was having me followed. I spoke with their men. One was Russian, the other Albanian. Charming chaps. Clearly illegal. So who was it? And what are the two of you doing together? I didn't think you were friends."

"We're not," Warren assured him, chuckling, "But Ruth and David made the connection and he's not such a bad guy for a billionaire. This is a unique event. I've never had a box seat behind home plate before."

"I thought you'd enjoy his insights, Michael. They're very different from mine. Come on, don't be a sourpuss. I'll tell you whatever you want to know."

"OK, tell."

"I had lunch with my brother today as I told you. In D. C. We ran into

Larry McWhirter at a recently 'discovered' hole-in-the-wall in Arlington. The name will amuse you. The El Paso Café. He was with a young lady of your acquaintance. Our little National Security Advisor. Well, in fact, she came in while we were chatting and hotfooted it to the powder room. She didn't venture over to the general's table until Pascal and I had said our goodbyes. She ordered her favorite cocktail, an awful concoction of Juarez, that's the house tequila if you can believe it, with Chambord, cranberry and lime. Blood red. Bet you can't guess the name."

"Dracula's Highball."

He made it sound like 'eyeball' and Lamy laughed.

"Not far off. 'Vampire's Kiss'."

"More than appropriate," Warren said.

"She didn't stay long, maybe twenty minutes. No time for a main course. Just a second cocktail and a Banana Xango."

"What is that, pray tell, and what the devil is shambore?" Michael asked, his post-nap mood remaining uncharacteristically grudging and grumbly.

"A cheesecake filled ice cream patisserie washed down with bad tequila and a dash of French raspberry liqueur. Why worry, she's got great teeth."

"So what was the upshot of your chat?"

"I found out it was them."

"Who were having me followed?"

"That's what you asked, isn't it?"

"How?"

"From McWhirter's face."

"Did they have David and Fernando killed? Warren said he thought whoever did it was sending me or us a warning."

"Could be. But I doubt those two are that organized."

"Warn me about what exactly?"

"Take a guess."

"To shut up. So everything goes back to the plutonium. I'll never escape this, will I? I feel like I've been sprayed with identity napalm! If I hadn't been such an idiot to follow that tiger David and Fernando would still be alive! What an insane position to be in!"

Lamy and Warren fell sympathetically silent.

Michael stared glumly at the darkened trees of Central Park flashing past on either side and thought of Brandy and glanced at Lamy and from the tiny twinkle playing at the corners of his eyes he suspected he was thinking of her too.

"I had my own chat at lunch with the stilt man we saw in Times Square
. . "

"Maxwell Forman," Lamy said, "No shit."

"Ha! I knew you knew him!"

"I know his name, Michael. I never met him."

"He was once a student of mine. I'm pretty sure he took the same
portraiture class as David," Warren chimed in, "I had no idea at the time
what was ticking away inside him. Like David, he didn't have much gift
for painting but his street routines and one-man shows have turned out to
be brilliant. And very courageous."

"He told me he knew who Bartolomeo Vespucci is."

"Who?" Lamy asked with interest.

"Everyone."

Lamy chuckled again.

"Maybe true but not much help."

§

At that moment in suburban Maryland Brandy was being bound and
gagged by three men in suits. They dragged her from her modest bungalow
and threw her into the rear of their Ford Explorer and what she didn't
know was that Melissa and Cindy were already dead.

§

The limousine eased its way out of the park and took a left on Fifth
Avenue.

"He mentioned some advertising guru chappie called Bernays,"
Michael said, remembering and looking at Warren, "He told me you'd
interviewed him on his hundredth birthday. That he'd had an influence on
Goebbels. Can't say I'd ever heard of him."

"How did his name come up?"

"We were talking about how the majority of people don't seem able to
take in what's so obviously going on around them. Like the manifestations
that appeared on television the other night. Did you happen to see them?"

"Yes."

"Good lord. Like their general lack of reaction to him as 'Lon Cheney'."

"Well, I'd say it's pretty simple. Most people's worldview doesn't encompass such nastiness and they'd rather not believe their own eyes than come to grips with it. And then 'Bush's Brain', a cynical little shyster named Karl Rove, and others like the vice-president have sold them the idea conspiracy theories are un-American and 'outrageous' and being trumped up by Hollywood faggots or left-wing eggheads or anyone the average man in the street automatically dislikes and they blatantly ramp up the level of fear that's genuinely out there and then use cliché catchphrases like 'saving our way of life' and 'they hate us for our freedom' and 'togetherness' and 'security' and 'strong defense' to cajole and reassure. It's brilliant and bulletproof. They got it all from Bernays."

"What was he like?"

"Smart, charming, highly egotistical. Like Walter Lippmann, he believed the herd had to be kept in its place. Nothing new there. The rich have always cultivated a slave class, the masses, the plebs, the *hoi polloi*. Nowadays the whole world is their strip mine."

"And he was Freud's nephew?"

"Twice over. His mother was Freud's sister Anna. His father's sister Martha was Sigmund's wife. It didn't take him long in conversation to drop the name."

Lamy had been amazingly quiet but offered, "Too much is made of the evil genius thing. It would have been the same without him. Population growth, mass production, the lightning advance of communications technology. And people have always been incredibly stupid. Bleeding-heart intellectuals in every period of history have despaired of this and lately been urging neuroscience to come up with an 'intelligence pill' as the solution. Nothing of the kind in sight, of course, and now for the last half century we've had television which is the total opposite. Trouble is, we can sit casually bemoaning the crassness of the marketplace and the callousness of the powermongers but in truth we're dyed-in-the-wool elitists just like Bernays."

"Not exactly," Warren interjected, "Though it would be pointless to deny I have a high opinion of myself, and am in many ways as you describe, it's also true that, like all artists, I've spent my life trying to create alternate pathways to the general cultural Juggernaut. It's no guarantee of riches but I'm lucky. I've always had enough money to satisfy my needs. Lucky, too, I never had more. I don't know how you cope with it. The truth is that no matter how much I may feel myself apart I don't think my life is ultimately more valuable than anyone else's. There has never been any honest way to make such a judgment. You can't blame Bernays for the rapacity of his adherents. Even an old fraud like him would have been appalled by 9/11."

"I'm sure some of the people directly involved were too but they seem to have come out the other side with their guilt neatly swept under the rug. I doubt Bernays would have had much problem either. Humans have a bottomless capacity to ignore troublesome feelings when it suits them. Since you mention it, I cope just fine. There's nothing necessarily evil about money. I give plenty away. I could give it all away but you have no idea how much time that would take. At least to do it carefully and sensibly. It flows in as fast as I could dish it out. I don't have enough years left. I'm handing everything to a trust when I die. There's no way to be pure in this world."

"Still, we're not murderers," Warren said quietly, "If so, only indirectly."

"I am. I told Michael and David. I killed three young guerillas in Colombia. And didn't you ever pull the trigger in those soft Italian hills? Maybe it was kill or be killed but we did it. What about you, Michael?"

Michael looked at them both sadly.

"I've been unimaginably lucky. I have absolutely no right to complain about anything. I was born into the first and only generation in England that has never been ordered to pick up a weapon and kill. I've never been shot at and never been bombed. But I know what murder feels like now."

§

The College of William and Mary in Williamsburg, Virginia, was founded in 1693. It is the second oldest institute of higher learning in the United States after Harvard and counts among its illustrious alumni presidents Jefferson, Monroe and Tyler and sixteen signatories of the Declaration of Independence and also enjoys the dubious distinction of spawning the first 'secret society' among its students, the commonly known 'Flat Hat Club' or, less commonly but more formally, *'Fraternitas, Humanitas, Cognitioque'*, 'Fraternity, Humanity, Knowledge', the members of which in Jefferson's time were only six and according to the future statesman, who was once numbered among them, 'served no useful object'.

The current Chancellor, however, held very different views about the value of secrecy and had made an abrupt change of plan due to a phone call that caused him to abandon his dinner companions and dessert of *Kaiserschmarrn mit Äpfeln* and the last few golden gulps of *Trockenbeerenauslese* and was winging his dyspeptic way home from the *flughafen* at Wien-Schwechat.

Stanza Fifteen

§

The president feigned sleep on the flight and let Laura and Condoleezza and Andrew Card cope with his mother. The preacher's daughter from Titusville and the 'bulbous-eyed' matriarch from Flushing and Rye sank several stiff gin martinis which made their mutual ordeal much more bearable.

It was unfair of the media to call her 'bulbous-eyed'. Graves' disease is hardly the fault of its victims and it was not really newsworthy that, soon after her own diagnosis when her husband, and even beloved Millie who had faithfully served as First Springer Spaniel during their four-year stint on Pennsylvania Avenue, began to suffer the same affliction, the Secret Service was prompted to have the drinking water at the White House, the vice-president's residence on Observatory Circle and the compounds at Camp David and Walker's Point in Kennebunkport analyzed for an excess of lithium and iodine.

Besides, as leaven to her crustiness, the septuagenarian from whose loins the latest occupant of the Oval Office sprang had on many an occasion exhibited a pungent wit. It was she who irrefutably exposed his priapic predecessor as a liar by saying, 'No man ever forgets oral sex no matter how bad it is.' And she spoke often about the importance of literacy which when your eldest son stands up in public and poses questions like 'Is our children learning?' is really quite laudable.

The two reverends, Kathleene and Kirbyjon, who had opted to sit apart and appeared to be in hushed discussion of some abstruse religious topic for the entire journey, were in reality brainstorming about ways to further enhance and entrench the 'ripple effect' set in motion by the 'inspired spirituality' of the president's belief that 'God had handed him this crisis.'

The subject of their concern had refused a sedative for his obvious nerves saying he needed to stay physically sharp and even as they boarded the Marine One Whitehawk at Kennedy he remained monosyllabic and aloof but everyone knew the pressure he was under and how important the moment was for him and respected his wish to stay focused and kept their distance.

To be mad is a terrible thing but worse is to fear that any moment one may go mad without warning. The boyish man once nicknamed 'Temporary' found no rest behind his pulsing eyelids but with every parched swallow and nervous knuckle clench was desperately trying to keep at bay another dervish dance of hallucinatory images. By maintaining rigid focus he had so far succeeded but the effort had only tightened the knot in his stomach.

Even the sight of Lady Liberty in the distance and the Empire State Building bathed in the luminous patriotism of red, white and blue as the huge chopper and its security escort brushed the edges of Manhattan did not ease his condition.

§

From Michael's point of view the limousine's arrival at the stadium couldn't have been timed more perfectly. They crawled up the Major Deegan Expressway and it took at least another half an hour to move the four hundred yards from the 157th Street exit to the corner of Ruppert Place but they were stalled a stone's throw from the main entrance just as Marine One came in to land on the left field side of the adjacent diamond in Macombs Dam Park.

Lamy told Mike the driver to open the sunroof so Michael could stand and from that vantage a few inches above the bobbing heads he could make out two parallel lines of mounted police keeping the crowd in check and creating a broad passage from the aircraft to the stadium. A dozen Secret Service men appeared in the distance and then the president. He was wearing a green USAF bomber jacket and walked briskly across the floodlit concrete with a man dressed like a pilot. His two right forefingers were thrust outward as pitchers do when they hold a baseball and he rotated his arm from the shoulder to loosen it as they went. Michael could only glimpse their progress in the gaps between the uniformed riders and the stout rumps of the horses and it reminded him of the staccato flicker of a kinescope.

As the president was ushered into the building Michael looked in the other direction and was at first delighted and then appalled to see Maxwell Forman in his costume and makeup as 'Lon Cheney' being knocked over and shoved roughly into the back of a white and blue striped New York police van and his stilts tossed after him. It happened very quickly and was obscured for the most part by bodies in the foreground so it was hard for Michael to believe what he was seeing but as he was about to duck down inside the limousine again and tell the others something even more disturbing met his eyes.

He could be forgiven for not knowing the huge neon letters high above the tiered bubble of the entrance normally shaped the words 'YANKEE STADIUM', but his ignorance didn't lessen the wonderment that shook his frame as he glanced up and saw the sign flashing 'WAKEUP AMERICA'!

"Good lord," he spluttered and then shouted, "Louis! Warren! For god's sake come up here and look! Do you see what I'm seeing?!"

The two polymath skeptics rather awkwardly poked their heads skyward and confirmed that they did.

"We'll walk from here," Lamy said and dropped down again.

After a moment Warren followed suit but he had to tug Michael hard by the sleeve several times to get him to tear himself away and join them.

They stood a few paces from the great white car watching in awe as the sign kept flashing the message every few seconds and Lamy told Mike to pick them up at the far end of Ruppert Place when the game was over.

"For the last seventy-eight years it spelled Yankee Stadium," Warren said.

"Why is no one responding? Is it invisible to them?"

He was wrong. A group of Japanese tourists were pointing up and laughing and one of them was taking a photograph.

"Maybe they see it but interpret its meaning differently," Warren suggested.

"How?"

"That it means 9/11 was a wakeup call and we darn well ain't going to let it happen again."

Lamy guided them through the crowd past the mounted officers and beyond the door where the president disappeared to another entry for the field boxes. It was far less choked with people but once inside they had to pass through a metal detector and submit to the same scrutiny as everyone else. The police were armed with automatic weapons and Michael had seen many with Alsatians on tight leash and Lamy told him the dogs would have been used to sniff every corner of the vast complex.

Even with all his connections and vast wealth they had to wait their turn and join the line and as they shuffled slowly along Lamy treated them to a stunningly detailed history of the surrounding area, the franchise, the stadium and the game of baseball itself, beginning with Abner Doubleday and Jacob Ruppert, the brewer and congressman who purchased the 'Yanks' in 1915 with his partner, the quaintly named Tillinghast L'Hommedieu Huston, an appellation originating a thousand years ago in Normandy with a crusading Knight of St. John deemed worthy the title 'man of God', and then bought Huston out for a million and a half in 1922, built the stadium in 1923, guided the 'Bronx Bombers' to extraordinary success in the years that followed and managed the club until his death in 1939.

He described the 'Murderer's Row' lineup who won the pennant with an incredible 110-44 record in 1927 and went on to sweep the Series in four from the Pittsburgh Pirates, how Babe Ruth hit sixty home runs that year with an average of .356 and Lou Gehrig as cleanup hit forty-seven and batted .373 and Michael asked for clarification of what it all meant from time to time and then suddenly they were talking about Marilyn Monroe and 'Joltin' Joe' DiMaggio and Michael told them he had once met Arthur Miller at a staged reading of his play 'All My Sons' at a theater club in Garrick Yard and Warren said he knew Miller well but didn't much like him despite his staunch refusal to name names before Senator McCarthy's House Un-American Activities Committee and the undeniable effectiveness of works like 'The Crucible'.

"DiMaggio hated him," Lamy said in conclusion.

His discourse had certainly passed the time.

As they mounted the few stairs to the front row boxes Michael's ears were greeted by a deafening wall of sound, the tumultuous din of fifty-seven thousand excited and rowdy fans. He had to shout to be heard over the uproar.

The massive stadium with its countless flags waving and flashbulbs popping and banners unfurled over the edges of tier upon tier of seating soaring endlessly upward into the night sky was incredibly impressive.

"It's like I imagine the atmosphere as the gladiators entered the Colosseum," he yelled and Lamy and Warren nodded.

"And then some," Lamy mouthed back.

§

The Whitehawk landed in Macombs Dam Park about forty minutes before game time and the president had been shown to a private dressing room where he freshened up and changed jackets, donning a dark navy windbreaker over his blue Ivy League shirt with the letters FDNY emblazoned on the back in remembrance of more than three hundred firemen and rescue workers who lost their lives when the towers collapsed. An involuntary shiver passed through him as he put it on but he dismissed the sensation as nerves.

He had then been taken to the umpire's quarters where he kibitzed for a few minutes with a Secret Service agent who was buckling on a gunbelt and shoulder-holster and a bristling array of weaponry. The agent had a walkie-talkie clipped at his neck and was readying himself to join the umpires on the field with everything hidden discreetly under one of their uniforms.

The president had time to autograph a few baseballs before going to the warmup room where he was strapped into a bulletproof vest by another agent and tossed some practice pitches to the Yankee's second-string catcher Todd Greene to gauge the difficulty of attempting a strike thus encumbered.

On most such occasions the ceremonial throw is lobbed from in front of the pitcher's mound but the president had no intention of doing so. He prided himself on having guts when the chips were down.

§

The First Lady, First Mother-in-Law and the rest of the president's party had been met at the steps of Marine One by the chairman of the American Shipbuilding Company and long-time owner of the Yankees, the controversial seventy-one-year-old billionaire George M. Steinbrenner III, who wined and dined them for half an hour in his suite where they were introduced to his wife, Elizabeth Joan Zieg, his sons Hank and Hal and his daughters Jessica and Jennifer Steinbrenner-Swindal, and they

195

were now sitting with the family in his private box above third base and, like everyone else, waiting for the president's arrival.

Lamy gave Michael the highlights of Steinbrenner's story on the way through security. He had been a football coach and owned a professional basketball team and dabbled without distinction as a Broadway producer before an unsuccessful bid to purchase the Cleveland Indians in 1972 and then buying the Yankees in 1973 for ten million dollars from media giant CBS with a group of investors that included Nelson Bunker Hunt, who made a fortune from Libya's oilfields before Muammar Gaddafi nationalized them and then lost it because he and his brother attempted to corner the entire world market in silver, and John DeLorean, a name Michael knew well because he designed and manufactured the DMC-12 sports car but whose later arrest for trafficking cocaine and the not guilty verdict following his claim of being the victim of entrapment by the FBI were dim in Michael's memory.

Steinbrenner had run into legal troubles of his own soon after the purchase. In 1974, he was indicted for obstruction of justice and making illegal contributions to the re-election campaign of Richard Nixon. After pleading guilty he was fined fifteen thousand dollars and suspended from Major League baseball for two years but was pardoned by Ronald Reagan on the last day of his presidency in 1989.

Under Steinbrenner the Yankees had won nine American League pennants and six World Series titles, four of them in the last five years. He was also, like Lamy, a breeder of thoroughbreds and owned the Kinsman Stud Farm in Ocala, Florida. His horse Dream Supreme had been widely expected to win the sprint at the Breeder's Cup but for some reason it hadn't made the cut at the last minute and 'The Boss', as Steinbrenner was called, didn't attend.

The teams were introduced and stormed up onto the field one by one and the excited expectation in the stadium rose to bursting point. To the right of them, in what Lamy informed him was the 'Yankee dugout', a news cameraman at the top of the steps began rapidly backing away and the mellifluous voice of Robert Sheppard came over the public address system, saying "Ladies and gentlemen, the president of the United States," and the man peeled away to one side and there was the born-again boy from Midland striding alone toward the mound with a baseball in his left hand and suddenly the entire structure began rocking with the chant of "U.S.A., U.S.A., U.S.A, U.S.A."

196

The president reached the mound and stood on top of it and turned around to face home plate then raised his right hand high with his thumb pointed upward and if it was possible for the ecstasy of the crowd to grow wilder and noisier it did so and despite being acutely aware of the tragic irony of that extraordinary moment Michael found it utterly thrilling.

Then something truly beyond explanation happened.

The stadium froze in time. There was a total galactic silence. The triumphant figure of the 43rd Commander-in-Chief stood stock still with hand upraised as if he had been chiseled from ancient marble. All the players in right and left field, all the photographers and journalists and umpires, the loyal men and women of the Secret Service and every one of the fifty-seven thousand jubilant fans, whether standing or sitting or somewhere in between, congealed in a voiceless and motionless pose.

Everyone, as far as Michael could tell, except himself and Warren and Lamy and some tiny scattered pockets of others and before their astonished eyes, starting on the raised dirt around the stone-struck president, then more and more rapidly until the vision covered the playing field and finally filled every possible interstice between the staring insensate souls in that colossal space, ghostly figures began to appear.

At first children, hundreds of starving children, all the downtrodden bombed and bloodied children of the world, dressed in rags but uncomplaining, many blind or horribly scarred, missing hands or hobbling on the stumps of legs, a fortunate few with cumbersome prosthetics and then, as the swirling mirage spread, mothers and grandmothers with fists upraised and howling in accusation, some weeping or tearing their own flesh, some mute with agony holding their burnt or broken, dead or dying babies in their arms. Surrounding them by the thousands, insurgent and unstoppable, the hollow-cheeked figures of men, brandishing fifth-hand weapons of every description, the overpriced detritus of an evil trade, bandaged and splinted, bearing the makeshift litters of fallen comrades, chanting legends of future victory to ease their pain. A furious threadbare legion of the emaciated and dispossessed, the brutalized and bludgeoned from every defrauded corner of the forgotten world, all seeming to move inexorably forward toward Michael and home plate yet never getting a hair's-breadth closer.

Then, as though some monstrous hidden dial had been turned, the tumult of their voices coalesced and they were suddenly still and chanting, "U.S.A., U.S.A., U.S.A., U.S.A., U.S.A."

Michael felt as though his very sanity was about to float away but after less than ten seconds of this tragic incongruity the entire ghostly army dissolved into the air and vanished as inexplicably as it had appeared, the stadium sprang back to life and the president popped the ball into his right hand and with an almost casual motion of his arm tossed in a perfect strike.

There was a moment of hushed wonder at the unexpected beauty of it and then a Vesuvian eruption of applause and whistling and yells and trumpet blasts and the chant of "U.S.A., U.S.A., U.S.A." resumed even louder and wilder than before and more banners were unfurled proclaiming 'Home of the Brave' and 'United We Stand' and 'USA Fears Nobody – Play Ball!' and the president, who must have been relieved but seemed eerily calm about it, strode back manfully toward the dugout.

Todd Greene, who caught the pitch, was the first to reach him and shake his hand, closely followed by Diamondback manager Bob Brenly who Michael could just hear saying, "Very nice throw, Mr. President, good stuff, great stuff," and then Joe Torre of the Yankees, less effusive but equally congratulatory, and as Broadway star Max von Essen launched into 'America the Beautiful' the president shook a few more hands and paused for a quick photo op before disappearing again down the steps.

Warren said to Michael later it was a pity the full eight stanzas of Katharine Lee Bates poem are seldom sung. Particularly the last two which, after the familiar refrain 'America, America, God shed his grace on thee', finish with 'Till selfish gain no longer stain the banner of the free' and 'Till nobler men keep once again thy whiter jubilee'. The last 'whiter' was perhaps a little worrying but still.

Miss Bates, he told him, was a professor of English literature at Wellesley, a women's liberal arts college near Boston, founded in 1895 and one of the original 'Seven Sisters'. Her only other work to survive in the popular consciousness was entitled, 'Goody Santa Claus on a Sleigh Ride'. She was a lesbian and she and her lover of a quarter century, the distinguished economist, Katharine Coman, were forced to live the clandestine lie of a 'Boston marriage' in Victorian America.

Michael turned to his companions as the song finished, 'And crown thy good with brotherhood from sea to shining sea', but he was beyond words.

"You'll see him arriving up there in a minute." Lamy had an oddly unsettled look on his face as he pointed to the Steinbrenner box and handed Michael a small pair of binoculars. "Take a gander. Your lady friend's there."

The Yankees were on the field and several were jogging on the spot in the cold night air or doing deep kneebends or stretching to stay loose as their starter, Roger Clemens, began his warmup throws and Michael fidgeted to find a focus. He had to ask Lamy to guide him to the right place but finally came upon it and landed by chance on the First Lady. They had met in El Paso and she had been very sweet during the embarrassing idiocy of the beauty pageant. She was smiling, pleased for her husband's success no doubt, and saying something to his mother.

Michael roved the spyglasses slowly around the box and found a lot of other people who he didn't recognize, all chatting to each other happily, and then came upon the National Security Advisor and nearly jumped out of his skin because she was looking directly back at him through a pair of identical binoculars. She held his gaze for a long moment but then turned away as the president entered the box and everyone got up to congratulate him.

Michael watched spellbound as their jollity changed to dismay and it became apparent that all was far from right with their pitching hero. He lost his balance and stumbled forward on the stairs and two of the men caught him just in time and had to help him to his front row seat beside Laura and when he got there he sat down in a rigid and unnatural position staring straight forward and despite everything she was clearly asking him he didn't seem able to say a word.

§

The sleeper town of North Laurel, Maryland, and the seedy Valencia Motel where Hani Hanjour and the other alleged hijackers of American Airlines flight 77 were staying on the night of September 10th, which according to the official report slammed into the west wall of the Pentagon at 9:38 the following morning, lies to the west of the Baltimore-Washington Parkway and just to the east and south of Fort George Meade. The shining black glass headquarters of the National Security Agency, which dwarfs in size and number of employees sworn to lifelong secrecy both the CIA and FBI combined, is located here and, surprisingly, some little-used and lonely roads pass through an uninhabited wetland on the Patuxent River close by and, because they had time to kill, Brandy's abductors took her there.

The Ford Explorer pulled off the road into a thick clump of trees and the men stripped her naked and bound her to the top of a half rotted-out picnic table with her arms raised and tied around one end and her buttocks nearly hanging over the other. Two of them held her legs wide open while each man took his turn to rape and sodomize her. She was bleeding profusely and leaking excrement but they threatened to strangle her if she made a sound.

§

"He's there," Michael said, "But it looks like he's had a stroke or something. They're talking to him but he doesn't respond."

Lamy took the binoculars.

"Who knows," he said after a moment, "Maybe he saw what we saw."

"Maybe everyone did," Warren added.

"Did they put LSD in the beer?" Michael asked incredulously, "What in the name of His Satanic Majesty happened here just now? Did we all see the same thing? Did you see thousands upon thousands of people? Third world people? The ones who are being blown to smithereens as we speak in Afghanistan. All howling and bloody and walking directly at us? Is that what you both saw?"

Warren nodded gravely.

"You're right," Lamy said, still holding the binoculars to his eyes, "Looks like Card has told Steinbrenner to bring in a doctor. He's on the phone. And yeah, I saw what you saw. Shit, I'm starting to believe you *are* this guy Vespucci and you're a godammed hypnotist."

Michael was still shaking.

"It was the weirdest experience of my life. How can one possibly explain it? How can one explain any of it?"

Warren shrugged uncomfortably. He too was at a loss.

"Yup," Lamy said, "A doctor just came in and sat beside him but he's making little 'no' gestures with his hands. He must be coming round."

He lowered the binoculars. Clemens was ready and the leadoff batter for the Diamondbacks, second baseman Craig Counsell, was standing at the plate.

"They're gonna start. Let's watch. I've got no explanation."

Stanza Sixteen

§

By the top of the third inning the Yankees were leading 1-0 on the strength of a solo home run by their catcher, Jorge Posada, in the bottom of the second and the fans hardly noticed when the president and his wife and mother and the rest of his party made a discreet exit from the box and didn't return.

But Michael did. He hadn't been able to find much interest in the game after so extraordinary an occurrence and borrowed Lamy's binoculars to keep an eye on the events above. The dark bride of Vyacheslav had refrained from looking his way again but Michael felt sure she was itching to do so.

Lamy provided a constant supply of useless information on the players and the minutiae of the rules and the strategy of the managers and Warren seemed to have either digested or decided to postpone thinking about what had happened and appeared to be thoroughly enjoying himself.

"Your boy has left the building," Michael told them.

They weren't surprised.

"Yeah, I wouldn't have expected him to stay," Lamy said.

"No one would," Warren explained with an ironic smile, "Everyone here can appreciate how busy he must be."

During the changeover in the middle of the first inning Lamy had whispered in Michael's ear that the two older gentlemen joking together about six seats to their right, both sportily decked out in the caps of their respective teams, were none other than Rudolph Giuliani, former U.S. Attorney for the Southern District and now the 107th mayor of New York, who Michael had misnamed 'Giancana' without having a clue that his father had been a small time enforcer for the Mob and spent time in Sing

Sing for armed robbery and assault, and John Sidney McCain III, scion of two four-star admirals, decorated war hero, thrice-elected senator from Arizona, and unsuccessful Republican challenger to the current Commander-in-Chief.

Giuliani had stared at them without embarrassment or apology over the top of wire-rimmed spectacles as Lamy whispered and Michael felt certain the chilling spookiness of the look wasn't simply in his imagination.

§

As she hunkered deep down into the collar of her Jil Sander Barbados wool trenchcoat while crossing the blustery tarmac at Kennedy to board Air Force One the Vulcan commander took another call from the general.

"Our boy did good, huh?" she said before he could speak.

"Who gives a shit! That little prick Scooter just summoned me to a fucking midnight meeting up at OC."

Observatory Circle, the vice-president's residence.

"So?"

"So what's it about?"

"I don't know. Honestly. Say no if you want."

"It's not a fucking cocktail party. It was a summons."

"So go then. What's your problem? I'll be there. Look, whatever it is, and I truly do not know, it's nothing beside what we're dealing with here. Ever since he threw that pitch he's been a basket case. Total fucking nervous breakdown if you ask me. We'll have to dress up some clone to talk to the UN."

"Is the Vaderman poisoning his Jack?"

"Could be. Consider yourself fucking lucky sitting there in your slippers. I've got mummy for the next hour and she's stinking."

Normally that would have aroused a chuckle but it didn't.

"Go," he said.

§

As he did, Helen was forcing herself to wake up from a frightening dream. She had understandable difficulty getting to sleep because of the excitement of her morning departure for New York and by three o'clock when at last she had been able to drop off she was almost instantly overtaken by a strange nightmare. She was a little black girl in a calico dress walking barefoot and alone through what appeared to be a sharecropper's outbuilding in the Deep South, an old wooden barn with the roof half gone and loose boards flapping in the hot wind.

She walked into stall after empty stall searching for someone or something and came upon dozens of dead piglets lying in their own filth. Then behind her she heard a furious hissing and turned in terror to face an enormous rattlesnake that lunged at her with dripping fangs but she was agile and dodged it as it missed her time and again.

Then she was transformed into a great sow and dashing to and fro around the snake, stamping on it with sharp hooves. Finally she pierced its throat with her tusks and tore it wide open and as she tossed the flailing carcass high in the air the whole building crumbled away.

§

When the game ended it was midnight and Michael was chilled to the bone. He consumed four hotdogs just for the onions and mustard and, though Lamy and Warren clearly had a marvelous time, in his opinion the game of baseball itself was a crushing bore and notwithstanding the obvious excellence of the pitching staff on both sides he thought most of the players were lousy.

The fans, however, were ecstatic and their excited chatter of 'didya see this' and 'didya catch that' and 'what about that guy Clemens' and 'ain't Rivera somethin'' as everyone shuffled toward the exits got on his nerves like nails on a blackboard. How could they be so happily ignorant? So utterly naïve and blind? He turned as they filed out the box-holder's door and gestured silently up at the sign. It was still flashing 'WAKEUP AMERICA' and yet no one was surprised. What was a cosmic joke to him was for them a comforting reassurance.

Mike was waiting at the end of Ruppert Place as instructed and they were seated in the limousine before anyone spoke.

"Did you watch the game?" Lamy asked over the intercom.

There was a small television in the middle of the dashboard.

"Yup. The Rocket's had one hell of a year."

Michael knew the nickname of the winning pitcher very well. Lamy told him at the outset about Clemens' great second season and his incredible 20-3 record and his sixth Cy Young award.

"How about the president?"

"Damn fine throw."

"Notice anything strange while he was on the mound?"

"Yeah, they morphed into some kind of Arab army. Did you see it?"

"Yeah, we could see it."

"No kidding? It's crazy what they can do these days. Pretty weird but pretty cool in a way."

"How so?"

"Well, they're the guys we're after in Afghanistan, no? And also kind of like the people we're over there to protect. So I guess it was meant to be symbolic. The president giving the victory sign and holding the pose to give time for the other stuff and then throwing a perfect strike. Pretty damn cool."

"How long did it last?"

"Maybe ten seconds."

Lamy switched off the intercom and looked at Michael.

"And there you have it," he said.

"Are you saying it was orchestrated? I don't believe it."

"No, I'm saying there's nothing that can't be interpreted to suit the mindset of the onlooker."

"And no problem that doesn't become even more complex when you look at it the right way," Warren added.

"But what made it happen? You can't tell me all these things are some kind of bizarrely motivated subliminal manipulation as your man seems to think. Even if what we saw was holographic wizardry of some sort it would still be impossible to make a whole stadium full of people freeze on the spot. And why would they want to do that anyway even if they could?"

"Any ideas, Warren?"

"None whatever. You've got an old rationalist here who's starting to believe in witchcraft."

They were almost motionless in the traffic snarl.

"Drink anyone?" Lamy asked.

"God yes," Michael replied.

Even Warren nodded assent.

"Why not? Since we've all gone mad."

Lamy poured three generous tumblers of Sazerac over ice and handed them round and then sat back and sighed.

"So what do you want to do?" he asked, "Is it back to the hotel or would you both like to come to Mattituck for the night? Your sister gets in around 1:15, did you say?"

"I suppose that would be more convenient for you," Michael replied, "Since you're being so kind."

"Makes no difference to me. I'm happy to stay in town. I keep an apartment on Washington Square. I'll get Mike to pick us all up in the morning if you want. Or we can meet at Arty's Deli at ten and he'll find us there by eleven thirty."

"I think maybe a good night's sleep is in order," Warren suggested.

"I guess since they called off the dogs you won't have to worry."

"I guess not," Michael agreed without conviction.

§

Things were rather slow getting started at Observatory Circle. Both the man they called 'Doctor K', or simply 'the Doctor', and the National Security Advisor were late due to dense fog at Andrews Air Force Base and Dulles International that delayed the arrival of their respective flights from Wien-Schwechat and Kennedy.

There were already more than a dozen limousines parked along the winding drive to the old mansion, which had been built in the Queen Anne style in 1893 for the superintendent of the observatory, and yet the house itself appeared as though its occupants were long abed. There was no welcoming light in the doorway or on the broad veranda as the last two attendees glided up to it through the swirling mist in their chauffeured Cadillacs, both at precisely the same time as it happened. It was eerily suggestive of some haunted palace in the imagination of Edgar Allan Poe as the cars were met at the front steps by soldiers in jackboots carrying old-fashioned kerosene lanterns.

The building had undergone extensive renovation before the Cheneys took occupancy. Merely for maintenance, it was said, and to enlarge some aspects of the main floor but really for a massive security bunker which was now within weeks of completion three full levels beneath the basement.

The reputed master of *realpolitik* from Bavaria and the champion of global dominance from Alabama acknowledged each other with their eyes but didn't speak as they were ushered to the privacy of separate rooms where the evening's costume and a tray of refreshments were laid out for them. But no sooner had the National Security Advisor sat down at the dressing table to glance disparagingly at her bleary reflection in the mirror than there was a loud knock on the door.

"Come in," she said curtly.

It was the general with a sloshing martini glass in his hand, looking extremely upset and more than a little self-conscious in the dress uniform of *ein Schutzstaffel-Oberst-Gruppenführer.*

"Two of my girls are dead!" he blurted in despair, closing the door, "We're here to execute another. My favorite. The most beautiful. Cheney fucks her too for god's sake. So do half the others. What's the point? She's harmless. You have to stop it!"

She put her hand up to silence him and finally was forced to interrupt.

"Three things," she snapped, "First, shut up. Then swallow. Then get out."

"It's all gone too far."

"Oh, fuck off, Larry, and grow up. What does she matter?"

"Her flesh is too sweet to be destroyed," he blubbed.

The girl from Birmingham jumped to her feet and snatched up a heavy metal jewellery box from the table, hurling it with deadly accuracy at his head. It smashed into the lattice of thin blue veins on his right temple with a painful greasy squeak. Blood instantly spurted from the wound and before he could react she charged at him and began kicking viciously at his shins and slapping him hard about the neck and he could only protect himself by retreating from the room.

"Don't ever bring your bitches up to me again, you self-pitying shit! I'm going to enjoy tearing out her fucking eyes!" she screeched as he fled.

Her heart was pounding and she returned unsteadily to the table and downed a triple shot of blackberry brandy.

"Fucking weak-kneed fucking mama's boys the whole fucking cheeseball lot of them," she muttered.

She poured a second glass and looked up to see the Doctor in the doorway, dressed only in a long-tailed shirt and underwear with calf-length socks held taut by clip-on elastic suspenders below a pair of hairy knees, dangling a shiny black riding boot from each hand.

"I need your help," he said in a guttural rumble.

'Christ, another one drowning in mucus,' she observed to herself sourly.

The Doctor shuffled to the bed and sat without invitation and she came to him obediently and helped to cram the stiff boots onto his swollen legs.

'What fucking next?' she thought.

Despite heavy deodorant his loins reeked of sweat and stale piddle.

"How was the game?" he asked.

"I hate baseball," she replied, "But his pitch was an ace."

"*Ja*, I heard," he said with a satisfied chuckly grunt.

The effort of shoving down on the boots was making his face red.

"What about these things that have been happening? Childish antics. Mount Rushmore, Ground Zero, the stadium. It's Rove, isn't it? Fucking amateur. You tell him I want it stopped. And quickly. It's not working."

With a final heave she forced the second heel into place and nearly fell to her knees with exhaustion.

"What if it's not him?" she said, struggling to regain her breath.

"Don't be stupid. His ham-fisted methodology is all over it."

He got up and made for the door.

"Let's get this over with," he mumbled irritably, "I'm tired. If Larry doesn't like it I'm sure we can find a solution."

§

When Michael entered Room 137 at the Belleclaire he found four message slips thrust under the door. All from Luciano Perretti and Jim Gonzalez and the first dated back forty-eight hours to Sunday evening. They also called late Monday afternoon and twice since the president tossed his ceremonial strike. Michael wasn't surprised. It was part of the job description that desk clerks pretend to an efficiency they don't possess.

He didn't recall telling the two salvage workers where he was staying but assumed they must have tracked him down by process of elimination or perhaps even called the magazine. They were either at Ground Zero for the memorial or at the stadium to witness the transhuman legion on the march or saw the apparitions on the news and wanted to talk but it was too late to call them back now.

§

In the candlelit bunker, Brandy was standing spreadeagled and semi-naked in the center of an open half-finished space about fifty feet across.

Mascara and rouge had been sloppily applied to her eyes and cheeks and she was now dressed as a sick parody of Marlene Dietrich in The Blue Angel complete with top hat, elbow-length satin gloves, a close-fitting vest under bare breasts, a garter belt, fishnet stockings and high heels. She was still gagged with duct tape but her inner thighs and exposed groin had been scrubbed clean. Her ankles were tied to metal rings in the floor and her wrists were similarly bound above her head to a beam so she formed an 'X'.

There was a light rope around her neck into which an elaborate sequence of complex knots had been wound and from each knot a thin strand swagged out to the circumference of the gloomy space like the spokes of a wheel and each strand's end was looped round the black-leathered pinkie finger of a spectator.

The circle stood in hushed readiness as the Doctor and the National Security Advisor came out of the elevator. There were now nineteen *Oberst-Gruppenführer-SS* in glistening jackboots and full dress uniform, each holding high-peaked caps with shining visors under one arm, and two *Reichsführer-SS* with white belts and braiding over the right shoulder.

The *Reichsführer* from the elevator walked stiffly across the circle, stopping to kick at his squeaking boots, and embraced the second.

"*Guten Abend*, Richard," he said, pronouncing the name as a German would.

"*Guten Abend*, Heinz," came the straight-faced American reply.

It was followed by some audible snickering which was quickly silenced by an unamused look from the *Reichsführer*.

Two strands were being held for the new arrivals but before he came back to take his the first *Reichsführer* strolled slowly around Brandy and, after gazing at her in mock sadness for a moment, reached out to caress her cheek with the knuckles of a gloved hand.

"*Haben Sie keine Angst, Liebchen,*" he purred.

She was shaking with terror but would have spit in his face if she could.

He returned to his place and looped the waiting string over his pinkie and glanced meaningfully at each member of the circle. The general was on the far side weeping.

"*Halt den Mund oder sterben!*" the *Reichsführer* barked.

"*Die Masken,*" commanded the second.

At which each of the nineteen awkwardly donned a rubber Halloween mask formed in the likeness of one of Adolf Schicklgruber Heidler's close confidantes. Göring, Goebbels, Himmler, the two Bormanns, Speer, von Ribbentrop, Strasser, Röhm, Heydrich, Hess, Rommel, Dönitz, Raeder, Keitel, Kaltenbrunner, Jodl, von Schirach and Schreck. The two *Reichsführer* waited until the rest had completed the transformation and put on their caps with the eagle and swastika insignia and then both donned masks of the man himself.

The first Hitler cleared his throat.

"Wir sind das Ei.." he began gruffly.

"Und das Ich," intoned the second, completing the sentence.

"Wir sind der Keim," came the only female voice, chosen to wear the Goebbels mask because of her slender physique.

"Wir sind Leben," said a tenor male beside the general.

"Wir sind die einzigen Götter," the two almost sang in unison.

"Stolz.." growled the first Hitler.

".. und rauberisch,.." added the second without a vestige of gusto.

And other voices continued.

".. definieren wir.."

".. die ganze Wahrheit.."

".. und verbreiten.."

".. alle Phantasie."

"Wir wissen kein Himmel.."

".. noch Hölle.."

".. wir preisen aber unsterbliche Tod,.."

".. unser Meister."

Then they all spoke together loudly.

"Wir die machen alles beugen vor uns!"

And repeated louder.

"Alles beugen vor uns!"

And even louder still.

"Unsterbliche Tod, unser Meister!"

On cue they all turned their backs on Brandy which drew the strands up and over their right shoulders and despite the unfelt pressure on each innocent pinkie it had the effect of tightening the thin cord around her neck so inexorably that within less than forty seconds she was dead, rather like the joined fingers on a Ouija board may move the pointer without any one person seeming to initiate the motion.

Even McWhirter turned away but as the life ebbed from her he let go of the strand and fell to his knees overcome with racking sobs.

No one spoke as the Death's Head ghouls broke formation, casually released each strand without a backward glance, lit cigarettes and strolled to the elevator.

The general was beside himself with grief and guilt and crawled to her and cried her name and pulled himself up her limp body to kiss the dead white flesh of her breasts once more and the last thing he felt was the thump of a bullet that made thick blood ooze down the back of his cropped white hair.

Stanza Seventeen

§

At five minutes past eight the next morning Michael was still sleeping fitfully when his telephone rang. It was Gonzalez. His first thought was that Helen might have some problem but quickly realized she would already be in the air.

"Sorry to wake you, sir," Gonzalez said apologetically, "We've been trying for a couple of days now."

"Yes," Michael answered groggily, "I only got the messages last night. What is it? Have you seen the weird stuff on TV?"

"Yeah, everyone's talking about it."

"I was at the game last night."

"No kidding? We didn't take you for a fan."

"I was invited."

"Yeah, well, you probably didn't see it then."

"Oh, but I did."

"Really? We had some buddies there but they didn't see a thing. We figured it was only for the TV audience. What did you see?"

"Everything you saw."

"How in hell did they do that?"

"I don't think they did anything. I think everything that's happened is just like you two seeing Cheney dressed as Dracula."

"No shit?"

"No shit."

"Even the stuff at the memorial?"

"Even that. How do your buddies explain that one, by the way?"

"They found it kind of puzzling."

"I'm not surprised."

There was a pause and Perretti came on the line.

"Good morning, Mr. Davenport, Luciano here. Hey, look, we also wanted you to know they found the gold last night. Under Building 4. Two hundred million at least. They're moving it out this morning and just like we told you Giuliani has cut the number of firefighters down there to twenty-five. There's gonna be a big protest tomorrow. But maybe it's a good thing. So damn many are sick."

"What bank vault was it?"

"Canadian. Bank of Nova Scotia."

"Thanks for letting me know."

Michael asked again how their friends were interpreting what was going on and got much the same answer as Mike the driver gave Lamy about the appearance of the ghostly army from the Third World. About the pranks behind the speakers at the memorial there was more confusion but the consensus was the doppelgangers of Cheney *et al* were supposed to represent the scornful attitude of certain foreign powers to the nation's pain or mock the cranks and their nutty conspiracy theories. But even so, they thought it was kind of tasteless.

§

The subject was also of concern in the vice-president's office. Not the spin, the public seemed to be handling that just fine on their own, but the perpetrators.

"The Doctor thinks it's all Turdblossom," last night's Minister of Propaganda was saying to a rather tired-looking Cheney and his 'Cheney's Cheney', "He said he wants it stopped. I told him it was none of our doing but he wouldn't listen."

"Whose doing is it then?" the Snake fisherman snapped, "Mueller's way too stupid. Tenet's too scared. The NSA's on our side. Rogue Mossad? Liberal media executives? Frogs? Krauts? Chinks? Russkies? Who?"

"I wouldn't put it past Putin," Scooter offered timidly.

They ignored him.

"Or the Chinese. All those crappy knickknacks had to be made somewhere."

"What if it's no one?" the dusky *Oberst* in daylight's frilly cuffs asked less than patiently.

Cheney eyed her with disdain.

"I can't accept that. Someone is doing it. What about Vespucci? You said he was with Lamy. You said you saw his brother. Why was he here? Not just to have lunch. A guy like that doesn't fly from gay Paree seven hours and back in one day for nothing. There has to be a reason."

"What about inviting Vespucci here and asking him?" Scooter ventured.

The vice-president looked pleased with the idea in a slithery sort of way and sat back in his chair considering it.

The Vulcan *Gruppenführer* took a deep breath and remained silent.

§

In the offices of McWhirter and Associates, which were closed for the day, a press release was being hastily prepared to inform the world the decorated hero of Viet Nam and Operation Desert Storm, three time recipient of the Purple Heart, former deputy representative to NATO and recent Director of the ONDCP had died suddenly in his sleep of an apparent thrombosis. Though his doctors avowed they had no suspicion of any coronary problem they were quick to add such things can happen without warning to anyone.

There would be a funeral with full military honors at the National Cemetery in Arlington on Sunday afternoon. The Chairman of the Joint Chiefs, the Secretary of Defense and the vice-president were expected to be in attendance.

§

It was proving to be a difficult morning for the ever-loyal National Security Advisor and the rest of the president's personal staff because their boy was still in bed and let it be known by gesture, since he remained unaccountably mute, that he was taking the day off.

Thankfully it was already planned as a light one because of the ball game and the late return to Washington but the daily intelligence briefings and another with the National Security Council had to be cancelled and Andrew Card had to contact the House Speaker and Minority Leader and the Majority and Minority Leaders of the Senate and tell them to find their breakfast elsewhere. Later in the day there was also to be a meeting with the International Development Administrator concerning humanitarian efforts in Afghanistan but in all probability that would get scrubbed as well.

§

Michael lay back on the pillows for half an hour to gather his thoughts, after politely declining to join Perretti and Gonzalez the following afternoon in Union Square because Helen was arriving and they had unexpected family business, during which time he had to dissuade the doggedly insistent maid from entering to supply fresh towels or soap or toilet paper or bathing gel or maybe give the room a quick go round with the vacuum to freshen it up. Finally he despaired of trying and rose to perform his habitual morning ablutions.

'Shit, shower, shave and shampoo' once leisurely and satisfactorily achieved he decided to give John a call at the magazine and discovered that people all over Europe had seen the same apparitions on television as the American audience. The fact that discussion of these weird events was widespread in the media across the pond though barely a mention had been made by any major news outlet in America was laughably normal they agreed.

Nonetheless, Michael fibbed, several major articles about the extraordinary occurrences were already taking shape in his mind. He was still planning to return on the 7th but might stay longer if it seemed pointful and, not to worry, he would pay for the extra. As to rooting out the ultimate source of the phenomena, whether transhuman or not, neither had any need to imagine it would ever be possible.

Michael left the Belleclaire at fifteen minutes to ten on his way to Arty's for the rendesvous with Warren and Lamy. He looked up and down 77th and was, if anything, a trifle saddened to find no sign of either 'Nikolai'.

He bought a copy of the New York Times as he strolled up Broadway in the chilly morning sunshine and was amused to find an article, by one R. W. Apple Jr., that noted how the word 'quagmire' was being used more and more by the media in relation to the situation in Afghanistan following Secretary Rumsfeld's admission that U.S. forces were now 'on the ground' there in a liaison and advisory capacity. It had stirred up ominous comparisons with Viet Nam and Lyndon Johnson's hollow vow he 'would not send our boys to fight a war for Vietnamese boys' though there were still many, indeed a majority of the American citizenry according to the latest Times/CBS poll, who thought bombing the hell out of those damn towel-heads was less than they deserved and these included Senator McCain and the columnists Charles Krauthammer and William Kristol. Michael felt sure Lamy mentioned the last name after they watched the bloodbath at the Serpent Mound.

Warren was waiting inside as he arrived and they were seated at a cramped table by the window.

"Did you sleep well?" Warren enquired with a kindly smile.

"No," Michael replied with a grimace of understatement.

"I don't suppose Helen did either. I'm excited to see her."

"I'll be interested to know how you find her. She's grown up a lot."

"I imagine so. What's in the news?"

"Nothing special. Only this piece by R. W. Apple, Jr."

He placed the paper on the table so Warren could read it.

"I guess his father's 'Big Apple'," Warren observed drily.

He scanned the article as an aging waitress of indeterminable origin plonked down two menus and two glasses of iced water in front of them.

"No one pays attention to history," he said, "Here today, gone tomorrow. That's what the likes of Krauthammer and Kristol have always known. No one gets to take it with them so grab everything you can today. Posturing bastards like that are only interested in the easy acquisition of loot."

"Speaking of loot," Michael said, nodding out the window at Lamy who they could see emerging from the limousine, "I thought he said Mike would find us here at eleven-thirty."

"I don't suppose he taxis it any more."

"No, indeed. Silly of me."

Lamy came in and took off his coat and gave it to the waitress at the front to hang for him.

"Coffees all round?" she asked and they said yes and she departed.

Lamy was holding his cell phone and the twinkle in his eye made it evident he was itching to divulge some secret.

"Well, Bartolomeo, old buddy," he said with a grin as he sat, "Your presence has been requested at the White House."

Michael could only assume he was joking.

"I just got off the phone with your lady friend," he went on, gesturing with it, "She and Cheney have invited you to lunch."

"Rubbish."

"Nope, one hundred percent dead serious."

Michael began to laugh.

"Impossible. When?"

"I told her today was no good because your sister was arriving from Podere di Gesso so they settled on tomorrow at 12:30."

"Did they invite her too?"

"Of course, I didn't give them a choice."

"Where in hell is Podere di Gesso?"

"It won't keep them guessing long. Italian for Chalk Farm. Couldn't resist."

Michael was laughing so hard he started to choke.

"How was it they called you?"

"She claimed it was because she saw us together last night. They would never have tried the hotel. Too much like confessing."

Michael's hysterical wheeze forced him to quiet down. He could see Warren wasn't amused at all.

"I fear they intend 'having us' for lunch," Michael suggested, wiping away the tears with his handkerchief.

"Not to worry, we're coming too. That is, if Warren's available."

Warren raised his eyebrows in surprise but then smiled and said, "We have an appointment with the lawyers about David's will but it can wait. I wouldn't want to delay the nation's business."

Michael started to laugh again but quickly thought better of it.

"What the devil can they be thinking?" he asked, "It's impossible they really believe I am this chap. They've been following me for years. They know everything there is to know about me."

Lamy and Warren looked skeptical.

"There's obviously a serious doubt in somebody's mind," Warren said.

"We wait for revelation," added Lamy.

The table waitress brought their coffee and asked if they were ready. Michael had been nervously tucking into the ever-present pickles and ordered a tenderloin steak with fried eggs, Warren wanted a LEO, an omelet with lox, eggs and onions, and Lamy decided on a corned beef Reuben.

"So," he said as soon as she was gone, "Where to after we pick her up?"

"Are we disposing of the ashes today?" Michael asked Warren.

"We can. We'd have to get them from the funeral home."

"Where are you going to do it?" Lamy enquired.

"They wanted to be scattered in the sea."

"OK, why don't we pick them up on the way to Kennedy and then continue on to my place in Mattituck. I've got a private stretch of beach. Michael's seen it. It would be perfect, no? And you can all stay with me out there. Might be the safest thing, you never know. I'll set up a flight to Reagan International for the morning. I keep a little Cessna Citation at Gabreski. It's only twenty minutes from the house."

Michael and Warren looked at each other and shrugged in mute agreement. What could they say? As usual, Lamy had everything mapped out.

While they ate Michael asked about the Cessna and got a detailed history of the company and its founder Clyde Cessna, the 'birdman of Enid', who had his first successful flight over the salt plains of Oklahoma, a round trip of five kilometers, in a monoplane he called 'the Silverwing' in December, 1911, and was the first man to fly from the Mississippi to the Rockies. Lamy also described the CJ1+ model that he owned and added a long digression about the Bombardier company of Montreal in which he was a major shareholder and their 1990 acquisition of Learjet which he helped to facilitate and finished up saying he intended to sell the Citation within the month and purchase a new Bombardier Challenger 604.

Michael was not the least bit bored with Lamy's rambling, on the contrary he was growing more and more fond of it, and asked about the name Gabreski which he had rightly assumed was the name of a smallish local airport in Suffolk County.

At that point Warren took up the subject and had even more to say about it than Lamy. He had known Colonel Frances Stanley 'Gabby' Gabreski well. He was the son of Polish immigrants and the most famous American flying ace of WWII with twenty-eight Luftwaffe kills, surpassing the record of Eddie Rickenbacker in WWI. He was stationed at Pearl Harbor when the Japanese attacked and attempted with members of his squadron to scramble and intercept them but by the time they could get airborne it was too late. In July, 1944, he was forced into a crash landing and was captured, spending nine months in a *stalag* in Barth, Pomerania, before being liberated by the Soviets in April, 1945. He was also a flying ace in Korea and went on to a distinguished career with the USAF though on retirement had put in a brief and frustrating stint as Director of the Long Island Railroad. He was still alive, Warren told them, and living not far away in Huntington.

After breakfast Lamy summoned the limousine. Michael insisted on paying the bill and they went first to the Belleclaire where he packed an overnight bag and then to the funeral home on Bleecker for the two urns and Warren's apartment on Spring for another overnight bag and on the way Lamy mentioned a report earlier that morning on Radio France Internationale claiming Osama bin Laden spent ten days in July being treated for a kidney infection at the American Hospital in Dubai and received a visit from Larry Mitchell, the local station chief of the CIA.

Why hadn't Mitchell arrested him? They had no doubt about the answer. Bin Laden is a creation of the CIA and always has been an American intelligence 'asset', Lamy said, and reeled off a long list of occasions on which he had clearly been so starting with the rise of the Mujahideen and the collapse of the Najibullah regime in Afghanistan, which effectively brought an end to the ten-year Russian occupation, then the 'Islamic brigades' and the civil wars in Bosnia, Kosovo and Macedonia and twelve years later 9/11.

"He's probably playing golf right now with Poppy Bush. The family fortunes are more closely intertwined than legs in a whorehouse."

Lamy chuckled and launched into the connection with Pakistan's ISI and the $100,000 Mahmoud Ahmad, the chief of their military intelligence, ordered sent to the account of Muhammad Atta in Florida. That between September 4th and 13th Ahmad was in Washington and met with CIA Director Tenet, Deputy Secretary of State Armitage, Secretary of State Powell, the Chairman of the Senate Foreign Relations Committee Joseph Biden and the National Security Advisor, though she rather clumsily denied it. That he was breakfasting at the Capitol on the day of the tragedy with the chairmen of the House and Senate Intelligence Committees, Bob Graham and Porter Goss. And let's not forget, he added, Osama's brother, Shafiq bin Laden, was Poppy Bush's guest of honor at a meeting of the Carlyle Group at 9AM that fateful morning. And then what about the hastily arranged departure of bin Laden family members before any other commercial airlines were allowed to fly and the discreet withdrawal of bin Laden accounts from Carlyle in the weeks since.

Such was the detail of Lamy's discourse that without Michael having noticed the passage of time the limo was drawing up outside Terminal 7.

"British Airways what?" Lamy asked.

Michael had to fish a crumpled piece of notepaper from his pocket while answering, "Oh, yes, um, it's, um, BA 0173."

"I'll wait outside with Mike. I've got some calls to make. You two go ahead."

§

In a quiet corner nook at The Cock and Hen in the Ballyhackamore district of Belfast, nestled on Lord Street between Albert Bridge Road and Castlereagh, Loomis Consterdine was staring into his third gin and Italian wondering whether to flee the country on the instant or keep a hastily arranged dinner date with an old NSA colleague who had just flown in to George Best airport from Washington that afternoon.

McLeaves Lock Restaurant, named for the third lock on the disused Lagan canal and the only one to have survived intact, had become an habitual haunt of his since it was within the confines of the Police Service's Newforge Country Club and conveniently located half way between their headquarters on Knock Road and his rented house in Upper Malone and more than that they grilled a tolerably rare steak but Larry McWhirter's sudden demise coupled with the unexpected and suspicious arrival was putting him off the idea of food altogether.

§

"There are historical precedents," Warren said, as they waited in the crowded terminal for Helen to collect her luggage and pass through security.

Her flight was on the arrival screen showing twelve minutes early and already landed so they were hopeful she wouldn't be long.

"What?" Michael asked.

"Historical and physical as well."

"What are they?"

"Lourdes, for example, a delusion that has persisted for a hundred and fifty years. Our Lady of Fatima and all the countless Marian 'appearances' throughout history. Yes, sure, the Catholic Church fosters such irrational nonsense but people sometimes come away believing they're cured. I'm thinking of crowd psychology. Of the Nuremberg rallies, the Salem witch trials and Joseph McCarthy. I'm thinking of Poe's 'faintly luminous agitated vapors' that enshrouded the House of Usher. Of St. Elmo's Fire in 'The Tempest' and 'The Rime of the Ancient Mariner' and 'God's burning finger' laid upon the Pequod in 'Moby Dick'. I'm thinking of Bergson and Rupert Sheldrake's 'morphic resonance', the so-called 'hundredth monkey' effect. Of crop circles. Of Bell's theorem and dark matter. I'm thinking I don't know what in hell I'm talking about."

Neither of them laughed.

"The three weird sisters in Macbeth," Michael offered, "But I don't know how to put it better than David did. The pressure builds to a point it can't help but force a way through the cracks. Evil so prodigious it simply can't be kept secret."

Warren nodded thoughtfully.

"Perhaps we'll find out something about David and Fernando's murder," he said, "The invitation is transparently ridiculous but irresistible."

"I suppose with our jillionaire along they won't slit our throats."

"They're definitely stumped by the connection between you."

Helen appeared with an overflowing leather satchel slung over one shoulder and tugging a large suitcase. She looked slightly frazzled and was almost upon them before she saw their faces through the crush and when she finally noticed Michael waving her eyes filled with tears and as they came together they both gave her a hug in silence.

"It's wonderful to see you," Warren said quietly.

"You too," she replied, "What havoc has this lunatic been causing?"

"None at all," Warren reassured her with an ironic furrow of his brow, "We're doing our best to keep everything under control."

"Come and meet our host," Michael said, taking her satchel and suitcase in tow and steering them toward the exit, "We've got an impossible amount to tell."

§

The president spent the whole morning staring at the ceiling of the master bedroom and remained unresponsive to the tender ministrations of his wife and the not so tender remonstrations of his mother who had finally given up trying to get through to her wayward son and stormed out in a rage, calling him an 'irresponsibly stubborn little prick'.

Even the Reverend Kirbyjon, who managed several short visits to the room between conference calls with the Power Center in Houston and its affiliates in Denver, Dallas and Oklahoma City and sat calmly by his stricken leader's side and held his hand while he and Laura prayed fervently together to the Lord their God for guidance and assistance, was beginning to get bored with it.

He decided to read from the Book of Revelation in a last ditch attempt to dislodge whatever demons were possessing him and had come to the eighth verse of the twenty-first chapter.

" . . But for the fearful and unbelieving, and abominable, and murderers, and fornicators, and sorcerers, and idolaters, and all liars, their part shall be in the lake that burneth with fire and brimstone which is the second . . "

As his tongue brushed the roof of his mouth to begin the word 'death' and complete the verse his patient screamed, "Noo! Noo! Noo!" at the top of his lungs and threw off his catatonic state and the covers in a frenzy, leapt from the bed and dashed from the room and ran six or seven times up and down the central hall like a panicked animal before he could be restrained and he was now lying strapped to the examination table in the doctor's office two floors below under heavy sedation.

The reverend stood in the doorway with a comforting arm around the First Lady's shoulders and the National Security Advisor and Chief-of-Staff to either side staring unhappily at the nurses fussing over their feebly twitching mealticket.

"Thank Christ you cancelled the tours for today," he said.

§

What they told Helen on the ride to Mattituck was mind-blowing and by the time they arrived she still had more questions than answers but both Warren and Lamy thought they should go straight to the seaside for the ceremony since it was nearly four o'clock and overcast and the sky was already beginning to darken.

Lamy drove them to the top of the cliff in a dusty red Range Rover that was normally only used by Charlie making his daily round of the fields and orchards and they walked the last fifty yards down a sandy slope to a promontory that bracketed one end of the little bay.

Helen held David's urn and Warren Fernando's and they stood together on the rocks and tipped them and the wind quickly blew the ashes into a single stream over the choppy water.

"Rest in peace, my dear, dear friends," Warren said.
Helen was too moved to speak.
"Say hello to Ruth," Lamy added in a strange hoarse voice.
"I'm so, so sorry," Michael whispered.

Stanza Eighteen

you can't take it with you you say
we know it that's why we make hay
there's no pleasure like feeling
global tentacles stealing
a march the American way

§

Maxwell Forman was taken in the van to the Bronx House of Detention on River Avenue which was not more than two hundred yards from the stadium. He had been held overnight without charge and released the next morning.

But to be silenced in that way was a new and unpleasant experience and he spent the afternoon in Union Square where there was much talk and planning and bitterness about the mayor's deep cuts in rescue personnel at Ground Zero and even more about the apparitions which by now nearly everyone had seen.

The Internet was boiling with interpretations and fury that the mainstream media had not offered more than a few guarded and dismissive remarks on the subject and many in the square were calling for a protest at the Times Building and Rockefeller Center and there was growing enthusiasm for a mass demonstration in front of the White House.

Being a loner not a joiner Maxwell only listened but by five o'clock he had packed both 'Humpty Dumpty' and 'Lon Cheney' and all three were standing in line at Penn Station to board the next bus for Washington.

§

Charlie was waiting for them by the gate beyond the swimming pool as they returned from the beach and told Lamy that he would 'see' the Range Rover to the garage.

"When she's comfortable we'll need drinks all round," Lamy said with a smile and Charlie nodded and slowly drove away.

As they passed the kitchen Camilla came out, wiping her hands on a cloth.

"I am happy it is so soon again, Miguel," she said and gave Michael a kiss on both cheeks and he introduced Helen and Lamy introduced Warren and asked what was for supper and she gave him a motherly pat on the chest and told him, "You are too impatient to know everything, Wicho. Let it come as a surprise."

Charlie took care of their bags when they arrived and they had already been shown to their rooms and, other than the need for a brief pit stop after the chill of the sea, within five minutes they were all gathered in Lamy's study.

"Thank you for doing that," Helen said to Warren and Lamy, "It's strange. I never met Fernando and Michael will tell you I'm no sentimentalist but I could really feel how much they loved each other."

"That they did," Warren agreed.

"Maybe we'll get lucky tomorrow and flush out some specifics about their murderers," Lamy said, "However the information may come. What would you all like to drink? Helen, you've had one hell of a day so far. I hope the rest of it will be less of a shock. Please make yourself at home."

"I'm dying for a large scotch," she said, still taking in the room.

"Single malt?" he asked.

"Common or garden is fine," she replied.

"Rocks?"

"Just a splash of water, thanks."

Lamy smiled and said, "I liked you the minute I saw you."

"I'm parched. I'd love a Guinness, if Charlie has one," Michael said.

"Warren?"

"I'll join Helen with the scotch. But single malt sounds tempting."

Charlie appeared in the doorway and Lamy told him what to bring and he shuffled away without a word and as he was going Lamy turned and looked at them and threw up his hands in a gesture of hopeless submission to the whims of fate and laughed.

"Ain't life an adventure!"

§

Though the invitation to Mr. Michael Davenport and friends had come from both of them the 20th National Security Advisor and the 46th vice-president had very different agendas. For him the president's strange malaise smelled of nothing but opportunity yet for her it spelled the gravest danger. She had no doubt that Michael was simply Michael but for him belief didn't matter and the only issue was winning the game.

He secretly hated the poker-faced Bavarian *graue Eminenz* whose shadowy presence lay behind all his complots, supporting them yet also threatening them at every juncture, and would have loved to poison his *Apfelkrapfen* but, now that the general was gone and the president might well be on the way out, she felt a strong need to be securely in his good graces and once she was back in the seclusion of her office, after spending virtually every minute of the afternoon playing damage control on the rumors that seemed to ripple outward at the speed of light about the president's condition, she decided to risk giving him a direct call.

She was nervous as she dialed because, though there was no adjoining door, the sanctum of the grim *Reichsführer* from Casper was directly beyond her south wall and she sensed he was probably still in there.

Nancy Maginnes answered, the 56th Secretary of State's second wife now twenty-seven years at his side, eleven years his junior in age and at a minimum four inches his superior in height, the slightly horsey philanthropist scion of a patrician White Plains family, who was his student at Harvard and on his recommendation had become a lifelong associate of Nelson Rockefeller.

"Nan, it's Condi Rice," she said, almost whispering.

"Who?"

"Condoleezza."

"Oh yes?" the strange warble replied, "How nice to hear your voice, Miss Rice. What is it? Do you want Henry?"

"Yes, if he's not too busy."

"He's watching the news. I told him not to bother. It's bad for his digestion."

"I know what you mean. I just need him for a minute."

"He's very tired. He was so late from Vienna last night."

"Oh really? I'll try not to upset him further."

"Hold on then."

In the silence, despite her belief in reason and logic and their power over the emotions, she felt the south wall turning cold as ice.

"Hello," said the unmistakable gravel rattle.

"I've put it out there that the manifestations or whatever we want to call them should be stopped," she said, lying, "But there's more I didn't tell you and I really don't know where it's coming from."

"Is it true what I'm hearing about George?"

"Probably worse if anything."

"Should I talk to him?"

"I don't think that's necessary yet."

"What's the more?"

"It's hard to believe but Mueller's foot soldiers have been rounding up literally thousands of little plastic knickknacks of Dick."

"So what? Nancy has dozens of them."

A poor joke but it reminded her of the legendary tidbit about a journalist who accosted the Kissingers walking near Dupont Circle a few years after they were married and asked him if it was true he was sleeping with young boys at the Hotel Carlyle. Nancy grabbed the woman by the throat and was arrested for attempted murder.

"Ha ha, you know what I mean. Dick as a fish, Dick as a Chinaman, Dick as anything you can think of and always gushing blood from the mouth. Cheneybilia I call it. Mueller sends crates of the stuff to Eisenhower every morning. Scooter has taken over a whole warehouse for it in Bethesda."

"Shit like that is always happening. There are millions of me too."

"True but it's not helping."

"What are you going to do about George?"

"I've told the doctors to check him for everything. Ground glass, arsenic, fly glue, everything. By the way, I warned Dick to lay off Vespucci."

"Is he still here?"

"His sister arrived in New York this afternoon."

"Sister? I didn't know he had a sister."

"What we don't know about him would fill Yankee Stadium."

"Did she come from Rome?"

"No, London."

"Interesting."

Too much idiocy always made her feel faint, a feeling she did not like, and she knew it was time to end the conversation.

"Are you watching the game?" she asked.

"*Ja.* Steinbrenner wanted me to sit in his box but I can't stand him."

"It's better on TV."

§

As they drank their drinks and Charlie brought them another they were also watching the news and talking non-stop about the madness of the coming visit and the generally insane situation in the entire country.

"What do you think is actually the matter with him?" Helen asked after they saw a clip of Andrew Card blandly explaining it was fatigue and nothing more that made the president's doctors recommend cancellation of the day's appointments.

"I'd say unacknowledged guilt," Warren said.

It was hard for Helen to accept the idea of a conspiracy but after all they had told her she was beginning to come round.

"He's no dyed-in-the-wool villain like his father," Lamy offered.

"It's just possible he has a conscience," Warren added.

"Perhaps they're trying to kill him then," Helen suggested.

"I doubt it," Lamy said, "Contrary to their purpose. They're not stupid. Little George is the perfect front man. Likable, down home, easily corrupted. Unless Cheney himself has gone mad with ambition they'll want him in place. Cheney has to know his own fireside manner is strictly Hammer film."

"I still can't get why they want to see you," Helen went on.

The combination of whiskey and jetlag made it look like she was blushing. A beguiling illusion, Michael would have been quick to say.

"OK, I can more or less get why they think you're some Italian go-between or superspy or something because of what happened in Mexico but what do they think you've got to do with all this weirdness?"

"I think they think Louis and I are behind it somehow."

Charlie rapped on the doorframe and summoned them to the dining room.

"Coming," Lamy said and turned back to Helen, "And there's more to it. I'll tell you over supper."

§

The anxious protégé of Brent Scowcroft, a Mormon from Ogden, Utah, a former lieutenant-general in the USAF and vice-chairman of Kissinger Associates, who was both the 9th National Security Advisor under Gerald Ford, in which office he was preceded by the squat Yankee fan from Fürth and followed by the scaly-skinned geostrategist from the lesser nobility in Warsaw, Zbigniew Brzezinski, and the 17th under the First Father, in the blithely hypocritical footsteps of the current Secretary of State, need not have worried about *Reichsführer* number two behind the wall because he was seated comfortably in his Chippendale recliner at Observatory Circle and just making a first delicious dip into a recently acquired 1653 edition of Izaak Walton's 'The Compleat Angler'.

§

Much to Michael's delight Camilla's surprise was her Peruvian version of a traditional English Sunday dinner. Medium roast beef with pan-browned potatoes, onions, carrots, parsnips, peas, caulifower, baked marrow and Yorkshire pudding, topped off with rich gravy and savoured with pickled beets and strong horseradish. What a woman!

"You are an absolute miracle worker!" he exclaimed.

"*De nada*, Miguel. Wicho wanted a meal of welcome for Elena."

She and Lamy shared a conspiratorial wink.

"Thank you," Helen said, "It's quite magnificent."

Charlie brought several bottles of vintage Pomerol to accompany the feast and when Michael took an enthusiastic swig and declared it 'a fine English claret' Lamy smiled politely into his napkin.

For several minutes there was only the sound of cutlery and pure enjoyment and then Michael came up for air, wiped his mouth, took another swallow of wine and turned to Lamy.

"All right then, what appalling new secret have you got to tell us?"

Their host paused for a moment before speaking.

"I'm guessing they're not particularly bothered by the manifestations. I'd say they just want to be reassured about where you stand on the plutonium. They'd like to find out if you've told anyone. You never mentioned it in the articles you wrote on your experiences in Juarez. You only talked about vampirism and the murders of the young women not your role as Vespucci and the meeting with the Russians."

"It wasn't only the embarrassment. I'll admit I was also scared."

"It's a good thing you didn't," Lamy went on, "We saw the news about the general's sudden death. The coronary story is a blatant lie. He was as healthy as a horse. And I haven't yet told you something else. All three of the young women he was with at Belmont and who went with you to the party have disappeared."

Helen gave Michael a sharp questioning look but Lamy was sensitive enough not to elaborate.

Michael was horrified. Was yet more death to be laid at his blundering door? Why in the name of all the egomanic gods had he opened his stupid mouth?

"And Loomis Consterdine, who was head of the DEA and equally involved, didn't make it to a dinner engagement in Belfast this evening."

"How is it you always seem to know everything?" Michael asked in flustered amazement.

"Connections," Lamy replied without smiling, "Two and two generally make four. We've talked about that, haven't we? It seems Ms. Rice and whoever else was part of it at her level are doing some housecleaning. Anyone who knew about the plutonium and also anyone who may have heard your name."

"That would apply to the Russians," Michael observed glumly.

Lamy chuckled.

"Can you imagine them blabbing to the press?"

"No. But if what you say is true then you're all in great danger tomorrow, aren't you? Is that why they agreed to include you in the invitation?"

"Come now, Michael, they're not going to commit murder in the White House. But our safety afterwards very much depends on what you do. First, let me tell you a story that shows how close 9/11 was to being a nuclear event."

Lamy launched into an astonishing tale about a con-artist and informant named Randy Glass and a little-known FBI sting called Operation Diamondback, interlaced with asides regarding the two species of venomous pit vipers common to the United States, *crotalus adamanteus*, the eastern, and *crotalus atrox*, the western, and a digression about the World Series and the coincidentally-named Arizona team.

The operation, which bore fruit the previous June, uncovered an attempt by agents of Pakistan's ISI to buy Stinger missiles and nuclear weapons components for the Taliban and Osama bin Laden. The components included heavy water and enriched plutonium, the makings of a 'dirty bomb' which was one method under consideration for bringing down the World Trade Center. Not surprisingly, the ISI agents wanted to pay for some of the goods with heroin.

Glass, who was part of the sting, claimed he passed on the information in the form of a warning about a possible attack to former Florida governor and now senator Robert Graham and Robert Wexler, the current representative for the 19th Congressional District of Palm Beach, both Democrats, both of whom made fleeting admission of the warning at press conferences in August and then denied all knowledge subsequent to the day of 9/11 itself.

"Needless to say, none of the Pakistanis were arrested," Lamy concluded, "I would guess it will be Glass who comes out of it badly. The whole affair is being sanitized by the highest levels of our so-called government."

Despite the perfection of the meal Lamy's revelation about Brandy and her friends caused Michael to lose his appetite and when Camilla asked if anyone would care for more he only said yes out of politeness.

"So the FBI was selling the plutonium the Russians wanted Amado Portillo to hide in the Samalayuca?"

"Not that particular stash necessarily. They definitely had something to show though because the ISI brought the head of their own nuclear program to examine it."

"It makes the official story even more unbelievable," Warren said, "Because if the terrorists wanted it to be a nuclear event, which apparently at least some of them did, why didn't they fly one or both of the planes that took off from Boston into the power station at Indian Point. It was directly along their flight path and would have caused far more destruction and far more long lasting consequences."

They were silent as Camilla brought Michael another heaping plateful.

"Good lord," he said, "I'll never manage it. But thank you, you are a dear."

"Save room for some English trifle," she said breezily as she departed.

"Heavens," Michael sighed, "I believe she is the terrorist."

"So the thing is," Lamy added grimly, "Whoever they truly believe you are, they know you know about the plutonium."

Michael put down his knife and fork and pushed the plate away.

"Well then, I'm finally buggered. We all are. What have I done! I can't bear to think of it. Oh god, I'm sorry. Helen, you mustn't come. Stay for a day with Warren and sort out David's will and then go back to London and change your name. I'll go to Washington and promise them I won't say anything."

"Oh, do stop being an idiot," Helen reprimanded him.

"I think everything will be fine," Lamy began again calmly.

"If what?" Warren asked.

"Well, it's obvious someone there believes that a person named Bartolomeo Vespucci actually exists, whoever they think he is or what interests they think he represents. And they're afraid of him. So afraid they haven't dared to touch you all these years even though they doubtless suspect you aren't him."

"What are they going to do, inject me with truth serum?" Michael blurted.

"I'm sure they'd like to do that. But it wouldn't work because your safety and our safety lies in your continuing to tell the truth. That you are Michael Davenport. It will just prove to them that they've been totally unable to crack your cover. It was Michael Davenport they invited to lunch. They're too cautious to mention Vespucci by name."

"Then what you said is all guesswork!" Michael exclaimed, "How do we know they're even thinking about Vespucci!"

"Have you forgotten that 'Nikolai' told you as much?"

"Oh, shit, yes, um, I'm sorry, I'm rather upset," Michael mumbled.

"Who the hell is Nikolai, for goodness' sake?" Helen asked incredulously.

"He was one of two men who were following me."

"Why?"

"I really don't know. They wouldn't say."

"You talked to them?"

"Yes, we got to know each other quite well. Delightful chaps really."

Helen started to laugh.

"Only you could create such a muddle!"

"So you see," Lamy went on, "You won't have to do anything when you get there but be Michael Davenport and Helen Davenport. Whatever they ask, tell the truth. If they ask about our relationship and how we came to know each other tell the truth. If you mention David and Fernando, all the better. They won't dare to stay on the subject. If they try to find out what you know about the manifestations tell them exactly what you've seen and exactly what you think. There is nothing in the truth that won't ever more firmly convince them you are Vespucci. In fact, there is absolutely nothing that would convince them you were Michael

Davenport unless you say the name Bartolomeo Vespucci or claim you are him. And if, under the influence of the truth serum, they ask if you've ever heard of this man you can say, yes, he was an obscure 15th century Italian astronomer who once wrote a letter to Niccolò Machiavelli!"

§

By game time for game number four that evening the president recovered enough to be returned to the master bedroom on the second floor and Laura and the nurses propped him up on the pillows to watch. The results of the blood tests were all negative for any type of poison and his vital signs were staggeringly normal. Even at the height of his panic attack his blood pressure had remained at 128/78, astonishingly low for a man of his age and responsibilities. His heart rate, on the other hand, fluctuated between 150 and 180 and he had been sweating profusely like a man pursued but then that is precisely what he felt he was.

He didn't say a word nor take his eyes from the screen as Laura sat beside him and they watched together. Every few minutes during the broadcast the action of the game was interrupted by fleeting manifestations such as those with which the public was already familiar, the antics of the Mount Rushmore four, the accusing faces from the Third World, but as the game progressed these were taken over by the macabre and mocking confessional of an endless gallery of bland unrepentant faces, some known but most unknown, many evidently from the world of politics, some military, some corporate, nearly all American but with a few notable overseas exceptions, and every one spoke as though in a rush to detail their particular role in the tragedy and thus, in some weird way, to gain immunity from blame.

Laura started anxiously every time they appeared and watched the president closely for any adverse reaction but there was none. He didn't even seem to see them and by the end they became almost as commonplace to her and as unworthy of comment as the commercials. It was Hallowe'en night, after all.

The game was a tense seesaw but the Yankees miraculously came from behind with two runs in the bottom of the ninth inning to make it 3-3. Then, in the bottom of the tenth, as the stadium clock passed midnight and the calendar entered the month of November for the first time in Major League baseball history, Derek Jeter slammed a solo home run over the right field fence off Arizona's Korean closer Byung-Hyun Kim and the Yankees tied the Series.

To Laura's amazement and relief as her beloved stared blankly at the Yankee shortstop pumping his fist in the air, rounding the bases and leaping triumphantly with both feet onto home plate where he was mobbed by ecstatic teammates, she saw the tiny flutter of a smile crease the frightening deadpan of his lips.

There was a moment of inner struggle, as though to consolidate some deep and difficult insight, and then he whispered with needful intensity, "Yankees two, Diamondbacks two."

§

After consuming a small dish of trifle Helen asked Camilla if she might have a cup of tea with milk and sugar and when Camilla brought it for her she told Lamy she was very tired and would they please excuse her if she went to bed and he and Warren went off to the study to watch what remained of the game followed by Charlie with a tray of double espressos and snifters of fine cognac and Michael said he would return shortly and accompanied Helen upstairs.

"Despite what he says, I'm petrified," she told him as they reached her door.

"I know, so am I. I'm dreadfully sorry to have involved you in this madness. I would have told you not to come but they only called Lamy with the invitation when you were already in the air."

"It's awful for you, isn't it," she said sympathetically, "Awful that something so innocent could lead to all this."

"I don't know why it always seems to happen to me."

She eyed him ironically and they both started to giggle.

"Because you're such an absolute noo-nah," she said, pushing him lightly on the chest, "You stumble about with no peripheral vision."

"A veritable Mister Magoo," he concurred.

"Bartolomeo fucking Vespucci!" she exclaimed with a *commedia dell'arte* twirl, almost collapsing from mirth and fatigue.

"A superspy so fucking obscure he doesn't even exist!" Michael shrieked.

"But does you in with a whiff of his aftershave!"

The thought of Brandy stifled his laughter and they fell silent.

"It's horribly true," he admitted, "I went to a party after the races and one of the young women with the general got permission to take me back to the hotel in his limousine. She asked me who I really was and for some totally idiotic reason I said that blasted name."

"And they killed her because of it?"

"That's what Lamy seems to think. But maybe she knew too much about a lot of things. He said she was familiar with the vice-president among others."

"Including you, I suppose."

"Oh lord, dear sister, please don't ask."

She raised her eyes to heaven but resisted.

"And this woman Rice was part of that revolting affair in El Paso?"

"I'm really starting to believe so, yes."

"Why on earth would she want to see you again? I'd be mortified."

"Ah, well, but then you're human. At least, as far as we know."

Stanza Nineteen

§

Charlie woke them early for the flight to Washington and when Helen came down to breakfast she declared she slept brilliantly thanks to Camilla's wondrous meal and was no longer dreading the coming encounter but looking forward to whatever the day might bring. Michael was none too sure her altered mood was a good sign but kept it to himself.

She was concerned about what to wear on such an occasion and if Michael's jacket wasn't too old and rumpled but Lamy and Warren were dressed casually and said he'd be fine. There certainly wasn't time to go shopping and Michael was far too tall to fit any of his host's clothes and he told her not to fuss. She was bothered that she had nothing suitable but the combination of her job and the passage of the years had naturally enhanced the neatness of her tailoring and though she remained unconvinced they all told her she looked perfect.

Mike brought the limo at half past seven and on the way to Gabreski Lamy gave them a rundown on a few choice items from the morning papers. First, a New York hospital worker had died from inhaled anthrax and the fear of contamination had now spread as far west as a postal station in Kansas City. Second, the FBI had alerted eight states that terrorists might be targeting suspension bridges on the west coast but the information was unconfirmed. Third that Al Jazeera TV had received a letter from Osama bin Laden urging Muslims to rise up against the Christian crusade in Afghanistan and fourth, in odd synchronicity with Warren's comment about it the previous evening, the FAA had just created no-fly zones around all the country's nuclear power plants including the one at Indian Point.

"Anything about the baring of souls during the game?" Warren asked.

"Nothing at all. But I think that's about to change."

"How so?" Michael asked.

"Big demonstrations are set for both New York and D. C. tomorrow."

"Something really does have to give," Michael said, "The manifestations have been totally overwhelming. Whatever absurd interpretations are made of what went on last night how could it not be front page news? My editor told me yesterday the whole thing is everywhere in the European media."

"It's going to be quite a day," Warren said with a wry smile.

"I can't wait to meet the bastards," Helen added and the hint of ferocity in her voice made Michael frown.

§

The bastards in question were already in their offices in the northwest corner of the West Wing and were only slightly heartened by the news that the president was able to sit up in bed and had recovered his powers of speech sufficiently to ask for coffee and a burrito. The doctors insisted, however, that he remain in the First Family quarters and free from the burden of official duty for at least another day so they had taken the liberty of ordering a midday meal for six in the cosy atmosphere of the private presidential dining room.

At eight o'clock they convened in the Cabinet Room for the daily intelligence and FBI briefings and twenty minutes later with the Homeland Security Council. The day's agenda concerned aviation security legislation and the imminent visits of Jacques Chirac and Tony Blair and how best to phrase the announcement that, despite widespread international protest, the bombing campaign in Afghanistan would continue unabated through the month of Ramadan which the National Security Advisor was scheduled to make in less than an hour's time but inevitably the discussion reverted to the thorny problem of the apparitions.

"Jesus," the ferocious kisser exclaimed irritably, "I've just got off the phone with the Amir of Qatar, Hamad bin Khalifa Al Thani, and even he was grilling me about them. We won't have to worry about Ramadan, it'll all be questions about this other shit."

"What are you going to tell them?" Homeland Chief Ridge enquired.

"That I haven't seen any of it myself but I'm sure it's just some silly prank. We have far more important matters at hand."

"But who's behind it? Don't you have any idea, Bob?"

FBI Director Mueller was munching on a messy egg salad sandwich.

"Thought we did," he mumbled, "Thought it was coming out of Brighton Beach for a while."

"Condi and I have a line on the ringleaders," the second *Reichsführer* broke in reassuringly.

"Who?" Ridge and Mueller asked in perplexed unison.

"We'll know better after lunch."

As they left the meeting and walked back down the corridor to their offices the trim *Oberst-Gruppenführer* couldn't resist questioning, "You don't really think they are, do you?" to which the ichthyophile from the Tetons replied with a patronizing sneer, "You can't catch fish without your hook in the water, dummy."

"Granted," she allowed tautly, "Should we have mentioned any of this to the Doctor?"

"Fuck the Doctor," he hissed, "I wouldn't be surprised if it's him!"

§

Laura was feeling cautiously optimistic. George had slept calmly for the first time in months and as dawn crept through the windows the reverend Kirbyjon had led them in an uplifting prayer and though their old friend was departing for Texas forthwith she was hopeful if her beloved followed doctor's orders and she could whisk him away to Camp David for a quiet weekend before any of the threatened demonstrations began then he might just be on the fragile road to recovery.

Even the intrusion of the Attorney-General, who burst in the bedroom door as the reverend was bidding them farewell and insisted on singing 'Let the Mighty Eagle Soar' in its entirety at the top of his fervent lungs, was taken in merciful good humor.

"This eagle's place is in the sky,

You can see it in his eye,

Though he's cried a bit for what we've put him through.

He's soared above the lifted lamp

That guards sweet freedom's door,

In the dews, the damps, the watchfires of a nation torn by war.

Oh, he's far too young to die,

You can see it in his eye,

He's only just begun to fly,
It's time to let the mighty eagle soar, once more!"
And that was the merest fraction of it.

§

It took an hour and fifteen minutes for the little Citation to transport them from Gabreski to Ronald Reagan Washington National Airport which is located on the west bank of the Potomac in Arlington directly across from Fort McNair, the Naval Station Reseach Lab and Bolling Air Force Base, just to the southeast of the Pentagon and the National Cemetery and three miles straight south from the White House.

There were only five passenger seats and Helen sat beside Warren and most of the conversation on the trip concerned David and Fernando and the will and what on earth to do about the gallery but much of the time they sat lost in their own thoughts amid an uneasy silence.

Mike was the fifth passenger and when they landed and came down the steps to the tarmac a limousine was waiting for them and he took the wheel.

Michael had been hoping to spot some famous landmarks as they descended but Lamy told him they wouldn't see any since they were obliged to approach down the river from the south because of the always complex D.C. flight restrictions but he did just catch a smog-veiled glimpse of the squat vastness of the Pentagon in the last few moments.

"How the devil could anyone believe they flew a jumbo through such a hair-trigger gauntlet?" Michael asked, knowing no one woud bother to answer.

Mike swung the limo onto the Mount Vernon Memorial Highway at twelve minutes after eleven and they had about an hour to kill so Lamy told him to take a detour around the sights and with the aid of Lamy's running historical monologue they were entertained, educated and afforded fine views of the Pentagon, a snatch of the cemetery, the Lincoln, Jefferson and Roosevelt Memorials, the Capitol, the Mall and the Washington Monument and Michael was able to get photos of them all standing in front of every one before they rolled up to the White House.

Following the National Security Advisor's instructions Mike stopped at the entrance to State Place on 17th Street where there was a barricade. The guards knew the plate number of the car and allowed it to pass through and told Mike to park immediately on the far side. He would be able to take it no further and should wait with it until his passengers returned. Then all four were politely asked to get out and show identification and given a meticulous once-over with a metal detector wand. Lamy and Helen were told to leave their cell phones with Mike and much to Michael's disappointment he was not allowed to bring his camera. As they finished the procedure an 'in-house' limousine was summoned and they were driven to the southwest appointment gate.

There was a grand old Victorian structure to their left on their slow passage down State Place and Lamy told them it was the Eisenhower Building and housed the overflow staff of the president and vice-president, the offices of Management and Budget and the National Security Council among much else.

"We could be in London just here," Helen observed.

"An uninspired stab at Parisian Second Empire," Lamy informed her, "Mark Twain called it the ugliest building in America."

At a second gate another pair of guards rechecked their ID and they eased down West Executive Avenue and were deposited beside some steps that led to the colonnaded portico at the north entrance of the West Wing. The trees prevented Michael from getting much of a view of the mansion itself until they came up the steps. They were five minutes late and a broadly smiling Scooter was already there waiting.

After cursory introductions Scooter led them in through the lobby and down a corridor past the Roosevelt Room then took a right and, much to their surprise and Michael's delight, ushered them in to what he immediately recognized as the Oval Office. To be suddenly surrounded by so historic a setting was extraordinary but there was hardly time for him to take it in because the vice-president and the National Security Advisor were standing ready to greet them.

"Hello, Lou, you old dog," Cheney said pleasantly, extending a clammy hand, "And Mr. Warren Allen Jones, what a pleasure."

"I'm your long time admirer, sir," Condoleezza cooed, shaking Warren's hand also.

"I'd never have suspected it," he answered drily, "But I'm gratified."

"And Mr. Davenport," the vice-president said, coming to Michael, "Condi tells me you're a movie man."

Michael caught a look in her eye that left not the slightest shadow of a doubt in his mind she was the one but he didn't dare turn to share it with

Helen.

"Hardly," Michael demurred, "But she's kind to say so."

It was idiotic that he found himself nervous and tongue-tied. He put it down to the inevitable excitement of being in the room itself coupled with the irritating fact that high office, like fame, always seems to exude an irresistible and mysterious charisma. Also, the National Security Advisor had held his look without a trace of embarrassment and it had thrown him off balance.

"And this is your sister?"

Helen was trying to hold on to her resolve but finding it almost as difficult.

"Yes, I'm Helen Davenport."

"I understand you're newly arrived," Cheney went on, "Welcome. Thanks for taking time out to visit us."

"We're very pleased to be here," she said.

"Good, good. Well now, we're on kind of a busy schedule so if you don't mind we'll just go straight in."

He led the way down the private corridor to the dining room which passed by the presidential lavatory and, for the time being at least, could only be accessed via the Oval Office because the president ordered the door from it into the main corridor to be permanently closed.

"I'm sure you've heard the president's a tad under the weather. Nothing serious but it means Condi and I have to step up and do a bunch of pinch-hitting."

In the dining room an elegant table was set for six and two butlers stood ready to serve.

"We have wine laid on but anyone care for a cocktail?" Cheney asked.

They all said wine would be just fine.

"Please sit beside me, Ms. Davenport," Condoleezza said, "And Michael, you next to her beside Dick. Gentlemen, we have you opposite."

The vice-president took the president's normal place in front of the windows and Condoleezza took Laura's chair. Michael and Helen were facing Healy's portrait on the west wall and he enquired who it was.

"George's favorite," Cheney informed them with his trademark smirk, "John Quincy Adams. The only other president who was the son of a president. Can't see why he likes it otherwise. Poor bastard looks as if he's about to croak."

They were all a bit surprised by the coarseness of the comment but managed to chuckle politely nonetheless.

"So Lou," Cheney went on, as one butler poured wine and the other dished up an appetizing-looking salad of red peppers, corn and butternut squash, "Neither Condi nor I can figure how the three of you came to be sitting together at the game the other night. How did an old shitheel capitalist like you come to be friends with our brilliant philosopher of the left?"

"We aren't," Lamy and Warren answered almost simultaneously.

"We were thrown together by love and mutual acquaintance," Lamy said.

"He was having an affair with a friend of mine's sister," Warren explained.

"And my sister Helen was once married to that friend," Michael added.

The vice-president let out a mirthless guffaw.

"That's it, huh? Small world. Who was the lucky guy?"

"No one particularly well known," Warren replied, "He owned an art gallery near where I live in Soho. David Giudice was his name."

Michael was watching their eyes for the slightest reaction.

"David died last Sunday," he said, "That's why Helen came to New York."

"Really?" Condoleezza responded sympathetically, "I'm so sorry."

"He left her everything in his will."

"We think he was murdered," Helen chimed in bluntly.

"No kidding?" Cheney said and then asked, "Are the NYPD looking into it?"

"Unfortunately not," Lamy responded with an ironic smile.

"How come?"

"They're calling it a suicide. A double suicide as a matter of fact."

"He was found dead in bed with his lover," Warren added.

"But you're sure there was something fishy about it?" Cheney asked without so much as raising an eyebrow.

"No doubt in our minds," Warren replied.

"Ain't that a son of a bitch," Cheney concluded, "Well, I'm sure I can speak for Condi when I say we both sincerely hope you'll get to the bottom of it. Helen, you have our condolences."

The first butler served the main course, filet mignon *au poivre* with button potatoes and asparagus tips, without waiting for them to finish their salad and the second was replenishing their glasses when the vice-president abruptly told them to leave and come back in fifteen minutes.

"Is the food OK?" he asked, "We mostly live on sandwiches around here."

"It's very good," Michael replied, "And the wine is delicious."

The waiters had made their exit.

"So look," Cheney began, "We're kinda desperate and we figured you might help. When Condi saw the three of you at the game she phoned me and we agreed we couldn't find more appropriate people so we invited you here for your opinions and advice."

"What about?" Lamy asked.

"You were there so you know what happened," Condoleezza said, picking up the thread, "And you must know about the other things, everyone does. We'd like your take on why it's happening and who's doing it. We'd have to say we're pretty much stumped."

"Even with the best intelligence in the world," Lamy joked.

"If it were funny we'd laugh with you, Mr. Lamy," she said seriously, "First 9/11, which was a colossal sequence of unlikely screwups, and now this."

"I'm afraid we have different viewpoints on the first," Warren cut in.

She smiled and held his eye.

"I'm aware of that, sir. We'll just have to agree to differ though I can promise you you're wrong. It's the latest occurrences we want to talk about. They're coming from every corner in a baffling variety of ways and some of them are quite frankly incomprehensible."

Michael could feel the vice-president's subtle scrutiny as he spoke.

"At the stadium particularly," he agreed, "The other oddities, the apparitions on television and the messages on signs, could be some technological wizardry that I wouldn't have a clue about but what happened at the stadium was truly beyond anything I've ever known."

"Thousands of figures couldn't have been conjured up before our eyes like that by any currently available means. To say nothing of the fans and players and the president being frozen in hypnotic silence," Warren added.

"So how do you explain it?" Cheney asked.

Warren gave a small sad laugh.

"Funnily enough, it was David Giudice who put it best. What were his exact words, Michael?"

Michael had by now perfected the rendition.

"The subcutaneous pressure of overwhelming guilt erupting like pus from a pimple."

He was sure a sudden flush of blood colored the vice-president's normally ashen cheeks but at that moment the door slammed open and he turned in his chair to see the First Lady with her face even redder and a trifle breathless.

"What in hell is going on, Dick?" she demanded.

It was not the tone Michael associated with her. Not the slightly querulous self-deprecatory drawl he became enchanted with in El Paso. There was something dark and fierce and almost fish-markety in it and her usual glazed expression was sharp-etched as though some homuncular stonemason were chipping at ice cubes behind her eyes.

"Since when do you get to dine in here without George?"

But before either the vice-president or National Security Advisor could form a response she recognized Michael and struggled to recover her familiar manner.

"Why, it's Mr. Davenport, isn't it? I'm sure it is. In El Paso you looked so . . different. Almost Italian. What a nice surprise. What brings you to Washington?"

Michael was already on his feet. He didn't know whether to curtsy or shake her hand and wisely decided on the latter.

"Um, ah, lunch," he stammered with a vague explanatory gesture at the table, "It's wonderful to see you again."

"Look, hon," Cheney began without apology, dabbing the sides of his mouth on his napkin, "We needed a quiet spot. George won't care. Why not join us? Have you had lunch? How's the patient doing by the way?"

"How about being polite and introducing me to your other guests," she said, cutting him off.

"Sorry, Laura," Condoleezza apologized, rising and relinquishing her chair, "Please say hello to Michael's sister Helen who has just arrived from London. To the famous Mr. Warren Allen Jones . . "

Clearly the name rang a bell because her famously Chinese eyes became even more narrow and slanted.

" . . And have you ever met Mr. Louis Lamy?"

"Mr. Lamy keeps a very private countenance," she teased with a sly smile, "He's never come to one of our fundraisers and he always gets an invitation."

"We each survive in our own way," Lamy acknowledged pleasantly.

Condoleezza had cleared her plate and place setting to one side between the First Lady's chair and Lamy and pulled up another seat for herself.

"Sit, Laura," she said graciously, "I'll call Gerry to bring you some lunch."

"I'm not hungry," came the still unforgiving reply.

"Have a glass of wine then."

"No, thank you. I'll take some carbonated water."

She sat and the National Security Advisor pushed her own glass forward.

"I haven't touched it," she said.

Neither did the First Lady.

"Anyone care to tell me the subject of this little get-together?" she enquired, "I declare you seem strange lunchmates."

They bounced back and forth with a rough rehash of the dialogue about the manifestations concluding as before with David's pithy encapsulation in Michael's mouth, though this time it came out less than perfectly.

"Um, ah, he described it as the overwhelming pressure of subcutaneous guilt erupting like pus from a pimple."

"I believe it was the subcutaneous pressure of overwhelming guilt," Warren corrected, "But what's the difference?"

There was silence as they waited for the First Lady's reaction.

"So you understand them to be transhuman phenomena," she said matter-of-factly, "Well, hear, hear, so do I."

Michael was very surprised she used the word.

"Jesus, Laura," Cheney said scornfully, "Please tell me you're not turning into Nancy Reagan. This place was a nightmare of séances and voodoo and exorcisms. Your father-in-law told me he once sat through lunch in here with a Congolese witch doctor. There has to be a reason for all this shit."

"Some things are beyond reason, Dick," she said, rising to her feet, "And I've got a pretty clear idea what they are. Michael, I hope you and Helen will join me in the Yellow Oval Room at four o'clock. I'm going to have George brought through for a cup of tea."

She offered no word of apology to Warren and Lamy for not including them in her invitation but swept out the door without further comment.

"Jesus!" the vice-president exclaimed, tossing his napkin on the table.

No one else spoke.

"OK," he said, "Let's quit fucking around. Whose guilt?"

The National Security Advisor had barely taken two nibbles of her food.

"Oh, come on, Dick," she said in hasty admonishment, "Everyone thinks it's us, you know that. Mr. Jones does. He said so."

"It's kind of hard to believe a few untrained Egyptians could have pulled it off by themselves," Lamy countered.

Cheney was suddenly on his feet and shouting.

"I don't care what people believe! And I don't give a rat's ass what you think, Lou. You didn't get to be a billionaire by rocking any boats. And you, Mr. Jones? It's a given what commie-sympathizing intellectuals jerk off about. Who cares what you say. Nobody listens. No, I care about what people like Michael and Helen think. Or should I call you Elena and Michele, *Signor?*"

He was leaning forward with his hands on the table, glaring triumphantly at Michael over the top of his glasses. The expression was a mixture of bottled rage and purest sycophancy and Michael couldn't stop himself from laughing.

"Jesus, Dick," the *Oberst-Gruppenführer* from Alabama muttered in disgust.

"Where did you say she was coming from, Lou?" the second *Reichsführer* went on, "Podere di Gesso. Kind of an interesting little joke. Or little slip maybe?"

"Joke," Lamy answered blandly.

"But *why*, Lou, why the joke?" he continued, pressing the point, "Why, if you don't know who Mr. Davenport really is?"

"Because I know who you think he is," Lamy replied levelly, "And I happen to know you're nuts."

The vice-president's breathing had become a labored rasp and he was forced to refrain from immediate response.

"Sorry to disappoint," Michael said apologetically, "I haven't the faintest why you think I'm someone else . . everyone assumes I'm English without even asking . . but I really am just plain old Michael Davenport."

He could see the vice-president had broken out in a sweat and his eyes had lost their focus and, as an unpleasant odor wafted over the table that reminded him of a childhood visit to the zoo at Drusilla's Park in Alfriston with his mother and the rank smell of the snake house, Cheney blurted dismissively, "Yeah, well, thanks for coming," bolted headlong for the door and was gone.

They looked at each other in amazement.

"You're right, Mr. Lamy, he is nuts," Condoleezza sighed, "We've been having a tough time. Dick has to meet with the Austrian Chancellor in just a few minutes. The meeting's in the Oval Office so we're either going to have to stay in here until it's done or leave before it happens. It's stupid but George ordered maintenance to close up the door to the hall behind me so, I'm sorry, there's only one way out. As to all the other stuff you'll have to forgive us. Everything has been upside down since 9/11. The attacks never stop in here."

Warren had tired of her posturing and said, "Tell me something, Miss Rice, have you honestly never heard the name David Giudice?"

Michael observed her tiny rueful smile with fascination.

"Oh, Mr. Jones," she answered with bone-weary patience, "We really aren't the monsters you take us to be."

§

The mortal enemy of the Snake is the Pig and equally so in reverse but it is less known that the secret friend of the Pig is the Tiger and Loomis Consterdine, being a Tiger, decided to play on that fact.

He had finished his third gin and Italian at a gulp and instead of keeping his dinner engagement at McLeaves Lock drove the red Jaguar XK8 coupe provided as one of the perks of his advisorship to Upper Malone where he hastily gathered up a suitcase of essentials. He left the car parked in front of the house and walked about two hundred yards to the high street where he caught a bus to Wellington Place in the center of Belfast. Once there he hailed a taxi that took him along the opposite side of Victoria Channel from George Best International down West Bank Road to the ferry dock for Stranraer. He had to wait just over two hours for the 22:35 and boarded it as a foot passenger.

The boat arrived at the head of Loch Ryan on time at five minutes to one in the morning and he paid a half asleep but delighted Scottish cabby two hundred and fifty pounds to take him the fifty-five miles to Glasgow Airport where he knew there was a conveniently located Holiday Inn on Caledonia Way. As he got out of the car he handed the man another hundred pounds and with a friendly wink asked him to keep his mouth shut.

He walked in the door of the hotel at twenty minutes to three, took a room under the name of John Martin and after a few fitful hours of sleep caught the 9AM Continental nonstop to Newark, New Jersey, using a passport with the same alias. He was standing at the Hertz counter in the terminal as Michael and the rest were being greeted outside the West Wing by Scooter Libby.

While still in the nook at The Cock and Hen he had briefly considered trying to negotiate a favor from the Russians in Brighton Beach but it had quickly become obvious to him they would balk at such a potentially hazardous request and that he could rely on no one but himself if he were to avoid sharing the general's fate.

§

As they were about to make their exit through the Oval Office a page came with a message from the First Lady for Warren and Lamy. She had not intended to be rude but had several appointments in the East Wing between two and four and merely wanted a moment to reacquaint herself with Michael and if they could spare the time would they please stay and regather for dinner in the family dining room in the residence at half past five. They were welcome to make themselves comfortable in the meantime in the Red Room, the Green Room or the Blue Room, whichever they preferred.

The National Security Advisor escorted them through the Rose Garden to the residence and they decided the Green Room would be most commodious and had the least monochromatic atmosphere and she left them there.

"Thanks for coming," she said pleasantly as she hastened away, "I'm kind of allergic to the irrational but I suppose I'll just have to get used to it."

Once she had gone they looked at each other and laughed.

"What do you want to do?" Lamy asked, "After such absurdity."

"I'm sure they knew David's name," Helen said.

"Oh god, yes," Michael agreed, "But you could never pin them on it."

"Don't you mean pin it on them?"

"What's the difference?"

The sad truth made them fall silent.

"So what do you want to do?" Lamy repeated.

"We can't leave now," Michael said, "It's just too fascinating. You go ahead if you need to. You don't want to leave, do you, Helen?"

"Well, I would but I don't see how we can."

"What about you, Mr. Pinko Intellectual?" Lamy asked Warren.

"Oh, no, I'm with Michele. I'm enjoying myself. You must have made quite an impression on our lady in El Paso, *Signor.*"

§

The always carefully accoutred *Oberst-Gruppenführer* had gone straight back to the West Wing and though she was dying to poke her head in the door of the Oval Office and shout, "Way to go, Dick!" she resisted and once in her own quarters immediately dialed the Doctor's private line at Kissinger Associates.

"You know who just called me?" said the crocodile croak.

"Who?"

"Connie."

"You're kidding. Where is he? Still in Belfast?"

"He's coming up here in a few minutes."

She processed the import of the information in a nanosecond.

"Did he say what he wants?"

"Don't be dumb, *Liebchen.*"

"Please don't call me that. It makes me nervous."

He chuckled and started to cough.

"What are you going to do about him?"

"I don't know," he said after clearing his throat, "What do you think I should do?"

"I'm past caring. Look, I have to tell you something. Dick and I invited the guy you think is Bartolomeo Vespucci here for lunch today."

There was an ominous silence.

"Why?"

"We wanted to find out what he knew."

"Did you?"

"No, he never took off the mask."

"What did you expect?"

"I agree it was stupid. But the thing is, he came with his sister and Laura saw him. She recognized him from El Paso and now she's going to have tea with them."

There was a longish pause for strategic rumination.

"So?" he said finally, "She thinks he's Michael Davenport, doesn't she?"

She had to bite her tongue in order not to shriek.

"That she does."

"So it probably doesn't matter."

"OK."

"Just keep him away from George."

She couldn't bring herself to tell the whole truth.

"The doctors have told him to stay in bed."

"Good."

There was another pause and more sputum rattling.

"But I wish you wouldn't do these things without asking me, *Liebling*. I don't trust that shifty little prick in the office next to you."

"He's not there, thank god. He's chatting with Schüessel."

"Ha!" the *Reichsführer* spluttered joyfully through a protracted prize-winning gargle, "Two boring shitheads who deserve each other!"

§

The second butler came into the Green Room moments after the National Security Advisor's departure and asked if they would care for any dessert or post-prandial refreshments. The strained peculiarity of lunch had barely allowed for the consumption of anything substantial though Michael did manage most of his main course and he and Warren were now happily devouring two large helpings of apple pie and vanilla ice cream. The butler also brought pots of tea and coffee and, on Michael's request, a bottle of expensive Napoleon brandy.

They were discussing the oil of Benjamin Franklin above the fireplace and trying to decide whether the great 18th century polymath looked more like Lamy or Warren in his blue velvet jacket and curly gray perruque squinting through horn-rimmed spectacles at a pamphlet and it came down in Lamy's favor but only after he had reminded them of Franklin's epigram, 'I don't mind so much being old as being fat and old.'

"Wasn't it Franklin who said 'I look at democracy as two wolves and a sheep voting on what to have for dinner' or something like that?" Michael asked.

"No," Warren replied, "But he did say, 'A countryman between two lawyers is like a fish between two cats'."

"Or pepper steak between two Dobermans," Michael observed wryly.

"It's how I felt just now," Helen concurred, "God, this is like waiting for a firing squad!"

"Have a brandy," Michael suggested, "It'll make the time pass."

Lamy was leaning back on a chair with stocking feet up on an antique table scanning a copy of the day's Washington Post and suddenly burst out laughing.

"Listen to this," he began, "There were earlier versions of this during Reagan and Poppy Bush and Junior has been chipping away at it since he took office. Now he's finally had the brazen balls to do it full out."

"What?" Warren asked.

"He signed a bill called Executive Order 13233 two days ago which basically shuts the door on public access to presidential records past and present. No one will be able to find out what the bastards have been doing unless the bastards themselves agree to it!"

"I feel lawsuits prepping as we speak," Warren said.

"Yeah, yeah, so what?" Lamy countered, "That'll take decades."

"A bit silly though, isn't it?" Helen said, "It's a confession he has something to hide."

§

In the Treaty Room directly above their heads, pacing back and forth across the patterned Victorian carpet in his pajamas and bare feet between the portrait of McKinley signing the Spanish Peace Protocols of 1898 and Healy's 'Peacemakers', a depiction of Abraham Lincoln among his advisors at the end of the Civil War, rapping the magnificent table at which Ulysses S. Grant once convened his Cabinet with the knuckles of alternate hands in an endlessly repeated syncopation at every nervous pass and in his mind by this action holding on to the gossamer threads of sanity, the harried subject of their chat could be heard muttering over and over in time to the rhythm of his steps, "Yankees two, Diamondbacks two."

Stanza Twenty

§

At 350 Park Avenue there stands a thirty story office block that resembles an old coal-fired power station where the topmost levels shrink inwards and represent the central smokestack and the 26th floor of this rectangular glass and steel phallus, though absent from the lobby directory, is occupied by Kissinger Associates and as its founder was struggling to empty his bladder in the beige marble bathroom of his sanctum he was summoned by his secretary's voice on the speaker above his head.

"Mr. Consterdine is here for you, sir."

"Wie ein Lamm zum Schlachten," the *Reichsführer* gurgled mirthlessly under his breath giving his shriveled manhood a final shake.

§

At two minutes past four, as the National Security Advisor and the Chief-of-Staff fielded a relentless barrage of calls from the media concerning the widespread reports of bizarre phenomena that were now too frequent to suppress or deny, the page entered the Green Room and informed a now slightly tipsy Michael and a fast asleep Helen the First Lady was awaiting their pleasure in the Yellow Oval Room on the floor above.

"Oh god," Helen murmured as Michael gently shook her, "Can't we just go home?"

"Come along, Sleeping Beauty," he said, "Further adventure awaits."

§

The upshot of the brief but ever so jocular and friendly reunion between the Water Pig and the Earth Tiger on the 26th floor was an invitation to supper.

"You go on ahead," the *Wasserschwein* warbled, "I'll tell Nan you're coming and meet you there."

The Pig occupies a roughly equivalent place in the Chinese calendar to the zodiac Scorpion and the Pig's motto is 'I preserve' but the motto of the Tiger is 'I win' and the Tiger, in the manner of Aquarius, was already on his way.

§

"I'm sorry," the First Lady said, "But the president is still not himself and won't be able to join us. It's very kind of you both to have stayed. I hope the staff haven't been ignoring you."

"Not at all," Michael replied.

The room was enormously oval and yellow as its name implied and filled like all the others they had seen with artworks of astounding quality.

"Please let's be comfortable by the fire."

Michael didn't know if his hearing was playing tricks but as they sat down he was certain he could hear muttering in the next room and a regular intermittent rapping that provided a rhythmical accompaniment.

"Tell me again the names of those movies, Mr. Davenport," she asked shyly as the butler served them tea, "I did try to remember."

"It's hard for me to remember them myself," he said.

"That's because they don't exist," Helen blabbed with sisterly malice.

The First Lady appeared confused. It was the same expression he had seen in the glare of the television lights in the ballroom in El Paso and now, as before, he found himself tenderly sensitive to her feelings and decided to tell her the truth.

It took even more time than usual because of the delicacy of the situation and he could feel Helen's mounting impatience with his rambling narrative but in the end he told the whole story of the tiger and his kidnapping by Amado Portillo and how he came to be sitting beside her on the judge's platform, tactfully avoiding the meeting with the Mafia dons and without mention of his ridiculously clinging Italian alter ego.

"It's a marvel you survived," she said sympathetically, though Michael could see her confusion hadn't entirely been satisfied, "I always wondered what happened after your friend pulled the gun."

The Secret Service had immediately whisked her out of harm's way and she hadn't seen the pandemonium that followed nor did she seem to know anything about the events on the hotel balcony, nor of Chuck and Cecilia Portillo's deaths and Amado's decapitation in the mouth of his great beast.

The strange noises in the next room continued unabated and Michael finally enquired with a smile if there was perhaps a séance taking place.

"No," Laura answered, trying her best to make light of it but her face flushed an alluring pink, "It's George. Something half scared him to death as he was making that pitch. Oh, I'm so sorry, I'm talking to myself, for heaven's sake. How would you know? You wouldn't have any interest in baseball."

"Oh, no," Michael said in earnest and suddenly excited contradiction, "I saw it. I was there with Mr. Lamy and Mr. Jones."

The First Lady looked at him in surprise and paused.

"What did you see?"

Michael did his best to describe the frozen onlookers and the spectral army of the downtrodden and she went completely still for a moment. Only her lips kept moving as though in silent prayer.

"Oh sweet lord," she whispered at last, her eyes tearing in wifely desperation, "You've just got to have a talk with him."

§

After his meeting with the Austrian chancellor, which he was barely able to sit through due to the rage boiling inside him, and approving a press release about the nomination of a new ambassador to Gabon and follow up phone calls to the Speaker of the House and the Transportation Secretary and preliminary discussions with the Chief-of-Staff about the forthcoming visits of both the Brazilian president and the prime minister of Ireland which had somehow been foolishly scheduled for the same day and more issues to do with the president's continuing absence and what the options were if he remained of insufficiently sound mind to address the United Nations in ten days time, the vice-president departed for Observatory Circle and as soon as he was traveling popped another nitroglycerine, got on his cell and put together a lightning and long overdue revenge on the man who was not only at fault for his embarrassment at lunch but who he was now convinced lay behind all his current difficulties.

§

Loomis Consterdine also owned a country house though not in an enclave of the super rich like Heinz and Nancy. It was near the little town of Cold Spring on the Hudson River just south of Poughkeepsie where he had for so many years been the superintendent of the police. The area looked similar in every geographical aspect to the rolling woodland of Connecticut but the most cursory examination of its residential acreage would reveal it was only inhabited by members of the upper middle class.

He kept the property to will to his children after his wife died and though he was intending to try and live there when he was done in Northern Ireland he had never much relished roaming round its emptiness alone.

What he didn't know as he drove the shiny rented black Lincoln sedan up I-95 toward his rendesvous with the Kissingers was that two of the gentlemen whose help he ever so briefly thought of enlisting over three gin and Italians in the Cock and Hen in Ballyhackamore were on their way to Cold Spring in a slightly battered pale blue 1973 Mustang.

Two gentlemen Michael fondly called 'Nikolai'.

§

The National Security Advisor, on the other hand, was hoping to make an early night of it. There was nothing she could do to protect herself from the First Lady's whims and though she could feel the storm clouds gathering she knew she could rely on the simple fact of her femininity to keep herself safe and dry. Yes, she knew of the plan for the towers. Yes, she had lied and obfuscated for the plotters. Yes, she had shared in their sick celebrations and several times prostituted her body for the cause. Yes, she was guilty of ordering the deaths of two innocent queers and had done the Doctor's bidding by putting a bullet in the head of an old friend and, yes, there was plenty more but no one was going to lay dark deeds at her door. Her blackness, her self-madeness, her womanhood and her solid Christian background would prevent it if she just kept smiling and her chin up, dressed well and talked the talk of reason quietly.

§

Laura was unable to cajole George into coming out of the Treaty Room and joining them so Michael and Helen went back down to the Green Room for a few minutes before supper. He helped himself to another large snifter of brandy as they told Warren and Lamy, amid fits of the giggles, what had transpired at tea.

They listened for the president's footsteps pacing above them but only once or twice heard the faint rap of knuckles and couldn't truly be certain what it was.

At five-thirty precisely the page entered again and told them to come and led the way past the grand entrance of the North Portico and across a corner of the State Dining Room with its massive chandelier and fireplace and Healy's 1869 gilt-framed portrait of a seated Abraham Lincoln in evening dress hanging above it and on into what is sometimes called the Family Dining Room.

It too was enormous but a circular table had been set for six in the center in an attempt at providing intimacy and to their collective astonishment the slumped figure of the president was already seated with his head bowed as if he were about to give the blessing. He back was to them but Laura, who had clearly brooked no further refusals and somehow pulled on an elegant navy blue dressing-gown over his pajamas, was standing ready to greet on the far side.

"He's here but not truly with us, if you know what I mean," she allowed in a soft, oddly jocular drawl, "Please sit anywhere you like."

As they did, Michael and Helen to the right and left of their hostess, Warren and Lamy to the left and right of the president, they could see he was in another world, staring intently at folded hands that were constantly fidgeting and muttering rapid-fire but indistinct sentences they eventually began to recognize as the play-by-play sportscast of some imaginary baseball game.

"I don't know whether it's possible for all of you," the First Lady began as the butler served a delicious-smelling corn chowder and his black assistant poured the wine, "But I'm going to ask Michael and Helen to stay with us tonight."

A tingly and uncomfortable thrill passed through Michael's blood and he had the idiotic thought that he had been transported through time to the castle of the Macbeths. Was it the *faux* candle sconces on the walls or the brandy? He was no casting for King Duncan but what about one of the murdered grooms?

"I know George will want to watch the game and I think, if you'll only watch with him and tell him the things you told me, that he may come out of wherever he is and talk to you. I hope you and Mr. Jones will consider watching with them too, Mr. Lamy. I know you were together at the third game and Michael told me you all saw what happened when he was making that damn pitch."

She stopped and dabbed at her eyes with a napkin.

"I'm sorry but it's been so awful since that moment," she went on, "Oh, he was a troubled man before but he always seemed able to control it. He was having bad dreams he said and felt like he was being pursued. I know it sounds ridiculous but he claimed it was Mr. Cheney who was somehow persecuting him. They never really hit it off from the start. Anyway, we prayed some and the reverend Graham and his lovely wife joined us by satellite and he got better."

She stopped again to control her tears but couldn't.

"Oh god!" she exclaimed, "Something terrible and frightening took over his mind that night!"

Michael wanted to reach out and touch her hand to comfort her.

"I'll certainly stay," he said, restraining his natural urge, "I don't know what good I can do but I'll stay."

"I don't see any reason why we all can't," Lamy added.

"Neither do I," Warren confirmed.

"Can I ask a question?" Helen said.

No one replied but she didn't need a response.

"I'd like to ask Mrs. Bush . . "

"Please, I want you to call me Laura. I told you that."

"Sorry, yes, Laura . . it's rather difficult, I don't know why . . anyway, I'd like to ask what *you* saw and what you think was happening?"

The First Lady took a sip of wine and smiled sadly.

"I've got through for so long pretending not to see or think," she admitted in an almost inaudible voice, "I'd feel disloyal if I started now."

§

The pressing subjects of the moment were avoided for the rest of their meal and for the entirety of another candlelit supper in an immense gated mansion set amid artificial lakes and rolling lawns at the end of a forested cul-de-sac known as Henderson Road in East Kent, Connecticut.

Nor was anything of consequence uttered in the now less than pristine living room of Loomis Consterdine's house near Cold Spring.

The two expatriate Mafia hirelings never agreed about anything and as they downed a six-pack of Schlitz and carelessly tossed around the detritus of takeout Dennyburgers and fries they nearly came to blows over the functioning of the TV remote.

Finally, in the cozy den between the Master Bedroom and the Yellow Oval Room on the second floor of the White House residence, in a paneled subterranean study in East Kent and nestled behind the camouflage of darkness in Cold Spring, everyone was sitting more or less comfortably in front of a television and the game began.

And so did the manifestations.

The Boy's Choir of Harlem barely got through the first phrase of the Star Spangled Banner, 'O say can you see . . ,' before ghostly visitors began to appear on the field.

This time it was the victim's turn. Corporate executives in frayed and bloody suits, secretaries in prim outfits holding up missing limbs, a grim parade of headless police and firemen, the severed torsos of pilots and passengers and flight attendants and a million gruesome body parts of every shape and size filled the broad expanse of green. Everything danced in macabre counterpoint to the national anthem and as the choir was concluding with the words, 'O say does that star spangled banner still wave . . ,' all the disparate bleeding pieces coalesced, 'o'er the land of the free . . ,' and joined into the recognizable shapes of the human beings they once were before their lives had been so mercilessly snuffed out. And in the silence following ' . . and the home of the brave' all two thousand, nine hundred and ninety-six figures, who took no apparent order as they reintegrated, turned outward to the fans in perfect unison and stared at them for a few brief seconds with expressionless faces before suddenly vanishing.

The president rose from his armchair as though hypnotized as he watched and ever so slowly approached the television and the other occupants of the room were torn between his progress and the impossible phantoms on the screen. A few seconds after their disappearance Helen, who hadn't seen the previous occurrences, rushed out and they heard her being violently sick in the adjoining bathroom.

"The Day of the Dead," Lamy whispered, "How fitting."

In the stadium itself, however, everything was proceeding as if nothing had happened. The fans were roaring as the Yankees took to the field and their starter, Mike Mussina, went through his warmup pitches.

"Are you all right, dear?" Laura asked but the president made no response.

She was perched on the edge of her seat but relaxed a little when he turned and shuffled back to his armchair. Michael noticed with some surprise that he alone didn't appear to be upset but was smiling a strange smile.

"I don't know if it was purely my imagination," Warren said, "But I thought I saw Ruth."

The First Lady enquired who she was and when they told her she nodded but was too moved to speak.

Helen returned and Michael asked if he could get her anything and she took a tiny sip of his brandy but said she didn't want anything more.

Over the course of the game, which in Michael's opinion was staggeringly dull except for the occasional reappearance of one or more of the ghostly victims who, though quite apparently invisible to the participants, would playfully stand in the path of a base runner or wave their hands before the eyes of a batter or take part in an argument between a manager and an umpire or let a throw or a swing or a promising hit pass directly through them, he drank the remainder of the bottle and a third of a second Laura was kind enough to ring for when she saw the first was empty and by the bottom of the ninth, when an almost identically miraculous turnabout happened to the previous night and Scott Brosius hit a game-tying two-run homer off the hapless Diamondback reliever Byung-Hyun Kim, he was quite shamelessly drunk.

By the end of the twelfth, after three innings of overtime, when the stadium went berserk as the Yankees came from behind for the second straight time and nipped the Diamondbacks 3-2, he was fast asleep.

And he wasn't the only one.

In Connecticut, to the Doctor's intense irritation, his dinner guest had also dropped off in his recliner and try as he might he was unable to wake him. Nancy had long since protested her boredom with the whole affair and gone to bed and so he gave up and, muttering a few choice German epithets, retired as well.

And in the damp forests of Cold Spring, where the curtains were drawn and the lights off and the shorter Nikolai occasionally peeked from behind to look for the arrival of their puzzlingly tardy victim, the taller Nikolai, whose real name was probably Vladimir, had raided the liquor cabinet. Like Michael, he was unimpressed by America's National Pastime and knocked off a full bottle of Southern Comfort along with a half of Peppermint Schnapps, an unopened 1997 Christmas gift from Kissinger Associates that still bore a small folded card tied with red ribbon around the neck, handwritten in neat secretarial script 'To Connie, a true Friend and honest Patriot'. He was snortling great racking snores on the carpet as his swarthier, more laconic companion, whose name might just possibly have been Nikolai but since he claimed himself Albanian most probably was not, morosely surfed the channels for some porn.

Only the president didn't seem tired as the Yankees' designated hitter, Chuck Knoblauch, stormed across home plate with the winning run, and a bleary-eyed but hopeful Laura and virtually comatose Helen nodded in mute agreement with Lamy and Warren's observation that he appeared to have come to some inner resolve as he grinned his crooked grin and whispered, "Diamondbacks two, Yankees *three*."

§

It was well after midnight when the game ended and Loomis Consterdine, who hadn't really been asleep, waited another full hour before putting his plan into action. He knew the paranoid *Reichsführer* had double-bolted the study door behind him and it took most of that time to quietly remove the hardware and open it again. He reminded himself he would have to replace everything very carefully.

There were glass French sliders leading to a broad patio and a dozen shallow curving stone steps up into a manicured garden but guard dogs constantly roamed the property and alarms might sound if anyone made so late a departure and, in any case, that wasn't his intention. He was well aware that bringing any kind of weapon would have been pointless since metal detectors were installed at every entrance.

He left his loafers in the study and did his best to ascend the stairs to the bedrooms without making a sound. There was an elevator but it would hardly have suited his purpose. He was by no means certain whether his quarry slept alone and he crept along the softly-illuminated hallway listening like a thief at each doorway.

At the second last he heard rhythmic wheezing but a bright light shone from beneath. He stood stock still for a moment then very gently tried the handle. To his surprise it wasn't locked and, as he peered through the slowly widening crack and the room revealed its garish clutter to his astonished gaze, he saw his hostess lying flat on her back on the black satin covers of an enormous bed wearing a full-length frilly black negligee and peignoir. Every lamp was ablaze and a padded black mask covered her eyes. The ends of black earplugs were visible protruding from each ear. Long strands of white hair sprayed out in all directions on the pillows. Bony fingers were folded on her breast as though in rehearsal for the coffin and gnarled white toes poked above the bedstead. Her lungs emitted an eerie plaintive whine.

The door to the ensuite bathroom was open and all the lights were on there too and there was another door closed on the far side so, rather than retreat to the hallway, the nightstalker padded across to it and listened.

The puffing and blowing and spluttering in the room beyond gave no doubt as to its function and its occupant. He took a deep breath and a capsule from his jacket pocket and silently turned the knob.

This room was completely dark but the spill from behind made his passage clear and without hesitation he strode to his victim and popped the capsule into the slimy gaping cavern of his mouth.

The model for *'Doktor Merkwürdigliebe'*, who derided soldiers as 'dumb stupid animals' and 'the pawns of foreign policy', made an instinctive murmur of objection but didn't rouse and, after a few preparatory sucking motions with his fleshy lips to gather sufficient saliva, swallowed it.

§

At five in the morning Michael awoke in the Lincoln Bedroom still wearing his clothes and hadn't the slightest idea where he was. His head was swimming with nausea, his back was sore from the lumpy mattress and he desperately needed to pee but it was all forgotten in an instant as his eyes focused and he became aware of the president standing by the bed in his pajamas, staring down at him with a daft smile on his face and the bottle of Napoleon brandy dangling from his hand.

"There are ghosts on the lawn," he whispered.

Michael was too thunderstruck to speak but the president was gesturing him to follow to the window and he rose from the bed and did so.

"It ain't fog. It's ghosts," he slurred quietly, "There, beyond the trees."

It was not yet dawn and the obelisk of the Washington Monument shone in the distance.

"Yes, yes, I think I see."

There was a strange purple mist rising from the grass and what appeared to be a slowly growing army of spectral figures sprouting from it, staring straight up at them exactly as they had done in the stadium less than nine hours ago.

"They want me to speak to them."

"Yes, yes, sir, I think they do. I think they surely will."

"We've seen them before, haven't we?"

"Yes, indeed we have."

"You saw them last night on TV."

"Yes, sir, we all did."

"You were there at the stadium."

"When you threw the pitch. Yes, sir, yes I was."

For goodness' sake, Michael chastised himself, it was time to stop calling this appalling twisted war criminal 'sir'!

"Do you know what they want me to say?"

Michael paused and picked his words carefully.

"I imagine they'd like to hear the truth."

The president turned and searched his eyes without speaking and the urgent need to urinate reentered his consciousness with a vengeance.

"Is that . . what *you* want me to do?" he asked at last.

"Me?"

"You and your associates."

"You mean Mr. Lamy and Mr. Jones?"

The president let out a weird sarcastic cackle.

"Don't fuck with me," he said, grinning drunkenly, "I know who you are."

Michael was too tired to argue and the boy-man the frat house once dubbed Temporary kept grinning and took the last swig of brandy.

"How can you drink this shit?" he joked good-naturedly and suddenly turned deadly serious, grasping Michael by the lapels and whispering with crazed intensity, "I have bad dreams. Very, very, very, very, very bad. I need them to go away!"

They were swaying together like two long lost drinking buddies but though the president's inebriation was fresh Michael's was stale and it pushed him to a cold straightforwardness.

"I can understand why," he said levelly, "Guilt works like that."

"Guilt?"

"Yes, guilt. The overwhelming pressure of subcutaneous guilt erupting like pus from a pimple. Or is it the other way around?"

The president looked confused.

"What guilt? Whose guilt?"

"Yours."

"Mine?"

"Of course. You're a coward and a thief and a liar and a mass murderer."

The president paused to consider and loosened his hold on Michael's jacket, his drunken mind momentarily caught off guard by the bluntness of the statement.

"I could have you killed," he sneered, but it was more kneejerk reaction than actual threat.

"That won't stop the dreams."

"No?"

"No. Only the truth can do that. That's what they've come for."

The president looked down at the silent multitude on the lawn. The number had increased by many hundreds as they stood in the window.

"It wasn't me," he muttered, "It was my father and all those other pricks."

"All the more reason to give them what they want."

The president paused again and Michael sensed some vague concept gelling inside his brain.

"But will that give *you* what *you* want?"

The absurdity was beyond tolerance and Michael pushed him away.

"I don't want anything!" he shouted.

"You and your goddam continental associates?"

"Oh hell's bells, think what you like, I've got to pee!"

§

As Michael dashed for the Lincoln Bathroom the three NSA operatives who raped Brandy in the Patuxent marshland were hidden in their Ford Explorer in a draw-off near the corner of East Kent Road and Henderson.

The commuter traffic along East Kent was light but they were nervous about their mission and had even been thinking of abandoning it altogether. It was Friday and they had been told the Doctor would be leaving before six but they knew nothing of the reason for such an early departure.

A secret breakfast meeting in the 26th floor boardroom at 350 Park Avenue with a small group of American corporate executives seeking a merger with Yukos Oil and members of a shell philanthropy known as the Open Russian Federation, a funnel for Yukos' owner and Russia's richest man, Mikhail Khodorkovsky, to lavish vast sums in high places. Others attending would be the ubiquitous Poppy Bush, Britain's Lord Rothschild and Lewis 'Scooter' Libby.

They also didn't know, though they might have been relieved to hear it, that the Doctor was already dead as a doornail from cyanide poisoning. If they had they wouldn't have blown away the driver of the rented Lincoln sedan speeding toward them through the murky dawn. It wasn't the stretch limousine they'd been told to expect but they were hoping it would pass as an excusable mistake.

Stanza Twenty-one

§

The president was gone by the time Michael returned from his pee and since there wasn't much hope of getting back to sleep he went to the bathroom again and washed his face. After feeling about the wall for more than a minute he found the main light switch and saw that some angel had been thoughtful enough to leave his overnight bag on an antique armchair by the colossal bed and was happily able to shower and shave and comb his hair and dress in fresh underwear.

It was not possible for him to fully appreciate where he was though he had heard of the existence of the bedroom and he did pause to admire the portraits of Andrew Jackson and Lincoln and a youthful Mary Todd Lincoln and sat to read the copy of the Gettysburg address on the desk but of the signing of the Emancipation Proclamation here on New Year's Day, 1863, his secondary modern education had not made him aware.

He looked out the window at the vaporous horde still coalescing on the lawn and then went in search of Helen. He crossed the East Sitting Hall and entered the Queen's Bedroom though he didn't know that was what it was or even if it might be where she was. The lamps were on beside another huge canopied bed and the covers were thrown back but no one was there. Then he heard a familiar sigh from the next room and found Helen already dressed and awake and pacing idly up and down.

"Aren't you tired?" he asked kindly.

"Aren't you still drunk?" she replied less so.

"Yes, sorry," he said, "But I'm surprisingly all right. I've just had a little chat with George. If you think I'm drunk wait 'til you see him. It seems to have given him his voice back though. Come on, I have to show you something."

"Did you know the fucking queen slept here?"

"Really?"

"And Winston bloody Churchill."

"Amazing. Come on."

"We had to carry you to bed, you horror."

"Who?"

"Warren and me and Mr. Lamy."

"Sounds like some awful lyric. I said I was sorry. Come on."

"Admit you're a horror."

"I admit it, for pity's sake. I'm a horror. Now shut it and come on."

They passed through the East Sitting Hall and entered the Lincoln Bedroom and Michael told her what it was and she told him she knew but the First Lady said Lincoln never actually slept there though it was apparently his bed which had been brought in from somewhere else.

"She also said his eleven-year-old son, Willie, died in this bed and the room was well-known to be inhabited by ghosts."

"What did the poor lad die of?"

"He caught a chill riding his pony and it turned into typhoid fever."

"Well, cheer up, I shouldn't be surprised if the bugs are still lurking about on the pillows. Come over to the window. I'll show you ghosts."

§

By seven o'clock a crowd of living protesters was gathering on the north side of the White House across Pennsylvania Avenue in Lafayette Park and Maxwell Forman was entertaining them, stilting about in their midst dressed in a costume that cleverly represented the president in disguise as his alter ego, Humpty Dumpty, sitting on a wall.

At the same time an even more defiantly angry group was amassing in New York's Union Square. Firemen and rescue workers and the families of the murdered dead readying to march to Ground Zero and demand that Rudolph Giuliani rescind his order slashing manpower to the site.

In the Yellow Oval Room Michael and Helen and Warren and Lamy, who had snatched a few hours sleep in the East and West Bedrooms across the hall, had been served breakfast and informed that the president and First Lady would join them shortly and they were looking out through the doors to the Truman Balcony at a vast assembly of ghosts that now stretched by thousands upon thousands far beyond the fountain on the

South Lawn and almost covered the Ellipse. Not only those who perished in the towers and the offices in the Pentagon's west wall but also the unfortunate planeloads who debarked at Wright-Patterson and surrounding them an even vaster number from the trumped-up killing fields of Afghanistan, all standing perfectly still and silent, patiently waiting and staring up at the balcony.

§

Loomis Consterdine's story, which he would certainly have stuck to if he still had any sticking to do, would have been that his host had become depressed by the ever-increasing international outcry against him, most recently Rigoberta Menchu, the political activist and 1993 Nobel Peace Prize laureate from Guatemala, which together with the threat of extradition and trial for his involvement in Operation Condor, had pushed him, like his role model Castlereagh, to the desperate resort of suicide.

The vice-president, on the other hand, had been relying on banner headlines about a despicable terrorist assassination that might at least temporarily deflect the public's demand for some explanation of the relentlessly disturbing manifestations and, at a stroke, rid him of a hated enemy.

Now all he had was a mess.

He was in his car on the way to the White House from Observatory Circle when Scooter called him with the news that everyone was in the boardroom except the *Wasserschwein Reichsführer* and an executive assistant had just informed him of a frantic communication from Nancy saying he appeared to have died in his sleep.

This was immediately followed by a coded message from a secret number at the National Security Agency telling him something had gone wrong with the hit and the ex-Administrator of the DEA had inexplicably been slain in his stead. He had no need of nightcrawlers to fish out the plotline after that.

And hard on the second came a third from Andrew Card dropping a bomb potentially far more dangerous than the first two combined.

The president had miraculously recovered his powers of speech during the night and was insisting his Chief-of-Staff arrange an impromptu press conference because he was intending to make some sort of unscripted statement before eight o'clock to a myriad of ghouls gathering on the lawn below the Truman Balcony.

It wasn't surprising the *Metallschlange Reichsführer* from Casper shouted at his driver to step on it and reached into his pocket for the vial of nitro.

§

The National Security Advisor had turned her cell to mute and television off the previous evening and took a pill while listening to Glenn Gould's incomparable 1955 recording of Bach's 'Goldberg Variations' on her headphones so she was thus, by contrast, amazingly calm.

She arrived at the West Wing before six and quickly sized up the situation and was standing by the window of the Chief-of-Staff's office looking stoically out at the South Lawn while he charged about the room in circles like the proverbial headless chicken fielding an endless string of calls.

§

In Cold Spring the television was tuned to CNN's Morning Report and Leon Harris and Daryn Kagan were trying their best to keep up with the incoming flood of breaking news but both 'Nikolai' were now soundly snoring.

§

At seven thirty-seven a crew of technicians entered the Yellow Oval Room and began setting up microphones and speakers and lights on the Truman Balcony and five minutes later the president and First Lady made their appearance.

He was dressed in an open-necked blue-striped shirt under a crisp blue suit and looked remarkably fit and alert. He crossed the room briskly to shake Michael's hand.

"How ya doin' now, you dog?" he whispered with a wink, "Or wouldn't that be *cane* in your lingo. How would you say 'hair of the dog' in Italian?"

"I haven't the faintest idea," Michael groaned.

"Well, c'mon, let's have one anyway. I need your support out there. We're up in ten minutes."

He turned abruptly to the others.

"Anyone else care to join us?"

They didn't have time to reply.

"Sure you do. Cocktails all round," the president commanded and circled his right forefinger high in the air.

Michael looked at Laura expecting she would try to stop this insanity from going any further but she was beaming from ear to ear with approval and before anyone could object the butler was pouring out tumblerfuls of Jack Daniel's.

Michael remembered what Lamy had said about the stuff and glanced at him but he just shrugged and smiled resignedly.

"OK," the president began when everyone had been served, raising his drink in a toast, "I want to thank y'all for coming and I know Laura thanks you too. She thinks of you fondly from that time in El Paso, Mr. Davenport, and I want to thank you as well for your kindness to her on that occasion."

He stressed the words 'Mr. Davenport' while flicking his eyebrows up and down like Groucho Marx and the sheer imbecility of it made Michael shudder.

"I don't know why or how," he went on, "But our time together and the little chat Michael and I had in the wee hours has made me feel a whole heck of a lot better and I'm gonna talk to those people out there because not only is that what I think they want me to do but also because it's damn well the right thing too."

"You're going to confess?" Helen asked, "I don't believe it."

The president stopped and eyed her quizzically.

"If confess is what they want, little lady, then that's what I'm gonna do."

"How long are you intending to talk?" Warren said but the president didn't catch his irony because at that moment the vice-president burst into the room with the Chief-of-Staff and the National Security Advisor on his heels.

The Metal Snake immediately saw the whiskey glasses and roared, "Christ all fucking mighty, Laura! What in hell is going on?"

The president opened his mouth with the full intention of telling his nemesis where to go for speaking to his sweetheart that way but was suddenly struck dumb because in his mind the vice-president had turned a brilliant radioactive orange and was rapidly swelling, ballooning up to the ornate yellow ceiling in an instant and filling half the room, transforming before his terrified eyes into an enormous fire-breathing serpent with huge clanking metal wings. He dropped his glass to the floor and covered his ears in pain as the dragon repeated, "What in hell is going on?" in a deafening amplified screech.

Michael had no idea why the president was staring like a madman and trying to muffle some nonexistent noise but he'd had quite enough.

"Look, you miserable arsehole," he began loudly in his best theatrical voice, advancing a few angry steps toward the vice-president, "I don't know what kind of power you have over this poor devil but why don't you just crawl back into your hole and fuck off. George has got something to say and he's damn well going to say it whether you and your filthy henchpeople like it or not."

Warren and Helen and Lamy couldn't decide whether it was the whiskey or some profound staunchness rising from deep within his Saxon genes but he strode to the president and smacked him hard across the face, then rotated him roughly by the shoulders and marched him toward the balcony like a naughty schoolboy.

Michael heard Laura scream, "Dick, no!" but he didn't flinch or turn back and so didn't see the vice-president pulling a gun nor his sister leaping like a tigress on the grim *Metallschlange Reichsführer* from behind and gouging her fingernails into his face and didn't realize as the gun discharged three times harmlessly into the oval ceiling that the twice-charged drunk-driving felon from Wyoming's heart exploded into a thousand shrieking pieces in that moment nor that he let out a wide-mouthed gasp of terror at what they all later agreed could only have been the hellish vision of his legacy before falling stone dead on the yellow rectangular carpet with his darling Helen right on top of him.

He didn't see any of it because he was walking with the 43rd president of the United States out onto the Truman Balcony and into the hopeful morning sunshine of a brand new day.

Coda in basso ostinato all'infinità

But the president's confession to the gathered ghosts didn't quite come up to Michael's or anyone else's expectations.

To begin with he was extremely jumpy and kept trying to snatch a peek over his shoulder. Only after Warren whispered to Michael that the vice-president was dead, and Michael relayed the information in the president's ear, did he relax a bit and begin to reveal something resembling the truth of what really led to that awful day. Before long, however, his speech became little but self-serving circumlocution and avoided laying blame on most of the real heavy-hitters, including his father and the *Wasserschwein Reichsführer*, who he didn't know at that point was dead. The vice-president conveniently took the brunt and underlings and scapegoats were named aplenty. Some well-publicized arrests followed and much legal action initiated but, though many in the media were quick with their praise, his words weren't ultimately remembered as any great contribution to the general level of clarity.

The president became almost immediately reclusive again afterwards because the Diamondbacks returned to Bank One Ballpark in Phoenix for the sixth game of the Series on Saturday, November 3rd, and crushed the Yankees 15-2, racking up a record-breaking twenty-two hits, and on the Sunday they went on to win.

Diamondbacks *four*, Yankees three.

§

The horrific manifestations continued undiminished but no consensus arose about their origin or meaning and they faded once more into the background.

Michael did eventually pen several articles about them using both versions of David's phrase as the key concept but they didn't create much of a stir.

He had always been fascinated by the Chinese calendar and wanted to write about Helen being born in 1960 just eleven days before the end of the Year of the Earth Pig but she forbade it.

He knew in the very marrow of his bones, however, that the plutonium was still ticking merrily away in the Samalayuca.